'There,' announced Beverly and pointed to a patch of beach some fifteen feet from a group of naked youths strumming guitars. Placido spread the towel as ordered, this was going to be worse than he feared.

The guitars broke into an uptempo jig as the youths took in the girl's spectacular build: swelling bosom and violin-curved hips barely contained by a cerise bikini. She unfastened her top and bent to step out of her panties, her big brown breasts swinging free like ripe fruit.

Beverly took the suntan lotion from the grim-faced Placido and rubbed it lovingly into her body – all over her tits and her full, rounded buttocks and into the crack between. One of the boys whistled, and Beverly gave him the benefit of a shy smile. Unlike Placido, she was enjoying herself hugely . . .

Lust on the Loose

Noel Amos

HEADLINE

First published in 1993
by HEADLINE BOOK PUBLISHING PLC

10 9 8 7 6 5 4 3 2 1

ISBN 0 7472 4100 7

Phototypeset by Intype, London
Printed and bound in Great Britain by
HarperCollinsManufacturing, Glasgow

HEADLINE BOOK PUBLISHING PLC
Headline House
79 Great Titchfield Street
London W1P 7FN

Lust on
the Loose

Somewhere in the Home Counties in England. A balmy evening at the end of a long hot summer. In the secluded grounds of the large mansion a swimming pool glistens beneath lanterns strung from the trees. This is a very private spot for a very private party. Nobody objects as the music booms louder and the action grows hotter.

The barbecue is finished but the drinking isn't. The pool is inviting. The first guest hits the water fully clothed, others strip to their underwear, soon no one wears anything at all.

The men are hairy when naked, broad-shouldered and tattooed. The old ones carry too much flesh, the young bucks are firmly muscled and tight of stomach. The women are all young, long-legged and full-bosomed. They take part in the horseplay with enthusiasm, breasts bouncing and bottoms quivering. Liberties are taken but the girls just giggle. It's as if they were paid to have fun.

As the evening stretches into night, nobody leaves. The communal laughter fades, urgent business is at hand. Mattresses have been spread by the poolside; naked and willing, the guests lie down in each other's arms. Men and women embrace and roll apart. They find new partners, new configurations. The men are lusty and insatiable – in public they all have something to prove. And these women, beautiful, skilful and utterly shameless, are happy to help them prove it. A frenzy of lust grips the entire company.

A sudden noise breaks the spell. There is a crack of wood and a shout of anguish. A figure falls from a tree. The revellers stare in disbelief to see a young man with a camera around his neck picking himself off the ground on the far side of the pool. Before anyone can react, he runs off into the darkness. And then the men go after him.

That signals the end of the orgy but, for some, it's just the start of the affair.

One

A FAIR COP

1

In a shabby Soho office, one-up from an Asian dry-cleaners and one-down from the business premises of a curvaceous whore, Billy Dazzle surveyed his in-tray with a jaundiced eye. The quarterly rent demand stared right back at him. Billy turned his gaze to the telephone. It did not ring. As he had been cut off the previous day this was no surprise. Beneath the rent demand was a politely indifferent letter from P. Starch, bank manager and supposed friend to the small businessman, refusing a further overdraft and indeed requesting the immediate repayment of the facility outstanding. A matter, obvious even to the optimistic Billy, that would be far from facile to arrange. There was no getting away from it, Billy Dazzle, upwardly mobile, streetwise private eye, was broke and Dazzle Investigations, launched in the optimism of the Enterprise Eighties, was about to go belly up in the Nasty Nineties.

Billy reached into a squeaky metal filing cabinet. There might just be some solace left in the bottle of malt whisky donated to him last Christmas by Betsy Toast, the soft-hearted strumpet from upstairs. That, of course, had been when he was in her good books after dealing with a coachload of stroppy punters on the stairs. Now he owed her money. He upended the empty bottle and watched as the last few drops of golden liquid plopped into his coffee cup. 'Boozing at ten in the morning, you pillock,' he said out loud. 'What would your mother think?'

'What will your glamorous lady visitors think?' said a voice from the doorway. 'That's more to the point.'

Billy looked up to see a smiling bottle-blonde in a scoop-necked scarlet vest and a black pelmet skirt large enough to make a decent handkerchief.

'Patsy Fretwork,' he said. 'You're the last person I expected to see.'

'That's because your phone's on the blink, you berk, or I'd have made a proper appointment.'

She tottered towards him on wickedly high heels, a brass band of rings, bangles and other jangly fashion accessories accompanying her progress. The effect was distinctly tarty, especially the sight of her plump bronzed thighs and the blatantly unbrassiered breasts jiggling under the thin cotton top. Billy's depression suddenly began to lift.

Patsy leaned across the desk to plant a lipsticky kiss smack on his lips, affording him a tantalising glimpse of dimpled cleavage as she did so.

'Blimey, Patsy, you look terrific,' he said.

'And you look bloody awful,' she replied. 'What if I was a rich and powerful new client about to give you a lucrative commission? Finding you unshaven and half pissed with your phone out of order is not very impressive.'

'I'm not pissed and if you were a rich client you'd be the first I've seen in months.'

'Poor Billy.' She plopped herself down in the chair

facing him and reached into her handbag. 'As it happens, I've come to do you a good turn.' And she removed from her bag a large white envelope. 'You remember that job you did for me last year?'

'Patsy, please. How could anyone ever forget spending six hours up a tree taking photographs of gangsters having it off with naked women.'

'Indeed. Just your kind of thing. Don't tell me you didn't enjoy it.'

'You're joking. It half killed me. And after I fell out of the tree your husband and his pals would have finished the job if they hadn't been blind drunk and naked.'

'Well, you were brilliant and so were the photographs. That's why I've come.' And she opened the envelope to reveal a thick sheaf of £20 notes. 'There's a thousand pounds in there. That ought to pay the rent on this poxy place for a few more weeks.'

Billy resisted the overwhelming impulse to grab the money. He looked deep into Patsy's big blue eyes and read only amused sincerity.

'But Patsy, you already paid me. Months ago. Don't tell me you want me to go after Danny again. Desperate as I am, I haven't completely lost my marbles.'

'Don't worry, Danny legged it to Spain last year. You're safe.'

'What have I got to do then?'

'Give me the rest of the photographs. I want the negatives, too. The lot. And all this is yours.'

As Billy reached into his filing cabinet for the large jiffy bag containing the photographs in question he racked his brains for potential flaws in this proposition. To be honest, he'd be better off without a collection of photographs incriminating Dangerous Danny Fretwork,

Britain's most sought-after criminal and two-timing husband of the fair Patsy. And a grand, in cash, unreachable by P. Bastard Starch, was a lifeline.

'OK, it's a deal,' he said.

She grinned and tossed the bundle of notes into his lap. He grabbed them eagerly. 'Patsy, you're an angel. An angel with tits.'

'Charming.'

'They're the best kind. Spreading sweetness and light in this world, not the next.'

'Does that mean you want to look through these photos with me?'

'I think I'd better, to check they're all there. Provided you won't be upset at seeing your old man on the job in black and white.'

'Huh,' Patsy snarled nastily. 'I suspect that's all I'm ever going to see of that bastard from now on.' And she upended the bag, scattering dozens of prints and plastic envelopes of negatives across the desk top.

Patsy crouched over them, spreading the prints out and turning them the right way up. Billy came round to her side of the desk and helped her. They stood thigh to thigh, their arms and hands touching and brushing companionably as they reached across each other.

'There's some pretty horny ones as I remember,' he said.

'Like this?' Patsy pointed at a photograph of a half-naked couple entwined on a poolside lounger, the man's face buried between the woman's big breasts, her hand tugging a stiff prick free of his swimming trunks.

'This one's better.' Billy showed her a shot of a hefty fellow between the legs of a slender girl in a wet T-shirt, her face set in fierce concentration as she splayed her pussy lips wide to receive his large member.

Patsy giggled. 'I know that bugger,' she said. 'He made a pass at me one New Year's Eve. Perhaps I should have said yes.'

There was silence for a few moments as they continued to shuffle through the stack. Patsy leaned heavily against Billy, her soft round hip pushing comfortably against him. Then she said, 'You must have been very frustrated while all this was going on. Stuck halfway up a tree with a hard-on and all the action just out of reach.'

'It was just a job, Patsy. I was gathering evidence of your husband's infidelity and pernicious conduct. You weren't paying me to have a hard-on.'

She laughed. A tough, sexy cackle. 'I thought a stud like you went round with a permanent erection. I mean, you never know when it might come in handy in your line of work.'

He slipped his left hand under the hem of her ridiculously short skirt and slid it upwards. She didn't move a muscle. And as they continued to look at the photographs of the orgy his hand roamed gently over the generous cushion of her bottom.

Billy was right, there were some pretty horny pictures – twosomes, threesomes and more, participants engaged in all sorts of amorous arithmetic both in and out of the water.

'Look at that randy cow,' said Patsy in awed tones. 'I've never done that.'

The atmosphere in the small office seemed to thicken. By now Billy had edged the insubstantial fabric of Patsy's panties away from the soft flesh of her buttocks and he was stroking, pinching and moulding the firm flesh with lascivious abandon.

Then he felt the presence of her hand on his belt buckle, unfastening and unzipping to give her knowing fingers access. Still their eyes were glued to the array of lewd images spread out in front of them.

'Well, Mr Hard-On,' she breathed, 'what's your favourite? What turns you on the most?'

Without hesitation Billy flipped over a shot of a rounded and voluptuous female bottom bent over a chair, the cheeks creamy white, the valley between dark and tempting, the vaginal pouch just visible through wisps of curly hair; in the corner of the print a stiff-standing male organ, coarse and glistening, the helmet fat and engorged, stood ready for action.

'I've got a better arse than that,' said Patsy in husky tones. 'Have you got a better cock?'

She had her fingers wrapped round him by now, frigging him with practised ease inside his trousers.

'More to the point, Mrs Fretwork, I've got the only cock that's available at present and that's what counts,' said Billy, lifting her apology for a skirt almost to her waist.

She sprawled forward over the desk, across the jumble of prints, while he eased her panties down the bronzed flesh of her soft plump thighs. As he lifted one foot out of the tiny garment she spread her legs apart and he looked upwards into the thatch of dark hair that covered her crotch. The long pink lips of her vagina were clearly visible, glistening with her evident excitement.

'What are you waiting for, Billy?' she whispered. 'Go ahead and fuck the arse off me – I want my money's worth out of these bloody photos!'

2

'Daddy was right,' said Sophie Stark to herself, as she lay motionless on the bed. 'I'm crazy. There's no doubt about it.'

She eased her shoulders against the bedhead. She was getting stiff but she didn't dare move sufficiently to give herself proper relief. Not until she had decided precisely what to do about the naked man beside her.

He was stretched out along the length of her, his head on the pillow nuzzling into the curve of her left breast, one arm encircling her waist. He had been sleeping for over an hour now but she had not closed her eyes. This was by no means the first gentleman-caller Sophie had invited into her bed but it was the first time Detective Sergeant Stark had gone quite this far. There was a lot of gossip about her. They said she'd stop at nothing to get her man. But this was the first time she had lured a wanted criminal into the sanctuary of her own bedroom and fucked his brains out for half the night.

'Crazy,' she repeated to herself.

It hadn't exactly been premeditated but the moment she had clapped eyes on the surveillance photos of Crispin Kingsley, elusive pimp and white-slaver, she had felt the familiar lurch of lust in the pit of her stomach. He

was stunningly beautiful – tall, suntanned and built like
a loose-limbed sprinter. His flashing smile and eyes of
innocent baby blue exuded public-school integrity. It
didn't matter that his real name was Herbert String or
that he had a list of convictions ranging from dope-
dealing to indecent assault. Sophie knew, though she
never exactly spelled it out to herself, that given the
chance she'd let him into her pants. Then she'd turn him
in.

So far, things were going according to plan. She'd
allowed him to pick her up at Evangeline, the tacky
night club he used as a local. Fortunately long-legged
redheads in mini-skirts were just his type. The rest of the
evening was now very pleasurable history. She hadn't
expected him to be such a charmer, he had manners and
style, he was fun. He also had brilliant lingual technique.
He'd had her knickers off going up the stairs to her flat
and licked her out in the hall. She'd come twice before
they'd even got into the bedroom. And then he'd got to
work with his cock, a long elegant appendage that he
used on her with such confident expertise that she even
considered proposing an unspeakably filthy weekend out
of town. Fortunately by the time she had recovered her
breath her good sense had prevailed. Charmer though
he was, if she went off with a villain like Kingsley there
was no guarantee she would ever return.

Now she had had her fun she was in a quandary. It
was five o'clock in the morning. Her quarry was sleeping
peacefully beside her. Somehow she had to immobilise
him and get some help.

She rolled towards the side of the bed, hoping to slip
away without waking him. At once his grasp tightened
and the arm around her waist held her fast. His eyes,

their lashes impossibly long, snapped wide open and he smiled up at her from beneath the white bulge of her breast.

'Good morning, darling,' he said and fastened his sculpted lips over her nipple.

'Don't, Chris,' she said but she could feel the betraying tingle in her flesh as his mouth caressed her.

Suddenly he was all over her, hugging her to him in an urgent embrace, kissing her hard, one hand kneading the softness of her buttocks.

'For God's sake,' she cried, tearing her mouth from his and wondering frantically how she could subdue this gorgeous male who had emerged from a deep sleep instantly rampant. She could feel the evidence of his condition digging hard into her thigh and knew it would be thrusting deep inside her within the next minute if she didn't divert him.

'Chris,' she breathed into his ear, 'would you like to try something different?'

That had an effect, though by now his fingers were at the lips of her pussy, teasing them apart.

'What are you proposing, Steph?'

For a second that took her by surprise. Then she remembered she had told him her name was Stephanie.

One finger was now inside her, a second followed, widening the breach. A thumb was ever-so-gently nudging her clit.

'Have you ever had a feminist fuck?'

The hand slowed.

'What the hell is that?'

'Let me out of bed and I'll show you.'

'But I'm enjoying what we're doing now.'

His fingers had resumed their insistent probing. She

vainly clamped her thighs together as a ripple of pleasure shuddered through her belly.

'Chris, *I'm* not doing anything. It's all you. It's great – ooh, that's nice – but sometimes a girl likes to have things her own way. I can't believe you're a *complete* chauvinist.'

That stopped him. Chris was very concerned about his self-image.

'So what is it? Girls-on-top time?'

'Sort of – but with a few variations. You'll love it, macho man. I can guarantee that you're going to get fucked like you've never been fucked before.' *And how*, added Sophie to herself as she slithered out of his now-relaxed grasp.

She began to feel more confident as she scrambled in the second drawer of her dressing-table where she kept her underwear. She now had an idea of how to get out of this mess. As she hunted in the drawer she stuck her rear end out provocatively and wiggled it for his enjoyment.

Kingsley wolf-whistled. 'Very feminist,' he said, 'just my kind.'

Sophie slowly turned and walked back to the bed, making sure to jiggle her breasts and flash her most lascivious smile. Not that she had to pretend to be on heat. He lay back with his hands folded behind his head. The sheet was on the floor. In the dim light his body was a golden brown all over apart from a broad strip across his loins. His cock lay fully erect against his belly, the fat red tip rudely gleaming against the white flesh. Sophie couldn't take her eyes off it. God, she was wet between the legs.

'OK, lover,' she said, 'you just lie there and do as I

14

say.' And she straddled his body on all fours facing his feet. Very slowly she lowered the fork of her crotch until she judged it to be about six inches from his face. He had to be gazing right up her sopping pussy. *Crazy and shameless*, she thought to herself.

'Oh boy, Steph,' came a voice from between her legs, 'you've got some ass.'

She made no reply but felt his hands on her upturned rump, spreading her cheeks. Then came the first licks as his knowing tongue began to meander across the tops of her inner thighs. She shivered. This was going to take all her concentration.

With Kingsley thus occupied Sophie began surreptitiously to loop a stocking around his left ankle like a cord. She tied the other end to the bedpost.

'Hey, what are you up to?' he asked.

'Shut up and suck,' she replied, settling her bottom squarely on his face. He didn't protest.

She quickly began to wind a silk scarf round his other foot, at the same time trying to ignore the sensation of his mouth and tongue on the most intimate portion of her anatomy. But some things cannot be ignored and, as he licked in long, agonisingly slow strokes from the tip of her crack to the rose of her anus, she felt the unmistakable onset of orgasm. Her hands worked furiously at the knot in the silk. His tongue fluttered sensationally over her throbbing clitoris. She pulled at the material, it held fast to the righthand bedpost. He flick-flick-flicked with his tongue and she came in a rush, grinding her pussy down onto his lips, squeezing his face between her thighs and moaning an incoherent litany of lust.

There was silence for a long moment, broken only by her ragged breathing.

Finally he said, 'What the hell have you done to my feet?'

She pushed herself up and turned to face him. 'Didn't I tell you I was kinky? I love to tie men up. Now, don't worry, the best bit's still to come.'

'I hope *I'm* still to come,' he said but she didn't reply. Instead she hooked her leg over his body and poised herself above his straining cock.

She gave the big tool an exploratory squeeze and a pearly drop of juice swelled from the tip. 'Poor thing,' she said, 'he's feeling a little left out.' And she fed the fat head between the lips of her vagina and sank down.

'Ooh baby, that's more like it,' said Kingsley. 'I think I like this feminist fucking.'

'You *think*! I tell you this is the best lay you'll have for years.' She swayed forward and dangled her breasts temptingly above his face. The big white globes swung like ripe fruit.

'What do you think of my tits?'

'Magnificent.'

'Don't touch. You can only look.'

'Why?'

'That's the rules. No tit-fondling or I'll have to tie your hands.'

'You *are* kinky.'

'You bet.'

Then they were struggling. He trying to squeeze and pinch her breasts, she cunningly winding a stocking round his wrist and tying his hand to the bedpost just as she had fastened his feet. He laughed, it was fun submitting to this spunky redhead who was bouncing on his cock and pushing her succulent breasts into his face. He lay back and suckled happily at her nipple as she turned her attention to tying down his other hand.

Sophie was exultant. She had him now – in every way. She leaned back and grinned down at him exultantly. He pulled experimentally at his bonds. They held. He pulled harder. They still held.

'Gotcha,' she said.

'Looks like it,' he replied. 'Now what are you going to do?'

Sophie had fully intended at this point to make tracks for the phone next door and summon assistance. But somehow it was not easy to unhitch herself from the warm pole of the beautiful cock throbbing deep inside her. Nevertheless DS Stark prided herself on her professionalism and here was the opportunity she had schemed for. The sacrifices she made in the call of duty!

'Sorry, Chris,' she said as she reluctantly raised herself from his body, allowing the stiff and eager penis to slip from between the puffy pink lips of her pussy. It made an unhappy wet plopping sound as it flopped back against the tautly muscled flesh of his belly.

'Hey!' protested her abandoned lover and he yanked viciously against his bonds.

'Now, now,' she admonished, sliding a teasing finger down his chest and into the sticky knot of curls above his angry-looking cock. 'I'll be back soon. The waiting is the best bit. It'll make you appreciate me more.' And she slid her hand between his legs and cupped his balls, squeezing gently. She had the bugger all right, though it might be prudent to tie him tighter.

He began to complain more loudly as she fetched belts and a dressing-gown cord and began to reinforce his bonds.

'Cut it out, Stephanie,' he said firmly, 'a joke's a joke

17

but now I've had enough.' Then, as she took no notice but continued to bind his wrists, 'Look, you silly cow, I'll give you such a belting if you don't let me go right now.'

Sophie realised she had to do something to shut him up or else he might wake the neighbours. She wadded up a pair of panties and thrust them into his mouth, then tied them firmly into place with another scarf.

She surveyed her handiwork with satisfaction and smiled. The gorgeous gangster was spreadeagled helplessly, his once-powerful cock now wilted and wet against his thigh, his eyes bulging and his face red with fury. Trussed and tied, this turkey wasn't going anywhere.

She took her CID badge from the bedside table drawer and flipped it open so he could read it.

'Sorry, Crispin,' she said, 'you've just been comprehensively shafted.'

3

Billy's second surprise visitor showed up approximately sixty seconds after Patsy had made a noisy and affectionate exit, clasping the bag of photos to her well-handled bosom. Billy was slumped in a chair, the sound of Patsy's retreating bangles still jangling in his ears, when the brisk clack of an approaching pair of shoes had him reaching for the trousers still concertinaed round his ankles.

There was no discernible lapse in time between the perfunctory rap on the door and the entrance of a severe young woman in a charcoal grey suit and spectacles. Apart from the discreet gold crucifix at her pale throat, she wore nothing that could be construed as decoration – no jewellery, no make-up, no perfume. Her skirt fell below the knee, her stockings were dark, her shoes were low-heeled lace-ups, her hair was scraped back and her mouth was turned down yet Billy's heart leapt to see her. Like Patsy, she was as welcome as the sun in February. The presence of Ms Katherine Crisp, solicitor, could mean only one thing. Work.

She took in his dishevelled state at a glance and sniffed. Her thin pink lips were pulled into a disapproving sneer as she said, 'When I passed that blonde slut on the stairs I thought I might find you half naked.'

'And did you consider that an enticing prospect, Ms Crisp?'

She ignored the question. 'I wouldn't have thought entertaining prostitutes in office hours would enhance your business.'

'Correction. That was a valued client.'

'Really? It looks as if your friend forgot her fee.' Katherine picked up the envelope of bank notes from the middle of Billy's desk. In doing so she revealed beneath it a photograph – it was Billy's favourite bum shot – evidently a parting souvenir from Patsy. The solicitor dropped the envelope as if it had bitten her.

'I can see I'm still your detective of choice, Ms Crisp.'

'You disgust me, if you want to know.'

'It's nice to know your affections are constant.'

'Your phone's not working.'

'I've been cut off. Won't you sit down?'

'No, I don't know what I might catch. Get dressed, if you want a job. I'll meet you downstairs. I'm not staying here to be polluted.'

Settling himself into the passenger seat of her white Golf – brand new, top-of-the-range, he observed, doubtless with clean ashtrays – he said, 'If I'm so despicable, how come you make use of my services?'

'Because, Mr Dazzle, if your drain is blocked you need a plumber who doesn't mind getting his hands dirty.'

'And I suppose you've got a bunged-up drain for me to tackle? I have noticed that all your jobs seem to involve me bugging someone's bedroom or stealing their personal correspondence.'

'Not this time, I hope. My client is very respectable.'
'So?'

'She is a highly successful show-business representative with an office in Mayfair.'

'Oh God, a bloody agent. This is not a blocked-drain situation, it's a cesspit.'

Ms Crisp cut inside a taxi as she accelerated into Berkeley Square. 'If you don't want the job, Mr Dazzle, you can walk back. But I'd suggest that a so-called businessman who can't pay his phone bill can't afford to pick and choose. Besides, you'll adore Imogen. She's the kind of inspirational woman who will be a good influence on you.'

He laughed without much joy. Recently women had only inspired him to spend money, shed tears and lose sleep.

'There are some kinds of influence,' he said, 'that I can do without.'

She parked the car outside a solid and imposing Victorian mansion with brass plaques on the door. The only dirt on the pavement was a poodle turd. They had arrived in the heart of Mayfair.

Billy was smiling. In reality he had no objections, he was already calculating his Mayfair-sized fee.

Almond Associates oozed wealth and class: a fashion-plate receptionist sat in a large anteroom with high ceilings, wedding-cake mouldings, marble fireplaces and mahogany panelling – all doubtless polished and perfumed and prettified on a daily basis. The office of Imogen Almond herself was on the first floor and reached by a staircase that would have graced the set of *The Merry Widow*.

Imogen was waiting for them at the door. Cool, slim fingers pressed Billy's in a firm handshake.

'Hello, Mr Dazzle,' she said. 'Do you always walk around with lipstick on your nose?'

Billy gulped. In her high heels she was as tall as he was and a pair of wide-set eyes of limestone grey bored directly into his. She was in her early forties but with barely a wrinkle to show for it. Blonde, elegant and expensively clad in caramel cashmere, she was as immaculately groomed as a champion show-jumper. Billy fancied her rotten immediately.

'Katie, darling,' said this imposing presence, 'why don't you pour us all a glass of wine so we can break the ice?'

Ms Crisp positively dimpled to be so addressed and jumped to fiddle with a bottle and some glasses standing on a low table in front of a sofa and a straight-backed dining chair. Obviously this was where the get-to-know-you process was to take place. Billy sat as instructed, surreptitiously dabbing at his nose with a tissue and observing La Crisp in a new light. In all their dealings he had never seen her smile before, it brightened her up no end. His regard for the woman who had induced this reaction was climbing.

Imogen Almond sat next to Billy on the sofa. Ms Crisp handed them both a full glass and perched herself on the chair opposite them. The elder woman began to speak.

'I run a very special business here, Mr Dazzle. I represent a variety of artists from opera singers and concert pianists to performers whose talents are less rarefied. I don't have many clients and I don't have a big staff – despite appearances,' she added, as Billy's gaze flitted round the vast room. 'I like to keep the whole business of representation as personal as possible and my clients treat me as a friend or a sister or a bossy aunt – whatever. Each relationship is different. With some I run their entire lives, I tell them what to eat, what to wear and which shoelace to tie first. With others I just negotiate the deals and tell them where to show up. You get the picture, Mr Dazzle?'

'Please call me Billy.' There wasn't much else to say, she hadn't got to the point yet. Ms Crisp was pouring herself another glass of wine, she'd probably heard all this stuff before.

'There's one thing I hate. That's parting company with an artist. Sometimes that's inevitable and, frankly, sometimes that's to my advantage. But sometimes a client will threaten to leave and I won't want them to go. Particularly when I have worked very hard to bring them to the brink of success.'

There was a pause in the monologue. 'That must be very frustrating,' said Billy, aware he was expected to react. 'But what can you do about it?'

'I persuade them by whatever means are available. Non-violent means, of course,' she added, seeing a look of alarm cross Billy's face. 'Don't worry, the means I prefer are entirely pleasurable.' And she placed one long, exquisitely manicured finger on his thigh. 'That's where you come in.'

'Katie,' she continued, 'bring me the book that's lying on the desk will you, darling?'

In a rustle of skirts Katie rushed to do so, handing Imogen a large black album and reseating herself clumsily on the chair in a manner that displayed a flash of stockinged thigh. Billy noticed that her glass was empty again. He placed his own, virtually untouched, on the table in front of him to accommodate the portfolio which Imogen was opening across his lap.

'I bet you know who this is,' she said as she began to leaf through the pages for his benefit. A tousle-haired blonde with a snub nose and sky blue eyes strutted her stuff before him. In some shots the hair was up, in others down, she wore leotards and boxer shorts, T-shirts wet and dry, mini-skirts and thigh-high boots, she lolled on golden sands, sprawled on Formula One racing cars, splashed in pools, clowned around with a cheesy grin and posed deadpan in tiara and floor-length evening gown. And the one constant in all these images was the emphasis, by some magic of the flesh or art of the photographer, on her breasts. To Billy and, he guessed, to every man who had ever ogled these pictures in papers and magazines, this girl's breasts seemed to zoom off the page and thrust themselves into his face. The two-dimensional image seemed to carry three-dimensional weight. He could feel the warm mass of these mammaries in his hands, imagine the yielding cushion of flesh pressing against his chest as he gazed into the void of that blue-eyed stare, taste the salty sweetness of those perfect raspberry nipples fed into his mouth after a marathon of lust . . .

'Yes,' he said at last, 'of course I know her, it's Tracy Pert, the tabloids' top totty for the past three years.'

'Didn't I tell you, Imogen?' La Crisp spoke for the first time. 'I said he was an expert on crumpet.'

'What do you mean?' complained Billy.

'Katie did mention that you had considerable expertise in certain areas,' Imogen added.

'What I said was,' Ms Crisp continued loudly, 'that if

ever you went in for *Mastermind* your specialist subject would be bimbos of the twentieth century.'

Billy stared at her, more out of surprise than wounded feelings. The solicitor's glass was empty but so was the wine bottle.

A strand of dark curly hair had come loose and now coiled prettily down her long neck, and her skirt had ridden up over her crossed legs to reveal, praise be, a suspender strap and a flash of porcelain-white thigh.

She met Billy's amazed appraisal of her charms with a sudden smile that turned her usually cross and sulky face into a picture of sweetness and light. 'I imagine,' she went on, 'that you would be unbeatable with a subject like that.'

Billy smiled back. The ballbreaker had been replaced by a tipsy flirt, it was a hell of an improvement.

'You come recommended, Billy,' said Imogen. 'Katie thinks very highly of your talents and I always back her judgement.'

Now the two women were smiling at one another in a conspiratorial fashion and Billy began to feel a trifle uneasy. Just what was this funny set-up?

'But what's this got to do with Topless Tracy?' he asked. 'Surely you don't represent her?'

'As it happens, I do. The glamour industry is a sideline of mine. As well as the actors and singers and concert performers, I also handle Tracy.'

'And now,' chipped in Katie, 'Imogen would like you to handle Tracy, too.'

'Very neatly put, darling,' said Imogen.

'Eh?' said Billy stupidly.

'Go on, Billy Dazzle, admit it,' said Katie, 'you'd just love to get your hands on her chest.'

'Well, of course I would. So would ten million readers of the *Daily Dog*. I'm only human.'

'That's a matter of opinion,' muttered Katie with a return to her accustomed tartness.

'You see, Billy,' cut in Imogen, 'I have been having a little trouble with Tracy and I've come to the conclusion I need some outside help. As you know, she has been a fantastically successful model for the past few years but a career in the glamour business is necessarily short-lived.'

'Gravity dependent, you mean.'

'Precisely. So I have been steering Tracy in other directions. Into fashion, into music, into acting. She'll never be Liza Minnelli but she's not without talent.'

Billy said nothing.

'I've been quite successful on her behalf and now I'm on the brink of a breakthrough movie deal for her. But – and I admit this to you in strictest confidence – we have had something of a falling out. She won't talk to me and neither will her family. I suspect she's fixing herself up with another agent. I need to know what's going on before I set up a meeting with Orlando Verdi. Do you know who I mean?'

Billy nodded. That fat piece of pizza had put together more movie deals than a jumbo jet of Hollywood executives. The problem was that all the films stank. But who cared about that? Obviously not Imogen.

'And you need me to find her?' asked Billy, light suddenly illuminating this unlikely interview.

'Not really. I know exactly where she is, she's staying at the Asquith round the corner while she's shooting a walk-on for TV and pretending she's already a big star. I'd like you to see her for me.'

'But why can't you go?'

'I've already told you. We've had rather a big row. She won't see me or Katie. She won't return calls. We've been there, we've tried and as time is short we've decided we need a different approach.'

'A *masculine* approach,' said Katie. 'Tracy has fairly predictable taste. She likes tall slim men with designer stubble in Armani suits and loud ties.'

'Men with dark wavy hair, pale blue eyes and the wherewithal to pour champagne down her throat all day,' said Imogen.

' – and the stamina to keep a stiff cock up her all night,' added Katie in her most business-like tones.

Imogen placed her hand on Billy's arm, taking the material of his jacket between thumb and forefinger. 'You do have an Armani suit, I take it?'

As they left the building, Billy hissed angrily in Katie's ear. 'You've got some nerve. Don't you realise I'm a professional private detective. I'm not some bloody stud-for-hire.'

She turned to face him on the steps. 'In that case, why didn't you say no?'

'Because – ' He wanted to explain that the pair of them had so unnerved him that only now had he realised precisely what he had agreed to do.

'Don't tell me that an unscrupulous opportunist like you wouldn't kill for a job like this. If you ask me, you should be paying us.'

'But you *are* paying me, aren't you?'

She made no direct reply but began peeling £50 notes from a wad she had taken from her briefcase. 'This is for a retainer and the suit,' she said.

'That reminds me, what with my phone being cut off . . .'

She peeled off more notes and thrust the bundle into his hand. 'All right. Pay some bills. I'll keep account for Imogen. If you do this properly there are a few other tasks you may be able to help her with.'

'Really?' Billy gratefully pocketed the cash as she turned from him and walked briskly to her car. Obviously he had now been dismissed.

Billy watched her retreating back with interest. He had never noticed that little wiggle in her walk before. As she bent to put the key in the lock, her buttocks rounded enticingly beneath the constriction of the tight grey skirt.

'Hey, Katie,' he called, 'just what was it you said to Imogen about me?'

But she was inside the little car, firing the engine into life. She didn't look at him as she pulled away.

He headed towards Bond Street with a spring in his step. For once in his life his pockets were bulging with cash, and he had just been hired to sleep with the nation's biggest sex symbol. Things were looking up.

4

The call Sophie had been expecting came as she sat hunched over her desk the next morning, trying to avoid the eyes of her colleagues. They were whispering about her, she knew. They often did but this time they really had something to gossip about. This time she had gone too far.

Which was precisely what DCI Ambrosia Spicer was about to say to her face to face. 'In my office, Stark. Right now.' That was all she'd said on the phone. Sophie feared the worst. Severe reprimand. Disciplinary proceedings. The sack. Sophie made her way upstairs with a heavy heart.

Ambrosia Spicer was the most senior policewoman in the building. As such she was respected, reviled, speculated upon, schemed against, lusted after and frankly loathed by every male in the force. Even the women treated her with suspicion. And yet to see her petite eight-stone frame shaking with fury as she bested her coarser colleagues in an argument or to observe her strength of will bearing down on some mean-spirited villain in an interrogation was inspiring. Sophie worshipped her. And as she stood smartly to attention on the carpet in Spicer's office she knew she was for it.

Ambrosia was at her desk leafing through a sheaf of type-written pages. Eventually she looked up at Sophie. Her light brown hair was short and stylish, though in need of a cut. Behind her tortoise-shell spectacles her eyes were bright like a bird's and there were frown lines around the mouth, pulling the full lips down at the corners. She wore neither lipstick, nail varnish nor wedding ring but the middle finger of her right hand bore a faint nicotine stain on the first knuckle. She looked tired.

'I've got lots of problems, Stark, and one of them is that I don't know where to start. Did you know I've been up all night?'

Sophie didn't answer.

'But then you've not been getting much sleep either, I gather. Did you know they call you Starkers?'

'Yes, ma'am.'

'It's a bit obvious, really, with a name like yours but some of your behaviour does ask for it, wouldn't you say? I mean being caught in flagrante with a wanted man . . . I'd call that pretty blatant, Starkers. And you were starkers at the time, weren't you?'

'I—'

'No, don't tell me. Let me read to you what Constable Napless has to say.' And she paged through the report in front of her until she reached the passage she wanted: ' "When I entered the room with Sergeant Bacon the first thing I saw was this great big bottom bouncing up and down. There were two people on the bed, a man and a woman and she was bouncing up and down on his penis which was in a state of erection. As far as I could tell they were both stark bollock naked. I was amazed at what I saw and could not move. Then Sergeant Bacon shouted out, 'For God's sake, Sophie,' and the woman turned to look at us. Then I recognised her as Sergeant Sophie Stark. Her mouth was hanging open but she did not say anything to us but carried on bouncing like she was riding a bucking bronco, up and down, with her hair flying and everything, you know, bouncing. I'd never seen anything like it in my life. It was then that I came over funny and I don't remember anything else." That's from Napless's statement taken last night at his hospital bedside.'

'How is he, ma'am?'

'Oh, he's much better now the shock of seeing you in action has worn off.'

'I know it doesn't make up for it but I am terribly sorry about Constable Napless, ma'am.' And she was, why on earth Mark Bacon had turned up with a dummy like Hapless Napless she couldn't think. Mind you, she hadn't intended anybody should catch her in such an embarrassing situation.

'What I can't fathom, Stark, is why you were actually on the job when the help you had summoned made their expected appearance. I understand that you seduced Kingsley in order to apprehend him and I can understand that subduing a vigorous young man of his type might call for considerable expertise. But having succeeded in tying him up and then ringing Sergeant Bacon for assistance why in God's name didn't you leave him alone?'

There was a long silence. Sophie stood stock still though inside she was squirming. Ambrosia stood up and walked round her desk to stare directly into Sophie's face.

'I know Kingsley is a pretty boy,' she continued, 'but

am I right in thinking he's also particularly well-hung?'

Sophie tried avoiding Ambrosia's burning gaze but couldn't. Her cheeks flushed.

'Eh? Tell me. Has he got a big cock?'

'Yes, ma'am.'

'And you like that, don't you? You're just crazy for a big cock. Say it.'

'Yes, I am.'

'You couldn't resist another go, could you? While your pal Bacon was heading over to your place you thought you'd just climb back on board for another ride. Admit it.'

'Yes, ma'am. I didn't think they'd be round so soon.'

'Tell me,' Ambrosia was very close now, her face within an inch of Sophie's, and there was just a hint of amusement in her eyes as she asked, 'was it worth it?'

Indeed it had been, catastrophic though the consequences might yet turn out to be. After Sophie had rung Mark Bacon and requested his help in untying and arresting Kingsley she had unlocked the front door and then returned to the bedroom to get dressed.

At first she hadn't looked at Kingsley, she felt a degree of remorse at making love to him and then trussing him up for capture. On the other hand, he was a villain and he deserved what was coming to him.

The room was a complete tip and she had quickly bundled up the clothes on the floor and returned them to the dressing table. Then, as she bent to retrieve her panties from beneath the bed, her eyes fell on the loins of the naked man spread out in front of her. His cock was at full stretch, a great white tower soaring from the dark hair of his groin. As she looked at it from such mouth-wateringly close quarters, it began to jerk and twitch. Kingsley was arching his back and waving his cock in front of her like a flag. She glanced up at his face and saw a look of desperate need.

Careful, she told herself, he can't move, he can't talk but this bastard is still dangerous. On the other hand, she thought, as unthinkingly she stretched out and clasped the meat of his tool in her palm, on the other hand the poor sod is due to spend the next few years without any kind of feminine release. It's not his cock's fault, she thought as she slipped her lips over the taut red glans. It's a shame such a beautiful big cock like this won't have some proper comfort for years.

The next thing she knew she was sitting on top of him, the petals of her cunt poised over that long white stem. She took it into her slowly, savouring the fat solid heat of him sliding within her. She moved gently, slowly up then slowly down, agitating the length of his organ with the slick sucking warmth of the hungry mouth between her legs.

Leaning forward she dangled her breasts in his face, drawing her nipples delicately across the skin of his cheeks, then rocking from side to side and smacking the weight of them against him so he could remember the exact feel of a great pair of tits throughout the long breast-less years that lay ahead of him.

Emotional now, aroused to a fine pitch by the captive male beneath her and the nobility of her giving, Sophie began to fuck in earnest, grinding down on that massive pole faster and faster. She sat back on it so it thrust right up through her centre and reached behind her to stroke and fondle the furry eggs of his testicles. There was a grunt from deep in his throat and she became aware that he had been crying out all the while, the noise not completely silenced by his gag, and the realisation of his silent passion thrilled her. Without quite knowing what she was doing she placed both her hands on the flat of his stomach and stretched her thumbs back to rub over the spot where the base of his member emerged from her pussy lips. And she began to play with herself rhythmically, scratching at the nub of her clit as that special feeling began to build within her.

Next she was stroking herself shamelessly and riding as hard as she could, the orgasm building with the irresistible pull of a great wave. And then the door opened and somewhere in her brain she realised that the asked-for assistance had arrived – early, dammit! – but she couldn't stop now, couldn't possibly stop until he came and then, my God, he did, in an explosion of spunk fountaining up into her as the wave broke . . .

Was it worth it? Ambrosia wanted to know.

'You bet,' replied Sophie. 'The best fuck I've ever had.' And that's *my* career down the tubes, she added to herself.

But DCI Spicer didn't seem to have heard. She had walked away to the window and was looking out into the summer sunshine. Sophie noted the stylish cut of her beige linen suit, the curve of her hip, the upright tilt of her head. How old would she be? Forty, forty-five, no more than that. She was very attractive, whatever her age.

Ambrosia turned to face her again, her reverie over. She started on a new tack, her voice pitched low, her tone less aggressive.

'You know they're all a bloody lot of chauvinists in here, don't you? Because I'm a woman I have to be twice as good as the rest of them to get on. If I slip up,

I'm out and they'd like that. It's all politics where I am. You know what I'm saying, don't you?'

'Well, not exactly, ma'am.'

'I'm saying that us girls should stick together. I'm saying that I'm tempted to give you the benefit of the doubt and that's the kind of benefit you wouldn't get from a male officer. But I want you to tell me why I should.'

'Oh.'

'Go on. Tell me why I should go to the trouble of smoothing over Hapless Napless and gagging your so-called buddy, Bacon, and generally putting the lid on this.'

'Well, I suppose that if you didn't it would rebound on you. It would be embarrassing for all female detectives. What will you do about Kingsley, though?'

'Oh, he won't talk. A macho man like him trussed up and half fucked to death by a saucy piece of skirt. He'll just treasure the memory in his lonely bunk. But you're evading the question, why should I give you another chance?'

'Because I'm good. And I always get my man.'

'That's what I wanted you to say – even if it is not entirely accurate.'

'Oh?'

'There's one that got away, isn't there?'

'There's only Danny Fretwork and he legged it to Spain. He won't be back.'

'Do you want to bet?

'Why would he? He'd be a fool.'

'Well, Miss Stark, even the brightest of us make mistakes and, like you, Danny sometimes keeps his brains in his pants.'

'Anything you say, ma'am.'

'Quite. We'll talk about this later.' Ambrosia scribbled something on a pad on her desk and tore off the slip of paper. 'Be at this address at eight o'clock tonight.'

Sophie took the piece of paper. She was confused.

'It's my flat. I'm cooking. Wear something casual.'

Sophie stood where she was, uncertain she had heard correctly.

'Get going. I'll see you later . . . Starkers.'

5

No elaborate subterfuge was required for Billy Dazzle to infiltrate Tracy Pert's hotel suite. Or even, for that matter, to see her adorable 42-inch double D-cup bazookas in all their awesome glory. In the event, she simply welcomed him in and stripped off.

Not, of course, that Billy hadn't planned a cunning means of entry. Togged out as ordained in a brand-new designer suit of grey slub silk, a bottle of pink champagne in one hand and an ostentatious bunch of blooms in the other, he announced himself to Reception as Signor Orlando Verdi. After only a few minutes, Reception snootily indicated that he should take the lift to Room 320. He did so and was greeted by a seemingly waist-high blonde in a towelling robe with a shower cap on her head.

'Allo,' she said cheerfully in piercing Cockney, 'you must be from the paper. You're a bit bloody early but never mind. Are those for me? Ta ever so. You open the fizz and I'll find something to bung these flowers in.'

And that was that. Billy had no qualms about switching identities. In fact, being a reporter was better, he could ask as many leading questions as he liked and she'd not smell a rat.

'Ooh, these roses are lovely, aren't they? Even if I can't get 'em all in this funny vase.'

'That's a chamberpot.'

'Really? We used to 'ave a bucket when we were little, all six of us would piss into it and I got to empty it in the morning.'

Billy's incredulity was obvious. She winked at him and laughed.

'Well, we would have done if we hadn't been living in a three-bedroom house in Stratford with bathrooms en suite. Me dad's a builder so we got the lot. Put in a sauna when I sold me first pictures. Swimming-pool went in last year.'

She stood back from the floral display which she had been arranging throughout her speech. Somehow the roses seemed to fit exactly right and she gave him a big grin of satisfaction. Obviously she wasn't as much of a dingbat as she appeared.

She couldn't have been more than five foot tall and her hair was piled messily on top of her head, with blonde corkscrews escaping haphazardly from beneath the cap. In her fluffy pink mules and bulky robe she was far from a picture of nubile temptation. On the other hand, the amateur photographer in Billy recognised the potential of her enormous blue eyes and high cheek-bones, the flawless complexion and the pouting lower lip.

He handed her a glass of champagne which she downed in one gulp.

'Right then,' she said, 'where shall we do it?'

'Well—'

'I rather fancied the bathroom, meself. Come on.' And she thrust her empty glass at him and set off, leaving him to follow.

Somewhat bemused by the turn of events Billy grabbed the bottle and headed after her through the door of the sitting-room and into the bedroom. The room was empty but the sound of running water from behind the door in the far corner betrayed Ms Pert's whereabouts. The door opened a few degrees and Tracy's head popped out.

'Have you ever interviewed anyone in the bath before?' A slim naked leg appeared from behind the door, the foot prettily pointed, fuscia pink toenails gleaming. 'Give me a minute,' she said, 'then I'm all yours.' Head and leg then vanished.

Billy looked frantically round the room. Evidently he had been mistaken for a reporter about to do an interview and in that capacity he was missing a couple of vital accessories. He put the champagne and glasses amongst the clutter on the dressing-table and searched his pockets in vain. Whatever the virtues of Gio. Armani suits they do not come equipped with pencil and paper.

'OK, Maurice,' came Tracy's voice, 'I'm ready.'

Billy grabbed the phone pad and pen from the bedside table, snatched up the champagne and stepped eagerly into the bathroom. Whoever this Maurice was, he was missing out.

Tracy Pert, Britain's Bustiest Beauty (according to the *Dog*), was reclining in an enormous bathtub filled almost to the brim with steaming froth. Only her beaming face rose impishly above the bubbles and, to Billy's heartfelt disappointment, of the National Treasure Chest there was no sign. Yet the thought of what pink and succulent feminine delights were concealed by a mere carpet of foam set his imagination racing. As he sat on the stool at the side of the bath he smiled his best wolfish smile and handed her a replenished glass.

'What do you think?' she said, stretching out one rosy arm to take her drink. 'I read that all the big stars do this so I got some bubble bath special. Only don't tell Pandora. Cheers!'

They clinked glasses conspiratorially, Billy ogling the dimpled hollows of her throat as the steam rose and the bubbles popped around them. What Maurice may say to Pandora he had no idea but he, Billy Dazzle, was on a separate mission and so far he was doing brilliantly. All that he desired was in his grasp, so to speak.

'Right, Tracy,' he began, 'tell me all about your role in *Two-way Letch*.' That was the title of the TV sitcom she was shooting – he knew that much.

'Oh Gawd,' she moaned, 'must I? It's only a walk-on, more of a wobble-on, if you ask me. They didn't hire Tracy Pert the actress, they hired a pair of charlies. As I see it, I'm being exploited.'

'Oh dear,' said Billy sympathetically, recharging her glass. The bubbles were bursting fast now. Delectable areas of Tracy-flesh were gradually inching into view. 'But if you think that, how do you feel about the glamour photos that have made you famous?'

'Oh, I love them, they brought me millions of fans. But that's all in the past, now I want a proper career to fulfil me as an artist and a woman.'

Billy loosened his tie. The heat in the small room was stifling. He was sure he could just make out the tip of one delicate pink nipple bobbing in the surf. He continued his Maurice act, pretending to scribble notes as he did so.

'I understand your agent is about to launch you into a whole new career.'

'Oh yeah? On my fat fanny! She's the one who's

holding me back. She's got all these fancy people on her books and they get all the high-class gigs. Me, I just get the wobble-ons.'

And Tracy polished off her third – or was it her fourth – glass of champagne, banging the receptacle down on the tiles dangerously as she warmed to her theme. Billy had spotted the second nipple now, its pretty crinkled nose peeping out of the foam, while beneath the suds the bulk of her entrancing bosom lay as yet unseen.

'Do you know,' she said, 'she's organising this big charity gala in aid of dead cats or something. It'll be a real nobs' night out at some mansion in the country, diamonds and tiaras on show, you know. And she's got all her posh clients in on it, that Italian singer Melissa Whatsit and the composer Sebastian Silk and Brick Tempo – I love Brick Tempo, I'd die to be on the same stage as Brick Tempo – and that smartarse cow won't let me in on it. If you ask me, she's the worst exploiter of the lot. She'll take fifteen per cent of my boobs till they drop to my belly button and then I'll be on the scrapheap. I'm a woman and an artist and I'm *not* just a pair of tits!'

Tracy shot bolt upright in her fury and suddenly there they were, the Nation's Number One Knockers, dangling in front of Billy's pop-eyed gaze in all their swollen rosy-pink free-swinging glory. Enough to make a man's mouth water, his palms itch and his trousers swell – all of which reactions hit Billy at precisely the same moment.

'Well,' demanded the steaming nymph, 'what do *you* think?'

'I think,' replied Billy, goggle-eyed, 'that those are the most fabulous breasts I've ever seen in my life—'

41

As soon as the words were out of his mouth he knew he had made a mistake. He was cut off by a wall of water as, furious and spitting, Tracy lunged for him, catching him by the collar and plunging his head into the bath.

Despite her extravagant proportions Tracy was only a small woman, but she was fit, energetic and fighting mad. A few minutes before Billy would have died for the pleasure of getting into the tub with her, now it looked as if he was going to do just that. She held his head under with manic fury, at the same time trying to bash his skull against the side of the bath. Then there came a terrible ringing in his ears and it was this that saved him.

Billy lay panting and spluttering on the floor for a full minute before he realised Tracy was talking on the telephone. He had noticed the receiver hanging above the bath during the interview. Thank God for ritzy hotels, he thought.

'But he's here, Pandy,' Tracy was saying, 'and I think I've half drowned the bugger.'

Still shocked, Billy listened in a daze. And, despite the evident dangers in so doing, he openly admired her dripping curves. She stared right back at him as she spoke.

'No he hasn't. No beard, no hair except on his head, lots of it, curly black, blue eyes, broad shoulders, about six foot and not bloody bad if you like that sort of thing.'

Just as he had concluded he ought to take it on his toes out of her delectable presence she winked at him and plonked the handset back on its rest.

'So,' she said, 'you're not here to do an interview.'

'No.'

'And your name is not Maurice.'

'No.'

'But you like my tits and you're soaking wet.'

'Yes.'

'Well, why don't you get out of your clothes and do something useful? Like soap my back.'

What man could refuse an invitation like that? Billy wondered. And though there had to be a catch he began to strip.

6

'MY DANNY IS A DIRTY DOG' blazed the tabloid headline. 'By the Woman He Left Behind' read the more modest sub-heading. Sophie devoured the story on sight, her hands shaking as she leafed through to its continuation on the centre pages of the *Blizzard*. Her gin and tonic stood untouched on the shelf just by her chair and the panoramic vista of the Thames at dusk, as seen through the window of Ambrosia Spicer's Docklands apartment, no longer held her admiring attention. She only had eyes for the stirring prose of Mrs P Fretwork, as told to Pandora Britches.

Though I sussed in those early days that my Danny was on the fiddle, I knew he couldn't be up to anything really bad. I thought he might be a little late with his VAT or taking advantage of loopholes in the tax laws but nothing more serious than that. He was, after all, a bright young businessman keen to make his way in Margaret Thatcher's Britain of the early eighties.

Nor did I believe the rumours that he had a string of girls on the side. We used to laugh together at these attempts to blacken his name by those envious

of his entrepreneurial talents. Of course I was madly
in love with him back then and completely blinded
by his phenomenal powers as a lover.

'This is garbage,' said Sophie, 'Patsy Fretwork must
be bloody hard up.'

'And fed up,' said Ambrosia, eyeing her protégée
keenly as she reclined on the sofa opposite her.
'Wouldn't you be if your two-timing husband had kicked
you out of his villa on the Costa del Sol to shack up
with a stable of bimbos? And you were left minding the
fort in Ilford with a Keep Off sign on your back?'

'I thought they no longer cared what the other got up
to.'

'Don't be daft. They're husband and wife. They've
been married ten years. They may leave each other
stone cold but you can bet they are *very* interested in
who the other is bonking.'

'And who *is* Patsy bonking?'

'No one. Danny's boys keep an eye on her and she's
off limits to anyone who wants to stay healthy. The poor
thing is very frustrated, I hear. They say she's turned to
girls.'

Sophie looked at Ambrosia sharply. Ambrosia smiled
back and said, 'Why don't you finish the article?'

It turned out he was wanted on one count of
murder, three of manslaughter and a whole string
of protection and racketeering charges. But what
really hurt was the revelation that his gang would
regularly meet up at a house in Kent for wild 48-
hour sex orgies. These were attended by society
groupies and show-biz personalities together with

specially selected high-class prostitutes who made sure things went with a swing. There were always plenty of beautiful people who got a thrill out of rubbing shoulders and a whole lot more with the criminal element.

Don't miss tomorrow's sensational instalment when I name names and expose what went on at these poolside sex parties.

'I have a hunch,' said Ambrosia. 'Once Danny reads this, I think he'll be back.'

'But why should he? Surely he's got people here who can sort it out?'

'So? This is very personal, it requires hands-on attention. *His* hands on *his* wife. I don't think he'll trust some third party to do it right.'

'But if he comes back he's risking a life sentence.'

'First we've got to catch him, Starkers.'

'Please don't call me that.'

'Why not? It's very appropriate. It is, after all, the condition you were in when you let Danny Fretwork get away last time.'

'Ah.' Sophie blushed. 'So you know about that?'

'I know, Starkers, that you attended one of these so-called poolside orgies posing as a high-class tart – one of your regular disguises, I suppose. I know that you took part in the entertainments there, presumably with the intention of getting your hands on Dirty Danny but the evening ended in fiasco and members of your back-up team barely escaped with their lives. The next day Danny popped up in Spain and two years' worth of painstaking investigation by yours truly and many other dedicated officers was put on hold. And quite possibly consigned to the scrapheap.'

'But I nearly had him! I was at the point of luring him into the bushes where Sergeant Bacon was waiting to make the collar when that bloody idiot fell out of a tree.'

'What bloody idiot?'

'I don't know. Some man. He was hidden up a tree, out of sight. He nearly fell on Sergeant Bacon. When he ran off we all saw he had a camera. A lot of Danny's boys gave chase but he got away.'

'Unlike Sergeant Bacon.'

'Unfortunately. But Mark is very brave. I've tried to make it up to him.'

'I'm sure you have, Starkers.'

Sophie squirmed with embarrassment. 'Ma'am, give me another chance. He's the only one who's ever got away from me. Let me try and put the record straight.'

'Don't worry, that bastard won't get away this time. My team will maintain a watch on all points of entry into the country and on his known haunts. We'll turn over our informants and dig up what kind of information we can. You, however, are not a team player. It seems to me your presence spells potential disaster to all those around you. I'm going to turn you loose to employ your special skills as you think fit. You report directly to me.'

'Oh, ma'am, I don't know how to thank you.'

Ambrosia, stretching one trim leg elegantly along the sofa so her skirt rode up her thigh, said, 'Actually, Starkers, I think you do.'

7

Billy was not the kind of fellow who was generally averse to a spot of striptease. His experience of it in pubs, clubs and, more than once, at boozy parties was almost entirely pleasurable. But then, it had never been him doing the actual stripping.

Now, in the steamy confines of Tracy Pert's hotel bathroom, with the piercing baby-blue peepers of the nation's top glamour girl fixed upon him, he felt seriously embarrassed. His smart new jacket lay in a soggy heap on the floor and he hopped awkwardly on one foot as he pulled off a sock.

Tracy lay back in her still-foamy bath, her magnificent curves entirely hidden from view, a critical smirk spread across her pretty features.

'You look a right prat,' she said cheerfully. 'It's funny how a woman doffing her togs is dead sexy but you guys haven't a clue how to go about it.'

Billy angrily ripped open his shirt, sending a button pinging against the mirror over the sink.

'Ooh, that's more like it,' said Tracy. 'You've got a nice chest. I don't like them too muscley.'

'Neither do I.'

'Oh, I know what you like.' And she sat up, cupping

her breasts in her hands, the soapy water running down the valley between the creamy hills. She jiggled the plump gourds on her palms, lifting and spreading the damp pink tit-flesh, revealing them to his hungry gaze in all their glory.

'Oh, Tracy,' Billy groaned, transfixed by the sight of her. Her slender fingers moved over the quivering opulence of her bewitching bosom with practised ease. Now she began to pinch her nipples, pulling the bright pink nubs erect, giving herself evident pleasure.

'Well,' she said, her voice suddenly low and husky, 'aren't you going to help me? Or are you just going to stand there till I've shrivelled up like a prune?'

With shaking hands Billy unbuckled his belt and dropped his trousers to the floor. His thin white cotton briefs could barely contain his excitement. For his part, this was not a shrivelling situation.

'Ooh,' murmured Tracy in appreciation, 'there's more to you than meets the eye.'

Billy said nothing but shucked the inadequate garment down his thighs and kicked it beneath the sink. The time for talking had passed as far as he was concerned.

''Ere,' squawked Tracy as he dropped to one knee and plunged his arms into the bath, one sliding under her thighs, the other circling her back.

'Oy,' she shouted but he fastened his lips over hers, cutting off the sound. Her mouth was warm and welcoming and those eyes he had once dismissed as vacant now blazed into his. She kissed him back avidly, hooking her arms round his chest and hanging onto him as, in a great torrent of foam and water, he pushed himself to his feet lifting her bodily out of the bath.

She squealed in surprise and pleasure as he carried

her out into the bedroom and tumbled her onto the big double bed. Then they were all over one another, squeezing and groping and giggling. He buried his face between her breasts, taking first one nipple between his lips then the other as she cradled him to her.

Both were in a hurry now and there wasn't time for finesse. She had one hand on his cock and the other between her legs as she spread herself beneath him. She aimed, he thrust and both groaned with pleasure as his cock slid in one smooth movement deep into her dripping pussy.

It didn't last long. Billy was already at fever pitch but so, thank God, was she. She had her ankles wrapped around his neck as he began what was meant to be a disciplined shafting and soon turned into a wild ride way off the road and out of control. Her wicked little tongue was in his mouth and her fingers were raking his back as he humped into her, holding her fast by the bum cheeks, diddling her bottom hole with his little finger.

He groaned out loud as she took her lips from his and sank her teeth into his neck. He pushed his finger into the ring of her anus. She bucked her loins furiously back and forth, revelling in the sensation of cock and finger filling her at the same time. He dipped his head to her breasts and she hugged his face to them as he nibbled and sucked and licked deliriously, his mind a jumble of lewd visions. He shot his spunk deep into her just as she came too, shrieking her pleasure into his ear.

They lay in a tangle of limbs, panting, wet from the bath and the sex, unable to speak. Tracy planted a gentle kiss on Billy's bruised neck. Finally she whispered, 'If you're not Maurice – who the bloody hell are you?'

8

'I think we should start,' said DCI Spicer, 'with an inspection. Why don't you show me the equipment you will be using to lure Britain's most wanted man into custody?'

'Ma'am—' Sophie was standing to attention on the Turkish rug in front of the sofa. Back straight, heels together, arms by her side – in her off-duty best of crisp turquoise blouse and cream silk skirt, she felt distinctly silly. And vulnerable.

'Take off your skirt.'

'Oh ma'am, please.'

'Off with it, Stark. I want to have a good look at the Metropolitan Police Force's secret weapon.'

With trembling hands Sophie unzipped and slid the feather-light garment down her long legs till it pooled in a discreet ring around her gleaming black stilettos.

'You do know what I'm talking about, Sophie, don't you?'

'No!'

'Come off it, Starkers. You know just what I mean. I want to see what it is that all these street-smart villains are prepared to risk their liberty for.'

And she leaned forward and fixed her beady stare

straight ahead of her on the sumptuous form of DS Sophie Stark clad, from the waist down, in just a pair of high-heel shoes and a wisp of panty cut high on her glistening hip, describing a deep white V over the dimpled plain of her belly. Sophie knew the dark thatch of hair in her groin was clearly visible through the thin cotton and, though bereft of only one garment, she had never felt so naked in her life. And she knew what was coming next.

'Off,' ordered Ambrosia.

Sophie opened her mouth to protest but it was useless. Her panties joined the ring of material around her feet.

Ambrosia leaned further forward till her nose was just six inches from the thick chestnut thatch that concealed Sophie's most secret nooks and crannies.

'Feet apart,' said Ambrosia.

As if in a dream, Sophie obeyed.

'Now, show me.'

'Ma'am, *please!*'

'Show me, Sophie. I want to see this special place of yours. Every detail of it. I want you to demonstrate to me that your equipment is in full working order for the greatest assignment of your life.'

'Oh God,' said Sophie but her fingers were already at work, gently opening herself up, spreading the pearly pink lips along the length of her split, automatically delving between them to emerge glistening with her own juices. Her knees trembled. She was violently aroused.

'Good girl,' said Ambrosia, as if she were praising a favoured child. 'Run your finger all the way round, just on the inside.'

'God, ma'am, I feel such a—'

'Slut?'

'Yes.'

'If I were a man I daresay I'd agree. But I'm not and you aren't. You're a hot-blooded woman with a gorgeous body and an enviable lack of inhibition. You should be proud of yourself.'

'Oh, ma'am – do you really think I'm gorgeous?'

'I wouldn't lie to you, Starkers. Now, slide your finger up your cunt. To your clit.'

The tiny pink nub of flesh stood proudly visible between Sophie's rhythmically moving fingers.

'That's right. Keep doing that and use your other hand as well. Push your fingers inside.'

'Oh. Ohh.' The little cries came bubbling from Sophie's throat. She couldn't help herself.

'You're very wet, aren't you?'

'Yes, oh yes.'

'Faster. Harder. Another finger.'

'Ohhh.' Her knees were shaking as she manipulated her sopping pussy shamelessly before the other's all-devouring gaze.

'That's it, Sophie, that's beautiful.'

'Oh God, oh God!' Her busy fingers were a blur.

'You can come now, Sophie—'

'Oh, OHHH!' Sophie's legs gave way.

'—if you haven't already done so, that is.'

There was silence, broken only by Sophie's heavy breathing as she squatted in a heap at Ambrosia's feet. Then Ambrosia leaned forward and began to stroke Sophie's tangled mane of auburn hair.

'That was very impressive, my darling.' One elegant, ringless hand slid round to the nape of Sophie's neck and gently urged her head forward. 'Unfortunately, I need you to run through your entire repertoire before I can end the inspection.'

'Oh, ma'am—' but Sophie's protest was terminated

by the firm application of a pair of lips to her own. The kiss was prolonged. Ambrosia Spicer tasted faintly of Martini and cigarettes but as the slippery, knowing tongue invaded her mouth Sophie trembled with pleasure.

9

Billy was adrift on a sea of pink and gold, his face nuzzling into the slender neck of Tracy Pert, damp blonde tendrils in his mouth, his oh-so-relaxed body buoyed up by the pneumatic perfection spread out beneath him. As his cock reluctantly melted in the warmth of her honeypot, he was already contemplating the myriad carnal delights ahead once batteries were recharged and sap rose anew.

'Oh Tracy,' he moaned, kissing the delectable porcelain-fine skin of her throat, 'you are adorable.'

'And you're a bloody imposter,' she replied in less-than-loving tones. 'What do you mean, pretending to be Maurice? Writing all those notes and things – you've got a bleeding nerve. And you're bloody heavy.' A small sharp fist whacked into his ribs. 'Get off.'

'Tracy, darling, moments like this shouldn't be spoiled by contemplation of the mundane . . .'

'I'll spoil your face if you don't let me up.'

Billy retreated to one side of the bed, taken aback by her sudden change of mood.

'I suppose I do owe you some sort of explanation,' he said, desperately trying to think of one. 'I'm here on behalf of Orlando Verdi.' It wasn't that far from the truth.

'Who?' said Tracy, sitting up and fixing him with a beady suspicious stare.

'The Italian film producer.'

'Never heard of him.' She continued to glare at Billy, her outsize breasts wobbling deliciously.

'He made *Dino the Dolphin*.'

'Really?' The fierce expression on her pretty face suddenly froze. 'So who are you?'

'Billy Dazzle, freelance film consultant and all-round factotum to visiting dignitaries.' This was better, Billy was on home ground. He gave her his warmest smile and moved a little closer. 'I'm a Mr Fix-it. I get things done.'

'Well, that's true.' She was visibly softening now and her eyes had strayed down his body to his groin, where Billy's big tool, briefly refreshed and inspired anew by her presence, was now perceptibly lengthening across his stomach.

'Since I badly needed to see you and we didn't have an appointment I just seized my opportunity.'

'In more ways than one,' she said.

'Can you blame me? Every man in the country would kill to be lying here with you.'

'You're a bloody big fibber, Billy Razzle.'

'Dazzle, please.'

She was laughing now, her lovely titties shaking just inches from his face. He leaned over and sucked a long pink nipple into his mouth, rolling it between his pursed lips. She did not object, indeed she slid one hand round his neck and pulled him closer; the other hand coming to rest in the tangle of hairs on his chest. But the interrogation was not over.

'So what does this film director want me for?'

Billy had no doubt what that fat lecher would want

from a delectable young woman like Tracy but he was certainly not going to tell her.

He placed his hand just above her knee and idly began to trace patterns on her satin-smooth skin.

'Is he going to offer me a part?'

'Of course.'

His lazy fingers dabbled upwards to the baby-soft flesh of her inner thigh.

'What part?'

Biting back the urge to say 'a nymphomaniac with big tits and no lines', which Billy secretly supposed to be the truth, he began to improvise a scenario which would at least ensure that he got the chance to fuck her again.

'Shakespeare,' he said, insinuating a finger into the soft blonde curls that covered the plump mound of her pussy.

'Shakespeare,' she repeated, her voice tinged with awe and puzzlement, at the same time spreading her legs to allow ease of entry to his prying hand.

'Actually, Shakespeare's daughter. It's a historical drama set in seventeenth-century England.' His index finger was swimming knuckle-deep inside her now, her moist flesh engulfing it like a hungry anemone.

'It's not strictly historically accurate, of course, but you know what Italian film directors are like. You play Shakespeare's unknown daughter who inherits her father's talent but who is persecuted because women weren't supposed to do that sort of thing then.'

'Blimey,' was her verbal response, her physical one was to wriggle her loins rhythmically as Billy introduced two more fingers into her cunt. She had also, seemingly unconsciously, grasped hold of his prick and was frotting it gently up and down.

Billy continued his narrative. 'You see, your character

writes all these plays but no one will put them on because you're a woman. There's only one thing for you to do – you form your own company composed entirely of women, which was taboo in those days because females didn't even get a look-in on stage.'

'Hasn't changed much, I bet they only let birds on in the first place so they could look up their skirts.' Billy kissed her hastily before she could expand on her theme. She kissed him back enthusiastically, sucking on his tongue and prolonging the contact till they both ran out of breath.

Her legs were spread wide now and the juice was flowing as he diddled her hard, waggling all four fingers deep inside her, working on her stiff little clit with his thumb. The cock-frotting ceased as she bucked her hips up and down in an ever-increasing tempo, her incredible bosom shaking like a jelly, her breath coming in short hard pants.

'Don't stop,' she cried, 'don't stop, don't stop, DON'T STOP!'

Billy didn't stop. It would have been most ungentle-manly, but by the time she had finished coming he felt as if he had sprained his wrist.

She lay back on the bed, her big titties still shuddering in time with her ragged breaths, her blue eyes aglow. She smiled at him smokily.

'What's she called?' she asked.

'Er – ' for a moment Billy was lost, right now there was only one thing on his mind and that was sinking his enormous hard-on into some portion of her glorious anatomy.

'What's my character called in the film?' Tracy repeated.

'Juliet,' said Billy hastily, 'Juliet Shakespeare – romantic, eh?'

'Oh yeah, that's great. I could really get into a part like that. When do I get to meet the Italian guy?'

'Tomorrow morning. In the meantime . . .' he gestured towards his neglected tool.

'Where?'

'Well – ' this was tricky, he couldn't spill the beans about Imogen just yet, at least not before his immediate physical needs had been attended to. 'I've got to make a phone call. Tracy, do you think you could . . . ?'

'Make the call now,' she was grinning from ear to ear.

'I can't get hold of him right now. Tracy . . .'

'You know, I rather enjoy watching you squirm around with that big boner.'

'Tracy, please.'

'I suppose you want to fuck my tits.'

'Um . . .'

'All guys want to fuck my tits. They act nonchalant for a bit, do the missionary, go down on me, all the usual. Then it's, "Would you mind, Trace, if I put my chopper between your knockers just once?" and then every bloody time after that they're spunking over my charlies while my fanny is dying of neglect!'

Billy's heart sank as he saw her getting steamed up again. She certainly had a chip on her chest and there only seemed to be one way to stop her losing her rag. He pounced. She screamed. He smothered and kissed her. She kicked and pummelled him. They rolled over and over on the bed. They hit the floor with her on top and, by accident, design or bloody miracle, the mouth of her pussy landed smack on the helmet of his upstanding cock and slotted over it like a warm and friendly glove. She stopped fighting at once and began to kiss him with furious passion, gripping his thighs between hers and grinding down with serious intent. Billy met her thrusts happily, this was more like it.

And then the doorbell rang.

10

Ambrosia Spicer's cunt was very like her mouth; enigmatic and expressive by turns, full in the lip and curling from a smile of menace into an open kissable pout. She kept it smooth-shaven the length of her slit, from the hood of her clit to the pretty puckered star of her anus; above, her groin was furred with soft perfumed curls, a shade darker than the hair that framed the commanding beauty of her face.

Sophie, on her knees, contemplated the glory of the naked loins fully exposed to her gaze beneath Ambrosia's now-upturned skirt. Her heart was beating fast and a tick of nervous excitement pulsed in her belly, the shameless exhibitionism of her own orgasm had simply whetted her appetite. For once it was she who was being sexually coerced and she loved it.

'Well, Sophie, what do you think? Do I appeal to you at all?'

'Oh ma'am. I think you are beautiful.'

Ambrosia chuckled, a low throaty gurgle that swelled into full-blown laughter. 'Don't you know, Sophie,' she said eventually, 'that you should drop the formalities along with your knickers? In these special circumstances you can call me Ambrosia.' And she shifted position slightly so that the mound of her pussy was thrust further into prominence, the light from the table lamp falling on the glistening wisp of pubic fur and the twin furled lips of her labia. The vertical smile was mesmerising to Sophie and she leaned closer to lay her head on the pale thighs thrust towards her in a welcoming vee.

'May I kiss you, please, Ambrosia?' she said, sliding one hand over the fleshy curve of the other's hip, lifting the irrelevancy of DCI Spicer's skirt out of the way to expose more of the smooth skin of her stomach dipping down into that entrancing, bewitching sexual junction.

'Oh do, please. Be my guest. In fact, that's an order. Starkers.'

One that Sophie had already anticipated, placing trembling lip to trembling lip, tentatively tickling with her tongue between the delicate folds, insinuating it gently into the hot musky mouth of Ambrosia Spicer's sex. The taste of Ambrosia was subtle and complex, at first briny and tart then rich and resonant, like full-bodied wine, as she probed deeper with her tongue and sucked keenly at the other's juices. The genital embrace was now urgent and open-mouthed and Sophie circled Ambrosia's hips with her arms, grasping the firm rounds of her buttocks in her hands and hugging the cup of Ambrosia's cunt to her lips as she drank deeply.

As she did so a groan rose from Ambrosia's throat and burst like a bubble into the silence of the room. And somewhere in Sophie's head the thought occurred that this was the first sound she had heard Ambrosia utter that was not tainted by sarcasm, cynicism or anger. She liked that and clasped the other woman feverishly, eliciting further moans of unadulterated passion.

Sophie drew back momentarily to flicker her tongue

over the hard nub of the clitoris and felt the shock wave of her caress ripple through Ambrosia's loins.

'Oh yes,' she cried. And she groaned louder this time. 'Oh yes, Sophie. Please, oh please.'

Sophie was playing with her now, teasing round the clit, sucking open-mouthed and rolling the long lips between hers before plunging her tongue deep into the bubbling honeypot between Ambrosia's legs. And now the pot was about to boil over as Ambrosia's loins bucked hopelessly out of control and her small strong hands, both buried in Sophie's hair, pulled her head urgently into her crotch.

'Oh yes, eat me,' she yelled, 'eat me, suck me, lick me out, you gorgeous cunt-sucker . . . OH!' And the stream of obscenities melted into an incoherent howl of sexual release as she came spectacularly in Sophie's face.

'The funny thing is, Starkers,' she said a few moments later as she stroked Sophie's dishevelled mass of hair, 'that was only meant to be an examination of your technique.'

Sophie lifted her head from the other's lap, her eyes huge and glistening in the dim light. 'What do you mean, Ambrosia? Were you were testing me out?'

'Of course, my darling. You passed with flying colours.'

'But why? Have I got to go to bed with a woman?'

'Probably. If you want to track down Danny Fretwork you may have to fuck more than one.' She laughed ruefully. 'Lucky bitches.'

11

At first Billy didn't realise quite what was going on. There was a funny bonging noise and, more seriously, Tracy had frozen in the act of humping gleefully on top of his straining cock.

'Oh shit,' she said forcefully.

'What's up?'

'It's someone at the door.'

'So? Let them come back later. We're busy.' And Billy squeezed the pliant buttock in his grasp, urging her to continue what she had been doing so deliciously well.

But Tracy wasn't listening to him, she was already untwining her delectable limbs from his.

'I think I know who it is and she won't go away. If I don't answer she'll get the manager to let her in, I know it.'

'Well, get rid of her, Tracy, tell whoever it is they're interrupting a very important meeting, which they are. Apart from anything else we're discussing your movie career.'

This last remark was born of desperation as Billy watched the big-titted nymph pull on a robe and tuck those gorgeous knockers out of view. His cock seemed a yard long and made of solid steel. He gestured at it pathetically as he wailed, 'For God's sake, Tracy, you can't leave me like this!'

She turned to him from the door and hissed, 'Shut up, you berk – she mustn't know you're here. I'll try and keep her out but if she comes in this room she mustn't see any sign of you. Or that's the last poke you'll get out of me.'

Then she was gone, shutting the bedroom door behind her and Billy heard her call out, 'Coming!' as she rushed to answer the insistent ring.

'Wish I bloody was,' he muttered to himself as he pulled himself to his feet and padded disconsolately to the bedroom door. He could already hear voices on the other side.

'Pandora – what are you doing here?' said Tracy.

Pandora – the silly witch who had rung up while he was being drowned in Tracy's bath. He might have guessed.

'Darling, are you all right? What did that bastard do to you?'

That must be her, Maurice's pal and obviously a wild hysteric. She sounded like one, all cut-glass vowels with no pauses for breath.

'I was so worried. When Maurice told me he couldn't make it and you said there was a man in your bathroom I felt this stab in my guts. I felt so responsible. I just dropped everything and you know how difficult it is at the moment—'

'Pandy—'

'So what happened? Who was he? How did you get rid of the swine? You've got to tell me everything.'

'There's nothing to tell. He was just a fan and I let him in by mistake—'

65

'Darling, I knew it. I wish I'd been here, I shouldn't have left you.'

'It's OK.'

'No, it isn't. Have you reported it to the management? Did you call the police?'

'There's no need—'

'Well, I'm going to do it right now.'

'No, Pandy, No!'

Just the thickness of a door panel separated Billy from this conversation and he was a fascinated though somewhat perturbed audience. Short of a miracle there was no way Tracy was going to get rid of this busybody in a hurry. The chances of him resuming his delightful acquaintance with the multi-talented Ms Pert were shrinking as fast as his recently rampant cock.

There was now silence in the other room. Billy was puzzled. Obviously Tracy had found some way of shutting the silly cow up and he wondered what it was. There was a keyhole in the door. Billy dropped to his knees and applied a curious eye.

The view was not brilliant but it was good enough to reveal Tracy's means of shutting Pandy's mouth. She was kissing it.

Billy's mind was boggled and his eye was glued fast to the hole which afforded a view of the large chintz sofa on the other side of the suite. Sprawling across it was a tall slender woman dressed in flat shoes, a denim skirt and a floppy white shirt that gave no indication of her superstructure. Her dark hair was tied back off her face which, from what he could see of it, was oval-shaped with a long nose and big black eyes. But it was hard to make out what she really looked like through the small but energetic form of Tracy who was kissing her with the kind of zeal that Billy had recently become addicted to.

This, as they say, was something of a turn-up. Billy could see the headlines in his mind's eye: 'Nation's Number One Sex Symbol Is A Dyke', 'Topless Tracy Digs Girls', 'Britain's Bustiest Beauty Swings Both Ways'. The *Daily Dog* would have a field day.

The embrace was continuing even as Billy's mind raced with the implications of the scene. Tracy had now removed the other girl's big round spectacles and they were settling in for a comfortable snog. Pandy had her hand inside Tracy's dressing gown and, in a trice, those heavy free-swinging boobs were out in the open again and being squeezed and hefted and pawed over once more, this time by female hands. Evidently neither man nor woman could resist them. It could just be, thought Billy, that Tracy's tits were the answer to all her problems. Evidently Pandy had been sufficiently mollified by them to prevent her calling the police.

'If only I hadn't got this special assignment,' she was saying between alternate kisses, left then right, on the uptilted tips of Tracy's boobs. 'But you know how important it is to my career. I'm not supposed to leave that woman for a moment, otherwise I'd be here to look after you.'

'You mustn't worry,' replied Tracy, 'I'm fine. I can look after myself better than you. He was a harmless sod and I got rid of him with no problems.'

'But Tracy, suppose he'd attacked you! I bet he wanted to. I can't stand the way those men look at you, stripping you naked in their heads, polluting your body in their minds. I bet he wanted to sully and ransack every inch of your beautiful body!' She accompanied these remarks by redoubling her assault on Tracy's luscious form, pulling the dressing gown wide open and feverishly thrusting a hand between Tracy's perfectly proportioned thighs.

Tracy sprung back as if scalded, pulling the robe tightly around her as she did so. Pandy looked anguished. Billy knew just how she felt.

'Oy, Pandy, lay off. There's no time for any of that now. Haven't you got to get back to work?'

'I've got a couple of hours, actually. To be honest she's rather a nice woman. She's promised to keep her head down till I get back. So why don't we go to bed, darling? I've got time.'

That brought Billy up short. Here he was, stark naked, with his clothes spread halfway round the bathroom and soaking wet to boot. Frankly, he didn't care two hoots about Pandy and would have strolled out under her nose if it didn't mean all chances of getting his leg over Tracy again would stroll out with him.

Behind the door, the conversation had taken a new twist. Pandy was demanding boudoir rights and Tracy was denying access to that facility. Hysteria returned to Pandora's voice as she drew the obvious conclusion.

'You've got a man in there, haven't you?' she shrieked. 'That bastard never left!'

Billy was quick on his feet when he had to be. In fact, he took a professional pride in it.

'The things I do for a good screw,' he muttered to himself as, thirty seconds later, he lay on his back beneath the bed, his once-beautiful new suit now sopping wet and scrunched up beside him on one side, the empty champagne bottle and two glasses on the other. And not a moment too soon.

He heard the bedroom door crash open with a bang and the sound of raised voices suddenly silenced. Tracy spoke first in triumphant tones.

'See, Pandora Britches! You wouldn't bloody listen. There's nobody else here. Where's all this sisterhood you're always on about? "Men are pigs", "You can only trust a woman" – all that. You obviously don't have much faith in me.'

'Oh, Tracy, I'm sorry,' said Pandy in contrite tones.

But Tracy hadn't finished. 'You haven't looked in the wardrobe yet,' there was the sound of banging doors, 'or under the bed.'

'You bloody fool!' thought Billy as a hand flicked up the valance in front of him and there, for a split second, was Tracy's pretty pouting face. For the second time that day she winked at him and then was gone.

'Please, Tracy,' cried Pandora, thoroughly repentant by now, 'I don't know what came over me, I'm so, so sorry, my darling, I didn't mean to doubt you . . .'

'Oh, shut up, you daft cow,' said Tracy in gentler tones, 'it's all right. Why don't you go next door and pour us a gin? I'm just going to take a crap.' And on that unanswerable exit-line Billy heard her disappear into the bathroom. Doubtless to wash the spunk out of her pussy, he thought to himself in admiration. It was a pity, he reflected, that she'd never get the chance to play Juliet Shakespeare – she'd be bloody good.

The bed above him sagged dangerously close to his nose as the defeated Pandy flung herself upon it. A moment later he heard a sob catch softly in her throat. Then another. And then came a torrent of tears. As she cried, the bed above shook with her every tremor and Billy felt his heart softening towards her. He fantasised about appearing from beneath the bed and telling her she'd been had. He'd then proceed to lend a shoulder to cry on and, in due course, other vital parts of his anatomy to soothe the anguished female breast. From there it would be easy to demonstrate the pleasures of the male-female connection, perhaps even with the help of the pneumatic Tracy – who was certainly taking her time. Punishing the silly bitch above him, he thought, returning to the uncomfortable reality of his present position as he heard the sound of the bathroom door opening.

'Pandy?' he heard Tracy say, concern in her voice as she registered her companion's distress.

A wail of pain split the air and the mattress above Billy began to shake once more. She was off again.

'Come on, Pandy. Don't cry, my love. There's no need.'

The crying took on a new intensity and the mattress suddenly dipped further towards Billy as Tracy evidently chose to comfort the bawling woman at close quarters. It seemed to work for the howling ceased almost immediately to be replaced by a lot of snuffling and sniffing and nose-blowing.

'There, that's better,' said Tracy. 'How about that G and T, eh?'

'No,' Pandy's voice was tear-stained and pathetic, 'let's stay here a moment. It's nice like this.'

'I bet it bloody is,' said Billy to himself. The artful cow, he knew just what her game was.

Sure enough there was a suspicious silence, broken finally by a slurping, sticky kind of noise, as of two hungry mouths coming up for air. Then a kind of scratchy, slithery noise as of clothing being readjusted to allow lustful fingers access to sensitive portions of anatomy. Billy could picture the anatomy in question, it had a powerful effect on him. His cock had once more resumed rock-hard rigidity, which seemed to be its perpetual state when in the proximity of Tracy Pert.

'Don't, Pandy,' he heard her say, 'we mustn't, we don't have time, I don't feel like – oh!' More twisting and slithering noises. The mattress above him seemed to flex and ripple.

'Oh God, Pandy,' came Tracy's voice again, 'oh you are wicked!' And the groans of a woman approaching orgasm split the air.

Beneath the vibrating bed, Billy also groaned out loud. His mind racing with carnal images of the love-making he could not see but could picture with vivid clarity. His cock was a stiff and swollen bar that reached painfully to his waist and cried out for release. How long could this torment continue?

Above him, Tracy came in a cacophony of pleasure and smoothed her hands up Pandy's long slim legs to return the favour . . .

12

For a small woman Ambrosia Spicer had a very large bed. Sophie reclined on it luxuriously, her mass of auburn hair spread across the pillow, her blouse open to reveal the swollen mounds of her sumptuous breasts, her knees raised and parted as instructed. She was watching her superior officer slowly divest herself of her clothes, taking her time to smooth out the creases from her skirt and hang up her petticoat and put away her shoes. There was something rather dangerous about her, decided Sophie, dangerous and sexy. Her pale flanks and sloping belly seemed to glow in the dim light and the smudge of brown curls at the crest of her slit made her pussy mound look especially large and prominent. Sophie stole a hand between her legs and began to gently fondle her own sex fur. She had only been to bed with a woman once before, she'd been drunk then and the whole thing had been just a giggle. This was different. It was a bit frightening.

'What are you thinking about, Sophie?' asked Ambrosia, finally removing her brassiere and turning to face her.

'I'm just watching you. You're very lovely.'

'You like my tits?' She jiggled them with her hands.

'When I was your age I wanted them big like yours. But now I like them because they're too small to fall.'

Ambrosia sat beside Sophie on the bed and put her arms round her. 'What's up, Starkers? All this girl stuff getting you down?'

'What did you mean about me sleeping with other women? I know we're . . . I mean, this is great but I don't usually—'

'Fuck women.'

'Exactly.'

'Frankly, Sophie, I don't either. And neither did Patsy Fretwork until recently.'

'What's she got to do with it?'

'Everything, as well you know. To get Danny you're going to have to cosy up to Patsy, she's the only reason he'll come back. We've been through all this.'

'I know, but I didn't realise I had to seduce Danny's wife!'

'Well, you might not have to. But to get to Patsy you have to suck up to that snotty dyke on the *Blizzard* who has got her stashed away somewhere.'

'Pandora Britches?'

'Exactly. There's nothing La Britches likes better than to break in new converts to her kind of sisterhood. My information is that she persuaded Patsy to spill the beans to the *Blizzard* by putting her head up her skirt.'

'Good Lord, I didn't think Patsy was like that.'

Ambrosia chuckled throatily and slid a hand between Sophie's legs. 'We're all like that if there's nothing better on offer. And where Patsy's concerned, there isn't.'

'So I've got to do her too?'

Ambrosia inserted two fingers into Sophie's sticky cunt. 'You do what you like provided you get Danny.

I'm just suggesting a line of enquiry, one you might rather enjoy. God, you're soaking down there.'

'That's not surprising, considering what you're doing.'

'You have an insatiable quim, Sophie Starkers. How would you like something long and hard up it?'

'Like what?'

'Like a thick meaty dick.'

'I don't believe you have anything of that nature about your person, Ambrosia.'

'Look in that drawer. On your side of the bed.'

'You haven't got a vibrator?'

'Something better. It's a piece of equipment that's more impressive than Danny Fretwork's. It's the final test to see if you're up to this special assignment.'

'Oh God, Ambrosia,' exclaimed Sophie as she extracted the false penis from the bedside table drawer, 'it's obscene!'

'Pricks tend to be. So do dildos.'

Ambrosia took the object from Sophie and strapped it round her so that, from out of her loins, sprang the incongruous sight of a false penis curving wickedly upwards beyond her belly button. It was bright pink, fantastically veined and ribbed, capped with a puce head the size of a fat ripe plum.

'What do you think?' asked Ambrosia, waggling the great truncheon with an experimental thrust of her hips. 'Think you can take it?'

'Do I have a choice?'

Ambrosia did not reply but knelt between Sophie's legs and carefully spread apart her swollen rose-coloured labia. Slowly and tantalisingly she ran her wet fingers around the top of the pretend penis, then up and down its shaft. Taking careful aim at the gaping pussy hole before her she asked, 'Are you ready, Starkers?'

Sophie's big eyes were smouldering with unspoken need and her whole body was trembling with anticipation. But her voice was loud and firm as she cried out, 'For God's sake, Ambrosia, get on with it! Shove it up and fuck me silly!'

For once, her superior officer was only too happy to obey.

13

Pandora Britches came many times before she went, though not nearly as often as Tracy. In his uncomfortable position beneath the bed, Billy reacted to every howl and moan of pleasure, to every shift of limb and to every sticky sucky sound made by the two randy women lying just inches above him. To be so near and yet so far was torture itself. Each climax sent an electric thrill through his aching cock and in the silence that followed he waited anxiously for sounds to indicate that the lovers had had enough. But inevitably the silence was filled by a giggle or a whispered endearment, then by a kiss or a slap and the pair of them would be at it again, moaning and growling and making those squishy sex noises that drove him wild with longing. As he listened, a truly captive audience, his cock twitched and drooled, the juices pooling and drying on his belly in an itchy sticky mess. Above him the awe-inspiring pageant of female lust played on interminably.

There was not much conversation. Every so often Pandy said, 'I really must go now,' causing Billy's hopes to rise – only for them to be dashed as the grunts and gurgles of girl-fucking were resumed.

At last the sound of breathless goodbyes, followed by

the click of the bedroom door, signalled Billy's liberation.

He crawled out from his hiding place and surveyed the scene of the debauch. Tracy was sprawled naked across the ruined bed, the sheets in a tangle, the pillows on the floor. Her whole body was rosy and glowing, as if marked with the fingerprints of her lately departed lover. Her big beautiful breasts lolled seductively, the twin saucers of the areolae dark pink smudges in the dim light, the nipples swollen and erect. The sparse blonde curls of her pussy were plastered stickily together revealing the pink and puffy folds beneath. The musk of female passion was thick in the air. Billy felt distinctly left out.

Tracy gazed blearily at him. 'I'm sorry, Billy, I just couldn't get rid of her.'

'It didn't sound as if you tried too hard. To be honest, Tracy, I'm a bit surprised at you. The Working Man's Number One Wanton having it off with another woman. I'm shocked.'

'Well . . .' Tracy smiled feebly at him – at both ends.

Billy gazed at her with undisguised longing. Her behaviour had not rendered her any the less desirable. Rather the reverse. His cock swung in front of him like a boom, even more painfully stiff than it had been at any point during the whole ordeal.

'You do look funny,' said Tracy. 'How long are you going to stand their pointing that great big thing at me? Why don't you come here and give me a cuddle?'

'I'll say this for you, Tracy,' said Billy as he snuggled down beside her and wrapped his arms around her delicious dimpled form, 'you've got some stamina. It sounded to me as if that Pandora had finished you off for good.'

'Oh, belt up. I'm partial to the girls if you must know but I just can't do without *this*,' and as she said it she swung a leg over Billy's hip and cunningly captured the bulb of his cock-head in the nook of her crotch. Billy needed no further invitation and slid sweetly inside her to the hilt in one smooth rush till they were joined belly to belly.

'Oh God, Tracy,' he breathed, 'that's better. Under the bed, listening to you, was just torture.'

'Ssh, Billy,' sighed Tracy, drawing his face to the luscious mounds of her tits and feeding a fat pink nipple between his lips. Wriggling the firm flesh of her bottom against his thighs, she began the process of relieving his tensions and mending his bruised ego. She gently posted up and down on his body, cradling his tense and desperate cock deep within her, soothing its hurts and easing its frustrations.

Billy lay back and took his medicine. Such sweet medicine it was. He nuzzled and sucked at her opulent titflesh as she worked her magic on his aching loins till all the aches and pains of his long wait were soothed away. And then, more urgently and with tantalising skill, she began to rekindle his desires.

She leaned sideways away from him, still holding his cock captive in the skilful mouth between her thighs. Her hand was now at the junction of their bodies, palming his balls, fluttering along his shaft to the point where their hair meshed, fingering him like a clever flute-player in a teasing tuneful fashion that set his pulses racing and his member thrusting urgently into her sweet crack.

'You are a sexy witch,' he breathed into her face, fondling and pulling her big lolling tits, thumbing the pebble-hard nipples, sucking on her pouting lower lip.

'I've got to live up to my reputation,' she responded, continuing her titillating ministrations. 'You poor boy, you're so stiff, so hard, you must have had a terrible time listening to me and Pandy. I hope this makes up for it just a little. Your balls are so big,' she said, cupping and jiggling them. 'I bet you're just loaded with spunk for me. Why don't you let me have it? I can take all you've got. Don't wait for me. Come on, shoot it up me! Up my cunt! Fill me up with spunk!'

'Oh Tracy, I—' Nor surprisingly Billy was not capable of withstanding this kind of treatment and he thundered into her in a rutting fury as his cock fountained his pent-up lust deep within her irresistible body.

'God, Tracy,' he panted as he lay on his back, recovering his breath, 'that was probably the most wonderful fuck I've ever had.'

'Until the next time,' she replied.

'No, I mean it. I think you're incredible.'

'So what are you going to do about it then?' she asked. 'I mean, weren't you going to turn me into a film star or something? Wasn't there a phone call you were going to make?'

'Oh yes,' said Billy, glancing at the clock on the bedside table. 'Unfortunately I don't think I can get hold of him right now, it's too late. I've got a meeting first thing in the morning and I'll fix something up then. I promise.'

He smiled at her happily, his kinks now cheerfully smoothed out. 'So what's with Pandy, Tracy? Leaving the sex out of it, she doesn't seem your type.'

'I suppose not. She's got more brains than all my family put together. A lot less commonsense, mind you. She interviewed me for *The Rag*, it's a feminist mag she edits on the side. She says it gives her a break from the sexist trash she has to write in the *Blizzard*.'

'What does she do for the *Blizzard*?'

'Women's page stuff, price of nannies, all that sort of thing. Only now she's got a big assignment, that's why she was in such a flap. She's holed up with some gangster's moll doing her story – Danny Fretwork's wife.'

'Christ!'

'What's up?'

'Nothing. Go on, tell me why you've got your paws in each other's knickers.'

'God, you're crude. That's one of the reasons why I like Pandy. She values me as a woman. She encourages my artistic aspirations. As far as she's concerned I'm not just a pair of tits.'

'Well, I value you as a woman too, Tracy. You're a caring, nurturing sort, I can tell. Frankly, I value women like you much higher than any man I know.'

'Come off it, you're a sexist pig like all the rest. You're quite cute though.'

'That's just as well because I don't think I can leave just yet. My clothes are still soaking wet.'

'Oh dear,' she said.

'In the circumstances I hope it won't be an inconvenience to you if I stayed here for a bit. Maybe we could order something from room service to keep us going.'

'Keep us going for what?' she asked suspiciously, her eyes widening as she glanced down his body to where his red and glistening tool stretched in sticky splendour across his belly.

'Well, Tracy, there are one or two things we haven't yet got round to. Don't get me wrong but I'd hate to be the only guy you've slept with who hasn't had the pleasure of fucking your magnificent tits.'

'Oh no. Honestly, Billy, I don't think I'm up to it.' But she couldn't disguise the grin that was already spreading across her pretty face.

'I might have known,' she said as he straddled her torso and laid his stiff and gleaming tool along the creamy ravine between the sumptuous hills of her marvellous breasts. 'I suppose you expect me to hold my tits around your cock while you jerk off over me.'

And she did just that, hefting a big boob in each hand and folding the soft mass of tit over his rigid member.

'Oh God, Tracy,' moaned Billy as he began to pump his cock in and out of the valley of flesh, 'that's *fantastic*!'

'It should be,' she muttered, bestowing long licks on the top of his helmet on each up-thrust, 'how else do you think I became a star? Now, hurry up and cream my tits!'

Two

BONKING USA

14

Billy presented himself in Reception at Almond Artistes shortly after the opening of business the next morning and was admitted to Imogen's office at once.

She looked him over with a sly smile on her face. He knew he looked a sight. The once-impeccable suit was crumpled and still damp, his hair was a tangled mess and a bite mark showed clearly beneath his left ear. Nevertheless success shone from his unshaven features.

'Been on the razzle, Mr Dazzle?' said Imogen slyly. 'I presume it's mission accomplished.'

'And a tough one it was too,' said Billy. 'I can't tell you precisely what I've been through.'

'I wouldn't want to know. So, what's the story? Has Tracy got another manager?'

'No, but she's got a new friend. A close one. A feminist journalist called Pandora Britches has been telling her that displaying her breasts to the nation is not the best use of her talents. So now she wants to be taken seriously as an artist. There's an obvious solution to this,' added Billy, 'give her a spot in your charity gala for dead cats, or whatever it is, and she'll be sweetness and light once more.'

'Oh hell.' Imogen's face lengthened.

'What's the problem? Surely that's easy. You are arranging the event, aren't you?'

'Well, yes and no. I can't have a page-three pin-up on the same bill as Melissa Melone and Sebastian Silk.'

'Why not? It's all in a good cause, surely? Can't she just jiggle around to her new record? I guarantee she'll impress all the gents.'

'I can see that she's impressed you but we can't have her doing that sort of act in front of the great and the good – it's meant to be a cultural occasion and not a live sex show. Though I suppose it might loosen up a few starched shirts to have her flaunt herself in public. The tabloids would go for it.'

'There you are then,' said Billy.

'Not quite. I don't have the last word on who performs. Have you heard of Candida Kensington?'

'The rag-trade heiress?'

'She's the real inspiration behind this gala. Poor Pussy Rescue is her new thing.'

'What's that?'

'It's in aid of abandoned cats, it aims to fund luxury catteries and sponsor kitten adoption. It provides grants to have catflaps fitted, buy rubber mice and calves' liver for neglected moggies. It's a very fashionable cause right now.'

'Never heard of it.'

'You obviously don't live in the real world, Billy. Anyway, this is her do and she asked me to recommend likely performers. Naturally, many of my people were delighted to take part, particularly since it is bound to be one of the big events of the summer season. It is going to be prestigious. Sebastian Silk has composed a special suite of songs in honour the occasion and they will be premiered by Melissa Melone, the world's leading soprano, whom I recently had the honour of adding to my client roster. There's also the Marian Mucus *corps de ballet* and many other distinguished performers from the quality spectrum of the arts.'

'What about Brick Tempo?'

'Yes, he's also appearing. Brick is one of the most brilliant live acts to have survived since the sixties.'

'He's also a dope-head and a sex-fiend. I wouldn't have thought he'd fit the image.'

'You'd be surprised at the appeal of the artist who is a reformed rebel. Though I must admit you've put your finger on one of my main anxieties. Katie was right about you.'

'I'm sorry?'

'She said that you were not just a pretty face.'

'Really? That tight-arsed Katie Crisp said that about me?'

'She obviously hadn't seen you after a night on the tiles with Tracy Pert. You're a complete mess, you know.'

'Sorry. I thought you'd like my findings as soon as possible. Now I'm on my way home to clean up.' And crash out for twenty-four hours, he thought to himself. Delightful though it had been, the encounter with Tracy had knocked nearly all the stuffing out of him. On reflection, forty-eight hours should do the trick.

'So, Billy,' Imogen was saying, 'assuming I agree to include Tracy – and if it would solve my problem I must confess I'm all in favour – it's now a question of persuading Candida Kensington, who is one of the biggest snobs I have ever encountered. It's worth a try but you'll have to help me out.'

She picked up the phone and tapped out a number. Before Billy had time to draw breath she was speaking. 'Candy, darling, how are you?'

The response was fulsome and as she listened, making the odd sympathetic murmur in her turn, she motioned Billy to take a seat. Finally she spoke again. 'Candy I've met the most wonderful young man and you simply must see him as soon as possible. He's wild about Poor Pussy Rescue and is burning to make a contribution. I think he's just what you've been looking for.'

She paused to listen to the other's response, then her face crinkled into a smile and she made an elegant thumbs-up gesture at Billy as she said, 'Why, that's marvellous. He's called Billy Dazzle and he has the most fabulous baby-blues. Your search is over.'

Imogen replaced the phone, a triumphant gleam in her eye. 'There we are, that's fixed. She'll give you lunch today, just the two of you. Why don't you try and work some of that famous Dazzle magic on her?'

'But Imogen—' Billy was flabbergasted by this sudden turn of events '— couldn't this wait for another day? I'm not at my best just now, I need to go home and—'

'Don't worry, Billy, I have every confidence in you. Go and see Katie, she's next door. She'll straighten you out and give you Candy's address.'

Billy stared at her blankly, unsure whether to protest further. And what did she mean about a search being over?

Imogen fixed him with a steely glare. 'You're not going to let me down are you, Billy? I'd be most disappointed to discover that you were overrated.'

Katie Crisp took one look at Billy and pulled a disdainful

face. Without pausing to wish him good morning she ordered him into a lift and they ascended to the top of the building in a frosty silence.

Upstairs there was no evidence of the business of Almond Artistes. Here were expensive service flats and Katie led Billy down a richly carpeted hallway, through a sumptuously decorated bedroom and into a large bathroom. She turned on the bath taps and squirted some luxurious bath oil into the water.

'Take your clothes off,' she barked.

Billy stood rooted to the spot.

'Hurry up,' she said in her best schoolmarm voice, 'we've not got much time.'

Billy took off his jacket – what else could he do?

'You'll find everything here you need to turn yourself into a respectable human being, if that's possible. There's shaving gear and deodorant in the cabinet.'

'Look,' Billy said as he perched on the loo seat and slowly began to pick at his shoelaces, 'there's something I forgot to say to Imogen. I've got to phone Tracy about Orlando Verdi. She thinks she's going to star in an art movie.'

'I'll mention it to Imogen,' said Katie, now on the floor at his feet impatiently tugging at his shoes and socks, 'but first I've got to get you looking presentable, so hurry up.'

Billy got to his feet and undid his trousers. He had no intrinsic objection to undressing in front of La Crisp – especially if the arrangement were reciprocal. Alas, the current circumstances were rather akin to a small boy dropping his pyjamas in front of matron. He stepped out of the garment and stood before her clad only in his thin cotton briefs. Katie, still on her knees, unceremoniously yanked them down to his ankles.

'For God's sake!' yelled Billy in outrage.

'We have to clean your underwear as well, you fool,' she replied but she was staring intently straight at Billy's dangling genitals. For once Billy's cock was shy and retiring under the spotlight of feminine curiosity. But as Katie continued to scrutinise him he felt blood begin to flow in a familiar fashion. Sure enough, his tool was thickening, rising to the challenge of her gaze like an old warhorse answering the call to battle. Eventually it stuck, halfway to full erection, and waved in her face like an obscene carrot.

Frozen with embarrassment, Billy thought he detected a snort of derision before she finally said, 'So that's what all the fuss is about. I hope Candy Kensington is easily impressed.'

Billy retreated hastily to the bath. 'What do you expect? I've been giving my all to Tracy Pert as instructed. I'm not some performing flea.'

'Huh.' Katie was not appeased. She had now collected all of Billy's clothes and was evidently about to depart. She could not resist a parting shot, however. 'The insect analogy is revealing,' she said, 'though *worm* is the variety I would have chosen.'

After she'd gone Billy luxuriated in the foam and raged inside over the insults he had suffered. Katie Crisp was undoubtedly a haughty cow with a very funny way of getting her kicks. And the nastier she got the sexier she looked. The way she bristled with contempt seemed to make her flesh writhe against the stern confines of her severe suit. He couldn't forget that pristine patch of white thigh and the shapely suspendered leg that she had flashed at him the other night. Or the way the rounded moons of her buttocks had wiggled inside her tight skirt as she marched briskly ahead of him down the corridor a few moments ago. How he'd love to hold her across his knees and paddle the pearly white cheeks of her bum until they turned a flaming puce! That would teach her to sneer at his cock.

It was true, however, that the actuality of sex, as opposed to the distant prospect, was currently beyond him. He badly needed some sleep and didn't relish the prospect of meeting this Kensington woman. She sounded snobbish and cranky and temperamental – some of the character traits he favoured least. The assumption by Almond and Crisp that he was some kind of superstud was frankly ludicrous and he couldn't believe that any rich society hostess would welcome advances from the likes of him.

There was a knock at the door and a man's voice called out, 'Breakfast.' The door swung open and a tray bearing a coffee pot and other enticing accoutrements swung into view carried by a man in a white coat who was so tall that his head appeared to scrape the door lintel as he entered.

'Sorry to barge in, old boy,' he said, 'but I was told your need was urgent.'

The stranger smiled, an expression that transformed his cadaverous features. He placed the tray on top of the sink where it sat neatly to form an ad hoc table. 'Milk? Sugar?' he enquired as he began to serve.

As a grateful Billy watched him pour a life-saving cup of coffee he realised that the white coat was an apron tied at the front in the style of a professional waiter.

'Are you the in-house tea boy?'

'Chef, actually. From The Holy Mullet next door.

Mind if I join you?' he added, indicating a second cup on the tray. 'It'll save me coming back for this lot later on.' And he sat companionably on the loo seat and sipped his coffee.

Billy had been thinking. 'You're famous, aren't you? The Holy Mullet – that gets written up in all the fancy magazines. You're um—'

'Arnold Brie. Yes, I have recently been flavour of the month in certain quarters. Have a cookie, I've just baked them.'

'Blimey,' said Billy as he eagerly sank his teeth into the softest and most delicious biscuit he had ever tasted, 'I'm deeply honoured.'

'Oh no,' said Arnold, 'the pleasure's all mine. Actually, I wanted to talk to you and this seemed a good opportunity.'

'To me? Why?'

'Well, I'm told you're an expert on women.'

'What?'

'And I need help. I can't go to doctors or therapists or anyone like that because it's not that kind of a problem. I thought maybe I could consult you professionally.'

'I'm a detective!'

'But you specialise in sex cases, don't you? That's what Katie told me. And I have a case for you.'

'Oh. Christ, Arnold, you bake a bloody good biscuit. This breakfast is making me feel a hundred per cent better.'

'So you'll help me? I'll pay twice the going rate.'

'Well, put like that, maybe you should come to my office for a consultation. I'd give you a card but . . .'

At that moment the door burst open and in marched Katie Crisp, a miraculously clean set of clothes over her arm. Arnold leaped hastily to his feet to pack away his tray of goodies. And as he exited he grinned at Billy and said, 'Don't worry, I'll find you.'

15

A big barrel-shaped man, dressed only in a pair of swim-ming shorts and espadrilles, sat under an umbrella by the side of an Olympic-sized swimming pool, reading a newspaper. From the villa behind him emerged a statu-esque blonde, clad as extensively as he, bearing a tray of refreshments. She set it down on the table beside her companion and placed in front of him a tumbler filled to the brim and beaded with moisture. It was a scorching hot day.

The man did not look up but carried on reading intently. The woman extended her gorgeous frame along the length of a sun-lounger, arranged a pair of dark glasses on her head and leant back to lift her face to the blazing sun. Sun lotion glistened on the full mounds of her already bronzed and naked breasts. For a few moments there was complete silence save for the clink of ice in the woman's tall gin and tonic as she lifted it to her lips.

Suddenly the man leaned back and threw the news-paper from him in obvious ill-temper. Its pages flew apart, settling like fallen leaves across the woman's all but nude body.

'Oy!' she objected loudly. 'What'd you do that for?'

She pronounced 'you' as 'yow'. She came from Birmingham.

'Read it,' he ordered, 'read the fucking thing for yourself.' And he drained his beer in one long gulp.

'No thanks,' replied the girl, pushing the paper away and rearranging herself comfortably, 'you know I'm a victim of an impoverished education. I can't read.'

'You can read cheques well enough. And designer labels, when it suits you.'

'That reminds me, you owe me some money. I popped into Malaga yesterday. I bought a new dress to replace the one you ripped off me on Saturday night. Actually, I bought a few. I know what you're like.'

'Fucking country!' he muttered. 'Fucking sun! Rotten beer. Fucking funny food.'

'What's got into you?'

'Fucking brainless tarts who ought to keep their mouths shut.'

'That's a bit rich, Danny Fretwork. You shouldn't say that to a girl who's given you the best of her mouth already this morning. It's not my idea of fun to hand out blow-jobs before breakfast.'

'As it happens, Beverly, I was not referring to you, though I could have been. I was talking about Patsy.'

'Patsy? What Patsy?' she asked, suddenly alert.

'My wife, you silly cow.'

'Oh. I thought you were divorced.'

'Not yet and I'm likely to be a widower before I'm a divorcee.'

'Oh dear, oh dear. What's she done?'

'I keep telling you, read the paper.'

She groaned in a resigned fashion but languidly picked up a fallen page which by happy chance contained the first instalment of Patsy Fretwork's confessions to the *Blizzard*.

She tittered as she read and then laughed out loud in a high-pitched irritating shriek which set her expansive breasts quivering. Danny snarled at her. He'd go over and smack those big tits for her if she didn't shut up.

'This is a bit of a laugh,' she said. 'Did you really ask her to measure your dick with a ruler on your first date? She makes you sound like a right prat.'

Danny reached across and swiped the paper from her grasp with a great hairy paw. 'Shut up.'

'But you wanted me to read it, Danny,' she said, aggrieved.

He took one of her sumptuous breasts in his hand and squeezed it. Despite its size it disappeared almost entirely in his big fist.

'Ow!' she squealed. 'You don't have to take it out on me, Danny.'

'No, but I'm going to all the same. Take your knickers off.'

'Ooh, you big beast – what are you going to do?'

'You'll see.'

'We could go indoors. You know, have a siesta before lunch.' But she was already stripping off for him, removing her bikini bottoms seductively and dangling the scrap of fabric in front of his face. 'I'm not sure I want to be fucked out here in the open. You'll have to catch me first.' And she set off along the terrace, her breasts bobbing, her arse cheeks jiggling. Danny eyed her as she ran off, looking over her shoulder at him and giggling.

Inside he was burning up, he wanted revenge for his humiliation in the *Blizzard*. He wanted a heart-to-heart with his beloved Patsy. He could imagine the smirk on her face already. Just for now, a little workout with Bimbo Bev might relieve the pressure. He shucked off his swimming trunks, revealing a thick stubby tool emerging from the forest of hair at the base of his belly. He set off after her, moving swiftly despite his bulk, a great hairy powerful gorilla of a man.

Beverly allowed herself to be caught on the other side of the pool. Smack! A great palm descended on her left buttock, flattening its creamy curves, sending the breath out of her body. Smack, smack, smack. The hand came down again and again, whacking the white flesh, turning it scarlet.

'Ooh Danny, ooh! No! No!' she screamed, pressing her cunt mound hard down on his thigh in her excitement. 'Oh no, that's too much! Stop now, please.' And she wriggled again, harder and harder.

Danny reached for a bottle of suntan oil that stood on a nearby table and poured a large pool of ointment over her flaming buttocks. He kneaded her bottom fiercely, digging his massive fingers deep into the pink moons of flesh and making her squirm. He spread the cheeks wide and the perfect star of her bumhole winked up at him invitingly from the crack of her arse. Thrusting two fingers deep into the wet slit of her pussy, he took her in a pincer hold around the fork of her body and pressed the head of his thumb up into that tempting opening. Then, with his other hand, he aimed a large gob of lotion splat into her rear.

'Oh no, Danny, not up my bum, please.' And she wriggled frantically in a futile attempt to escape his grip.

'Now now, Beverly, you loved it last time.' And his thumb, its passage well greased, slid into the vestibule of her arse, disappearing up to the knuckle. She redoubled her efforts to shake him off but succeeded only in burying the digit further inside her.

'Oh God,' she groaned, a hint of resignation – and of excitement – in her voice.

'You see,' he said triumphantly, jamming his thumb up her back passage and thrusting his fingers simultaneously into her pussy hole, 'you love it, don't you. If I keep this up you're going to come, aren't you?'

She didn't reply but moaned wordlessly, her hips now bucking in time to his thrusts, her arse and cunt eagerly eating up the fierce fingering. Suddenly he stood up, lifting her with him and threw her face down on a nearby sun-bed. She flopped down like a doll, her big breasts splaying out from under her body, her legs spread to reveal her pink wet quim, her bum cheeks still raw and flaming from the spanking. Danny eyed her with a predatory gleam in his eye. He knew she loved his animal brand of fucking.

'Kneel up,' he commanded. 'Stick your arse out so I can see where I'm going to put my dick.'

She obeyed at once, pulling her knees under her and thrusting her bum out obscenely. Without being asked, she reached round with both hands and spread apart her cheeks, revealing every delectable millimetre of her hairless crack, from the distended eye of her pretty pink anus down to the splayed purse of her quim. Danny smoothed oil into his rock-hard organ. He had her well-trained, there was no doubt about that.

Then he was up her. His thick prong charging straight up her bumhole with no finesse, no civilities, just brute strength. A loud groan rang from her prone body as she took his weight and her slender frame rippled beneath him as he sawed in and out of her bottom, stuffing his fat organ up her rear tunnel with the energy of a sprinter. But this sprinter was determined to make the race last, he was out to extract every nuance of pleasure from the delicious body bent beneath him.

His stomach slapped against her quivering bum flesh as he bulled into her. He had both arms around her now, massaging and mauling a big soft tit in each of his massive hands. Little mewing noises were coming from her mouth as he prodded and pounded. He knew that she now had a hand between her legs, playing with her pussy lips and stroking the hard nub of flesh at the top of her slit as she sought her own satisfaction before he finished. The thought that she was wanking away beneath him while he fucked her arse sent an electric thrill through his body and he prodded and delved and pinched and smacked away at her wanton flesh on the verge of delirium.

And then he came, his energy redoubling in unbelievable fury, as he pumped, pumped, pumped and finally exploded deep inside her glorious bum.

For a moment he lay on top of her, a dead weight, panting his breath into her ear like a dog. Then he was on his feet leaving Beverly in a bruised and crumpled heap.

A slim Spaniard in a white coat was standing by the patio door, a tray of food in his hands. It was possible he had been there some time. Danny strode past him, his fat dick now dangling damply between his thighs, a big grin on his face.

'Placido,' he said, 'bring me a sandwich upstairs. And then get the car out, we're going to the airport.'

'Yes sir,' said Placido subserviently. But his coal-black eyes were not on his employer, they were focused on the still undulating thighs of his mistress and on the thick white slick of spunk that was oozing from between the cheeks of her rosy bottom.

16

Candy Kensington lived in a mansion in St John's Wood. It was extravagantly furnished with high quality antiques: Hepplewhite chairs and Chippendale tables, chiffonniers and armoires and bijoux writing desks and ornate gilt mirrors, lush brocaded curtains swagged and rouched, exquisite little watercolours and vast lowering oils of stormy seas and Venetian canals and shepherdesses. Cabinets bulged with crystal glasses and Chinese porcelain; bouquets of flowers, exquisitely arranged in oriental vases, filled the vast drawing-room with the fragrance of high summer. It occurred to Billy that, outside of a museum, he had never been in the presence of so much ostentatious wealth.

Candida Kensington herself was no less extravagantly turned out. Her cream summer suit was by Chanel, her snakeskin high heels were by Jourdain, her wristwatch was by Cartier – and Billy longed to discover who had designed her underwear.

Her features were animated. She smiled and laughed a lot, flashing small white teeth from long curling lips and her oval face frequently dimpling into a grin. Her big brown eyes never left his face, indicating some kind of urgent interest in him. Candy was not the most beautiful woman he had ever seen yet there was something about her which made him positively drool with desire.

Billy shamelessly ogled her slim tanned legs, which crossed and uncrossed in a faint fleshy whisper as she sat by his side on the vast chesterfield. He shifted uncomfortably, a plate of sandwiches concealing the kind of erection that had made last night's sojourn beneath Tracy's bed seem such agony. How could this be after an energetic night spent tussling with a voracious sexpot? It was a mystery to him why his sex urge had returned so conclusively. But the moment he had set eyes on the elegant society queen his carnal impulses had come flooding back, threatening to overwhelm him. He hoped he would not come in his pants.

He found it hard to take in what Candy was saying. He gazed with longing at her slender, finely manicured fingers as they raised a thin sandwich to her mouth and marvelled at her as she ate: the way her perfect glistening teeth crunched neatly into the bread, the exquisite manner in which her lips moved as she masticated and the sweet bob of her Adam's apple as she swallowed. He pictured those delicate fingers paddling through his chest hair, walking down his body to take a firm grip on his painful shaft. He couldn't help but imagine her bending that slender neck and taking the ripe red plum of his glans between those wickedly curling lips and nibbling it, grazing it with those tiny teeth – this was crazy! He had come here to undertake some cunning diplomacy and all he could think of was this rich bitch chewing on his cock!

He forced himself to make some kind of conversation.

'Do you have cats yourself?' he asked. There was certainly no sign of them if she did.

'Oh no,' she said. 'Unfortunately my home, as you can see, has far too many unsuitable objects in it and so it wouldn't be fair to keep any pets. It's a terrible shame but living with valuable things is such a burden and cramps one's life in so many ways.'

Billy really did not know what to say to that. He sat mesmerised as she crossed her legs once more. They were bare. He imagined kneeling at her feet and running his hands from her slender ankles, up her firm calves and then beneath the hem of her skirt – was she wearing panties? he wondered. Would the hair of her bush match the deep chestnut of her head? Perhaps she would have no hair down there at all, just a naked sex-mouth, as moist and succulent as a slice of ripe honeydew melon. And he could bury his head between her thighs, close his hungry lips over hers and suck the sweet juice that flowed from her very core . . .

He tried to concentrate on Candy and what she was now saying. It seemed she ran charity organisations for all sorts of species. Abandoned gerbils apparently were in need of special care and she was trying to reintroduce red squirrels into NW8. Billy decided that, whatever her other attractions, this woman was literally crazy about small furry mammals.

'Let's talk about your pussy,' he heard himself say.

'I'm sorry?'

'I mean, Poor Pussy,' he corrected himself, 'the Gala concert.'

'Of course, but do you mind if we do it upstairs while we're working?'

'No – ' Billy was puzzled, but he'd go upstairs with this woman any time, in fact the sooner the better.

She preceded him up flights of stairs with fine mahogany banisters and glistening brass carpet rails and along hallways hung with more paintings, which became less conventional and more contemporary in execution the higher they climbed. Billy hardly noticed a thing, his eyes glued to the graceful form ahead of him and in particular at the purposeful swivel of her buttocks as she ascended.

She lead him into a room that was obviously used as a studio. Sunlight flooded in from the high windows. Drawings and paintings littered the room, from large canvases to small pencil sketches pinned haphazardly to the wall. All the artwork contained the same subject matter – the male nude.

In a flash of insight Billy knew what Candy was going to say before she said it. For the second time that day a desirable woman was going to ask him to undress. She did have the grace, however, to be rather more diplomatic than Katie Crisp.

'Billy, I hope you won't mind just slipping out of your things and standing over there.'

Billy stared at her boggle-eyed, his cock so huge in his trousers that it seemed it might almost leap out of its own accord. This was going to be horribly embarrassing.

'You see, Billy, I've been searching and searching for just the right model to complete my programme design and I have a hunch that, with you, my search is over.'

Somehow he found himself removing his jacket. 'What programme?'

'For the Poor Pussy Gala. I'm designing the programme myself. It has a centre piece of an adorable kitten lying on a cushion and below are the twin muses of comedy and tragedy, male and female figures, bearing the theatrical masks. Look, you can see it here.'

Billy studied the sheets of paper on her slanted drawing table and could indeed see many workings of the design she was describing. The kitten was of a chocolate-box nature with a cute little bandage over one ear indicating, doubtless, that it had been rescued. A slim female figure reclined on the righthand side of the drawing, arms held aloft towards the cat, offering up the mask of tragedy. The figure was nude, with long slender flanks, narrow loins and pouting pear-shaped breasts. The face had almond eyes and curling lips. Billy recognised it at once.

'A self-portrait? It's the lips and the eyes, they are very distinctive.'

'Naughty boy,' she replied, batting her eyelashes at him. 'There's no other way you *could* spot me, is there? At least, not on such a brief acquaintance.'

By now Billy was down to just his trousers. He hopped up onto the small dais. Maybe he could get away with exposing himself just this far. But no.

'Oh, Billy,' she said at once, 'I think you'll have to take your trousers off. I'm awfully sorry but I couldn't get the proper lines of your body otherwise. You can, of course, leave your underpants on.'

Billy knew that such a fig leaf would hardly be adequate. Nevertheless he stepped out of his trousers and turned to face her.

He could swear she gulped. Certainly her eyes seemed to pop as she took in the extraordinary bulge in his skin-tight bikini briefs. His cock was lodged sideways and so its length was barely contained within the thin white cotton. He knew very well he might just as well have been naked. Every bulge and ridge of his magnificent tumescence was revealed to her thirsty gaze.

'My,' she said, 'you're just what I'm looking for. If you could place your left hand on your hip and hold your other arm up – yes, that's lovely.' And she began to draw.

The atmosphere in the room was pregnant with possibilities. The silence grew heavy, broken only by the scratch of her pen on paper and, to Billy's ears, the beat of his own heart which pounded in his chest like a drum. He could swear that his cock was twitching in tempo inside the tight confines of his briefs.

'About the Gala,' he said hesitantly, 'Imogen was telling me who was on the bill.'

She didn't reply but continued to sketch, staring at him intently.

'I must say,' Billy blundered on, 'it's a most impressive gathering, though I'm a little surprised at one or two omissions.'

'Oh yes,' she said.

'I mean for such a popular cause I thought you might be aiming at a rather broader audience. You know, have someone younger, just to keep up with the trends.'

'Like who?' she asked. Her attention now well and truly caught.

'Well, I know that Imogen has an exciting new singer on her books . . .'

'Who's that?'

'She's called Tracy Pert. She's just made her first record.'

'I don't think I've heard of her. Of course I'm not really up on who's in and who's out on the pop scene.'

'Tracy's very popular. Imogen has high hopes for her.'

'Have you seen her perform?'

'Yes, I have. Sort of. She's a friend of mine.'

'Tracy Pert,' Candy repeated to herself. 'Wait a minute. She's that pin-up girl, isn't she?'

'Yes, she's really very talented.'

'Good God.' The lead in Candy's pencil broke with a loud crack. 'And she's a friend of yours, is she?'

'Er, yes.'

'And I suppose she's the reason you're standing there with that silly look on your face and your penis half out of your pants.' Suddenly Candy was spitting blood. She was out of her chair and throwing Billy's clothes in his direction, her eyes blazing and the red flush of anger in her cheeks.

'You can cover up your equipment right now, Mr Dazzle, and then you can clear off. I tell you categorically that no lowlife slum child with elephantiasis of the mammaries is going to ruin my evening of classical entertainment. Got that?'

17

In the dining-room of Emmeline's, Pandora Britches' club, Pandy and Sophie shared a secluded corner banquette. It was an elegant room full of light though not of people. Which suited both parties.

The two women sized one another up. Pandora wore a crisp blue shirt and designer jeans, her hair pinned back in a wooden barrette and she observed Sophie through scarlet-framed spectacles that obscured half her face. She appeared purposeful and efficient, in contrast to Sophie who looked as if she had dressed in a hurry. Her auburn curls billowed untidily around her shoulders and the black lycra mini-dress, which showed off every sumptuous curve of her voluptuous body, was distinctly inappropriate in the asexual surroundings of the most aggressive women's club in London. Sophie oozed sex. The effect was entirely intentional.

'You're not exactly how I pictured you,' said Pandora, 'I expected someone rather more . . . well, rather less attractive.'

'Same here,' said Sophie. 'I thought you'd be dressed in tweeds. I've read some of your revues in *The Rag* – you come over as a hardline feminist dyke.'

'Well, I've got to trim my copy to the readership. I

also write for the *Blizzard*, don't forget.'

'How could I? That's why we're here. Where's Mrs Fretwork?'

'Patsy won't be joining us. I'm sure you understand.'

'Not exactly. It's her I want to talk to.'

'She can't go out while this big serial is going on. We can't have any of our rivals getting wind of her. They're beasts. They'd spoil anything, given the chance.'

'So where is she?'

'Somewhere secret.'

'Safe from her husband?'

'He's no problem, he's in Spain.'

'He can hardly be unaware of what she's saying about him every day in the *Blizzard*. He won't be happy.'

'So you think he might come after her? And that's why you're so interested.'

'Exactly. Of course, Danny also has many associates still active here. Apart from keeping Mrs Fretwork out of sight, I hope you are taking steps to ensure her safety.'

Pandora took a long sip of her mineral water and said, 'You're not offering police protection, by any chance?'

'Well, if you could put up with me for a bit . . .'

'You?'

'You thought I meant a couple of strapping male detectives, I suppose. No chance. It's me or nothing. I can assure you I can be very effective if it comes to the rough stuff. I've been trained. I also have other methods of enforcement.'

'I'm sure you do.'

'I'd keep out of the way, if that's what's bothering you.'

'I'm not sure that I'd want you to, you're far too attractive.' And she put her hand on Sophie's thigh beneath the tablecloth. Sophie did not attempt to remove it.

A waitress appeared and set a plate of crudités in front of them.

'Bring us a bottle of Louis Roederer Crystal,' ordered Pandora.

Sophie's eyebrows rose a notch.

'Don't worry, sergeant, I don't expect the Metropolitan Police to foot the bill. Or don't you drink while you're on duty?' Pandy was enjoying herself. Her hand was by now quite at home on Sophie's right thigh, roaming over the firm bare flesh, probing and squeezing as pruriently as any male suitor about to effect a boozy seduction.

'Actually,' said Sophie, eagerly raising the flute of pink sparkling liquid to her mouth, 'I only say no when I'm in uniform.'

'I should like to see you in uniform,' said Pandora, taking the hem of Sophie's skirt and slowly raising it upwards to her waist. The journalist studied the exquisite picture thus revealed, of creamy white thigh flesh and gently curving belly barely concealed by black lace panties. The bulging mound of Sophie's bush was clearly delineated beneath the thin material.

'I've always wanted to look at a policewoman's cunt,' she said.

Sophie returned her gaze. She was obviously being tested. 'You mean, in a public place? Like the dining-room of a club dedicated to the memory of women's suffrage?'

'Quite,' said Pandora, letting go of her skirt, leaving it bunched around Sophie's waist.

'It looks like your lucky day, doesn't it?' said Sophie,

pulling the gusset of her panties to one side and exposing a thatch of auburn pussy curls and the long crinkly lips of her pink quim. She held her other hand to Pandora's lips and pushed two fingers into her mouth. 'Lick them,' she ordered, 'make them nice and wet.'

Sophie lowered the moistened digits to her cunt and slipped them inside herself, pushing obscenely in and out, then sliding them to the top of her crack, splaying them in a vee, revealing her long erect clit to Pandy's eager gaze. The ripe smell of pussy rose in the air. Pandy sniffed it in eagerly.

'You're a little saucebox, aren't you? You must want to see Patsy Fretwork very badly.'

'I want to see her husband very badly,' said Sophie, continuing to play with her clit, the colour rising in her cheeks, her breath already beginning to shorten.

Pandy removed her spectacles, then slipped to her knees beneath the table and positioned herself between Sophie's open legs.

'Won't someone notice?' said Sophie. 'Or doesn't anybody care what you do in a place like this?'

But there was no reply from Pandy. Her mouth was otherwise engaged.

18

Billy returned to his office. There wasn't much point in going home, he knew he wouldn't be able to rest as planned. Frustration and humiliation were burning him up. His erection throbbed in his trousers, a painful reminder of the ignominy he had suffered at the hands of Candy Kensington. Yet it was an unnatural sort of hard-on, iron-hard and unrelenting. Something funny was happening to him and he couldn't work it out. How come he had been so hot for Candy after an energetic night with a sex queen like Tracy? In other circumstances he would have been overjoyed at this evidence of his virility. But now, having suffered the bum's rush from La Kensington, he was well and truly pissed off.

Suddenly the phone rang. He had been reconnected – well, that was something. He snatched up the receiver.

'You blew it,' announced the ice-cool tones of Katie Crisp. 'Candy's been bending Imogen's ear for the last half an hour. You're off the pay roll.'

'Well . . .' spluttered Billy, 'what about Tracy and Orlando Verdi, shouldn't I—?'

'Don't do anything. It's all covered. And you're out of it. Don't bother to invoice us, you've been paid enough already.'

'In that case, Katie,' said Billy swiftly, his tumescent state calling to mind her perky posterior and milky white thighs, 'now I'm not working for you, why don't we meet up later for a drink?'

But she had already rung off, the bitch. He chalked up another insult to be avenged.

Billy quickly dialled Tracy's hotel.

'You rat,' was the first thing she said, 'you didn't tell me you were working for Imogen.'

'How could I, Tracy? My job was to build bridges and I've done that, haven't I? Look, about Orlando Verdi—'

But she interrupted him, 'Yeah, I know. I'm going round there now and if I have to suck his slimy Italian dick before I get a deal I'm going to send my brothers after you. Don't think I wouldn't.'

'Perhaps I could see you later?' said Billy, clutching at straws. 'Let me take you to dinner, you can tell me how it went.'

'I know what you're after, Billy Dazzle, and you've had plenty of it already under false pretences. So you can get lost.'

She hung up, too.

Billy slammed the phone down. He wished he hadn't had the bloody thing reconnected now. He felt just as wretched as he'd been the other morning, before Patsy turned up out of the blue. And that was another thing : . .

He'd bought a copy of the morning's *Blizzard* on the way back to the office. He spread it open on the desk. Part two of the confessions of Patsy Fretwork stared him full in the face. What was more, some familiar photographs also confronted him. Bloody hell, the little

cow had only used his photographs of the poolside orgy
to spice up her story! Mind you, there had been that
thousand pounds and the tumble over the desk. There's
no such thing as a free fuck, he reminded himself.

He remembered with some pleasure the jiggle of
Patsy's plump little buttocks as he pumped into her and
her gratitude for the service so lustily performed. His
cock throbbed again in his trousers. He wondered how
Patsy was getting on with that voracious dyke, Pandora
Britches, whose byline was prominently featured on the
page next to her own.

He took from his desk drawer the one photo Patsy
had left behind, the shot of the bum of his dreams:
voluptuously rounded cheeks and flaring hips thrust
backwards to reveal a glistening, pouting quim – there
was no doubt she couldn't have used that in the *Blizzard*!
His penis throbbed even more urgently. God, this afternoon was turning into a nightmare.

The phone rang once more. Billy let it ring for a bit.
Doubtless more bad news. Eventually he picked up the
receiver without enthusiasm.

'Billy Dazzle? It's Arnold here, just checking to see if
you're in. I'm coming right round, if that's convenient.'

'Arnold?' The chef. The saviour with the coffee. Oh
well, maybe what he needed was a bit of male company.

'Come right over, Arnold, no time like the present.'

Funnily enough, by the time the chef arrived Billy was
feeling significantly improved in the stiffy department.
His cock had suddenly shrivelled up, the blood dashing
off to do useful work elsewhere in his system, leaving
his sex organ limp and somnambulant. For once in his
life Billy had no regrets about a vanishing erection. He
bade Arnold hello quite like the old Bouncing Billy.

Arnold folded his elongated frame into a chair.

'How did it go? Your meeting with Candy Kensington?'

'Badly, if you must know, and I'm not sure why you should.'

'Oh dear.' Arnold face fell in sympathy. 'I'm sorry.'

'It's nothing to do with you but thanks. What's up? How can I help you?'

'It's very embarrassing. I've got this problem with women.'

'Join the club.'

'No, it's not the kind of problem you'll have. It's my, er, size.'

'Better to be too tall than too short. Anyway, women don't care about that sort of thing. They're always telling me it doesn't matter what a man looks like. That's usually after they've dumped me for a dwarf with a Porsche, of course.'

Arnold did not laugh. 'No, it's the size of my, um, member.'

Billy composed his features to look sympathetic. 'Isn't all that stuff just in the mind? The girls always say they're not bothered if it's on the small side.'

'No, it's not that. It's too big.'

'Too big? I didn't know it was possible to be too big.'

'Take it from me, chum. I'm not kidding.' Arnold's face grew long and serious. His lank black hair fell around his face as he spoke passionately. 'I worship women. I watch them walking down the street in their short skirts and tight T-shirts. I see their cute little mouths and sweet jiggly titties and I just want to wrap them in my arms and protect them and – and—'

'Rip their clothes off and fuck them stupid. Arnold,

I know just how you feel, it's entirely normal. So what exactly happens when you've charmed them out of their short skirts and tight T-shirts?'

'When they catch sight of it for the first time and see how big I am – well, they mostly go into shock. One girl threw complete hysterics and another ran from the room.'

'Blimey,' said Billy, 'you must be something special.'

'Another women offered me a job in dirty movies. She was a producer, she said I could have a great career. But it's not me, Billy, I'm just a chef who wants a girlfriend.'

'Have you never actually found anybody to, er, accommodate you?'

'No, and until recently I'd given up hope. I haven't tried to go to bed with a woman for nearly ten years. You see, I fell in love and it was going all right until I got her into bed. Then she told me she just couldn't go through with it. She said my cock was monstrous. It cast a bit of a blight over our whole relationship. So I put girlfriends out of my mind. I threw all my creative energies into my cooking. Now I'm a star in the kitchen but it's not enough. And when I see blokes like you effortlessly knocking off crumpet like Tracy Pert, well . . . You'd feel hard done by, too.'

Billy nodded in agreement. He would indeed. Poor old Arnold.

'Anyway, I suddenly thought, given your reputation, you might be able to help. Maybe you could find me someone who wouldn't be put off.'

'Well,' Billy was thinking, 'you've tried professionals, of course.'

'Only once. She just laughed at me, said it wasn't

worth her while no matter what I paid her because she'd need a month off work to recover. She offered to toss me off into her knickers instead but it wasn't really what I wanted.'

Billy had the beginning of an idea. 'Suppose I do know someone . . . tell me frankly – how big is it?'

'It's not *that* big,' said Arnold, 'it just looks it. It's about twice the size of the average.'

'You mean about a foot long?'

'Yes. Well, maybe a bit bigger.'

'My God,' Billy breathed, 'that's certainly impressive. OK, let me just make one call . . .'

19

The sand dunes seemed to stretch for ever, pale and shimmering in the baking heat of the Spanish sun. It was the middle of the afternoon, still siesta time for the sensible but play time for the newly liberated – like Beverly from Brum. She walked gaily along the wet strip of sand that separated surf from beach, a floppy straw hat on her head, sandals and T-shirt in her hand. Behind her, grim-faced but mesmerised by the vision of those swinging hips and striding thighs ahead of him, trudged the coal-eyed Placido. This was Fun-Fun Beach where the sunbathing was nude and the dipping skinny, where dope was smoked openly and the boogying went on till dawn – and where no nice girl ever went because her very presence was an open invitation to all-comers. There would be hell to pay for this, thought Placido, if Signor Fretwork ever found out . . .

'There,' announced Beverly and pointed to a patch of sand some fifteen feet from a group of blond hippy youths, strumming guitars and passing a bottle. Placido spread the towels as ordered. This was going to be worse than he thought.

The guitars stopped playing for a moment or two then broke into an uptempo jig as the youths took in Beverly's spectacular build: swelling bosom and violin-curved hips barely contained by a cerise bikini which she was already shimmying out of. She put her hands behind her back to unfasten the clip of her top and shrugged her big brown breasts into view, tossing the garment at the unhappy Placido.

There were three boys and one girl in the watching group; all were naked. The boys smiled at Beverly and called out their appreciation in German. The girl scowled, crumpling her remarkably pretty face. She had very small pointed tits.

Beverly slid out of her bikini bottom, displaying her full and rounded posterior to the boys as she did so. Her arse had now recovered from the treatment meted out by Danny a few hours earlier and two triangles of white flesh, fore and aft, flashed into view. The sun sparkled on the blonde tuft of hair at the junction of her thighs. One of the boys whistled.

Beverly was enjoying herself hugely. Ever since Placido had returned from the airport without Danny she had felt as if the door to her prison cell had been unlocked. Which was a laugh really, considering that she hoped a key would soon be turned on Danny. The silly bastard had obviously hotfooted it to England. At least, that's what she had told that butch DCI Spicer when she had rung her from the post office on the way to the beach. Now she would be able to return home without a beef hanging over her own head, if Spicer played fair. She felt no remorse for Danny – he had turned into a pain in the butt, anyway. Funny how life sometimes just worked out right.

She took the suntan lotion out of Placido's hand and, still standing, began to smooth it into her skin. She took great care to rub it into all her most intimate crevices, lifting each breast and smearing the undercreases, running her fingers right into her bum crack and splaying her legs wide to get at the inner flesh of her upper thigh. Placido grudgingly palmed some oil across her back between her shoulder-blades. His touch was tender though his jaw remained set and his eyes blazed with disapproval. Beverly squirmed appreciatively under his fingers, flaunting herself shamelessly. If the Spaniard was going to be such a stuffed shirt, she had other fish to fry. She lay face down on the towels to wait.

It took less than five minutes before one of the German boys approached, holding out a half-empty bottle. He was big and muscular and walked with a confident swagger, his long hair hanging in damp ringlets to his bronzed shoulders. Between his thighs dangled a thick and meaty cock, foreskin peeled back to reveal the scarlet bulb of his glans. Beverly almost licked her lips as it bobbed towards her, coming to rest directly in front of her face as he knelt to offer her a drink.

The cheap firewater scalded her gullet and lit a flame in her belly. The boy was grinning and his big penis was swelling to stiffness right in her face.

'My name is Bruno,' he said.

Past his tanned left hip Beverly could see the others watching his progress. The girl sat between the two boys desperately trying to keep their attention. She was fondling a cock in each hand, both of impressive proportions, but the eyes of the boys were fixed on their friend.

'You are a very pretty girl,' he went on clumsily.

'Go away,' said Placido from behind them, 'she does not want you here.'

'Shut up, Placido. Mind your own business.'

'But Signor Fretwork . . .'

'Signor Fretwork will never find out, Placido. Now, why don't you just sit back and watch? You're very good at that.' And Beverly tipped some brandy into her hand and sprinkled it onto Bruno's fat erection.

He gasped as the alcohol stung the tender skin, then gasped again as she lowered her lips over his big tool and sucked half its length into the hot cave of her mouth. Behind them the boys cheered and the girl quickly lowered her head to the crotch of the one of her right.

Placido closed his eyes and muttered, '*Madre de Dios!*'

20

Despite her name, Betsy Toast, the whore from upstairs, was not of English extraction. Her real name was Gretchen Bockenheim, but in essence she was Californian through and through. Six foot tall with long flaxen hair that fell in a golden curtain to her waist, she glowed with sun-bronzed health as she admitted Billy and Arnold into her upstairs parlour.

Betsy was wearing her preferred costume of skimpy T-shirt finishing just below her ribcage – revealing a flat brown belly and loosely encasing firm breasts, prominent nipples pushing through the thin cotton – and tight denim shorts cut to finish high on her hips and just below the undercurve of the rounded moons of her buttocks: an outfit designed to show the maximum amount of her glorious tanned flesh.

She had once told Billy she had come to England on a modelling assignment but had fallen out with another girl who was sleeping with the photographer who was of course also sleeping with her. In the ensuing cat-fight her nose had been broken, debarring her from a modelling career, and she had simply fallen into whoring. Billy reckoned that fashion's loss was the horny punter's gain.

In any case he particularly liked her nose with its

prominent bump high on the bridge. It was the imperfection that gave character to her flawless oval face with its violet eyes and enormous full-lipped mouth, just made for sucking cock. When she had first moved in, some nine months previously, she had thrown a couple of freebies Billy's way to ensure neighbourly goodwill and Billy had been smitten. However, she had smartly reminded him that theirs was a business association by threatening to charge him a fiver a feel. From then on Billy had hardly been able to afford a decent grope.

Betsy shoved two mugs of tea in their direction and said in her nasal twang, 'So, how can I help you guys? Is this business or what?'

Billy glanced at Arnold, whose jaw had fallen at the sight of the bronzed vision in front of him and whose eyes were devouring every mesmerising inch of her. Billy decided he could safely forge ahead.

'Arnold has a little problem and I though maybe you could help him. It's a bit personal.'

'Of course it's personal – it's about fucking, right?' She looked at Billy quizzically. 'Are we talking a threesome here?'

Billy's slumbering cock rolled over in its sleep, as it were, nevertheless he quickly shook his head. 'No, Arnold needs some particular attention and I'm just advising him on where to get it.'

The violet eyes narrowed. 'You're not suggesting a cut of my fee, I hope.'

Arnold spoke up. 'I shall take care of Billy separately. I'm hiring him as my adviser in this matter.'

'Great.' She smiled, her dazzling pearly teeth flashing. 'Come next door, Arnold. Let's get it on.' She indicated the bedroom door.

'Hang on,' said Billy, 'there's something we've got to discuss first. You see – ' he stopped. He didn't really know how to say it, not with Arnold sitting there making goo-goo faces at Betsy. He decided to try a different tack.

'Look, Betsy, in your professional opinion, as an expert in the field of human relations – how big a cock can the average woman take?'

She thought that was very funny. She laughed for what seemed like five minutes, her breasts shivering enticingly inside her vest, her loose hair shaking around her face.

'I mean, how big can you take?'

'Honey,' she said eventually, 'no guy's got a dick I can't take.'

This was the crunch moment. Billy turned to Arnold. 'OK, Mr Brie, drop 'em.'

'Maybe things are moving a little fast,' stammered Arnold. 'Do you mind if I have my tea? I'm feeling a little nervous.'

'Oh right,' said Betsy, 'you need to relax, I understand. How about a joint? I've got some great grass. Mellow you out definitively. We could take it from there.'

'No,' said Arnold, 'I think the tea's just fine. How about a biscuit?' And he produced a paper bag from his jacket pocket and offered it first to Betsy and then to Billy. She shrugged and took one. Billy plunged his hand in eagerly. 'Arnold's a chef. The Holy Mullet. It's a big deal.'

Betsy didn't look particularly interested until she took a bite. 'Oh wow,' she exclaimed, 'this is great. You make 'em yourself?'

Arnold smiled modestly. Billy recognised the biscuit as similar to those he had had for breakfast. He tucked in. Betsy took another.

'Arnold's got one over a foot long,' said Billy, thinking he had better keep their minds on the subject. Betsy's eyebrows shot up. 'You think you can handle that?'

'No sweat,' she said, her teeth chomping, 'there are three or four places I can put a sucker like that.'

Arnold coughed, 'Well, it might be a little bigger.'

Betsy's eyebrows lifted a degree higher. 'Interesting. Are you in the *Guinness Book of Records* or something? Of course,' she went on ruminatively, 'it's not so much the length as the width. Come on, Arnold, let's get to it.'

In one sinuous movement Betsy gripped the bottom hem of her T-shirt and pulled it over her head, revealing her bare breasts. They were high and firm, not large but undeniably thrilling to gaze upon. The pale saucers of her areolae surrounded dark brown nipples seemingly disproportionate in size and fully erect. Suddenly Billy realised that she was turned on and that he himself was as ragingly tumescent as he had ever been in his life.

Betsy stood in front of Arnold and undid the button at the waist of her shorts. The zip descended with a deafening scratchy sound in the silence of the room. She turned round and presented her rear to Arnold, almost thrusting it in his face. 'Pull them off,' she ordered.

Billy noticed that Arnold's hands were trembling as he took hold of the denim and clumsily tugged downwards. For a moment the thick blue material stuck fast on her hips then, in a sudden rush, it crumpled to the floor, exposing her golden bum. The rounded contours of her buttocks were as smooth and pleasing to the eye as distant hills. But there was nothing remote about these thrusting curves which were scarcely covered by a thin strip of fabric that ran into the cleft between her cheeks. From the rear the fascinating quadrant of her pussy was framed by the undercurve of her bum and the succulent skin of her inner thigh.

Betsy let Arnold contemplate this delicious landscape for a moment or two, grinning at Billy over her shoulder.

'Do you want me to go?' he pantomimed at her. Her mouth formed a soundless 'No.'

She turned her body to face Arnold. The wisp of panty was cut in a vee across the plain of her stomach, the white scrap of material barely covering the prominent mound of her cunt. She offered her hips to him with a little jib of her pelvis. 'Go on, Arnold,' she commanded, 'finish the job. Take them off for me.'

Arnold needed no further urging. Using both hands he reverently inched the flimsy garment down her hips and along her sumptuous golden thighs, his long nose almost buried in the blonde curls of her pussy as he bent to complete this sacred task. Betsy put her hands on the back of his head and pulled him towards her crotch. Arnold plunged in head first, his hands sliding up the back of her thighs to grasp the soft cushions of her bum cheeks, his mouth opening as he lunged forward to burrow into her welcoming quim.

'Ooooh, Arnold,' she said in a voice that had dropped a full octave. 'Oh, that's good.'

Billy studied her for signs of professional play-acting but her eyes were closed and her smile was surely genuine.

Arnold lapped noisily and she allowed it for a full half minute before pulling herself free and bending to plant an open-mouthed kiss on his lips which neither of them seemed keen to end. She broke away first and pulled Arnold to his feet.

'Come on, honey,' she said, 'I think it's time we got to grips with this so-called problem of yours.'

Billy coughed and said, 'Why don't I just leave you two . . . ?'

This time it was Arnold who cut him off. 'Billy, this is the point where I need moral support.'

'OK.' This was the moment of truth after all. It would be a shame to miss it.

Betsy was wasting no time. She already had Arnold's jacket and shirt off, and she unbuckled his belt and pulled his trousers down in one movement.

Arnold wore what was probably the male equivalent of a reinforced brassiere – an elasticated jock-strap that finished at his navel. The extraordinary sight that met their eyes was of some two or three inches of white penile shaft emerging from the top of this garment, capped by the angry red head of Arnold's cock. It looked as if his dick reached almost to the centre of his chest.

There was a split second of silence before Betsy cried, 'Wow!' and pulled his pants down to reveal a veritable colossus of a cock, a white tower capped with a fiery red dome that rose and rose from the crisp dark hair of his groin.

'Why, Arnold,' said Betsy in awe, 'that's beautiful.'

Billy was struck dumb. Despite the throbbing evidence of his own masculinity he felt suddenly inadequate.

Betsy had fallen to her knees in front of Arnold and was assessing the problematic member. Hand over hand the shaft took four of her fists to measure out. She absentmindedly fondled the dangling eggs of his balls as she considered her next step. Suddenly she lowered her head and in one swift movement sucked the fat glans into her mouth. Her head bobbed a couple of times and her fingers ran up and down the great shaft, circling and spanning it. Eventually she ejected the helmet from her lips with an audible plop.

'Just as I thought,' she announced, turning to face Billy with a grin on her face and a gleam of anticipation in her eyes, 'the length is extraordinary but the girth is manageable.' She smiled up at Arnold. 'I think I can make you a happy man, Arnold, why don't we take a crack at it?'

The chef did not reply, instead he placed his hands under her armpits and lifted her up, pulling her to him in a great hug, one hand in the small of her back, fingers spreading down across the upper reaches of her arse, the other in the yellow curtain of her hair. She folded eagerly into his embrace, lifting her mouth to his kiss, pressing her belly against his towering cock. Billy thought they made a very handsome couple.

Arnold said hesitantly, 'About the money, Betsy, I'll pay whatever you want.'

'Shut up, Arnold,' said Betsy. 'Let's fuck.'

21

Placido was *not* a happy man. Beverly had been frolicking with the Germans for nearly an hour now and they were still going strong. Fully clad beneath the baking sun, the Spaniard sat by himself on the beach and watched every twitch and thrust of the action that raged only a few yards away. He had been in love with Beverly for months. He adored every voluptuous inch of her, hated his employer for the way in which he casually used her and longed to bury himself in her golden embrace. And to see her now!

Beverly was loving it. It had taken her barely a minute, it seemed, to urge Bruno into his first orgasm; jamming her lovely lips over the head of his fat cock, sucking and slithering up and down its solid length while palming his big hairy balls. He had squirted into her happily and collapsed onto his back to the applause of his fellows who had sat transfixed as Beverly, big breasts swaying, a dribble of spunk running down her chin, had risen to her feet and strode towards them.

Marlene, the German girl, had been pushed aside as Beverly sank herself on the thick spike the girl had been sucking and pulled the boy's face into the deep valley between her tits. The third boy had responded to her invitation to kneel and offer up his genitals for her examination. His tool was smaller than the other two but with pretty golden hairs and one pulsing blue vein standing out along its satin-smooth length. Beverly kissed and fondled it as she bounced on the big fellow beneath her. Then she had closed her mouth over it and set to work with her tongue and lips. In a moment both boys had come, shooting their jism into her with hoarse shouts of pleasure.

It had gone on from there. The Germans did not have much finesse but they had plenty of stamina. It seemed to the watching Placido that by now the German boys had used her in almost every way; first individually, then in combinations as their immediate lust was slaked and they searched for more inventive and comradely means of satisfaction.

Beverly was on her knees with Bruno at her head feeding his swollen cock down her throat, his hands buried in the mass of her expensively streaked blonde hair, now tangled with sweat and sand and spunk. At her rear, Dieter, the boy with the smallest penis, was sawing in and out of her pussy, every now and then reaching beneath her to pull and slap and maul her hanging mammaries. The remaining boy lay off to the side, urging his two compatriots on in incomprehensible but doubtless coarse German. Between his legs crouched Marlene vainly trying to breath life into his flaccid cock.

Placido was on fire, with anger and jealousy but above all with lust. The sight of the three bestial Germans gorging themselves on the perfect form of the English-woman he adored was agony. He longed to beat them off, to lay them out in a swift fistfight, and then to throw himself on Beverly and sink his burning penis deep inside her glorious body. But he knew that was not the way. This degradation was what she wanted. This wild uninhibited orgy was some kind of release for her after pandering to the whims of Danny Fretwork for months. She was a slut, he knew that, but she was a passionate one and he wanted her desperately.

Dieter was still labouring at Beverly's rear but his cock kept slipping from her wet pussy. He had a conversation with his pals in rapid German. They had loosened her up too much, he needed somewhere tighter. When he placed an exploratory finger on the puckered rose of her anus a shiver ran through her kneeling form. She took her mouth from Bruno's cock and hissed, 'Yes! Put it up me there! Stick it in my arse!'

Placido became aware there was a hand at his belt. He tore his eyes from Beverly's thrusting buttocks and looked directly into the eyes of Marlene. They were great pools of the palest blue and though the words she spoke were incomprehensible to him her need was written in that liquid gaze.

She had been ignored from the moment Beverly had made her first appearance. She had insinuated her slender form into the action whenever she could but she had been allotted only a bit part in the drama. The boys had allowed her to lick limp cocks to proud erections, and then promptly buried them in Beverly's wanton flesh; they had let her stroke their balls while they fucked; and they had made her lie beneath Beverly's pendulous bosom and suck on her thick rubbery nipples. Beverly herself had twice grabbed Marlene's head and forced it between her thighs to reach orgasm on the girl's skilful lips and tongue. But as for the aching void between the Marlene's own thighs, no one had volunteered to fill it.

Now she eagerly unbuckled Placido's belt as he sat transfixed by the lewd tableau in front of him. She cleverly unzipped him and reached into his pants to pull his cock free. His organ was solid and hard like stone, yet warm and pulsing in her hand, full of energy and life. Long and smooth, thrusting out from a forest of silky black hair at the base of his belly, his was a beautiful cock and Marlene exclaimed her excitement in breathless German. She urged him onto his knees so she could pull his pants down and lay bare his firm hard buttocks and soft lolling balls which she cradled in her palm as she bent to lick the tip of his elegant tool.

Placido felt as if he were in a dream. This strange German girl with the liquid eyes had stripped him and pulled his penis free to finger and fondle provocatively while, just in front of him, two husky lads were using the lush body of his employer's mistress, the woman he lusted for and was sworn to protect. The Germans were thrusting their cocks into her from both ends, Dieter now embedded firmly in the mysterious crack of her arse, Bruno bollock-deep in her beautiful face.

He felt a tug on his own tool and dropped his eyes to Marlene, now crouched in front of him and offering up her own arse for his pleasure. And what a delectable prospect it was, too! Though slender and boyish above the waist, Marlene was all woman below it. She was bent before him shamelessly, her legs apart, the full and rounded contours of her shapely buttocks upturned to reveal all she had, from the pretty dimple of her bumhole down to the hairy purse of her full-lipped pussy. Placido grasped the fat cheeks and squeezed, spreading her open wider, thrusting her two tempting holes into greater relief. He slid one finger, then two, between her buttery cunt lips and explored the sopping, slippery cavern within. She was so much on heat the juice was pearling down the insides of her thighs and the walls of her vagina fluttered round his fingers as he jammed into her more forcefully.

She said something in German to him over her shoulder. It was a command uttered through clenched teeth and it could only mean one thing. He sank the length of his iron-hard cock into her like a knife into butter and she howled the first notes of her long-awaited orgasm.

Other climaxes were approaching too. Ahead of them, Bruno's face was stretched in a grimace of pain and ecstasy as he neared his fourth or fifth come. Dieter was stuffing his slim blue-veined dick in and out of Beverly's arse-crack in a blur, smacking his palms on the seat of her magnificent rump, sending ripples through her trembling bum-flesh. Even the other German had stirred himself and he lay beneath the quivering trio licking the ends of Beverly's dancing tits which swung and dangled from side to side as her body flexed and twitched and danced to the music of the three-way fuck.

It seemed that they all came at once. Beverly sandwiched between the two boys, Bruno and Dieter erupting into her at both ends, Marlene receiving Placido's long-dammed-up torrent of lust as he drank in the sight of Beverly's beautiful bum receiving a cockful of spunk for the second time that day.

And when they had all slumped to the sand in exhaustion they heard the sound of claps and hoots and bravos from an audience that had gathered around them unseen.

Beverly raised her head from Bruno's crotch and sank

back on her haunches, spunk running down her legs and down the tawny hills of her heaving chest. She saw Placido nearby, his trousers at his ankles and his cock still jammed inside Marlene. Behind him were a motley group of onlookers, smiling and clapping, others already embracing and falling to the sand in search of their own pleasures.

Beverly caught Placido's eye and grinned. She spread her arms wide. 'I love it,' she said. 'You can't do this back in Birmingham.

'Now, are you going to take me home and fuck me properly?'

22

Betsy made Arnold lie flat on his back on the rug in front of the fireplace. It was a cosy room with chintz curtains, a comfortable sofa and Constable prints on the wall. Betsy had once told Billy that it was important to put her uptight English clients at ease before blowing their minds with her own brand of Bonking USA on the waterbed next door.

As Arnold stretched his length along the floor, Betsy began a remarkable series of calisthenic stretches – as if she were an athlete limbering up or a dancer preparing herself for a great role. Her gorgeous limbs weaved sinuous patterns and stretched in a sexual warm-up that sent shivers up and down Billy's already quivering member. Her culminating stunt was to stand on one foot and raise the other leg high above her head, the knee joint against her cheek, one hand firmly grasping her ankle – and the bulging mouth of her cunt fully revealed in the open hinge of her thighs. The gaping quim was like a rose in full bloom, its petals unfurled, its pink heart open to the world, its fragrance filling the room.

As she lowered her limbs, she said, 'I used to be a cheerleader when I was a schoolkid. We'd do the greatest warm-up routines. I tell you, they made you hot to trot. The guys on the team really appreciated it. No one cared much for football but we sure had some great parties after the game.'

By now she had straddled Arnold's body, one long golden thigh on either side of his hips, and was busy oiling his massive cock with precise care. The aroma of the oil mingled with the smell of sex in the air.

'I've seen some big wangs,' she went on conversationally. 'There were some guys on the Snakebucket defence who had enormous dicks but, Arnold, I tell you they just don't compare with your ivory tower.'

She gave Arnold's cock a final squeeze and put aside the bottle of oil. Then she ran a hand between her own legs and fondled herself experimentally. Billy noted that the fingers that emerged from her crack were dripping with her own juice.

'Here we go,' she said as she crouched over Arnold in a squat. Balancing on the balls of her feet, she pulled Arnold's magnificent machine perpendicular and aimed the great head into the slot of her cunt. 'Just promise me, Arnold, you'll stay completely still and let me feel my way. It's going to be fantastic!'

Billy leaned forward from his vantage point at Arnold's feet. From there he could see the red helmet slip easily inside the pouting pussy lips which jutted from below the curves of her creamy rear.

'Ooooh,' she breathed as the first three or four inches disappeared inside her and she slid her weight down his rigid pole. She paused for a moment and then lowered herself further, taking in more cock flesh.

Billy stared mesmerised at the sight, at Arnold's quivering thighs and his great balls lolling in the vee of his crotch and the column rising from his ballsack, the veins standing out along its length – and still some six inches remained for Betsy to take if she could.

'Oh Arnold,' she moaned, 'that's incredible, that's as much of a man, I think, as I've ever had before.' And she began to slide up and down in little jerks, bouncing on her feet, easing just a little more of his magnificent tool inside her on each downstroke.

Billy leaned around Betsy's body to look at Arnold. He was staring at the naked woman suspended above him, his eyes popping and his mouth open in a great O of wonder at the sight of his long-neglected pole disappearing inside her slim form.

Betsy had now stopped bouncing. She only had a couple more inches to go but it seemed that Arnold had plumbed the very depths of her and it was not possible for her to take any more – or so Billy thought. She had stopped moving completely and was balanced on the spar of his tool, her fingertips pressing on the flat of his stomach, her head thrown back and her eyes closed. A small moan came from her throat which grew and took on a higher pitch and grew again into a great howl. As he drank in the thrilling beauty of her quivering form, Billy suddenly realised that she was in the throes of a profound orgasm.

When it was over she seemed to slump and she sat down on Arnold in a tangle of buckled limps and wild golden hair. Billy gazed at her in awe. The remainder of Arnold's cock had vanished from sight. The entire limb was now hidden deep inside her.

Arnold clasped Betsy to him, running his hands up and down her silken back, squeezing the buttery flesh of her buttocks and rubbing the small of her back in soothing sweeps. Then he took her around the waist, his fingers encircling her slender body, and lifted her up, then down, little by little, gradually higher and higher so she slid up and down his great pole. Billy watched in amazement, he had never seen anything quite so rude or so thrilling as the elastic ring of Betsy's pussy engorging and disgorging the fat girth of Arnold's giant prick.

She was moaning again but this time there were words, obscenities rung from somewhere deep inside her way beyond the artifice of professional whoredom.

'Oh stuff me, Arnold, stuff it right up me! Shove that great pole into my guts! Oh Lord, I've never been so full of cock! It's incredible! Fuck it up me! Oh, I'm going to come again! Come with me! Shoot me full of spunk! Fill my cunt with spunk, Arnold! OH! OHH! OHHH!'

And come she did, and again and then again, as Billy sat transfixed, glued to the sight of that splayed pink clam between her legs slithering up and down Arnold's mighty weapon. And Arnold fucked on like a man possessed, as if he might never fuck again, as if he were making up for ten years of abstinence – which of course he was.

And then, just when Billy thought it might never end, when the tossing of her blonde mane and the jiggling of her tits and the bouncing of her buttocks made a kaleidoscope of flesh before his hypnotised gaze, Arnold shot his load. His balls seemed to pulse and twitch and the tool shaft buried itself inside her insatiable pussy in a manic blur.

For a moment both figures froze. Betsy screamed in ecstasy, a noise that was drowned out by a roar from Arnold himself. And then came the flood, a deluge of spunk flowing from her cunt lips down over his crotch and running in creamy rivulets down his thighs.

Like a balloon coming to earth, the pair of them subsided to the floor in a heap, their limbs entwined, their mouths together, their bodies still joined cock to cunt.

There was silence.

Billy, his balls aching and his dick throbbing, slowly got to his feet and crept from the room as silently as he could.

23

Sophie recognised Patsy Fretwork from her photos in the *Blizzard*. In the flesh she looked smaller and older, less of a bimbo in fact, with hard little creases at the corners of her mouth. She regarded Sophie with evident suspicion as she allowed her into Pandora's flat and led her in silence into a cluttered living-room blue with the fug of cigarettes.

'So you're Sergeant Sophie,' she said. 'I can see why she took a shine to you.'

'Where's Pandora?' asked Sophie. 'She shouldn't have left you on your own.'

'But you're here now, aren't you? The force's finest fanny has arrived to protect me from my own husband. How thrilling.'

Sophie looked round at the clutter – empty bottles, dirty glasses, rancid takeaway bags, overflowing ash-trays. It was a mess. Patsy looked a mess, too: her hair was ragged and unwashed, her blouse crumpled and, despite the bravado, she was obviously wound up.

'We'll have to move you,' Sophie said, looking round. 'This place it too easy to find. It's on the ground floor, the locks are no good, there's access from the garden at the back. And it's a pig sty.'

'Well, don't look at me, dearie. This is how the great journalist lives. The worst of it is that the fridge doesn't even work. There's no ice for the gin.'

Sophie pulled a face. 'I'll have it warm then.' And she flopped down on the baggy sofa amongst a pile of newspapers. A cat erupted from beneath her and scurried off with a mew of complaint.

Patsy fetched fresh glasses from the kitchen and poured two generous slugs of Gordon's. 'Cheers,' she said and lit up a cigarette. 'I've had lots of visits from the Old Bill in my day but this is the first time I've ever offered one a drink.'

Sophie raised her glass in salute and took a solid hit. Neat, lukewarm, it tasted disgusting and burned as it rolled down her throat.

'So, where's Pandora?'

'Dashed off half an hour ago, done up to the nines. She's got a girlfriend, you know.'

'Dozens, I imagine.'

'No, this is a special friend. She rang about an hour back and there was quite a conversation. She took it in the bedroom but I heard every word.'

Sophie took another mouthful, waiting for Patsy to continue. The gin didn't taste quite so bad now.

'It seems the loved one spent a torrid night of passion with a man and rang up to tell Pandora that, on balance, she preferred cocks to cunts. It was meant to be "let's cut out the naughties and remain good friends" – you know the kind of thing. However . . .'

'She talked her round?'

'They're having dinner. She said you were coming to babysit. I don't think she's planning to return tonight. Not until she's licked Tracy into shape, that is.' Patsy grinned knowingly over her glass and Sophie smiled back. Both parties could imagine what such a licking might entail.

'Maybe you're not so bad, considering you're the law,' Patsy went on, pouring them both another. 'You were a big hit at lunch. Pandy got back at four with your short hairs between her teeth.'

Sophie blushed. She didn't want to dwell too much on their lunch at Emmeline's but she had to hand it to Pandy, that woman knew how to suck pussy.

'It was you I wanted to talk to,' she said, 'about Danny.'

'Bugger him, he's in Spain with a big-titted tart from Brum.'

'Don't count on it, Patsy. We thought he might come back to shut you up. Now I can tell you he's on his way.'

'Really?' Suddenly she didn't look so cocky.

'I heard this evening. Your friend from Birmingham rang in to say Danny read the *Blizzard* this morning and went apeshit. He flew out this afternoon.'

'But didn't you pick him at the airport?'

'We missed him. I don't know how. I only know we hadn't got him by eight this evening. He could be here any minute.'

'Oh shit.' Patsy lit another cigarette and knocked back her gin. She gave Sophie a long, appraising look. 'You don't look like much in the way of protection. Why haven't I got a couple of beefy guys? Three, maybe – one to take me to bed and the others to stand guard.' She laughed boozily.

Sophie was beginning to feel a little woozy herself. 'Don't worry, Patsy, I might not look tough but I'm very . . . resourceful. If he shows up, he's mine.'

'Oh yeah?' The grin was back on Patsy's impish face. 'I might hate the bastard but he *is* my husband.'

'I don't mind assistance. We could take him on together.'

'Right!' They clinked glasses.

'Seriously, Patsy, we've got to get you out of here. We'll go tomorrow. I'll think of somewhere.'

'Make it a lumberjack training camp. Or a boys' sixth form college. Or the Chippendales' hotel suite. Somewhere there's men. Lots of guys with muscle and sweat and big swinging dicks.'

'Patsy, you're drunk.'

'And horny. I'm cock-starved. Danny's pals keep me so penned in no man dares come near me. I've had one fuck in six months and it was so fantastic I'm permanently on heat. I even let Pandora suck me off I'm so randy these days.'

'Tell me about the guy.' Sophie didn't want to talk about Pandora.

'He's a smart-arse, but cute. I had him tailing Danny and he took some great pictures of him bonking bimbos at this orgy. They ran some of them in the paper but most of them were unprintable. Billy's got a real nerve. He hid up a tree to get the photos and got so carried away he fell out, right in the middle of all these naked gangsters and their tarts. But he managed to run off and I got my pictures.'

'Who is he?' Sophie was all ears.

'Billy Dazzle. He's a private detective, though I don't know that he gets much work.'

Billy Dazzle – so that was the name of the clown who had upset her plans to capture Danny last time. Sophie slotted the information home in her brain. Patsy was gabbling on, warming to the memory of her recent tryst.

'I'd always fancied him but never did anything about it. I used to think I'd stay faithful to Danny anyway even though he was bonking half Romford. Silly cow. Then when I got the photos off Billy and we were looking at all these rude goings-on, I knew I just had to have him. There were some really naughty shots. All these great big willies thundering up sopping fannies, people banging away in groups – I wish I had them here to show you.'

Sophie was glad she hadn't – or else there was a good chance Patsy would spot her amongst the revellers, bending over to take her share of those great big willies. Sophie had not been able to divorce herself from the action, she recalled, after all it had been incumbent upon her to play her part to the full.

Patsy, in order to get more comfortable, had slipped out of her tight mini-skirt and sprawled in a collapsing armchair opposite Sophie, her plump brown thighs spread wide apart. Sophie's eyes were drawn to the black bikini panties drawn taut over the bulge of her pubic mound. In particular, she noted the smudge of damp now spreading in the vee of Patsy's crotch as she continued her tale.

'We just stood there looking at all these dirty photos spread out on his desk, discussing which ones we liked best and what turned us on. It was really exciting. He had his hand up my skirt, wandering all over my arse and I had his whopper in my hand. God, it felt good. The first I'd touched in months!'

Patsy had now slid her hand inside her panties, perhaps unconsciously, and was obviously fingering herself as she spoke.

'He pulled my knickers down and put it up me from behind, with me sprawled over the desk right on top of these photos. I think I came the moment he put it in, it just felt so fabulous. And he just went on and on, jabbing his dick in and out and kissing the back of my neck and saying these fantastic filthy things in my ear.'

'Like what?'

'Oh, all about how he'd always fancied me and the way my jiggling tits just drove him wild and what a great little arse I had and how he was going to pull out at the last moment and shoot his load all over my bum and rub the spunk into my cheeks.'

'Ooh, I like the sound of that!' Sophie was getting quite turned on herself. 'And did he?'

'No. He got so carried away talking about it that he couldn't hold back and he started ramming in and out of me till he shot off inside my pussy. I'm not complaining. I was so far gone I passed out for a moment. The funny thing was, when I came to I was looking right at this picture of Danny being sucked off. Once upon a time I'd have been shattered just to see it but, in the circumstances, I had to laugh. Pandora says that was a key moment in my liberation.'

'You told Pandora about it?'

'She wants to know everything about me, she says it helps her get the right feel for my story.'

A companionable silence fell. Sophie watched Patsy's fingers fluttering inside her black panties. Her other hand was in the open flap of her blouse rolling a stiff nipple between two scarlet fingernails. Her eyes were closed and her breath was coming in short hard pants.

'Patsy, does Pandora have a vibrator?'

'In the bathroom.'

'If I go and get it, will you promise to tell me the rest of what you and Billy got up to?'

But Patsy couldn't answer. Her hips were thrusting rhythmically as her fingers worked away beneath the damp cotton and the first moans of orgasm were already spilling from her mouth.

Sophie sighed in resignation and poured herself another drink. As the cries and moans of Patsy's pleasure filled the room she began to unfasten her jeans. A long night lay ahead.

24

Billy sat in his office in the dark. From upstairs came the sounds of Arnold and Betsy still in the throes of passion. It was incredible. How long had it been now? Three hours? Four? They had moved into Betsy's bedroom which was just above Billy's room. The wail of Betsy's umpteenth orgasm rang through his head like a bell. He absentmindedly nibbled one of Arnold's biscuits. He felt very small indeed.

The mystery of his permanent erection raged on. Between his legs glowed and throbbed the biggest boner of his life. After he had crept downstairs he had taken his cock out and looked at it, given it a good shake and, shivering with pent-up lust, in a few quick strokes had shot his load into a wad of paper tissues. That, however, had not solved his problem. His cock had remained obstinately erect, teak-hard and unyielding.

Now, some hours later, it was still as stiff as ever. He fretted. Perhaps this recent surfeit of sex had done him some physiological damage? Could he be suffering from some rare disease of the dick which meant it would never subside? That would be terrible. Imagine going round the rest of his days with a permanent erection. Think of visiting his mother or helping an old lady across the road – a lifetime of humiliation and embarrassment flashed through his mind. He'd have to have special clothes made. Throw out his entire wardrobe and invest in handmade garments designed to conceal the pole in his pants. And what about public toilets? It was a frightful prospect.

What Billy wanted was his equipment back to normal. He longed for the return of his regular appendage that went up and down on command, like an aeroplane undercarriage, so he could land and take off at will. There was no obvious advantage in life in being permanently primed for the act of fornication.

The phone rang once more, interrupting his depressing reverie. Who the hell could this be?

'Billy, it's Candy Kensington. You must come at once.'

Billy was astonished. He floundered. He had never expected to hear from her again.

'Billy, you must help me. This is an emergency.'

And indeed it did seem like one. This was a different-sounding woman to the haughty bitch who had thrown him out of her house earlier in the day.

'What's the problem, Candy?'

'Oh God, it's awful. I've got a spider in my bath.'

Twenty minutes later Billy stood in the imposing portico of the Kensington mansion. He knew if he had any sense he'd have gone home hours ago but the throbbing between his legs had not abated and the vision in his mind of Candy Kensington's long bare legs led him on.

As he stepped inside the door Candy threw herself into his arms, a sweet-smelling bundle of loose hair and soft flesh wrapped in a silk kimono. She was sobbing out loud, spilling tears into the crook of his neck.

'Oh Billy,' she said, 'I'm so pleased to see you, it's been ghastly.'

One hand between her shoulder blades, the other on the curve of her hip, Billy thrilled to the glow of her body heat through the thin material.

She held him close, embracing him with the whole length of her and seemingly unconsciously rubbing her belly against the spike of his erection.

'Come on,' she said at length and led him up the stairs and through a vast bedroom into a bathroom that was merely large; it glistened with mirrors and marble tiles and gold taps. The bath was sunken, with room enough for three. It made the spider seem positively minute. It sat peacefully by the plughole, probably the least malevolent insect in the whole of Northwest London.

'Right,' said Billy, deciding to make the most of this opportunity for heroism. He removed his jacket and handed it to the damsel in distress, who stood hesitantly behind him. In all honesty she did appear to be petrified.

He resisted the obvious temptation to turn on the bath tap. Instead he took a credit card from his wallet and a tooth glass from the sink.

'What are you going to do?'

'Just watch.' And he popped the glass over the spider and the card between the glass and the bath. The spider obligingly stood on it and was flipped into the tumbler. Billy held it aloft triumphantly.

'Would you open the window, please.'

Candy obeyed and watched in admiration as he cast the offending insect into the night.

'I don't believe in unnecessary violence,' he explained.

'My hero,' she said as she insinuated herself into his

embrace to bestow a valedictory kiss on his cheek. She pressed herself full against him once more, her soft belly yielding to the pressure of the iron bar in his pants.

As she felt it dig into her, a wicked grin formed on her curving lips. 'Is that on my account?' she asked, grinding her pelvis against him.

'Yes,' he replied. What else could he say? And maybe it was true. It had all started that morning when she had captivated and then spurned him. So, now, all he needed to do to cure his condition surely was to bury his aching rod deep within her pampered and perfumed body . . .

He looked down into her smiling face. Her eyes were large and brown and searching, one was flecked slightly with green specks – it made her look all the more beautiful. Her robe was coming loose and he could see the upper reaches of her breasts and the dark valley between.

'You were lucky I was in the office,' he said.

'Working late?'

'You could say that.'

'Imogen told me you were a private detective. How thrilling. It must be so exciting to do a dangerous job like yours.'

'Sometimes,' he agreed, declining to elaborate on the bold deeds of the day. He pondered the precise etiquette of his current position. Though she was in his arms, her gown loose and her swollen tits dangling almost in full view, he was still not sure of her. She struck him as skittish. If he made the wrong move she might just fly into a rage and chuck him out again.

'I'm surprised you don't have your own official spider-remover on the premises. Don't you have maids and flunkies?'

'They've all gone home. I like the evenings to myself. So I can be free.'

'To paint?'

'That kind of thing.'

Throughout the conversation they hadn't moved, except to get closer if that were possible. Billy was caressing the small of her back in a brotherly, frankly incestuous, fashion and she continued to bump her loins against his erect cock through the material of his trousers. The thin silk of her gown had now opened to allow one long brown nipple to poke free and nuzzle into his shirt front.

'You must let me draw you again.'

'OK.'

'Properly, this time.' Her hands were plucking at his shirt. 'Without any clothes at all.' She had his belt unbuckled and her fingers in his fly. 'Stark naked.' His trousers were around his ankles. 'Quite, quite nude.' And his cock and balls were in her hands. He kissed her. It seemed the appropriate moment.

The kiss was long-drawn-out. Her tongue was slippery and wicked in his mouth, just like her knowing fingers on his throbbing genitals. And his hands were busy too, roving from ripe dangling breasts to the rounded curve of her hip, down the slope of her belly to the soft fur of her crotch where her moist pussy lips opened eagerly to his touch.

She pulled him to the floor and they wriggled uncaring on the hard, cold tiles; she manoeuvring her body so her thighs closed over his face just at the moment he felt her hot mouth on his bulging penis. He lapped and sucked her deliriously, his hands on the firm flesh of her jutting bottom, squeezing and fondling the full softness of her buttocks.

She gobbled him with skill, using both hands and her mouth, laying her cheek along his length and nibbling

his balls, licking up and down the barrel of his tool and
sucking the big bulb deep into her face. Then, as he
went to work on her clit with the ridge of his tongue,
she attacked him with abandon. She bit down on him
hard but he didn't care. It felt good, it felt wonderful!
He jabbed his cock up, trying to jam it as far down her
throat as he could and she took it all. He thrust a finger
between her bum cheeks, sinking it into her bottom, and
that took her over the top. She came in great wheezing
shudders, bouncing up and down on his face, her full
breasts swinging and her hair flying. Her orgasm went
on and on but throughout it she never released her hold
on his bursting cock, which now gushed come down her
throat like water from a hose.

Afterwards they lay in a sticky heap for a long time.
Then she squirmed around on top of him to plant a wet
kiss on his lips. He held her tight, a silly grin on his face
– and his impossible erection still burning a hole in the
silky soft skin of her belly.

25

Joyce Gosling paged half-heartedly through the *TV Times*, already aware that there was nothing on the box she wanted to watch. She could ring Aunty Doris but the old duck was probably in bed already. She could have a nice long bath, wash her hair and paint her toenails – if Amanda hadn't already taken up residence in the bathroom. She'd read the paper, done the easy crossword and she'd made the casserole and crumble for tomorrow's lunch. She was buggered if she was going to clean anything at this time of night. Ray was out till God knows when – till the pubs closed at least. There wasn't anything for her to do.

What she'd really like, she decided, was some big strapping fellow to turn up unannounced, with a bottle of champagne under one arm and an enormous box of chocolates in the other. A few drinks, a few laughs and then off with her knickers and out with his big tool and they'd spend the night happily rogering. Sod the crumbles and the casseroles, some energetic screwing was the kind of entertainment she fancied. She hadn't been properly ploughed since Christmas Eve and that was only because she hadn't let Ray at the brandy till he'd done his duty.

The front door bing-bonged. Joyce's dreams were about to come true.

As she opened the door a bronzed and bearded shape lunged into the hall and threw both arms around her, grasping her well-upholstered form with the familiarity born of long acquaintance. 'Danny Fretwork!' she shouted in amazement. 'How the bloody hell did you get here?'

'Plane to Heathrow, tube to Woodford. No problem, my darling.'

'You just waltzed in?'

'A beard and a false passport, that's all it took. Stupid sods. You'll have to help me get the fuzz off, Joyce. I stuck it on in a hurry.'

He threw his shoulder bag down on the floor and marched into the front room, tugging her behind him by the hand.

'God, it's good to be back in England. I tell you, too much lying in the sun drinking cheap brandy makes your brain rot.'

'But Danny, if they catch you, you won't be so keen on merry England. Why have you come back?'

'Because there's some things a man has to sort out for himself.'

'It's Patsy, isn't it?'

'Precisely,' he growled, the smile gone from his face. 'I just need a few words with my darling wife and then I shall be off and out of it. But—' and here his expression lit up and he held his arms out once more to Joyce '—let's not worry about that tonight. Where's Ray?'

'At the pub.'

'So he won't be back for a bit?'

'If Ray returned before closing time they'd have run out of beer.'

'Great.' Danny had Joyce firmly in his bear-like embrace, one hand around her waist, the other unbuttoning her housecoat at the point where it ballooned generously over her chest.

'Danny,' she protested, 'lay off.'

'Come now, Joyce, you wouldn't deny a starving man.' The coat was open to the waist now, partially revealing a capacious bosom encased in a vast straining white bra.

'Starving? What are you on about? Don't tell me they've run short of senoritas out in Spain.'

'It's not the same thing, my darling. There's no substitute for English cunt in England and you are much better than that. You are Essex cunt, right here in Essex and that makes you number one in my book.'

Throughout this elaborate tribute to her charms, Danny had been at work stripping the feebly protesting Joyce down to her scanties. He slipped the straps of her bra over her dimpled shoulders. She made another attempt to push him off, holding one arm firmly across her chest.

'Come on, Joyce, don't be a spoilsport. Let's get those marvellous knockers of yours out in the open. You don't know how often I've longed to lay my face between them throughout those lonely months of exile.'

'Bullshit,' she replied. Nevertheless she lifted her arm, allowing him to peel the stiff white material from the ends of her creamy cones of flesh. Her massive breasts came free, springing into the room like great white footballs.

For a woman of her maturity Joyce's bosom was indeed magnificent, with just a little sag and spread which, to many an appreciative eye, only added to its character. And Danny's eye was indeed appreciative.

He grasped a big tit in each hand and pressed his face into the beckoning valley between, muttering as he did so, 'England!' Joyce tenderly stroked the back of his head; she was easily moved by a show of patriotic sentiment.

At that moment there came a thump on the ceiling and the sound of a high-pitched female voice yelling, 'Oh shit!'

Danny jerked his head back. 'Who's up there? I thought we were alone.'

'Blimey, it's Amanda. She's having a bath. I forgot all about her.'

'Amanda!' Danny's face creased into an enormous grin. 'I must just pop upstairs and say hello.'

'Danny, she's in the bath.'

'So? She won't mind. Meanwhile, why don't you rustle me up a little snack. Some proper English grub – egg and chips. And a bottle of beer. Perhaps we could have it upstairs, in the bedroom.'

'Danny Fretwork, you are wicked.'

'That, my darling, is my reputation!' And with a final squeeze of her dangling glories he slipped out of the door.

To be precise, Amanda Gosling wasn't exactly in the bath. She stood in the cramped and steamy bathroom with one towel wrapped around her still-damp curves and another wound into a turban around her wet hair. She screamed as Danny's hulking form burst into the tiny space but her cry soon turned to a girlish shriek of pleasure as she recognised him.

'Uncle Danny!' she squealed and flung her arms around his neck with predictable consequences. The ends of her towel around her middle burst apart and it slithered to the floor, leaving her naked in his arms. Danny clasped the moist nymph to him with fervour, his hands on the full rounds of her pert bottom.

'Amanda, my sweetheart,' he breathed into her exquisite pink ear, 'I've missed you.'

'I've missed you, too,' she replied, 'life hasn't been half so much fun since you done a runner.'

'You've missed the pocket money, more like.'

She didn't reply to that, instead she slipped her naughty little tongue into his mouth and rubbed her delicious front against his shirt. He could feel the warm dampness of her through the thin cotton.

'Let's have a look at you,' he said at last, holding her away from him. 'I want to see how you've changed.'

'You're just a dirty old man,' she replied but she took a pace back and pirouetted daintily in front of him. Not that 'dainty' was a word that sprang to Danny Fretwork's mind as he gazed at her. Amanda was a youthful version of her mother, with the long legs and flared hips of a showgirl and big high breasts that seemed to defy gravity. Danny stared in admiration at the swaying tits and rounded belly and the neat thicket of black hair at the crest of her split.

'My, Amanda, you've grown into quite a big little girl, haven't you?'

'You bet. It's been a while since I was little in any way at all, as you well know, *uncle*.'

Danny pulled her soft body into his arms, slipping one hand down the dimpled curve of her stomach to the inviting bush between her legs. For a moment she held her thighs pressed tightly together, denying him access.

'I can still use pocket money, however.'

'Of course.' They both laughed and she opened her legs to him, his thick index finger sliding straight into her wet hole. It slicked in and out, making a rude sticky sound.

'Ooh, yes,' she said and pulled his head down to her bosom to push one stiff raspberry of a nipple into his hungry mouth.

'Danny—' Joyce's voice rang out from downstairs '— do you want beans and tomatoes with your egg and chips?'

Amanda replied for him. 'Bung the lot on, mum, he'll need to keep his strength up.'

Danny said nothing, being occupied with other things. It was great to be back.

26

Placido was now a happy man. He had stopped listening to the demon inside his head which told him it wasn't right to be lying in Signor Fretwork's comfortable double bed with his arms wrapped around the sleeping form of his master's woman. He reckoned that he had earned at least one night of bliss after the trials of the day. The agony of Fun-Fun Beach still burned in his memory but was superseded by the glow of satisfaction that came from later events. Bringing Beverly home, washing the sand and semen from the nooks and crannies of her abused body, tending her cuts and bruises, fetching her mugs of strange English tea – these things had been a pleasure and not a chore. And when she had sleepily held out her arms to him and pulled him down beside her into the bed he had felt it was no less than his due.

And the way she had loved him! Without a trace of the whore he had seen in action on the beach and by the pool, but hotly and passionately nonetheless. Worshipping his body, cradling his big tool in the warm and wonderful tunnel between her legs until he had fountained all of his dammed-up lust deep within her. And then holding him there long after, reluctant to let him go.

Now she slept in his embrace, her head on the hair of his chest, her face as unlined and peaceful as an infant's. Placido did not know whether it was true what she said, that Signor Fretwork would not be back, and the implications of that were beyond him. However, he resolved to keep Beverly with him as long as he could, to protect her and love her and curb her excesses as his employer would surely wish. And if his reward was that he might spend the night in her bed, surely it was better than that she should be frolicking with hooligans like those German boys.

A bolt of anger consumed him. Those Germans! It gave him great satisfaction that he had taken their woman – both women in fact – for Marlene had accompanied them back to the villa. She lay asleep in Placido's own bed, a few doors away. Placido had felt it his duty to bring her with them when she had asked. Her companions were barbarians. It would not be right to leave a young girl in their company. At least here he could ensure that she absorbed something of the real Spain. He would make sure she saw things far removed from pot-smoking and nude bathing and other imported uncivilised activities. Tomorrow he would ask Emilio to take her into the village for the holy day. They were dropping a goat from the church tower. That should show her something of real culture.

The two women were on the sofa side by side. The gin had long gone but the lack of male company was still keenly felt. Despite the efficiency of the vibrator and its pleasing size it was no substitute for the real thing.

Sophie and Patsy had traded war stories of bedroom battles both honourable and dishonourable, of lovers past and lovers yearned for. And though laughter had been the keynote and the shortcomings of the male sex had frequently been the point of the stories, nevertheless the absence of a cock – two, at least, said Patsy – was palpable and the buzzing jumping machine in their untutored hands just didn't seem to do the trick.

'Oh shit,' said Patsy, as she clumsily sawed the big beast between the tender lips of her aching pussy, searching once more for the soul-stirring orgasm that was eluding her. 'I just can't handle this thing.'

'Then let me show you,' said a voice from the doorway and the overhead light snapped on, cruelly illuminating the chaos of the room and the embarrassingly intimate tangle of bodies on the sofa.

Pandora Britches had returned, a broad grin on her predatory face. She did not exude an air of content. She swiftly divested herself of her jacket and threw herself to her knees between their squirming legs.

'No,' she said in answer to Patsy's feeble enquiry about her dinner date, 'I did not have a successful evening. I've been insulted and abandoned but I'm delighted to see that you two are in a position to make me feel a whole lot better.'

'For God's sake,' cried Sophie as Pandora thrust a hand between her legs and rudely fingered her slippery slit. But it was an empty protest for the touch was instantly pleasurable and she knew that she would submit to whatever was required to keep this formidable woman sweet. Pandora's other hand had taken charge of the vibrator and Sophie saw at once from Patsy's astonished expression that Pandy knew just how to use it.

The journalist looked down with satisfaction on the

two women spread out in front of her, their bare legs scissoring open and closed in obscene harmony as she expertly steered them both to orgasm.

Candida Kensington's face was contorted with concentration. It always was when she sketched this quickly. Not that she really needed to rush for there was no sign that Billy's remarkable hard-on would ever subside. Nevertheless she hurried, for she felt the urge building within her loins once more. She had to have it again and that would make . . . God, she couldn't remember. They had been at it for hours and still the organ between his legs stood as proud and noble as ever.

She crouched in the vee of his thighs, her pencil flying across the paper. This was going to be good. One of her best. And there were many that were very good indeed among her collection. Of course, the model helped. How could she fail when faced with such a beautiful subject: snowy white skin, strong broad column, ruby red cap, a solitary blue vein pulsing – she stopped for a moment and leaned forward to suck between her lips the plump head of his pole. She couldn't resist.

She looked up at Billy's face. His eyes were closed and he appeared to be asleep. But how could he be with this formidable monument to her charms rearing up from his belly? This was turning into one of the most marvellous nights of her life. How could she ever thank him?

She supposed she could reconsider the matter of the Poor Pussy Gala. It's true there was room for this Tracy woman to do her act. It might be fun. She supposed it would keep some of the men interested. After all, the point of it was to get everyone to enjoy themselves and consequently cough up as much money as possible. If Tracy finished off the first half it would make a nice contrast with the Marian Mucus *corps de ballet* and send everybody off to the bar in a more upbeat mood. Yes, that might work.

She laid down her pencil. She could always do some more work later but right now she felt she deserved a little play. She reached out and took the stiff shaft in front of her in her hand . . .

Ray Gosling knew he had been hitting the bottle hard. Now he had obviously got to the point where he needed help. If he had to go to the clinic and dry out, so help him he'd go.

He stood in the kitchen, leaning on the sink to stop his whole body shaking. It had to be the DTs. He couldn't really have seen what he had thought he had seen. It was funny, though, how realistic the vision had seemed to be. Funny, too, the way it had gone on and on rather than just flashing in and out of his befuddled brain. But dreams were like that, weren't they? Only he'd had this one when he was awake and not asleep.

Up in the bedroom, on his bed, the sight of Joyce, stark naked, riding on a man's face, her quim pressed into his mouth, his tongue licking upwards, clearly seen between the dark wet curls on her mound, flicking between the elongated flaps of her pussy, delving upwards to the top of her crack to worm and tickle around the bright red nub of her clitoris. That had been so vivid!

And to see his daughter, Amanda, facing Joyce, bouncing up and down on the man's cock, that had been just as real. The way her mouth was all slack and her

163

eyes closed and her panting like that as if she was on the downslope of a shattering orgasm, her young tits jumping up and down opposite Joyce's great big slack ones that writhed and rippled in their turn. And the man beneath them: large, hairy and strong, his cock just glimpsed as Amanda rose up and down, squirming on the big fat shaft as if she were completely out of control.

And then the last bit, the thing that had sent him running downstairs into the kitchen to recover, when the man had lifted Joyce off his head, his big meaty hands disappearing into the soft flesh of her bum, raising her solid arse-cheeks to reveal the grinning face of a bearded Danny Fretwork. It was too much. It was some kind of nightmare warning that said to him very loudly, 'Stop drinking.'

At that moment a large hairy hand descended on his shoulder and Ray jerked upright to find himself in the bearlike embrace of his former employer and colleague – Danny Fretwork, as naked as a newborn baby, his thick cock dangling wetly between his monumental thighs.

'Ray, my man,' said this awful vision, 'I'm back. Have you missed me?'

Three

ALL TIED UP

27

'Do you know,' said Patsy as she dreamily placed a soapy mug on the tiny draining board of the kitchen galley, 'that a woman can have a hundred and thirty-four orgasms in one session? Well, maybe not every woman but one woman did. Under research conditions too – it's a scientific fact.'

'Are you all right?' said Sophie, dabbing a damp tea-towel over some cutlery.

The two of them stood side by side in the cramped quarters on board a Thames cabin cruiser called, in honour of the tousled form by Sophie's side, *Princess Patsy*. Technically it was owned by Patsy but the money that had paid for it, some years earlier needless to say, had been plonked down in cold cash by her once-loving husband. Over the course of an exhausting weekend the three women had moved it from its moorings a mile upstream to its current berth owned by the *Blizzard*'s proprietor, who also happened to be Pandora's uncle. On the bank a strategically placed police team kept look-out. Short of submarine, there was no approach to the boat that was unobserved.

The idea of using the boat had been Patsy's and the others had seized on it after some two hours of fruitless suggestions. Of course, thought Sophie, if they really wanted to avoid Danny Fretwork it was the last place they should be. But then, her intention was to lure Danny out into the open and nab him. And Patsy was the bait.

'Pandy showed me this article in yesterday's paper. They've been doing this research on the human orgasm. I didn't know those posh papers were full of so much filth. There's none of that in the ones I read.'

'Huh,' was all Sophie could manage.

'Mind you, it wasn't half interesting. It seems the best a man could do was sixteen comes per session. That's pretty pathetic really, isn't it?'

'Oh, I don't know.' Sophie's mind was suddenly enlivened by the thought of a big fat cock shooting off sixteen times in succession. She could do with a bit of that, she thought, just to wipe herself clean of Pandora's incessant abuses.

'I mean sixteen times compared to a hundred and thirty-four is nothing. Pandora says it demonstrates the inherent superiority of the female response.'

'I bet.'

'I reckon you might do more than a hundred and thirty-four in a session, Sophie. The way you go at it.'

Sophie smiled weakly. The betrayal of her mind by her body was the story of her life.

'Don't get me wrong,' said Patsy, 'I could go a willy any time but Pandora's opened my eyes to a whole new world of sensuality.'

Oh Christ. 'Look, Patsy, I'm going to slip off for a few hours to get some of my things and catch up on a bit of sleep but I'll be back by this evening. All the lads are well set up so there shouldn't be any chance of

Danny sneaking by while I'm gone.'

'That's a good idea,' said the third voice as the tall figure of Pandora Britches, dressed in a half-buttoned man's shirt, insinuated herself into the small space. 'Why don't you pop off for a bit and let Patsy and I get on with our work. We've got tons to do, haven't we, darling?'

'I would have thought you were just about finished,' said Sophie as Pandora casually looped an arm around her shoulders. 'Surely the *Blizzard* has milked everything possible out of Patsy's story by now.'

'Patsy and I have a new project – her life story. We think it'll make a great book.'

'But it's already been done in the papers,' Sophie protested, conscious that Pandora's hand had come to rest on top of her right breast. 'There can't be anything left to say!'

'Nonsense, that's just the tip of the iceberg, isn't it, Patsy? This will be much deeper. I need to probe into the wellsprings of Patsy's life, find out why a woman like her is attracted to the criminal fraternity, discuss it in the context of female subjugation. Besides, Patsy will go down a storm on TV chat shows if she wears one of her tight tops.'

By now Pandora's hand was inside Sophie's own top and sliding purposefully into the cup of her brassiere, prompting the policewoman to say tartly, 'So you're not above a bit of basic sexploitation?'

'You've got to sell your project otherwise your message won't get across. It's the iron fist in the velvet glove. That's why I work for the *Blizzard*.'

'Really? I thought it was because your uncle owned the paper.'

'Now now, darling.' Pandy's fingers dug into Sophie's right breast, tweaking her nipple painfully. The traitorous flesh swelled to erection immediately.

'Before you go, Sophie, come next door. There's a few things we should discuss.'

Patsy rolled her eyes heavenwards. Sophie began to protest but the words seemed to die on her lips as Pandy's wandering hand now crept downwards into the waistband of her jeans and across her stomach.

'Well, let's make it quick,' Sophie said feebly, allowing herself to be propelled in the direction of Pandy's cabin. She looked back at Patsy who grinned at her waspishly.

'Go for the record, Sophie. A hundred and thirty-five, remember.'

28

It had been a long weekend for Billy Dazzle, too. Half of it spent in furious carnal activity with Candy, alternately bonking and posing for her endless sketches until, on Saturday evening, his miraculous erection had collapsed like a punctured balloon. Candy had tucked him up in bed by himself in a cosy room and left him to sleep, waking him only to administer bowls of chicken soup made, so she told him, by her very own cook.

Now, on Monday morning, Billy felt refreshed and full of beans. His pleasure was enhanced by the luxuriant greenery of his surroundings as he sat in Imogen Almond's conservatory and waited for her to join him for breakfast. He had been summoned directly from La Kensington's mansion. After his heroics in Candy's bath and bedrooms it seemed he was back in good odour. And so, he reflected with some satisfaction, he deserved to be.

A door opened behind him and Imogen emerged dressed in a skintight leotard of shiny vermilion and black leggings. Her hair was tied back off her head in a ponytail. She wore no makeup and the colour was high on her cheeks. The tight lycra moulded every contour of her lithe body, compressing the full mounds of her

breasts into large concave saucers, emphasising the
gentle dome of her stomach and stretching in an enticing
vee between her legs clearly delineating the bulge of her
pubis. She was breathing hard and her chest rose and
fell as she panted. She looked like a wholesome, hearty
schoolgirl fresh from a brisk frolic on the playing fields.

'Sorry,' she said, 'I hope they told you I was in the
gym.'

'So this is how you keep yourself fit for the rigours of
business,' said Billy. 'I'm impressed.'

'You should try it,' said Imogen, grabbing a glass of
orange juice from the table. 'Why don't you have a little
workout right now?'

Billy began to protest but there was no denying the
firm pull of the hand that grasped his and drew him to
his feet. For a moment he stood his ground.

'Come on, Billy, some healthy exercise is just what
you need.

He followed her out of the door, his eyes glued to the
taut lycra stretched across the perfect moons of her trim
bottom as she walked ahead of him down a flight of
stairs into the bowels of the large house.

Imogen's basement was remarkably well-equipped for
a private gymnasium. There were two kinds of exercise
bicycle, a rowing machine, a complicated device with
rectangular weights for arms and legs and a sound system
that filled the room with raucous, breathy rock at the
touch of Imogen's elegant finger. She led him to a separate shower and changing room where she rummaged in
a cupboard and produced a towel and some sports clothing. She handed them over with a curt instruction to 'get
changed'. There was no turning back.

Moments later Billy presented himself in a white

sleeveless vest and a skintight pair of egg-yolk yellow
leggings that finished just above the knee, hugging his
thighs and buttocks, and moulding his cock and balls
against his stomach as precisely as vacuum-packed deli-
cacies on offer in a supermarket chill cabinet. Imogen
eyed him frankly and he was uncomfortably aware that
every bulge and curve of his body was on display – as
indeed was hers.

'We'll get you warmed up then,' she announced and
immediately broke into an energetic stretching routine
to the rhythm of the music. Billy followed her lead, as
was obviously expected. Imogen was a stern task-
mistress – and a very fit one. Notwithstanding her previous workout, she was eager to expend more energy
and she spurred Billy on with a demonstration of testing
aerobics, slapping his chest and buttocks, straightening
his legs and pulling on his arms and otherwise urging
him to put more oomph into his efforts. Billy began to
blow hard. In truth he was not much of an athlete. He
had the natural strength and energy of youth and was
pretty adept at dodging the traffic, running up escalators
and shinning down drainpipes. But as for hard physical
exercise concentrated over a period of twenty minutes
– that was a different story. Already there was a burning
stitch in his side and his breath was coming in quick
shallow gasps as he strained for air.

He remembered this kind of agony from a time some
years distant in his previous life as a City dealer. He
had joined the firm's health club in an effort to get to
know a female colleague better on the squash court.
But Clarissa's dancing tits and twitching derriere had
remained tantilisingly out of reach, both on the court,
where she had left him for dead, and in the shower

afterwards – where she had kicked him in the balls and left him writhing with the cold water full on. He had sworn off hearty birds ever since.

By now Imogen had mercifully brought a halt to the physical jerks and he was able to snatch a few deep breaths as she manoeuvred him into the rowing machine. The respite was shortlived. He was soon putting his back into it as required, keen to make as good an impression as possible this side of utter exhaustion. The thought that he might score in the shower this time spurred him on.

Obviously his efforts were paying off, for Imogen was smiling at him as she urged him on.

'That's more like it, Billy. I only have fit, strong workers on my team. Which reminds me, I've got another little job for you.'

Billy cocked a quizzical eyebrow. He couldn't speak.

'Last time we spoke I was impressed that you were able to put your finger on my main problem with the Gala programme – Brick Tempo. He's flying into London tomorrow and I want you to look after him for me.'

Billy's stroke faltered and Imogen laid a hand on his arm and indicated that he could stop.

'I'm putting him up in the flat above the office while he's in London. You'll be staying there too.'

'Christ, Imogen, you're not asking much. He's a legendary hell-raiser. He used to trash hotels with Keith Moon.'

'He's slowed down with age. He's still alive, after all.'

'If half the stories are true then *I* might not be very soon. Why is he appearing at the Gala anyway?'

'Candy insisted. She lost her virginity to his first hit.'

'Blimey.' Billy pondered this information. 'She must be older than I thought.'

Imogen patted his back, urging him to his feet. 'That's settled then. Excellent. Now I think you need a quick session with the weights and then a shower and a sauna will set you up a treat.'

Her cools hands on his skin – how could they possibly be so cool? – were nectar to his senses as she arranged him horizontally on the most fearsome of the machines – the one with weights at the head and the foot. It had straps, too, which she now buckled tightly, pinning him around the chest and waist. As she fastened the waist strap she turned down the top of his pants to cinch the broad belt tight, pushing the flimsy material down almost to his groin.

At that moment a door opened and Imogen grinned. 'You've turned up just at the right moment,' she said to the new arrival. 'Your victim awaits.'

And the inverted figure of Katie Crisp swam suddenly into Billy's vision. Her severe features gazed down on his captive form with evident satisfaction.

'Well, well,' she said, 'this looks like my lucky day.'

29

In the normal course of events Monday morning is undoubtedly the least exciting time of the week. This particular Monday morning was no exception in the lives of the many; in the lives of the few, however, it provided an introduction to activities never before experienced – such as bondage sex.

Billy Dazzle was one such novice, yet another was Patsy Fretwork. At the same time as Billy lay imprisoned in Imogen Almond's aerobic torture chamber, Patsy Fretwork was rendered similarly immobile in the main cabin of the *Princess Patsy* as she lay at the mercy of her newfound friend and lover, Pandora Britches.

She lay face down along the length of a small wooden bench, her hands and feet bound together with silken cords beneath the seat of the bench, a pillow under her stomach thrusting her naked arse high up in the air, affording Pandora unrestricted access to the most delicate and delightful portions of her anatomy.

Patsy could not see what was being done to her and yet it felt delicious. She could not cry out, for her mouth was stuffed with a rubber bung, yet she did not care. The sensation of being tied down, forced against her will to submit to Pandora's blatant manipulations was unbearably exciting. She felt something hard and solid probing at the lips of her pussy, at the same time something soft and slippery began to circle the tight ring of her arsehole. She forced herself to relax . . .

Pandy had begun the session by dribbling cool body lotion along the knots of Patsy's spine and into the exposed furrow between her buttocks. Then she had gently smoothed the ointment into her body, easing away her tensions, giving her time to adjust to the notion of being at another's mercy. By the time she had finished, Patsy had been lulled into a sense of security, trusting those strong and gentle hands which had now covered almost every inch of her flesh many times over.

The first slap had been a shock, like being suddenly awakened by being doused in cold water. It didn't exactly hurt, however, and there were kisses and caresses too. More smacks had followed on her upturned buttocks, but not in quick succession, Pandy allowing some seconds, even minutes, between each blow so Patsy could never guess when the next would fall. She found herself perversely looking forward to each stinging assault and the glow which spread afterwards through her flesh, in particular the warmth which was growing ever fiercer between her legs.

By now her cunt was on fire, thrust up and open, the lips quivering in the air begging for attention – and yet Pandora ignored it. Patsy was quaking with desire, aching for the void between her legs to be filled. It was strange. No man had ever made her feel like this. Though she knew this adventure with Pandora was simply an excursion away from the mainstream and her dreams would still be full of stiff and plunging willies, now she gave herself up utterly to the other woman. She would have begged for a cuntal caress if only she could have spoken. The rubber stopper between her teeth, like a great baby's dummy, served only to soothe her as she bit down on it, flinching from the blows on her behind. She thrust her pelvis down but the soft pillow prevented her from gaining any pressure on her aching clit. She strained up into the empty air as far as she could, silently begging for satisfaction.

Then came the bigger slaps, with something hard, maybe a slipper. It made a whistling sound as it descended and a crack as it smacked across both buttocks, causing her whole body to twitch and writhe. She bit down hard on her gag as a moment of fear suddenly penetrated her cocoon. But then Pandora's face swung into her limited vision and smiled at her. She kissed Patsy's brow and soothed the back of her neck in reassurance and then – at last – the journalist had set to work on her cunt.

Now she was in sight of orgasm, with the big hard rod of the dildo insinuated deep inside her pussy and the fluttering featherlike touch of Pandy's fingers on her clit, teasing and titillating. The warm glow from the slaps and spanks she had received had spread throughout her body. From the waist down she was on fire and she knew she would soon come off – coming as she'd never come before, not even with Danny at the height of their passion (thought that had been different, of course). She was completely at the other's mercy and she didn't care. It was out of her control, not her fault – she was guiltless. The pleasure was absolute and once Pandy pushed her over the edge she knew it would go on and on and on and . . .

30

'Steady on,' said the captive Billy as Katie Crisp slotted some evil-looking metal weights into the grooves by his shoulders. 'I'm not used to this sort of exercise, you know.'

'Don't worry, Billy,' said Imogen, reaching for a towel and rubbing her face and neck briskly, 'we know just the kind of physical exertions you like.'

'Eh?'

'Push!' barked Katie and Billy strained obediently against the bar across his chest. The weights struggled up a few inches.

'Harder!' commanded Katie and Billy pushed with all his might, lifting the dead weight upwards.

Imogen had now loosened her hair and was towelling it roughly. Suddenly she slipped one arm out of her leotard and pulled the garment down to dry her armpit. An amazed Billy found himself staring directly at a firm pear-shaped breast which wobbled deliciously as she rubbed.

'Again!' ordered Katie, prompting him to lift once more. He managed it more easily this time, did it without thinking, his gaze fully focused on the shuddering globe of flesh that rippled enticingly just a few feet away.

Imogen shrugged the other tit free, pulling the leotard down to her waist. She smiled at Billy as she did so, seemingly unconcerned by his open admiration. His view was suddenly blocked by the large and almost naked backside of Katie Crisp as she bent over to adjust the weights by his feet. In his amazement he registered that she, too, had stripped off and was wearing just a pair of scanty panties cut high on the thigh and revealing a rounded expanse of plump bottom flesh.

'Bend your knees,' she ordered. He did as he was told. 'Now straighten them.' And he found himself straining against two levers beneath his feet which acted on the weights she had been arranging. He laboured to please her, his mind in a turmoil, as he took in the half-naked women in front of him.

Katie now stood beside the seated form of Imogen. Her breasts were small and high, the nipples long, pink and, it seemed to Billy, disturbingly erect. Out of her severe solicitor's garb she was more heavily built than he had suspected. Her thighs were strong and full, her hips rounded and curvy, her belly domed and sloping. The mound of her cunt was barely covered by the thin material of her flimsy white briefs and a dark tangled mass of pubic hair sprang out from the gusset. Despite the physical exertions he was enduring he was once more definitively erect.

Imogen patted Katie's near-naked rump and said, 'I think he likes you, darling.'

'I think he likes both of us. But he's the kind of lecherous swine who'd fancy my granny.'

'I still think you should give him the once-over.'

Katie nodded and leaned across to place further weights on Billy's two piles. Suddenly he found that he couldn't move a muscle.

'Right,' she said, 'let's check out the equipment.' And she briskly tugged down the top of Billy's shorts, exposing his stiff cock. Slipping her hands between his legs, she casually pulled his balls out into the open. For a moment all three were silent.

Imogen leaned forward, resting her elbows on the exercise machine. Her breasts swung down fluidly, twin dangling tubes of flesh which Billy ached to lift and squeeze and fondle.

'Show me,' she said to Katie who at once took hold of the head of Billy's cock, pulling the organ up so it stood perpendicular, a pulsating tower rising from the plain of his belly. None too delicately, but nevertheless with practised ease, she peeled the foreskin downwards to reveal the pink gleaming helmet of his glans. She slid the skin up and down once or twice, forcing more blood into the head, turning it a deep red. A pearl of juice glistened in the eye of his organ.

'Mmm,' Imogen sighed appreciatively, 'what a big juicy one. I can understand how you finally won over Candy.'

'Not without a little help, though,' added Katie, squeezing and frotting the stiff flesh almost absent-mindedly.

'What do you mean "help"?' said Billy.

'Has it ever occurred to you,' replied Imogen, 'that to maintain an erection for forty-eight hours is not normal? It can't be achieved without a little extra stimulation.'

'We didn't intend it to work out quite like that,' said Katie, still manipulating him, 'it's not our fault. I think you should blame Arnold.'

'What's he got to do with it?' Billy was incredulous.

'Everything. The magic is in his biscuits, you dummy.

And you had second helpings, I understand.'

'Oh Christ!' said Billy, realisation suddenly dawning. 'You mean there's an aphrodisiac in his biscuits?'

'Didn't you wonder why you had a two-day stiffy?' chuckled Imogen, bending down to plant a gentle kiss on the angry red cap of his prick as it thrust between Katie's tantalising fingers. 'You poor lamb!'

'Wait till I see that bloody Arnold!' cried Billy.

'I wouldn't be too hard on him,' cooed Imogen, 'from where I'm sitting, it doesn't look as if you've suffered any permanent damage.'

'But I could have,' yelled Billy, reflecting that he had not only had second helpings of Arnold's cookies but thirds and fourths. 'You shouldn't have done it. You should have warned me. It's completely against my rights as a citizen.'

'Oh shut up, you toe-rag,' said Katie, 'a rat like you doesn't have any rights when it comes to fucking.' And she waggled Billy's big prong energetically from side to side, making it grow even stiffer.

'But I'm being abused! This is indecent assault.'

'Maybe,' said Imogen, 'but it'll never stand up in court.'

31

On the bank, from his observation post in an unmarked car parked on the road, DS Mark Bacon watched the rise and fall of the *Princess Patsy* on the water of the Thames. He wondered idly to himself how come such a large boat moved quite so much when there was no other river traffic in the vicinity. His fertile imagination supplied an answer that was doubtless only too true. This was a job that involved Sophie Stark and Mark well knew what that meant. In his mind's eye he conjured up visions of naked females jumping up and down on one another, breasts bobbing, hips grinding, hair flying as they cruised to multiple orgasms. He did not doubt that the reality was close to his dreams. He had worked with Sophie too often for it to be otherwise.

And so DS Bacon failed to observe the one thing he was on duty to spot, the sudden rocking of the boat on the water which could possibly have been made by a fifteen-stone man hauling himself aboard from the water side. In fact his eyes were focused more specifically on the small galley portholes which were affording him an incomplete view of a half-naked blonde woman with round plump tits whom he knew to be Mrs P Fretwork. At that moment Patsy looked straight at him, scowled and twitched the curtain over the porthole, blocking off the enchanting view.

'Daft cow,' she said to herself, aware that she had given some bored rozzer an eyeful. But it was not surprising, in her present mood, that she had forgotten the existence of the world outside. Her session with Pandy had absorbed her totally. In fact the encounter was far from finished. Now was, as she had put it to Pandy upon release from bondage, 'her turn'. Pandy was next door, trussed up in a similar fashion to the way she herself had been till just a few moments ago. Patsy took pleasure in that: the fact that Pandora trusted her sufficiently to do unto her as she had just dished out.

In truth, having the upper hand had refreshed Patsy. She had never been a dominant partner in anything before, and certainly not the guardian of a bound, gagged and naked reporter with a degree from Girton and a charge account at Harrods. As she had tied Pandy up she hadn't been sure exactly what she was going to do when in command. She assumed she would follow a similar programme of pain and pleasure as Pandy had dealt her. The funny thing was, once Pandy had been rendered silent and immobile, an urge had stolen over Patsy to give this pushy dyke who had been bossing her around for the past week something of a shock. Pandy would be bound to approve, for she was constantly urging Patsy to assert herself.

Unlooping the broad belt from Pandy's discarded jeans she had given her half a dozen hearty thwacks on her upturned buttocks turning the flesh a raw flaming pink and sending shudders rippling through the reporter's long slender frame. Then she had gone off in search of other means of torture, deciding that Pandy could stew in her own juices for a bit. After all, as she knew from her own recent experience, it only heightened the pleasure in the long run.

Searching for a tea towel which she could maybe soak and knot and turn into an impoverished flail, she had come to the galley. There she had boiled a kettle. A cup of tea was just what she needed at the moment. Doubtless a tea break would be frowned on at the best sex orgies but she was new to this sort of lark. It was then she had become aware of the prying eyes of the copper in the car. And it was there, a moment or two later, that Danny Fretwork discovered her.

It would have made a memorable encounter for the world at large. The big bronzed barrel of a man – Public Enemy Number One – dressed in a dripping wet-suit and transfixed at the sight of his estranged wife, her lascivious curves on full view in a pair of flimsy panties, balanced on a pair of high heels and clutching a mug of steaming tea. Unfortunately for the nation and in particular the readers of the *Daily Blizzard*, their intrepid reporter – who would surely have scooped the front page the next day – was not quite on the spot, being stark naked and trussed to a wooden bench in the cabin next door. Quite how she would have dramatised the epic encounter will never be known.

'Hello, Danny.'

'Hello, Patsy.'

'The kettle's just boiled. I'll make you a cup of tea if you promise not to chuck it at me.'

'Don't be stupid. You'd be scarred for life.'

'I thought that was what you wanted.'

'Leave it out, Pats. Do you mind if I just slip out of these wet things?'

'Go ahead. I've seen it all before.'

'That's true.' Danny's face split into a melon-sized grin. 'Me too. You're looking good. Have you lost a bit of weight?'

'Oh, you've noticed? Two stone. Through worry. It's a most effective diet, I've discovered.'

'What were you worried about?'

'You, you stupid bastard. And who you were fucking.'

'Ah,' he said pensively, eyeing the wobble of her tits as she dumped three sugars into a mug and stirred vigorously. 'If you'd lost two stone earlier maybe I wouldn't have been fucking anybody. Apart from you.'

'Get off. Screwing scrubbers is a reflex where you're concerned. Like farting. Don't tell me you'll ever stop.'

'That's not entirely true, Patsy.' He had stripped down now to just a pair of scarlet swimming trunks and was leaning against the sink sipping his tea, the mug entirely hidden in his huge grasp. 'Some of the birds I went with were high class.'

'High-class tarts, you mean. They cost you enough.'

'Look.' Danny raised his voice. He hadn't been entirely sure what he was going to do or say to Patsy when he finally caught up with her but he certainly hadn't pictured a conversation like this. After all, he was the aggrieved party. 'Now, look here,' he said again, gesturing with his mug and slopping scalding liquid down his naked chest. 'OW!'

'Serves you right,' said Patsy unsympathetically and then, in a gentler tone, 'Here, let me,' and she dabbed at him with a handy tea towel.

She was up close to him now, the top of her blonde head nuzzling into his chin. She smelt of deep musky perfume and of sex. She giggled suddenly. 'Here,

Danny. You've got grey hairs on your chest.'

'I should tan your hide,' he said gruffly.

'So that's what you've come all the way back to England for, risking your liberty. To beat me up. That's very clever, Danny.' The fleshy rounds of her breasts were pressing into his chest as she ministered to him. 'That's the kind of brainy thinking that made you king of the London rackets.' Her hard little nipples were scratching at his burnt skin, hurting him.

'Shut up,' he growled.

'Make me.'

The kiss went on for a long time, her small slippery tongue deep in his mouth and her arms around his neck, pressing the warmth of her tits into his flaming chest while his big hands were everywhere, up and down her back and under the flimsy panties to grasp the plump mass of her bum cheeks and run his fingers into the juicy well of her pussy.

They would undoubtedly have crowned their reunion with a breathless bonk up against the metal sink – she was already struggling to wrestle the blunt jackhammer of his cock out of his trunks and ram it up between her legs – when a sound from on deck made her pull her mouth away from his and froze her entire body.

'Patsy—'

'Be quiet!' she hissed.

'Hello,' came a voice from above.

'Oh hell,' she groaned.

'Who's that?'

'It's only one of the coppers.'

'*What!*'

'One of the coppers keeping a lookout in case you turn up.'

'Christ!'

'Don't worry, I'll get rid of him. Hello!' she called back up the stairwell, 'I'll be right with you.'

'I just brought the milk over,' said the voice, sounding ominously close. 'Why don't I bring it down?' They heard the sound of large feet on the stairs.

'*Christ!*' muttered Danny again, pulling open a drawer and grabbing a bread knife.

'No, you can't come down,' Patsy called back, frantically motioning Danny to put down the knife, 'I've got no clothes on.'

The footsteps halted.

'Oh dear, oh sorry, I, er—' the footsteps retreated clumsily.

'Danny, quick, where's your diving gear? Will he see it?'

'Not unless he goes poking around up there.'

'Don't worry, he won't have eyes for anything but my tits. You get lost somewhere, I've got to go and sort him out.'

And she was gone, wrapping a towel around her delicious body as she scrambled up the stairwell. 'Oh Mark,' he heard her say, 'it's sweet of you to come over. I was just in the bath.'

Danny leaned against the door, the red mist in his head and loins slowly clearing. He realised his cock was sticking out of his pants and that he was still clutching the knife.

'Bloody hell,' he said to himself, then picked up his wet-suit and padded silently down the corridor.

He soundlessly turned the handle of the first door he came to and slipped inside.

32

Billy was still protesting but, in truth, his complaints of ill-treatment were undermined by the reaction of his prick which thrust obscenely up into the air as Katie toyed with it. She pinched and stroked, smacking it playfully from side to side, grasping it at the base and waggling it like a stick – much to Imogen's amusement. She took her turn, too, licking the shaft like a lollipop; allowing Katie to slip the head into her mouth for a tantalising moment; then bending forward to roll the fleshy sausage between her wobbling tits.

'Lay off,' said Billy feebly.

'Why don't you shut him up, Katie,' said Imogen. 'The way you like best.'

Katie needed no second urging. Cleverly, for she never let go of his stiff-standing member, she sat herself astride Billy's torso and then dragged her knickers down until they stretched in a single band across the meaty rear of her thighs. Suspended above him were the twin pillows of her succulent arse, the furrow between them spread wide to reveal, in the gap between her legs, a veritable forest of thick black curls.

Billy's words of protest had died on his lips. He heard Imogen's voice, felt her breath warm on his ear as she bent her head to his face and whispered, 'Isn't she magnificent, Billy? Have you ever seen a hairier cunt?'

Billy shook his head and gazed in wonder as Imogen ran her fingers down the exposed crack, giving the winking brown star of her arsehole an impudent tickle before plunging her fingers into Katie's bush, combing out the thick fronds to reveal the split of her pussy. Billy watched mesmerised as the long and elegant fingers teased open the curling lips and plunged within, emerging wet with juice which glistened on the pale pink varnish of her nails. 'Isn't she lovely Billy? Aren't you just dying to taste her?'

Whether he was or not was immaterial for Katie's rump had now descended on his upturned face. To be honest, he had no heart to protest. It was gross, it was lewd, it was wonderful. The big cushions of her buttocks smothered him in a perfumed embrace and his lips opened automatically to meet hers. He explored her soft and juicy cave with his tongue. She tasted strong and clean, like the sea warmed by a hot sun.

She ground his head between the pistons of her thighs, almost cutting off his air, his ears muffled by the walls of flesh. He couldn't move. He thought of nipping her with his teeth but was conscious of sharp fingernails playing across his scrotum and the implied threat therein. In the dim distance he heard their voices and was aware of his genitals being manipulated, pulled this way and that with no obvious aim, it seemed, to excite him and yet doing just that, inching him towards a longed-for explosion.

He was almost drowning in her crotch now as the liquid seeped from her, salty and pungent, filling his mouth, running into his nasal passages. And then she was bucking and bouncing on top of him in an uncontrollable frenzy. The soft ovals of her bottom were shaking in his face and, far off, he could hear her cries as she satisfied herself on his mouth.

With relief he realised that supple fingers were bringing him to his own climax, wanking his prick, clinically milking him as he, too, shot off, erupting into the empty air.

Eventually Katie climbed off him. She moved slowly, as if she were half asleep, and Imogen came to her assistance. Billy gratefully sucked air into his lungs. He felt utterly exhausted. And used. And cheated.

They stood over him, gloating. Imogen's breasts were wet, sticky with his come. She stood there rubbing the spunk into her big tits with one hand, the other was round Katie's waist.

'Let's get you into the shower and wash that horrible stuff off,' Katie said.

'There's such a lot of it,' said Imogen, 'he's quite a little sperm factory. Perhaps we could keep him here and put him to stud.'

Katie giggled, setting her little tits bobbing. 'We could feed him on Arnold's biscuits and send in a new female every twenty minutes.' They both thought this very amusing and laughed out loud. Billy noticed that Katie's hand was in her luxuriant black bush, stroking the top of her crack.

'What shall we do with him now?' Katie asked Imogen.

'Let's leave him to cool off a bit. Recover his strength.'

'Hey!' said Billy, as it dawned on him he was to be left trussed up and half naked. 'Untie me at once!'

But they had turned away and were heading for the shower room.

'Let me up!' he cried, his eyes mesmerised by their rear view, Katie's prominent arse rippling as she moved, Imogen's by contrast neater and trimmer, set high on her long legs. Katie's arm was round Imogen's waist, Imogen's hand was fanned across the upper slopes of Katie's broad buttocks, her long index finger probing between the fleshy cheeks.

'Bitches!' he yelled after them but they did not turn round. Instead he heard loud laughter, then the hiss of falling water and he cursed beneath his breath. Lying in the sticky pool of spunk and sweat on his stomach, his thoughtless penis was once more fully erect.

33

Danny leaned against the cabin door behind him, listening intently. Maybe Patsy wouldn't be able to stall the policeman, maybe the big oaf would insist on coming below. But he could hear nothing apart from the pounding of his own heart and he rapidly came to the conclusion that Patsy had the situation well in hand. He was impressed with her. Certainly she had handled things smartly – and she looked fantastic these days. He still burned to fuck her. This revenge mission was not turning out quite as he had anticipated.

Only now did he begin to take in his surroundings. The first thing that registered was the smell. A thick pungent musk that thrilled his senses and immediately stiffened his prick. It spoke to him of expensive perfume – and of cunt. He looked around the dimly lit cabin and was thunder-struck by what he saw.

It could never be said that Danny Fretwork – the Randy Racketeer, the Hard-On Don, the West Ham Womaniser; these were just some of his tabloid nicknames – did not know what a naked woman looked like. Yet for a moment Danny simply could not register what lay in front of him. It looked like a female arse, a rounded and disembodied bottom which was pointing straight at him, the creamy smooth buttock ovals flushed pink even in the dim light. And between the wide-spread cheeks lay the glistening slit of a long-lipped pussy pouch just waiting to be crammed with cock. Despite the evidence of his eyes, Danny was flabbergasted. What the hell was going on here?

Danny considered the figure before him: a tall woman, shapely and slender, with long legs, bound in a crouch to a wooden bench, a pillow between her legs thrusting her rump high in the air. Her face was half glimpsed as she lay with one cheek on the bench, a scarf round her mouth in a gag, a swatch of dark hair over her eye. Was she asleep? Her body was moving, her breath coming hard and fast, a flush of excitement on her cheek.

Good God, what had he walked into? Could this be Patsy's doing? Patsy – a girl who had insisted on turning off the lights on their honeymoon night, a woman who only two years ago had threatened to cut off his bollocks with pinking shears when he had suggested a threesome. And now it seemed his stick-in-the-mud other half had shed two stone and turned herself into a right little raver, playing lesbian sex games. Only two minutes ago she had been more than keen to let him shag her up against the kitchen sink. There was no doubt a new spirit of sexual adventure had taken hold of his wife since his departure. And he'd been missing out on it!

In a small way he could make up for it. He pulled his cock free from his trunks and advanced on the milky pale buttocks rearing so invitingly in front of him.

To be honest, the arse on offer was a little bony for his taste but the long, well-juiced lips of the proffered vagina and the pink tunnel within were entirely to his liking. He slipped an experimental finger inside. Her body jerked at the touch and the soft walls of her gaping pussy seemed to suck in his finger like some hungry sea mollusc. She was wet, overflowing with juice. It had soaked the pillow beneath her and moisture glistened on the skin of her upper thigh and in the beard of her bush. The unknown woman's entire body appeared to be shaking. Her loins were twitching and writhing. She seemed to be in a state of perpetual orgasm.

Danny was in no mood to hesitate further. In a flash he had positioned himself behind her, lined up the broad red cap of his cock and pushed it into the gaping hole between her legs in one smooth thrust. Beneath him the woman's bottom leapt and quivered. Danny placed his hands on the firm rounds of flesh, opening her like a ripe fruit. His thumb pressed into the dimple of her anus as he savoured the honeyed handshake of her pussy along his pulsing shaft.

Below him Pandy reared and bucked, insofar as her bonds allowed. She was being ravished in a way that was entirely foreign to her. She did not even recognise the object within her cunt as a male member. She only knew that Patsy had somehow surprised her in the most thrilling and wonderful way: beating her and leaving her for so long and now finally giving her this miraculous thrill, the most ecstatic of her extensive and, to date, exclusively lesbian sex life.

Danny humped on, his half-crouched position not entirely comfortable and delaying the inevitable onrush of orgasm. But that made this anonymous fuck in the half-light even more delicious, for it prolonged the action. Both parties teetered on the brink as he fumbled at her flesh, now finding her splayed-out breasts crushed against the sides of the narrow bench and hanging down conveniently. He pulled and pinched the hard nipples, teasing them with his blunt fingers.

Pandy twitched beneath him like a woman in a fit, already at her peak but going higher. Her climaxes were overlapping, building on one another as exotic visions flashed through her mind – of Tracy's luscious tits wet and wobbling in her mouth, of Patsy's jiggling bottom flushing pink as she smacked it, of Sophie's sweet pussy lips parted to receive her kisses. And now she was revelling in the ultimate pleasure, on the receiving end of some miraculous *thing* that was warm and hard and vigorous and filled her so completely. It was unbelievable – impossible! How could Patsy . . . ?

But there was no time to question, no time to think, for she was coming, coming, coming in a series of distinct thrills – each separate spasm, like pearls in a necklace, adding to the brilliance of the whole.

Danny too was at the point of no return, pistoning his fat tool in and out of the hungry hole beneath him. He began to spunk on an out-stroke, creaming her slit in a sudden flood and continuing to jab and poke his cock inside her till his balls were quite empty of juice and he collapsed on top of her, sated.

The sudden weight on her back shook Pandora from her postcoital bliss. She tossed the hair from her eye and craned round as far as she could, a smile of fond gratitude on her lips. Which died there as she saw the dreadful but somehow familiar face of a naked male. And as the twin horrors of what had happened struck home, mercifully, she fainted.

It was at that moment that Patsy walked into the room.

34

Imprisoned on Imogen's cruel weight machine and transfixed by the sounds of uninhibited female laughter from the shower room, Billy Dazzle was sorely in need of a friend. So when the delicious vision of Tracy Pert loomed into view his heart leapt for joy.

'Bloody hell,' she said on catching sight of this captive male in a state of sexual arousal, 'Imogen thinks of everything these days.'

'Tracy! It's me, Billy Dazzle.'

'Of course it is,' she replied, 'I'd recognise that cock anywhere.'

As ever, Tracy looked spectacular in tight little shorts that already seemed to have disappeared up the crack of her bum and into the vee of her slit. She wore a loose T-shirt with enormous armholes through which could be glimpsed the transparent black material of her brassiere encasing the pink flesh of her sumptuous tits. Her hair was tied back in a loose ponytail from which blonde ringlets had already escaped to fall entracingly about her heart-shaped face. Her wide blue eyes sparkled with pleasure at the sight before her and her swollen pouting mouth split into a calendar-girl grin as she took in his indecent state.

'Blimey, Billy, you are in a bit of a state. What have you been up to?'

'Imogen and that cow Katie Crisp have been working me over.'

'I can see that. It doesn't look as if they've finished the job.' She took hold of his cock between thumb and forefinger and lifted it away from his belly. 'You still look ready for action, if you ask me.'

'Don't, Tracy. Just help me out of here.'

'Well . . .' she said, idly letting go of his member which smacked back against his stomach, 'I'm not sure that I want to. I've got a bone to pick with you.'

'I don't see why. I've just done you a big favour.'

'Getting me an interview with a fat and lecherous Italian film director is no favour,' she said, taking hold of his balls and jiggling them rather too strenuously for his liking. 'I not only had to suck his salami but he virtually had me swinging from the chandelier by the time I got him to give me a part in his bloody film. And it's *nothing*' – and here she began to squeeze menacingly – '*nothing* to do with Shakespeare.'

'Oh?'

'Not unless he wrote something called *Naughty Nights in Norway*.' And she yanked hard on his testicles.

'Ow! I'm sorry, Tracy, I'm sorry.'

'No you're not, you're hurting and that's much more satisfactory.'

'But I got you on the Gala programme, didn't I? That's what you wanted.'

'So?'

'I pulled out all the stops for you, Tracy.'

'I'm sure you did. I understand you spent a weekend bonking the sponsor just to get little old me on the bill.

It must have been tough going.' And she twisted her fist viciously.

'Lay off, Tracy! Why don't you let me up and we can talk about this properly. In fact, there's still an outstanding dinner invitation where you're concerned.'

'No dice. You're a snake, Billy, I'm not going out with you.'

'Not even if Brick Tempo comes along?'

That hit home, as Billy thought it might. Her wide blue eyes blinked even wider.

'Ooh, could you introduce us?'

'If you're very nice to me, Tracy.'

Her hand slid up from his balls to clasp his stiff-standing member.

'You mean that kind of nice?' she said as her fingers began a subtle rhythm, holding his shaft just below the head.

'That's a start,' said Billy, the pleasure now beginning to ripple along his throbbing spike, 'though there are one or two other things you could do for me.'

'Don't tell me.' Releasing his prick, she delved beneath her T-shirt and rummaged and wriggled until one hand emerged clutching a flimsy black strip of material. Then she slipped her hands into the waistband of her shorts and pushed them down her smooth tanned thighs. As she bent towards him Billy clearly saw the gentle shifting of her loosened breasts beneath the inadequate vest. She grinned at him wickedly.

'That's much more comfy,' she said, standing up to reveal herself clad only in socks, trainers and T-shirt which came just above the curve of her belly before it ran down into the delectable golden triangle at the junction of her thighs. Beneath the curls, the plump pink lips of her pussy smiled at Billy.

'Tracy, you're incredibly fuckable.'

'I know.'

'Why don't you help me get free of this damned machine so I can do something about it?'

But her grin had turned calculating and Billy watched in helpless anticipation as she straddled his hips, one satiny thigh on each side of his body. She took his cock in her fist and squeezed pearls of juice from its tip, then daintily spread the moisture along her pussy crack.

'I've always wanted a captive stud. Some big fat dick trussed up where I can get at it. It looks like you're it, Billy.' And she lifted the head of his penis to her golden slit.

'You're a rapist, Tracy. You're taking advantage of a helpless human being.'

'You bet.' And she slipped the bulging head of his tool between the coral-pink lips of her pretty cunt and lowered herself onto it. 'Ooh, that's lovely! You fill me up so nicely.'

'You should be ashamed of yourself.'

Tracy had already started a steady rhythm, grinding her adorable hips down onto his loins.

'Don't take it personally, Billy. Think of it as one woman's revenge for the inequalities of society.' She was riding him energetically now, bracing herself with one hand and probing the other into the junction of their bodies to rub her clit.

'You spend too much time with that dyke Pandora.'

'Not any more. I'm back on cock full-time.'

'What?'

'Why don't you talk rude to me, Billy? Here, tell me how much you love my tits.' And she reached into her loose T-shirt and pulled first one big rosy breast into view through an armhole and then the other.

'Christ, Tracy, that's obscene!'

'Yeah!' And she bounced them in her palms, pushing them together to form a platform of firm pliant breast-flesh and then pulling them apart, a rounded loaf of tit in each fist.

'Tracy, they are phenomenal – true wonders of the age. But I thought you didn't like men going on about them. Or was that Pandora's influence?'

'Oh shut up, Billy. Eat tit.' And she bent forward, pulling the vest upward over his head and tumbling her big mammaries into his face.

Billy felt as if he were drowning in a sea of perfumed flesh, soft yet weighty, firm yet yielding. He sucked in first one springy nipple, then the other, burrowing into the warmth of her in the half-light of the tented T-shirt. As he suckled and nuzzled the pain of recent humiliations slipped away. An observer of a psychoana-lytical mind would have drawn obvious conclusions from this infantile embrace – for which Billy would not have cared two hoots.

'Oh, Tracy,' he mumbled, 'this is incredible. I love fucking you. I love having my cock up you and your fantastic tits in my face.'

'Yes, Billy, yes.'

'You're a dirty cow, though. You're wanking yourself right now, aren't you?'

'Yes.'

'You're stroking your clit, aren't you?'

'Yes, yes!'

'Stroking your clit and sitting on my cock and rubbing your tits in my face, you horny little slut.'

'Oh Billy, I'm coming! Oh yes, oh YES!'

35

'I thought you'd murdered her,' said Patsy, drawing deeply on a cigarette.

'I don't know what came over me, Pats. I was in shock. And I never took you for a bull dyke pussy-licker.'

'I'm not. I was just experimenting. I'm a liberated woman now.'

They were sitting in the state room of the *Princess Patsy*, chain-smoking Pandora's cigarettes. Half-empty mugs of tea were lined up on the table.

'How is she, do you think?' said Danny. 'I didn't hurt her, I swear.'

'Even you couldn't hurt a woman like that, she's Teflon-coated. She's sleeping off the shock of having a willy up her. Honestly, Danny, how could you do it? Just because a cunt's there you can't go sticking your dick up it without permission.'

'Well, what about you? Cosying up to me in the kitchen with a naked woman tied up like a parcel next door. You've changed, Patsy.'

'So what's that to you?' She glared at him defiantly, her big brown eyes alight, her little jaw set firm. 'If you're going to kill me you'd better hurry up. Otherwise

I suggest you fuck off now before Sergeant Sophie comes back and locks you up for good.'

A heavy silence fell. Patsy held her husband's gaze, her eyes still blazing but the chin now beginning to wobble. Danny thought she looked absolutely adorable. He moved next to her and took her hand.

'Come with me, Patsy. Come back to Spain. You don't know how I've missed you.'

'You're right. I don't.'

'I still love you, Pats. Honest.' Danny kissed her cheek.

'Come off it, Danny.'

'You're still my wife.' He slid his arm round her waist.

'No.'

'You still love me, I can tell.' He planted a kiss in the hollow of her throat.

'No, I fucking well—'

But Patsy's protests were sharply cut off as Danny's mouth descended on hers, swallowing her words.

Danny was a big man and Patsy only a small woman. Nevertheless she could have fought him, could have bit and scratched and jabbed him in tender places as she had done on several previous occasions. But not on this one. Indeed she thrilled to feel his huge paws on her body again as he lifted her thin sweater to palm and fondle her tender breasts. And she made no objection as he pulled her ski pants over her soft rounded hips and shucked them off together with her tiny panties.

In truth Patsy was longing for his cock. She wasn't sure how she felt about the rest of him but she felt no ambivalence about the swollen hammer he carried between his thighs. She loved it, she always had. It was fat and bloated and irredeemably coarse and she just adored it thundering between her legs, filling her to bursting. There were no half measures with a cock like Danny's, it never held back, it never gave less than its all. Throughout the ups and downs of their stormy relationship it was a constant. And when she had seen it ramming in and out of Pandy in the final throes of a stolen fuck all she could think of was how much she wanted it inside her again.

'Get up,' she ordered him. 'Stand in front of me.' And he did so, enabling her to pull his trunks to his knees, releasing his fierce erection and swollen balls to her hungry gaze. For a moment she marvelled at the pulsing tower waving in her face then she took it in her hand and guided the big red knob into her mouth.

'Oh Patsy!' groaned Danny as her lips stretched wide and miraculously swallowed his engorged tool. 'You beauty!'

He bent to kiss the top of her head, nuzzling into her blonde locks, reaching beneath her to roll the hard pebble-points of her tits between his fingers.

As he trembled with the pleasure of her deep-throated caress and played with the dangling treasures of her chest, his eyes rolled heavenwards. Then they closed. Then flicked open again to see, staring at him from the open doorway of her cabin, the intrepid journalist and sexual deviant Pandora Britches.

Danny was dumbfounded, his loins throbbing to the ministrations of his attractive wife, his eyes bewitched by the sight of the woman whom he had fucked without the benefit of an introduction within the last hour.

She presented a very different appearance to his last sight of her. Tall, almost his own height even without shoes, she wore a white camisole vest that reached just to her naval and a pair of tiny bikini panties that described a deep vee over her stomach, ending high on the hips. Her incredible legs seemed to go on and on for ever. Her half-shut eyes glared smokily at him from beneath the fringe of the loose dark hair that tumbled to her shoulders. She did not look in the least like a tweedy lesbian, she had the air of a recently bedded man-eater on the prowl for seconds.

Danny opened his mouth to speak but she raised a finger to her lips and he remained silent, transfixed by her presence and by the insistent thrill of Patsy's mouth at work on his throbbing cock.

It was Patsy who broke the spell, coming up for air and finding herself under Pandora's keen scrutiny. She gasped in surprise. Pandy smiled.

'Would you,' she said, 'would you mind if I just . . . ?' and then she too was on her knees, one arm around Patsy's dimpled shoulder and a hand on Danny's hip as she leant forward and clumsily began to lap at his monstrous organ.

Patsy started to giggle. There was a note of hysteria in it.

'Show me, darling,' said Pandy, 'I've never done this before. I don't know what to do with a penis.'

Patsy did, however, and within a few minutes she was giving Pandy a lesson in the noble art of cock-sucking: how to lick and how to suck, where to nibble and where to tickle, how to titillate the frenum, how to gobble the glans, how to softly squeeze the scrotum and how to suck deep against the soft upper palate while frotting the base of the cock-shaft to hasten the suckee's ultimate pleasure . . .

Danny's brains were scrambled, though it wouldn't be

fair to say he didn't know if he were coming or going – he was definitely going to come. Patsy was aware of it.

'Careful, Pandy, I think he's about to—'

And he did, great gouts of spunk shooting into Pandy's face as she, unfamiliar in the ways of the male member, took the jet straight in the eye. But then, to Patsy's astonishment, she plunged his leaping tool deep into her mouth, sucking its fat pulsing length and chewing on it happily as it twitched and dribbled its last drops of come down her throat.

Pandora sat back on her haunches and tossed her hair away from her face. Her features were lit up by a big sticky smile and her eyes were sparkling. 'Fantastic!' she said. 'I never realised. Does that mean—' she asked Patsy ' – he can't fuck me now?'

Patsy laughed, an obscene throaty chuckle. 'You may be a bloody fast worker, Pandora Britches, but you'll have to wait. The next hard-on's all mine.'

36

Billy stood in the shower, hot water drumming on his head, steam in his nostrils, revelling in the release of tension that was slowly spreading through his abused body. The muscles in his thighs and arms throbbed from the unexpected exercise he had been forced to undertake; and around his waist the skin smarted from the belt which had been cinched tight and rubbed him raw throughout his ordeal. Katie, Imogen and Tracy had all taken advantage of him, there was no doubt. But his torture was the stuff of wet dreams. His mind's eye was full of ripe wobbling breasts and gaping salty cunts. A hard-on still pulsed between his thighs.

He stood with arms braced against the wall, water cascading over his head. Behind him Tracy pressed her pneumatic form the length of his aching body. Her slippery fingers soaped the throbbing barrel of his tool, sudsing every ridge and crevice. Across his back the twin peaks of her adorable breasts massaged the hurt from his bones.

'This is bliss,' he said. 'I think I'm in love with you, Tracy.'

She chuckled and ran her fingers from the rear of his scrotum up the crack of his arse, working the cake of soap between his cheeks.

'You promised to fix me up with Brick Tempo, remember?'

'Sure thing. I'm his new minder.' And he wriggled to the ecstatic touch of her flesh on his in the rain of hot water. 'Have you really finished with Pandora Britches?'

'I packed her in. Told her we should just be good friends.'

'I thought you and she were a hot item. You certainly seemed to be having a good time the other night.'

'She's a hypocrite. She wants to own me and yet she makes eyes at anything in skirts. Just like a man, in fact. Only, she doesn't have a cock. That's something of a drawback.'

Billy's mind had wandered, distracted by the sensuous massage of her soft and slippery titties up and down his spine. He could swear he could identify the separate points of her nipples within the all-encompassing cushion of flesh that serpentined across his skin.

'To be honest, Billy, I've got to thank you for putting me straight.'

'Eh?'

'That night at my hotel I realised I really preferred this,' and she placed both hands around his stiff-standing penis and squeezed.

Billy was lost in a whirl of sensation. The torrential hot water, the rubbery slither of Tracy's boobs, the insistent rub of her fingers on the shaft of his cock had him rooted to the spot. Her hands slid upwards across the flat of his stomach onto the broad sweep of his chest as he turned him to face her. There was an impish grin on her wet face as she arranged his limbs to her liking.

'Hold my bum,' she commanded and leapt up into his arms, scissoring her legs around his waist and reaching up to grasp the shower fitting above their heads.

Billy juggled and then caught her, though she was slippery as a bar of soap. His hands were now filled with her pliant buttock flesh and her magnificent bosom swung, pink and swollen, right in his face. He knew what she wanted.

For a moment they wobbled, his knees buckling, her hips shifting and flexing, his cock prodding the length of the deep slit of her arse until, miraculously, the head nosed into the notch of her wide-open pussy and stuck.

'Yes!' she cried and sank her pelvis down, slotting her delicious hole over his shaft. 'Give it to me, Billy, stuff it right up my cunt!'

And, despite his tired limbs and wounded pride, that's exactly what Billy did.

37

It's well-known that beds on boats are not large. Whoever builds medium-sized cabin cruisers does not put a high priority on providing maximum bonking space. Nevertheless there is no accounting for human ingenuity when the blood is up. Hence Patsy, Danny and Pandora now reclined in a mass of sweaty, sticky limbs on two small mattresses pushed together on the floor of the state room.

Patsy had been as good as her word. She had not allowed Pandy first use of Danny's next stiffy. Indeed she had quite shamelessly thrown herself on her back and lifted her knees to her chest, presenting the pair of them with the sight of her gaping honeypot, and commanded Dany to ram his dick home. What loving husband could fail to obey such an injunction? Pandora had been relegated to the role of interested bystander which, in truth, was only proper for a novice in the realms of heterosexual fuckery.

'Christ,' she had said as she knelt on hands and knees to observe up close the pistoning of Danny's slick and angry rod as it drove in and out of Patsy's hungry quim. 'It's so beautiful. What power! What energy!' And she had tentatively reached out a hand to touch the hairy jumping bollocks in front of her. From there the hand had crept upwards to tickle the base of Danny's throbbing cock at the point where it drove between the frilled lips of Patsy's pretty pussy.

Soon Pandora had both hands running over their most sensitive parts, hunting between their bodies, dipping into the dark hairy crack between Danny's muscular arse cheeks, and fondling his balls. Then, as their huffing puffing climax approached, Pandy's curious fingers delved into the top of Patsy's notch to rub the tiny nub of her clit and she threshed in orgasm like a landed fish.

Afterwards, in the balmy glow of gratitude, Patsy had settled herself between Pandora's spread thighs and wriggled her wicked little tongue in and out of Pandy's slit. Then she had sucked on the long fleshy vaginal lips, pushing two fingers deep inside Pandy's twitching hole while she licked and nibbled Pandy's clit to a spectacular climax.

This activity had, quite naturally, stimulated Danny's own interest and the moans of Pandy's orgasm had no sooner faded than he was inserting the head of his big tool into her well-oiled orifice, sliding it home with a grunt. This being Pandy's first proper fuck, in that this time she knew she had a cock up her, Patsy had intended to stay out of the action. But the sight of Danny's animal thrusting between Pandy's long and slender legs had enflamed her. In her newfound spirit of sexual adventure she had straddled Pandy's neck, her arse in Danny's face, and poked her still-hungry pussy back onto his mouth.

The three of them were joined together like that for an age, licking and probing and thrusting. Danny had his cock in the hot tight channel of Pandy's almost-virgin cunt, his face in the cleft between Patsy's pert twitching buttocks and his hands everywhere – full of breast and thigh and juicy quim. He was in heaven. If the entire Metropolitan Police Force had come aboard at that moment he could not for the life of him have stopped what he was doing.

Now, as he lay between two naked and well-fucked women, he reflected on his current situation. And burst out laughing.

'What's funny?' asked Patsy.

'It just occurred to me. I've achieved what I set out to do.'

'What's that?'

'Shaft the wife *and* the tabloid press,' he said, running a proprietorial hand over Patsy's pert right buttock and lightly smacking Pandora's smooth left one. 'Now you,' he said to Patsy, 'are coming back to me. Sell the house. Come out to Spain.'

'Are you two getting back together?' said Pandy, scenting a scoop.

'I don't know,' said Patsy. 'It's for me to say. I've got other things on. There's our book.'

'What book?' said Danny, instantly suspicious.

'I'm doing a book with Pandy. About my life living with a gangster.'

'What!'

'Don't get alarmed, Danny,' said Pandora. 'You should come in with us. Why don't the pair of you tell me your story? We could keep all the stuff about a woman coming to terms with the world of violence and racketeering. And we could tell Danny's side of it, about how he had to turn to crime to express himself and how he was exploited by society. You *were* exploited by society weren't you, Danny?'

Patsy laughed. 'Yeah. And we could get Billy Dazzle along to take some sexy photos to spice it up a bit.'

Danny's mind was racing, he wasn't all that enamoured at the turn this conversation was taking. 'Who the fuck is Billy Dazzle?'

'He's a private dick. He took those photos of your skinny-dipping party in Kent.'

'That's the bastard who screwed me up right and proper! He was working with the Old Bill.'

'No, he wasn't. He was working for me,' protested Patsy, but Danny wasn't listening.

'He signalled to them. He jumped out of a tree and they went for us. I had to leave the country because of him.'

'It was an accident. He didn't know the police were there.'

'That's only what he said,' interrupted Pandy. 'I know about this man. He's not to be trusted. He seduced a friend of mine. He hid beneath her bed and listened in on an intimate conversation.'

Patsy giggled. 'That does sound like Billy. But he's harmless, Danny, really.'

'No, he's not,' said Pandy forcefully, 'he's a cheap stud with the morals of a sewer rat and I don't see why you are standing up for him, Patsy Fretwork.'

Suddenly Danny sat up. His face was grim. He leaned over to Patsy and gripped her jaw in his huge hand, forcing her to look directly into his cold blue eyes. 'Tell me one thing, Patsy.'

Patsy glared back at him, unable to break from his grip.

'Has he fucked you?'

She did not reply.

'Well – has he?'

The silence stretched on. And on.

Four

LICENSE TO LUST

38

Brick Tempo was not exactly as Billy had expected. He bore no obvious resemblance to the rock star whose ever-changing image had been a fixture in the cultural firmament throughout three decades. Long gone was the sixties' Afro and droopy moustache, the seventies' ponytail and Old Father Time face fuzz, even the eighties' bouffant and designer stubble. The slouching man who stared blankly at him from the cushioned comfort of the armchair in Imogen's office wore a grey suit and scuffed brown shoes. His short-back-and-sides was stubbled with silver and a battered holdall lay across his lap. He could have been a bank clerk or a ticket inspector – except, Billy reflected, not even public servants looked quite so terminally depressed.

Imogen was making the introductions, explaining that Billy was to take care of Brick's every little need while he was in London, expressing her own great confidence in Billy's competence. Billy noticed that she was enunciating her words clearly with the volume turned higher than usual. He flashed Brick his warmest smile of welcome, added his own good wishes to the end of Imogen's speech and pressed Brick's hand firmly.

It was like gripping lettuce, nevertheless Billy was in

awe. This man had been famous throughout all of Billy's life. He had had million-selling records when Billy was in the womb. He had faced death and disaster many times yet he had survived. He had Been There. He was a walking soundtrack to millions of lives. He opened his mouth and the chills ran down Billy's spine.

'I feel like shit,' he said. 'Would you run me a bath?'

The Living Legend had so far not turned out to be a live wire. That first afternoon, Billy had settled him into the apartment, unpacked his bags and run him a bath. Brick had then requested dry toast and milkless tea, disappeared into his room and remained there till eleven the next morning. Billy had watched television till the small hours, alert to any movement from next door – there was none – till he had finally flopped onto the bed in the spare room.

He decided the next day, as he served more tea and toast to his silent guest, that this was like being a man-servant to a Trappist monk. His brain buzzed with questions that he didn't quite have the nerve to ask. What had it been like to play with Bob Dylan in Greenwich Village in 1962? Had Brick really got his leg over all of the Dancing Pretties onstage during his Get It Up tour? How had he managed to crawl down Woodsmoke Mountain after the plane crash which wiped out all the other members of the band? Most of all he wanted to ask for an autograph for his mum but he didn't dare.

'So, Brick—' he said as the rock star pushed his half-empty cup to one side of the table, 'what kind of a day do you want? The office has been fielding a string of requests for interviews from all the media. It would be good publicity for the Gala. Or would you rather hit the shops? We've got some musicians standing by, too, in case you want to run through any of your stuff before the performance. Just say the word.'

Brick did not say any word at all. Billy wondered if he had heard him. Remembering the way Imogen had spoken to him he said loudly, 'It's up to you.'

Brick slowly turned his head in Billy's direction. His eyes were empty slits.

'Imogen has asked me to look after you, Brick. Surely, there's something I can do.'

There was a long pause. Was the man deaf? Had thirty years of the electronic guitar damaged his circuits?

Brick slowly raised a hand and pointed to the sliding window that lead out onto the sunny balcony. He finally spoke.

'There's something you can do.'

'Yes?'

'Fix me up a chair out there.'

'Sure thing. Anything else?'

'Yeah. Get lost.'

Billy was thoroughly pissed off. Playing Jeeves to a rude relic from the so-called Swinging Sixties was not his chosen role in life. He was contemplating telling Imogen where to stick her job – and he knew just where – when the doorbell rang.

It was Tracy, her blonde ringlets cascading around the dewy fresh beauty of her heart-shaped face down to the shoulders of her smart powder-blue linen suit. She strutted straight past him on her three-inch heels positively bristling smart summery sex appeal. 'Where is he?' she demanded, tossing her artfully distressed leather attaché case onto the sofa.

'You're looking smart,' said Billy, struck by her change of style. 'What's with the fancy luggage?'

'I've brought my music. In case he wants to rehearse. So, isn't he here?'

Billy pointed to the balcony where the great man's cowboy boots could be seen resting on a cane chair. Tracy was through the french window in a trice.

'Hey – Brick Tempo!' she cried. 'We meet at last!'

Billy didn't hear a response but it may have been drowned in Tracy's onward gush.

This was incredible! effused Britain's Bustiest Beauty. She'd been brought up on the music of the great Brick Tempo and now here she was on the same bill as him, about to share a stage in honour of a Worthy Cause. To think that she, Tracy Pert from the East End, a singer/songwriter in her own little way with a record at number thirty-seven this week, funnily enough, should be teaming up with him was measure enough of how far she had come. Etcetera.

Billy still couldn't gauge the Tempo response. There was no sound of a male voice amidst the piercing tinkle of Tracy's chatter.

She had now moved onto the weather, the summer heat that was making silly old her so uncomfortable since she had foolishly put on a suit that morning. She had thought that just wearing the top would be cool enough but it really was scorching and, well, she just had to slip it off and let some air on her bare skin. Oh wow! That was better. It was so great to feel the heat on her body. Maybe she'd better slip out of her skirt, too. He didn't mind, did he? It was a bit of a cheek but he must have seen it all before. Back in the sixties they were half-naked all the time, weren't they? They were free then, they let it all hang out. She'd always envied that. She wished she'd been there in the sixties, was it as great as they said? Grooving in the raw to all that great music and letting their minds and bodies come together like in that John Lennon song . . .

'Billy.'

The deep rich male voice shook Billy out of a half-stupefied reverie as he watched the almost-naked Tracy, wearing just the briefest of pink cotton briefs, sway along the balcony, evidently heading for the rock singer.

'Billy!'

Brick's voice rang out again, clear and imperious, and Billy stumbled out into the sunlight, a part of his mind thrilling to the knowledge that the singer had remembered his name.

'Yes, Brick?'

He was reclining across two chairs, a big white Stetson in his hand.

'You still want to do something for me?'

'Of course.'

'Get Little Miss Big Tits out of here.'

A strangled squeak came from Tracy's lips and her adorable body shook in pain and fury as Brick clapped the hat on his face shutting her from his sight.

39

'My name is Danny Fretwork. Some of you will have heard of me. And to those of you who haven't – where the bloody hell have you been for the past few years?'

The picture on the large television was jumpy, obviously the camcorder operator was not experienced. Nevertheless the bronzed and beefy face of the nation's most wanted man was instantly recognisable to the small audience of policemen and women crammed into the small office. Among them, Sophie Stark shifted uncomfortably as she hung on Danny's every word.

'First of all, I've got to thank the proprietors of this television station for giving me the chance to send a few messages of public interest.

'To the readers of the *Daily Blizzard* I'd like to say I hope you enjoyed my wife's stories about me. It was a good laugh, but you people ought to know that her memory is what's known as selective. Very soon I hope to set the record straight and tell you all the whole truth. I promise you then you'll really split your sides.

'To my wife, I have only one thing to say and I said it to her face when I met her just a couple of days ago. Now I'm going public so it's on the record, witnessed by everyone who's watching this. Patsy, I love you, I can't live without you and I want you back living by my side. Our marriage vows are as sacred to me now as they were on the day we wed.'

A loud raspberry rang through the small room as Sophie's companions reacted to Danny's bug-eyed sincerity with predictable derision. But the laughter died on their lips as he continued.

'Here is my message to the coppers: what a load of tossers you are. You couldn't organise a bunk-up in a brothel. Here am I, strolling round London as you can see' – and indeed, as he swayed to one side, St Paul's could be clearly discerned on the opposite bank of the Thames – 'and you haven't laid a finger on me. Frankly, if I was paying British taxes I'd be disgusted.

'My final word is a personal message to Sergeant Sophie Stark. I hear you're a bit of hot stuff, my darling, but I'd advise you to hang your knickers up right now. You ain't sticking *my* dick in your trophy cabinet.'

There was a stunned silence in the poky office as Danny's face was replaced by a white blizzard of static.

Mark Bacon muttered, 'I didn't know you wore knickers, Sophie,' but nobody laughed as the lights flickered on and a grim-faced Ambrosia Spicer rose to her feet.

'That tape,' she said, 'was delivered to the BBC just after eleven this morning. They sent us this copy but tell us they'll be using it at the top of the one o'clock news. We are going to look complete mugs.'

'Stop it going out,' said a voice.

'We can't. If it had just been the Beeb we might have had a chance but it's also gone to ITN, Celestial and, we think, the satellite stations. We can't gag the lot.'

'Oh shit,' said someone.

'Precisely. The news media and the politicians will

have a field day with us, then the top brass are going to jump all over me. And you know what that means. If my tits are in the mangle I'm going to make sure your nuts are wrung out at the same time. So, get out there and find the bastard! He's not exactly inconspicuous, for Christ's sake. At least, after that tape goes out everyone in the bloody country will know exactly what he looks like!'

40

Billy felt awful. Tracy had been in tears as he had helped her into her clothes and he felt a genuine tenderness for her as she sobbed into the handkerchief he had thoughtfully provided.

'Oh Billy,' she wailed, 'how could he be so horrible?'

'Years of practice, I should think,' and he rubbed her back fraternally as she hung on his neck and spilled her tears onto his shirt front. 'When you've gone I'll go and sort him out.'

She sniffed loudly, obviously unimpressed. 'It's a nice thought, Billy, but don't be a hero on my account.'

'Why not, Tracy? I'm your devoted slave. Frankly, how he could turn down such an utterly gorgeous creature creature like yourself boggles my imagination.'

'Now hang on, you make it sound as if I just marched up to him and asked for a good shagging.' She pushed him away from her, instantly indignant.

'That's better, Tracy, you look much more like your old self.' And she did, her blue eyes blazed, her perfect complexion flushed pink with anger and her buoyant breasts bobbed deliciously between the unbuttoned flaps of her jacket.

'That's a very saucy outfit you've got on,' Billy continued, slipping a hand into the breach and cupping the rosy fullness of her left boob. 'I like the contrast between the severity of the cut and your natural curves.'

The nipple was big and erect beneath his thumb and she let him fondle her for a moment before she said, 'Thanks, Billy. I feel a bit better now.'

Billy pulled her close and kissed her, gently at first, then more urgently, his hands roaming lasciviously beneath her open jacket. She allowed him these liberties without responding then stepped away to button herself up.

'I'm sorry, Billy, but I'm not going to let you bonk me on the sofa with that pig sitting next door. I'll make it up to you, honest.' And with a sly squeeze of the obvious erection tenting his trousers, she was off down the corridor. Billy heard the front door slam behind her with pained regret.

Brick was reclining in the same position as before, stretched out across two chairs, the big white Stetson completely covering his face.

Billy removed the hat with a flourish, exposing the rock star to the full glare of the sun. For a moment the lined basilisk face remained motionless, then one eye flicked open. For the first time Billy caught a glint of life deep within the void.

'Uh,' grunted the singer.

'Did you have to be so fucking rude? That girl is a fellow artist, one of Imogen's top performers, she's also the country's biggest sex symbol. She's very upset.'

'So?'

'So – so she's gone storming off. She'll tell Imogen. She might tell the Press!'

'I'm shaking in my boots.' The eye snapped shut.

'Give me my hat back, Billy, and fuck off.'

'No.'

Both eyes opened this time and subjected Billy to the full force of their reptilian glare.

'No,' repeated Billy, 'not until you talk to me like a fellow human being. If you don't I might just throw your precious hat off this balcony.'

There was a silence. Then Brick slowly swung his feet off the chair and sat up. 'Oh shit,' he said, 'you'd better sit down, then. And *please* may I have my hat back?'

An hour later Billy had got to the heart of the matter. Once he had opened his mouth, Brick had scarcely been able to shut it again.

'Your friend, Tracy Whoosit, she reminded me of a gal I met in Australia once. Must have been in seventy-eight or nine. She was someone's PA or something. She sets up this lunch with me in a hotel suite and we're having all these fancy things and she's in this smart suit, very business-like. And then she puts down her fork and starts taking off her duds, talking all the time about these interviews she's set up for me and meantime just stripping off. Beneath this suit she's not wearing a stitch. And she has the most fantastic body, all smooth and pink and waxed and pampered, with cute little red toenails and a bare pink pussy with a neat little knot of blonde curls right at the top of her slash. And, just like Tracy, she has the most dick-standing gazonkas you ever clapped eyes on. Just the most sensational tits. All thrusting out on their own and yet moving and shifting like cream in a tub.'

'Did you throw her out too?' asked Billy.

'You're joking, man! I couldn't wait to get my face

between those danglers. I just dived in, knocked the table over as I recall and broke up all those plates and glasses. We had someone clear up the mess next day and they charged us extra and the papers ran a story about me smashing up the room. The truth was I was dorking this doll with the x-rated chest accessories for twenty-four hours straight. Yes sir, they were the finest titties I ever saw, till maybe the pair that just walked in here.'

'So why did you tell Tracy to leave?'

'Because, Billy, I can't do it any more. My dick gave up on me five years back. You remember that thing I had with Tania Tingle?'

Billy nodded. He remembered reading about Brick's last big romance, which had produced an X-rated video, a Gretna marriage, a Reno divorce and a schmaltzy remake of 'True Love' that had remained a late-night banker for FM deejays the world over. All of Brick's marriages had yielded significant commercial opportunities.

'That Tania finally blew my tubes. She was a witch. She used to give me this stuff, her nooky juice she called it, which meant I could stay in the saddle for twenty-four hours straight. We fucked like bunnies for six months, anywhere and everywhere. But the human frame has its limits. I'd try and tell her to slow down but she was hooked on her multiple Os. She finally decided I wasn't strong enough for her and she trawled the body-building scene till she found some poor schmuck who wasn't gay and went off with him. Poor sap. I sent a wreath to his funeral. I felt I should have warned him. So I guess I had a lucky escape. But Tania didn't just break my heart she stole my balls. Since she and I split I haven't been able to get it up. Not once.'

'Would you like to?'

'Are you kidding, my friend? If I got my dick back I'd give little old Tracy a hundred new suits for the pleasure of poking her sweet puss.'

'Really?'

'Sure thing. But I don't live on pipe dreams.'

Billy said nothing but he had just had a sudden flash of inspiration.

'In the meantime,' said his talkative charge, 'I sure could use some more tea.'

41

Sophie found Ambrosia standing, still and silent, in the middle of her office. Her shoulders were shaking and her left arm was held rigidly to her side, fist clenched, the knuckles white. Her right hand held a half-smoked cigarette that had burnt almost to the butt. Moisture glistened on her cheek. The blinds had been drawn and the air was blue with smoke.

'Oh, Ambrosia!' said Sophie as she closed the door behind her. 'It's not that bad, surely?' And she rushed to put her arm around the other woman to comfort her.

Ambrosia did not yield to the embrace but spoke in a low, urgent voice that dripped with venom.

'Your sympathy is misplaced, Sergeant Stark. You would do better saving it for yourself. For your information I am trying very hard to control my temper and my anger is directed principally at one person. You.'

'But, Ambrosia—'

'I know we have both enjoyed the pleasure of carnal relations with one another but I must insist that in this office you address me in a manner more appropriate to our respective stations.'

'Yes, ma'am.'

'I, on the other hand, can call you what I fucking well

like. And I am going to call you a dirty little tart who is more interested in sucking pussy than in doing her job.'

'But, ma'am—'

'Shut up. It is obvious from Fretwork's Jack-the-Lad video that he got on that boat. I can just about understand how Bacon and his cretins failed to spot him but I cannot comprehend how you could have done so. After all, you were on the damn thing, weren't you?'

'I had to go home on Monday. I was off duty for six or seven hours, I suppose. He must have got aboard then.'

'So what happened after that? Did you notice anything different about your two companions?'

'Not really.'

'Did it occur to you that they were keeping something from you?'

'No. Things went on much as before. They spent a lot of time working on this book project of theirs. They seemed to have got quite close. I was rather surprised by that. I thought at first that Patsy wouldn't put up with Pandora for long but now she seems to me to be rather taken with her.'

'Patsy Fretwork enjoys having her cunt licked, wouldn't you say?'

'Yes, but it was more than that. She seemed to absorb some of Pandora's ideas. I thought it was good for her, actually. Pandy was encouraging her to be more assertive.'

'So you noticed nothing different when you got back.'

'No, just that Patsy and Pandy were even more pally than before. All girls together, you know, lots of giggles. I realised then that they'd become good friends.'

'You all carried on diddling one another, though, didn't you?'

'I'm sorry?'

'Don't get coy with me, Sophie. You all sucked each other off, didn't you?'

'Yes.'

'And you carried on in the same way after you got back on Monday?'

'Not quite as much, actually. To be honest, ma'am, sleeping with women is not really my style. It can be pleasurable, of course, but it's not something I want to do exclusively. I mean, I might if an opportunity arose which, er—' Sophie ground to a halt.

'I see, so having it off with Patsy and Pandora was simply in the line of duty?'

'Well, you did indicate that I should.'

'And going to bed with me was simply in the cause of furthering your own career?'

'No, of course not, Ambrosia, that was entirely different.'

'Was it?'

'*Yes.*'

'I'm not convinced, Sophie. You'll have to prove it.'

'Oh, Ambrosia!'

'Now now, Sophie, what did I say about addressing me in the office?'

'I'm sorry, ma'am.'

'That's better.' Ambrosia sat on the chair in front of her desk and kicked off her shoes. 'I'm all wound up, I need to relax. Why don't you come here and help me?'

'Yes, ma'am,' said Sophie in resignation as she sank to her knees before the parted thighs of her superior.

'That's it, Starkers, I'm feeling better already. And

while you're kissing my pussy I'll work out exactly where
we go from here in the question of Danny bloody Fretwork.'

42

As Billy was boiling the kettle he heard the sound of a key in the front door. He glanced up to see Katie Crisp bearing down on him, grim and efficient in a starched white blouse and black skirt. Nevertheless Billy couldn't help but think of the perfumed mass of pussy hair and the creamy white flesh that this severe costume concealed.

She gave him her customary smirk and said, 'Playing housemaid, are we? Our little session the other morning must have done you some good.'

'Up yours, Katie,' he said cheerfully.

'You wish.' And she eyed the front of his trousers where once more, ever eager, stood the evidence of her effect on him. 'Can't you learn to control yourself? Or does my presence make it impossible?'

As Billy floundered for a suitable response she demanded, 'Where's the degenerate superstar? Not still in bed, I trust.'

'No, ma'am,' came the soft voice from the doorway, 'I'm right here.'

Katie was completely unfazed. 'Good. We can't have you lounging around all day. Important people want to meet you, God knows why. While you are here you must earn your corn, as I believe you Yanks say.'

'Yes, ma'am,' replied Brick obediently, 'whatever you say.'

'Hang on,' said Billy, 'Imogen told me yesterday that Brick had no fixed agenda, he could please himself.'

'That's all changed. Candida Kensington is holding a little lunch party for some of her friends and she wants him up there by one. I believe you know the way, do you not?'

'Now wait a minute, Katie, I don't know whether Brick would find that kind of occasion to his liking. I'm sure if I explained to Candy—'

'Billy, it's OK.' Brick had stepped forward and was now addressing himself directly to Ms Crisp. 'Whatever this young woman says is OK by me. I'm here to do a job. Besides, I might meet some nice English ladies who appreciate my kind of music.'

'You'll meet them all right,' said Katie, evidently unimpressed by the American's compliance, 'they'll all be old enough to have heard of you.' And she turned on her heel and left.

'Wowee,' whistled Brick, 'that's some gal. What wouldn't I give for some nooky juice right now!'

'That reminds me,' muttered Billy, heading for the phone.

Arnold Brie turned up half an hour later.

'Billy!' he cried, hugging him like a longlost relative. 'I've been looking all over for you. You've changed my life. I love Betsy. I want to marry her. We're going to open a gourmet restaurant in the country and have a litter of children . . .'

'Put me down, Arnold! What an impetuous fellow you

are. I wouldn't rush into anything with Betsy, if I were you. Now you're back in the swing, why don't you try out your wicked weapon elsewhere?'

'Well . . .'

'There's no time to talk now. Have you got the stuff?'

'Yes.'

'Follow me. And remember, you're a doctor.'

Brick was looking pretty cool in his tight jeans, cowboy boots and soft leather jacket so fine it hung on his broad frame like spun silk.

'I thought I'd best tool up for the ladies luncheon,' he explained as Billy and Arnold entered the living room.

Billy made the introductions and noticed with some trepidation that Arnold was awed by the great man's presence. He forgot to let go of Brick's hand when he shook it and gazed at him with mouth agape.

'As you agreed, Brick, I've been telling Dr Brie a bit about the problem you mentioned earlier. Dr Brie is a specialist in the area of fading powers and has experimented successfully with herbal tonics. There's just a chance he may be able to help you.'

Brick had been looking increasingly sceptical during this speech and now said to Arnold, 'Is this true, doctor?'

'Oh yes, no problem, Brick. Hey, it's really great to meet you, man.'

'You can give me something to perk my pecker up?'

'Absolutely. Here—' and Arnold produced a small vial with a dropper top from his pocket. 'Take four drops, two in each nostril, about half an hour before the action. You'll soon be boffing those groupies just like the old days. I guarantee it.'

'So it's like nooky juice?'

'Yes,' said Billy. 'Take some now, Brick.'

'But we're off to some old dame's lunch. I'm not likely to need it there.'

'Believe me, Brick, Candy Kensington's house is where a man needs nooky juice most of all . . .'

43

In the distance there was the noise of hearty conversation and the ringing of telephones but in Ambrosia Spicer's office there was silence. It was broken only by soft sighs and murmurings, the whisper of flesh on flesh and the occasional hiss of indrawn breath. And the rhythmic slick-slick sound of lubricated genitals being pleasured.

Ambrosia Spicer's skirt was bunched around her waist and her panties were crumpled around her left ankle. The regions in between were completely nude, laid bare by Sophie to kiss and stroke and fondle and admire. Sophie was a conscientious lover and she had taken her instructions to relax Ambrosia very seriously. So far she had relaxed her comprehensively twice with her mouth and once with her fingers and Ambrosia's large prominent cunt was flushed with its exertions.

Sophie rested her head on the other woman's thighs and contemplated the pretty sex delta ahead of her. The long slit lay open and exposed beneath the brown thatch of pussy fur at the top of Ambrosia's crack. The fleshy vaginal lips were curled outward like butterfly wings, revealing the pink and juicy entrance to the tunnel within.

'You have the loveliest pussy, ma'am,' said Sophie, but Ambrosia did not reply. She simply ran a hand fondly through Sophie's thick curls and then firmly pressed her head back into her crotch. Sophie opened her mouth to resume the cuntal kiss, reaching forward to grip the other's taut buttocks and slip a finger into the smooth divide between to gently titillate Ambrosia's puckered arse-hole.

The great detective began to relax seriously once more.

'Ooh, that's good. Mmm, yes. And now my clit. Flick it lightly with your tongue. Ohhh, yes. You know what I like, don't you? Oh Sophie Stark, I swear you are the greatest cunt-licker on the Force!'

Sophie gripped Ambrosia tighter, her palms digging into the soft buttocks to pull the spread pussy onto her eager lips and tongue. Her forefinger was rimming Ambrosia's bumhole from the rear, forcing itself into the tight ring of muscle while she ran the pointed tip of her tongue up and down the wet pussy slit from the front. The result was all too predictable as Ambrosia thrust her loins back and forth, forcing the finger up her arse and the tongue deep into her cunt.

'Oh yes,' she cried, 'yes, yes, yes, yes, YES!'

And she came in a final, bucking lurch that pitched Sophie backwards onto the floor and left her looking up at her superior's widespread thighs scissoring back and forth in her orgasmic spasms.

Silence was resumed. Both parties sprawled as they were, catching their breath. Within Sophie's loins there was an unbearable itch but she didn't dare do anything about it. Finally Ambrosia spoke.

'Look in the bottom left-hand drawer of my desk.'

Sophie obeyed. 'There's nothing in it. Just a truncheon.'

'Exactly. Bring it here and take your knickers off.'

'Ambrosia, you can't!'

'Oh yes, I can. Besides, I know you, you're mad about sex. You must be dying to come off. And since we all know how much you prefer a big thick staff to a delicate feminine hand then this will do very well.'

'You can't make me!'

But Sophie was already unfastening her skirt to reveal her long tanned legs and shapely loins barely covered by a wisp of panty that was undeniably wet.

'On your knees, your arse facing me. I'm going to fuck you doggie-fashion.'

'You're a bitch, Ambrosia.'

'You said it. Oooh, you *are* wet, aren't you? It's slipping straight in.'

'Oh God, Ambrosia! It's too big! I can't take it!'

'Nonsense, it's up you already.'

And it was too, some eight inches of wooden pole were buried deep in Sophie's snatch as she bent over in front of the still-seated Ambrosia. Her smooth broad bum cheeks were thrust high and spread wide to reveal the long furrow of her arse-crack, the pink star of her anus winking up at Ambrosia as she worked the truncheon in and out of the pouting pussy lips below.

'How do you like that, Sophie? You can play with your clit at the same time. In fact, that's an order.'

'Oh God, Ambrosia, this is so rude! Suppose someone comes in!'

'You weren't worried about that when you were sucking me. Besides, they're probably peeping through the keyhole.'

'Oh no!'

'I'm going to make you come lots, Starkers. It aids my concentration. Especially if I imagine I'm doing this to your friend Patsy Fretwork.'

'Oh Ambrosia! Oh, I'm coming! Oh! OH!'

'Patsy Fretwork is the one we've got to get to. I think I'll give that reporter bitch a grilling. I won't get anywhere but it might freak Patsy out.'

'Ambrosia, please! Oh God, I think I'm going to come again!'

'Then it'll be up to you to crack Mrs Fretwork. Got that, Sophie?'

'Yes, Ambrosia, yes!'

'Good. Do you want me to stop now, Sophie?'

'Don't you bloody dare! Oh, Ambrosia, that's *fantastic*!'

44

Billy watched Brick closely as they drove to St John's Wood in a taxi. Beyond asking Billy if he was sure Arnold was a real doctor – to which Billy had responded that he was an alternative practitioner – Brick had lapsed into his former state of sullen silence.

As they alighted outside Candy's house, Billy checked his watch. It was twenty-five minutes silence Brick had taken Arnold's wonder drops, at any moment now he should achieve lift-off.

A male flunky ushered them into the house – a young handsome male flunky, Billy noted. Doubtless he doubled as an artist's model as part of his duties.

Candy emerged in a cocoon of seductive perfume, her face a picture of ecstasy at the sight of her longtime idol. She offered him a slender hand and Billy watched with trepidation. This should be it, he calculated: the first touch of finely groomed female flesh on a man starved of sexual frisson for five years. This surely was the ultimate test of Arnold's skill.

Billy was not disappointed. As he later told Arnold, it was like plugging a man into the national grid. A bolt of electricity seemed to shoot from Candy's small hand into Brick's large one. His eyes flicked fully open for the first time in Billy's short acquaintance and all those grimly etched lines on his face suddenly danced into life as he bent forward and kissed Candy on both cheeks.

'I sure am delighted to meet you, ma'am. It's a privilege to be invited onto your Gala programme and into your lovely home.'

'How do you do, Mr Tempo?' said Candy, gazing upward into Brick's crinkly smiling face, familiar to her for so many years and now actually here in the handsome, larger-than-life flesh. 'I hope Billy is taking good care of you.'

'I've just got one complaint about Billy,' he said, his eyes dancing with mischief, his face close to hers, 'he never told me what a beautiful woman you are.'

'Oh, Mr Tempo!' Candy was a lost soul already, Billy could see that. He dropped his eyes to the crotch of Brick's jeans. Just as he thought – this could be a most interesting social occasion.

A buffet lunch had been laid in Candy's vast sunlit dining-room and her guests were well into the aperitif champagne by the time Brick made his entrance. The hum of conversation was already substantial but it noticeably kicked up a level after the rock star's broad shoulders appeared in the doorway. There was even a spontaneous burst of applause which Brick acknowledged with a modest wave of the hand.

As forecast by Katie, the ladies at Candy's lunch were of a certain age, best defined as 'middle'. However, they were all women who had suffered the passage of time with the wherewithal to cushion its worst blows. Here were trim, pampered and elegantly preserved females dressed to kill in the most lavish of designer garments.

But though they sported the most expensive accessories that the fashion houses of Milan, Paris and New York had to offer they were themselves far from simply decorative. These women wielded influence and chequebooks. Candy certainly knew her market.

Brick inclined his mouth to Billy's ear and said simply, 'Hot damn!' From then on he was borne away into the throng, with Candy on his arm, prodding and patting his handsome frame at every opportunity as she began the serious business of introducing him to wealthy wives, business executives, aggressive charity fund-raisers and even a newly appointed Cabinet minister.

A hand tugged at Billy's elbow and he turned to face a tall brunette with a crimson mouth. Her simple summer frock successfully showed off a body comprised of tempting curves.

'Excuse me, young man,' she said, 'are you associated with our guest of honour?'

'I'm with his management team,' Billy replied, trying not to look down the fascinating crevasse of her cleavage, 'I suppose you could call me his minder.'

'So you know all his movements?'

'Yes. It's my job to make sure he turns up.'

'I see. My name is Joanna Knickerbocker and this is my daughter, Nicole.'

Billy turned his attention to the intriguing figure by her side. Amidst this well-groomed throng Nicole Knickerbocker stuck out like a sore thumb. Her hair was a wild hennaed tangle and around her slender neck she wore a leather choker with silver studs. The lower half of her spectacular form was encased in black tights over which she wore a tiny pair of skin-tight blue shorts. On her top was a loose white vest with the legend 'Poll the

244

F**k Tax' which did nothing to distract from the elastic thrust of the pert boobs that billowed unrestrained beneath. Billy found himself gazing into a sulky face whose milky blue eyes and swollen pouting lips were drawn into an expression of utter distaste.

'Pleased to meet you, Nicole,' he said, his cock rearing in his underpants at this vision of teenage lust.

'Nicky insisted on accompanying me when she heard Brick was going to be here. We are both such fans,' said the elder Knickerbocker. 'It's about the only thing we have in common these days,' she muttered as an after-thought.

'I can think of something else,' chipped in her daughter in a squeaky voice loaded with venom. 'She can't keep her hands off men,' she said to Billy, 'randy old tart!'

'Youth is so embarrassing,' said Joanna, her hand on Billy's arm. 'The thing is, we would both so love to meet Brick properly, away from this crush.'

'Yes,' said Nicole, her face suddenly perky and pretty, 'I want to ask him what it was like to play with Bob Dylan.'

'And I'm dying to hear first-hand how he managed to escape from the plane crash on Woodsmoke Mountain.'

'Well . . .' said Billy, a multitude of lascivicious opportunities racing through his brain.

'*Please*,' implored Joanna, 'it would be so good for Nicky to meet someone from an older generation whom she admires. 'And,' she added, squeezing Billy's forearm meaningfully, 'I'd be most grateful.'

Billy finally managed to separate Candy from the throng.

'Oh Billy,' she gushed, 'isn't he cute? I could just eat him up.'

'You're not the only one. Just about every woman here is dying to kiss his feet.'

They looked across the crowded room to the knot of women surrounding Brick. He was smiling and answering questions and shaking hands but Billy thought he could detect a look of sheer panic in his eyes. And Billy knew what was causing it.

'May I confide in you, Candy?'

'Of course. We're old friends now, aren't we, Billy?' And she rubbed her hip surreptitiously against his thigh.

'Brick Tempo hasn't made love to a woman for five years. He can't. He's had a mechanical breakdown and nobody has been able to fix it.'

'Oh my God.' Candy looked genuinely shocked and Billy could guess why. 'That's terrible.'

'Indeed it is. But I think I've mended it.'

'The breakdown?'

'Yes. With a little help, of course.'

Candy's big brown eyes narrowed as she gave him a significant look. 'You mean he's like you were last week . . . ?'

'Quite.'

They both looked back at Brick who now had his arm round a willowy blonde with a long toothy face. As they watched he appeared to place his other hand into the neck of her blouse and paddle with the pale white flesh at the top of her bust.

'My God!' exclaimed Candy. 'That's the Honourable Vanessa Crumble – he's fondling her breasts in public!'

'He'll ravish your entire guest list on the floor if we don't do something. Think of it, no sweeties for five years and suddenly he's loose in the candy store. That's a man with a mighty appetite.'

'What are we going to do, Billy? There are reporters here. Scandal would ruin my Gala!'

'Well, Candy, as it happens I've got a plan . . .'

45

Betsy Toast was becoming suspicious. Amongst her usual clientele had been a crop of new punters who had been surprisingly reluctant to avail themselves of her services. She was used to men turning up at her door full of unlikely excuses as to how they came to be there. She wasn't fooled, however, because she knew what they really wanted – her high creamy breasts, long tanned legs and the pink treasure concealed in her golden fork. Though their desires may be masked by furtive grins and embarrassed smiles, she prided herself on cutting through the usual anal bullshit of the Brits.

These new visitors, however, were not like that.

First there had been a paunchy fellow in a fake-leather car coat who had exhausted himself by climbing three flights of stairs to her door.

'I'm looking for the geezer downstairs. Don't know where he is, do you, love?'

'What?'

'Billy Dazzle. Don't know where he is, do you?'

This kind of British double-speak always got on Betsy's nerves. She was an English major, after all. 'I know where he isn't, if that's what you mean,' she replied.

'Where's that?'

'Here.'

'He's here?'

'No, he's not here.'

'But I thought you just said he was.'

Betsy could see this obtuse exchange going on for ever. She decided to cut it short.

'Look, mister, pardon the cliché but my time is money and I'm wasting it talking to you. Do you want to party?'

'Eh?'

'You know – boogie, fool around, get your rocks off. Christ, man, we have a real communications problem. Do you want to fuck me – yes or no?'

Car Coat shuffled his feet and squinted shiftily at Betsy's protruding nipples before declining her offer. Then he produced a card and a £10 note.

'Look, love, do us a favour – when Dazzle shows up give us a bell on this number.'

'A bell?'

'A tinkle. On the dog and bone.'

'What!'

They'd sorted it out in the end to their mutual satisfaction. Betsy had relieved him of another nine notes, promised to undertake the telephonic service and jerked him off in the hall while he groped her breasts and tongued her big brown nipples. She'd not given it another thought until the second man turned up.

He was big, tanned and barrel-chested; he wore dark glasses and a baseball cap. Fortunately, he was easier to understand.

'Excuse me, young lady, I am looking for Mr Billy Dazzle.'

'One flight down.'

'He's not there at present – do you know where I can contact him?'

'Sorry, I don't.'

'Is he likely to be back soon?'

'Look, buster, he's nothing to do with me. We're in a separate line of business. His is closed.'

'I see.'

'But mine is open. Why don't you step into my showroom for a demonstration? I'm the model. All parts are movable if you get my drift.'

If he did he didn't want to; he disappeared downstairs without one curious glance in her direction, leaving Betsy snarling. She didn't often let a fish off the hook.

In the afternoon Barrel Chest was back. He'd changed his appearance and now sported a blazer, a tie and a beard but there was no disguising the tan or the torso. Betsy opened the exchange, she was getting fed up.

'Look, buddy, he ain't back yet.'

'I'm sorry?'

'You're looking for Dazzle, right? You were here this morning and, my God, that's some five o'clock shadow.'

'It's true I am trying to get in touch with Mr Dazzle but I've never been here before.'

'Oh, OK, so I can ask you for the first time today if you'd care to step next door with me and have what you Brits refer to as a nice time.'

For the first time she thought she detected a flicker of interest in his icy blue eyes. On reflection he was rather an attractive man.

On impulse she stepped right up to him and bumped her pelvis suggestively into his as she growled, 'Is that a pistol in your pocket or are you just pleased to see me?'

But he was gone, off down the stairs like a startled rabbit.

'Damn,' she muttered to herself, 'too corny.'

She returned to her parlour quite put out. Something else was worrying her apart from this last failure. She had felt something with her bumping pelvis and it wasn't an erection. Funnily enough, it might just have been a pistol . . .

46

So far Billy's plan was succeeding. While Candy addressed her guests in the dining-room Billy had ushered Brick to a first floor sitting-room equipped with easy chairs, occasional tables and, more significantly, a large and comfortable sofa. It had been difficult to tear Brick away from the women. He was almost frothing at the mouth with excitement.

'Christ, Billy, it worked – it WORKED! I've got a hard-on like a steel rail! Look!'

'No thanks, Brick, I'll take your word for it.'

'And all that hungry pussy downstairs – I feel like I could shish-kebab the lot of them!'

'Well, you're going to get the chance. Sit down and listen.'

Brick obeyed but he could barely sit still as Billy outlined future events; the somnolent sloth had been turned into a jumping jack rabbit.

'Candy is downstairs making an appeal on behalf of Poor Pussy Rescue. Then she's going to announce that those who are prepared to make exceptional donations to the fund can buy an interview with you. A personal interview. Alone. In here. On this sofa.'

'Oh boy!'

'Will you do it?'

'You're asking me to be a *whore*?'

'I'm asking you to sell kisses for the Milk Fund – like Monroe in *Some Like It Hot*.'

'Who's going first?'

'Minty Hush, the TV presenter.'

'Which one's that?'

'The doe-eyed brunette in scarlet and cream. The one with the cocksucker's mouth.'

'I'll do it.'

Things had got off to a slow start because Candy had insisted on 'a private word' with Brick before proceedings began – an interview which lasted a good ten minutes. Billy had dashed upstairs to investigate the hold-up and discovered Candy breathlessly quitting Brick's room.

'Hurry up!' he hissed. 'Minty's going spare.'

Candy smiled weakly at him as she hurriedly tucked her blouse into her skirt.

'Do I look OK?'

'Christ, Candy, you didn't fuck him, did you?'

'I couldn't resist, not after you'd told me he hadn't had a woman for five years.'

'You horny cow.'

'Don't be crude, darling.'

'You owe the fund a thousand quid.'

'Worth every penny, believe me.'

As it turned out Candy had used her time to excellent advantage. After she had ushered Minty Hush into Brick's presence she grabbed Billy's hand and dragged him to the next door along the corridor. This room backed onto Brick's sitting-room and was connected by a serving hatch with a sliding door which Candy had already opened a tiny crack. The crack, however, was sufficient for a pair of observers to view the goings-on in Brick's room. Thus, with Candy in front and Billy behind, his chin resting on the top of her head, the two of them settled down to watch events unfold.

Araminta Hush was one of the acknowledged beauties of the television age. Her face, with its enormous liquid brown eyes and full Cupid's-bow mouth, was made for the small screen. For the past twenty years she had been seen in various guises, as anchor-woman and field correspondent, as contentious interviewer and special investigator. It was not known whether she had a sense of humour, certainly she was never glimpsed on any programme that had a hint of frivolity. Come Christmas, when other reporters were tap-dancing with the professional comics, Minty was nowhere to be seen. Nevertheless it was guaranteed she would re-emerge in early January reporting on some foreign war, the mud and sweat on her brow only serving to accentuate her angelic good looks. But – to her everlasting chagrin – all her serious reports on the ills of the world passed over the heads of the heterosexual males in her audience. When it came to the gorgeous Minty Hush, masculine interest was purely carnal.

So Billy watched closely as she shook hands with Brick and sat beside him on the sofa directly opposite their vantage point. He was intrigued that a rock musician should be of interest to her.

'Araminta Hush,' Brick was saying in his deepest, most mellow tones. 'Don't I know you?'

Her porcelain cheeks blushed daintily as she said, 'Well, I am on television rather a lot.'

'No. I don't mean *that* – though I've seen you a bunch

of times and, my God, you're a shit-hot reporter, if you'll pardon my free speech – I mean haven't we *met* before. Years back. In the sixties.'

'Oh no. I've never met you before.'

'Whoa, Minty. Don't you be so sure. I used to tour England a whole lot back then. I went all over. Met a hell of a lot of girls but not many as beautiful as you. I couldn't forget a face like yours.'

Minty was squirming beside him, her slender legs crossing and recrossing. Billy realised with some surprise that she was starstruck.

'Where were you in sixty-eight?' Brick asked.

'I was in my second year at Cambridge.'

'That's it, then. We played Cambridge. Oh yes, I remember it clearly. You were one hot little blue-stocking back then, Ms Hush.'

'I don't know what you mean, Brick, honestly. I never went to a concert of yours in Cambridge. Really.' Squirm, squirm went her little bum in her tight cream skirt. Swish, swish went the silk of her stockings as she crossed her lovely legs.

'Stop shitting me, Minty, we were very close friends for a short while back then and I can prove it.'

'How?'

'You have a mole up the top of your thigh. Boy, how I used to love to lick that chocolate button!'

'Well, you're wrong. I don't have any such mole.'

'Says you.'

'I don't.'

'OK, if that's what you say.'

'But I *don't*.'

'Hey, no need to get upset. A gentleman always believes a lady.'

'But I don't, I tell you. *Look*.'

So there it was. She had pulled her skirt up above her knees and Billy realised with a thrill that she was wearing suspenders and stockings – who'd have thought it?

Brick made a careful study of the exquisite milk-white flesh presented for his inspection.

'As I recall,' he was saying as he took hold of the hem of her skirt and eased it higher, 'it was way up on the inside of the left thigh.' And he slid his long fingers up the creamy skin above her stocking top, probing into the ravine between her legs in search of the elusive blemish.

For a moment there was silence and Billy was deafened by the sound of his heart beating. His hand was inside Candy's brassiere, rolling the firm stub of a nipple between his fingers, but his attention was fully fixed on the action in front of him. Minty, he could see, was shivering like a flu victim as Brick made a scrupulous examination of her naked thighs.

'Maybe it's on the right side,' he said. 'It's been such a long time since I had the pleasure . . . Now where is it?'

Minty's legs were now spread across Brick's lap as he made himself free with her lower limbs, twisting and turning her flesh to his satisfaction and, in the process, laying bare her entire stomach and the wet wisp of matching cream that covered the thrusting vee of her pubis.

'Maybe it's a little higher – on the inside, if you get my meaning. Oh my, what have we here?'

Brick had now pushed the material of her panties to one side and was boldly examining her exposed groin. His brazen fingers combed through the silky bush of chestnut hair and opened up the delicate pink oyster of her quim.

'Well, Ms Hush, it looks like I owe you an apology, you don't have any marks on your skin whatsoever. But you do have the cutest, the most adorable and the juiciest pussy I've seen in a long while.'

Minty's pelvis bucked and undulated to his touch. Her upper body had flopped back along the couch, her eyes were tight shut and her breasts rose and fell rapidly as her breath shortened.

'With your permission, ma'am,' said Brick, 'I wonder if I may pay my respects in the appropriate manner?'

Minty said nothing but unceremoniously grabbed him by the hair and pulled his head down into her crotch.

She came twice before she allowed him up for air, her slender arms tense with unlikely strength as she held his face to her hungry snatch, her eyes shut all the while, her perfect mouth set in a rictus of effort.

Meanwhile, her face still held to the peephole, Candy had reached behind her and pulled Billy's penis out of his pants. Now he was bollock deep between the pouting lips of her honeypot as she bent forward, her elbows on the ledge of the serving hatch. Billy jammed his throbbing organ fast within her, cushioning his stomach against her pliant bum cheeks, determined not to shoot off until he had savoured every nuance of Minty Hush's seduction.

Brick was now cradling a relaxed and out-of-breath reporter against his broad chest. She ripped open his shirt and buried her face in the mat of hair beneath.

'Take your cock out,' she said, 'there's something I want to do.'

Brick stood, unbuckled his jeans and pulled his organ free. It thrust out from the sandy hair of his groin like a great club, gnarled and veined and as stiff as a baseball bat.

'Come here,' she commanded and he stepped up to her so the great organ swung arrogantly right in front of her pretty face.

She took it in both hands, one dipping to fondle the big furry balls at the base, the other halfway up the shaft. Bending the stem to her mouth, she ran her tongue up to the rim and over the glistening scarlet cap. She looked up at him and smiled beatifically. 'Ready?' she asked.

Billy's fingers were in Candy's crotch gently rubbing her clit and she squeezed her thighs together to still him for a moment. Both trembled on the edge of orgasm as they watched.

Minty placed her mouth to the swollen head of Brick's penis and spoke into it as if it were a microphone. In her best newscaster's voice she said, 'Testing, testing. One two, one two. This is Araminta Hush for *News at Ten*, alone with Brick Tempo, rock superstar, about to give head.'

Then, with a hysterical laugh, she thrust the obscene member between her incredible lips and began to suck.

Billy couldn't hold it any longer. His mind bewitched by the sight of the immaculate Minty chewing on Brick's fat cock, he shot off deep inside the palpitating channel of Candy Kensington's cunt.

47

Sophie found Patsy amongst the chaos of Pandora's flat. Pandy had been driven away in a police car some ten minutes earlier and Sophie had watched from across the road until she judged the moment right to catch Patsy off-guard.

'Christ,' she said as she edged her way in the front door past a heap of luggage in the hall and a pile of half-opened post that had been carelessly kicked along the carpet. The sitting-room was as cluttered as ever but it smelt worse. 'Christ,' Sophie repeated, 'this place stinks.'

'Pandy and I were going to clear up when we got back but your lot just took her away,' said Patsy.

'I'll give you a hand. We could sort it out in no time.'

Patsy lit a cigarette and tossed the spent match towards the overflowing ashtray. It fell short but she made no attempt to pick it up.

'No thanks. You just want an excuse to snoop around.'

'It's a genuine offer.'

'Oh yeah? Well, you needn't worry in any case. We've had three policemen poking around here for the past hour, the same guys who were watching the boat and being all chummy. Now they're marching about like

259

little Hitlers. What's going on, Sophie?'

'You haven't seen the news, have you?'

'No.'

'Let's go down to the wine bar.'

'Oh blimey,' said Patsy when Sophie described Danny's video. 'Fancy old Dan saying that about me on the telly.'

'He also said he'd seen you two days ago.'

'He said that?'

'Is it true?'

'Yes. He popped up after you'd scarpered on Monday.'

'How?'

'He got some diving gear and climbed on board from the river side of the boat. He's good at all that diving lark, does a lot of it in Spain. Bit of a laugh, eh?'

'I can assure you that my superior officer is not laughing. She's tough. Pandora is probably finding out how tough round about now.'

Patsy shrugged and swigged down half a glass of house white in one gulp.

'How could you do it, Patsy? The whole set-up was to protect you. Why didn't you at least tell me he'd been there?'

'A fat lot of good you are at protecting anybody, Sophie Stark. If you ask me, all you're good at is dropping your knickers.'

'You bitch! He could have killed you and I was trying to prevent that happening.'

'Well, he didn't. He still loves me and now everybody knows it.' She refilled their glasses and attacked hers thirstily. 'But I couldn't tell you, Sophie. I'm his wife. He wants me to go out to Spain and live with him. We could start over.'

'And you think that will work?'

'Why shouldn't it?'

'What about the bimbo in residence?'

'She can go back to walking the streets or whatever it was she did before she got her hooks into my Danny.'

'Oh dear, Patsy.'

'Don't you oh dear at me. Just because I've got him and you haven't.'

'I'll catch him yet. All this living happily ever after in Spain is just a dream, Patsy. He's going to see out his days in Parkhurst and I'd advise you to find another man.'

There was a strained silence between the two women. Sophie's harsh words had blown away Patsy's good humour like a chill breeze.

'Let's face it, Patsy, we're on opposite sides of the fence. However, it doesn't mean we can't like each other.'

'Even though I said you were only good at dropping your knickers?'

'I'm not the only one, sister slut. Why don't we get another bottle and swap rude stories? About men.'

'Aren't you going to ask me about Danny?'

'I thought I just did.'

'He poked Pandora.'

'What!'

'It was an accident at first. It's difficult to explain but she loved it. She thought having a big thick dick up her was wonderful.'

'There's a reason for that, Patsy. It is.'

Two bottles later Sophie had heard a blow by blow, lick by lick, suck by suck account of the orgy on the boat that she had missed. Reprehensible though it was, the salacious detail and the wine were making her pussy weep with frustration.

'You're getting turned on, aren't you?' said Patsy as she observed Sophie shift uncomfortably in her seat.

Sophie nodded guiltily. The image of Danny Fretwork on screen loomed large in her mind, she could imagine the twinkle of those pale blue eyes and the smirk of his roguish smile. He was an attractive sod all right. She vowed she'd have him properly before she put him away for life. Yes sir, stuffed and mounted in her trophy cabinet before he joined the Crispin Kingsleys of this world behind bars. God, it seemed an age since she had last had a man!

'He'd be such a darling, my Danny,' mused Patsy drunkenly, 'if he wasn't such a bastard. Mind you, I love it when he's like an animal. All dominating and passionate. I really got him going this time 'cos I made him jealous.'

'Oh yes?'

'He found out about Billy. He went completely apeshit. It must mean he still loves me, don't you think?'

'How did he find out about Billy?'

'I can't remember exactly. I made some joke about the rude photos Billy took and he got all excited. Like Billy was the reason he'd had to do a runner to Spain. And Pandy didn't help.'

'What do you mean?'

'She told him how Billy had got his leg over that Tracy friend of hers. She put the boot in good and proper.'

'He gets around a bit, this Billy, doesn't he? It sounds like he lives a charmed life.'

Patsy gave a harsh caw of laughter. 'It won't be charmed no more if my Danny runs into him. He said he'd sort him out good and proper.'

'Really?'

'There's not much chance of that though, is there? I reckon he's halfway back to Spain already, now me and him have sorted things out.'

'You could be right,' said Sophie, her stomach suddenly alive with nervous tension, 'but I wouldn't be so sure.'

48

At £100 a minute Brick had already earned Poor Pussy around £7000 and was showing no sign of flagging. Candy had happily filed away four substantial cheques, one of them drawn on the personal bank account of the Honourable Vanessa Crumble who had, so far, been the only one to cause Candy and Billy any anxiety.

'I know what's going on here!' she had said to the pair of them as they reappeared after the excitements of watching Brick entertain Minty. 'It's utterly disgraceful!'

'What do you mean, Vanessa darling?' said Candy in her sweetest tones.

'I mean that lewd and obscene acts are taking place in that room in return for money! I mean that Minty Hush and Petronella Smiles and God knows who else are lining up for a sex session with Brick Tempo! Well, I won't stand for it.'

'But Vanessa—'

'I am the new Minister for Transport, Candy Kensington, and I do not expect to be kept waiting!'

So it was that the Hon Crumble had jumped the queue and gone in next. In the circumstances Billy had felt quite justified in slipping into the adjoining room to watch Brick charm the politician out of her knickers. To his surprise, there had been no need. Vanessa had greeted Brick with an open-mouthed kiss that had lasted for a good thirty seconds as her hands roved without ceremony under the silk robe that had now replaced Brick's clothes.

Then she had simply hoisted her dress over her thighs and turned to present Brick with a broad nude bottom already prepared for the fray. Of knickers there was no sign – perhaps, mused Billy, busy people like the Hon Vanessa had no time for such inessentials.

'Shove it up me, Brick,' she had cried, bending forward over an armchair. 'Don't hold back! I want all of your degenerate groupie-fucking, rock-star cock up my passage right now! OH!'

Brick had complied at once, stuffing his bone-hard spike straight into the minister's hairy split without benefit of foreplay or lubrication. Evidently such niceties were not required in Vanessa's circles for she thrust her rump back at him with a will, howling out her pleasure.

'That's it, man, ride me like a horse! Give me all you've got! Debauch me, you beast, just like you've debauched thousands of innocent young girls! Fuck it up me and see what true-blue British cunt can do.'

Brick had responded to the spirit of the occasion by cracking his big hands – splat! – on the juddering mounds of her bum cheeks, leaving the pink imprint of his palms on her wobbling flesh. Then he had torn open her bodice to release the ministerial tits which had tumbled out to dance and jerk beneath her writhing frame as she took the rock star's thundering shaft from the rear.

Finally her legs had buckled under her and she had orgasmed with a piercing whinny, collapsing face forward onto the chair.

As Brick extricated himself from her still-twitching form Billy had been interested to note that his tool still stood at full stretch. Though it showed signs of wear it was evident that Arnold's miracle drops still gripped the mighty organ in a frenzy of desire. Vanessa raised her head to marvel at it, grabbing the bar of flesh in both hands to bestow a parting kiss on the red and glistening cap.

Next door Billy had adjusted his own bar of flesh, concluding that the new Minister for Transport was a good sport after all. If the PM ever created a Minister for Bonking she undoubtedly had the right credentials.

Brick was now on his fifth special contributor, Mrs Sadie West of West's chainstore jewellers, a five-foot fireball with an over-proportioned bosom and caramel thighs. She was bound to ring the cash register for Poor Pussy in a big way, being that Morrie West was a well-known contributor to charity.

Billy was debating whether to ogle Brick's progress with the West whoppers when Candy appeared by his side.

'I need your help,' she said in a low voice, 'too many people want to give.'

'That's a problem?'

'Too many of them are asking for a special audience with Brick. They know what's going on, they don't want to be left out.'

'That's too bad. I reckon he can manage a couple more and that's it. I'm taking him away.'

'But what about the others? I can't send them home with full purses and itchy cunts. I wouldn't be doing my duty as a hostess.'

'I'm sorry, Candy. A real star should not be too available to his public. Always leave them wanting more, that's the cardinal rule.'

'Maybe,' she said, prodding a long fingernail sharply into the centre of his chest, 'but not before everybody has taken the stage. And that means you. You're on in the Blue Bedroom in five minutes with Lady Florence Smart.'

'You're mad, Candy! They don't want me – I'm no superstar!'

'Maybe not but they all know you're connected with Brick. I'm telling them you're a brilliant young song-writer who is composing exclusively for him. Besides, we're not charging as much for you.'

'How much?'

'A tenner a minute.'

'That's outrageous!'

'Do you think so? Honestly, Billy, they're all so stea-med up they'd pay for anybody's cock right now.'

'No! I mean Brick can't be worth ten times more than me! That's insulting!'

At school Billy had done his fair share of amateur theatrics but on the bed in the Blue Room he saved his finest performance for Candy's Poor Pussy Rescue. As Lady Flo dangled her big boobs in his face Billy captured a rubbery brown nipple between his lips and gummed it enthusiastically. At the juncture of their heaving bodies he ran his fingers through the slippery folds of her cunt, searching for the magic button that would bring her release – and allow access to another of the randy sister-hood.

Without the benefit of Arnold's elixir he knew that the afternoon threatened to tax his most vital resources.

As the buxom dress designer Brandy Brazil approached the bed Billy announced, 'I only suck pussy, my cock's off limits!'

'Fantastic!' she replied, tugging off her panties to reveal a veritable forest of wild and tangled pubic hair. 'Down into the jungle, young man, and don't bother coming up for air!'

The French actress Monique Aragon insisted on sucking his penis till the spunk frothed on her bee-sting lips. 'It eez my specialitay. Ozzerwize I don' write no cheque. OK?'

Grace Garter, the schlock novelist, and her agent, Marilyn Savage, came in together.

'Be gentle with me!' pleaded an exhausted Billy.

'You must be joking!' said Grace as she settled her big soft buttocks squarely on Billy's face. 'Gentleness would ruin Marilyn's reputation, wouldn't it, darling?'

'You bet,' replied the piranha of the literary world as she snapped her sharp white teeth over the head of Billy's valiant tool.

His howl of anguish was muffled by a mouthful of hairy quim.

'Billy – Billy! Are you OK?'

A familiar voice was calling from afar and firm hands were shaking him by the shoulders. Billy's eyes opened reluctantly. Candy Kensington's big brown orbs were staring directly into his. Concern was writ large on her lovely face.

'Candy, I'm sorry. I don't think I can manage any more.'

She laughed. 'Don't worry, Billy, the show's over. You've done your bit. In fact, you saved the day.'

'Thanks.' He sat up wearily and took in the fact that Candy was as naked as he was. 'What's been going on? I hope you haven't been molesting Brick again.'

'Fat chance. I had to go to work just like you. Bianca Fleece is a hardcore lesbian and there were two others who swing both ways. I wasn't letting any of them out till they had paid their dues.'

'And what was that, exactly? I'd love to know your rate per minute.'

'Well, you shan't. But you *can* call me the best little fund-raiser in London. Now, shall we go and see if our honoured guest is still alive?'

Brick was more than just alive, he was bubbling with good humour.

'Hey, man, what a trip!' he cried, punching Billy on the arm. 'That's the most fantastic afternoon I ever spent in my life. You are a genius!'

Billy smiled modestly and Candy announced that her chauffeur was standing by to drive them both back. She'd take them herself if she wasn't so (yawn) utterly exhausted she could hardly stand. Billy sympathised but he thought he detected a hint of disappointment in Brick's eyes as he eyed Candy's carelessly buttoned blouse and its generous display of shadowy cleavage.

'There's just one more thing,' said Candy and she swivelled her eyes meaningfully along the hallway.

Billy turned to see, smiling at him in a predatory fashion, the statuesque figure of Joanna Knickerbocker. His heart sank.

'Oh God,' he muttered.

'They wouldn't leave. They said they were waiting for you.'

'Yoohoo, Brick!' called Joanna.

Billy squared his shoulders and stepped forward, it would be better to fob them off straight away with sincere apologies.

At that moment Nicole Knickerbocker stepped from behind her mother and shamelessly lifted her T-shirt up to her chin, baring her chest for all to see. Her huge pert breasts, pink bulging rounds of taut youthful flesh, wobbled hypnotically before their eyes. The words of excuse died in Billy's throat and from behind him he heard a gasp of indrawn breath.

Suddenly a broad figure strode past him, arms outstretched in welcome, as Brick bore down on mother and daughter.

'Hello, ladies,' he cried, 'I wondered where they'd been hiding all the pretty women! How'd you all like to come back to my apartment for tea?'

The Knickerbockers squealed acceptance with one voice.

'Once more unto the breach then, Billy,' said Candy with a sly smile on her face. 'I'm sure you can rise to the occasion.'

49

It was mid-afternoon when Betsy received her next unlikely visitor. Her mind had been taken off the matter by the arrival of Arnold with an armful of roses. She had entertained him in the customary way and consequently now walked rather gingerly to the door with just a flimsy wrap thrown over her aching charms. Arnold was a bruising lover. His compulsive talk of marriage was flattering but daunting. She wasn't sure if she was robust enough to withstand his romancing for any length of time.

These were the thoughts buzzing through her head as she opened the door to a pretty dark-haired girl in a denim jacket and a lime green mini-skirt that scarcely covered her crotch.

'Yeah?' said Betsy, genuinely curious. She wasn't used to female visitors.

'Sorry to bother you, but do you know where I could find Billy Dazzle?'

Betsy rolled her eyes heavenwards. 'For crying out loud! Who do you think I am? His fucking wife?'

The girl was completely unfazed and continued to chew a mouthful of gum in a noisy, loose-lipped fashion. Her big black eyes, however, darted curiously at Betsy, noting her dishevelled state.

'Got you out of bed, have I? Sorry. The thing is, he's not down in his office and I need to see him urgent. You're a brass, aren't ya?'

'What?'

'You know, on the game. "French chest for sale", that sort of thing. You sure you don't know where Billy Dazzle is?'

'No.' Betsy began to close the door.

'Here, hang about – can I ask you a question?'

'You already did and I can't help you.'

'No, something different. Tell me, how much do you charge?'

Betsy's irritation boiled over. She stepped forward and grabbed the girl by the collar of her jacket.

'Push off, you little bitch,' she hissed into the other's startled face, 'and don't you or any of your funny friends come and bother me again.'

The girl's lips froze in mid-chew and her pupils grew large with fright. An irate Betsy, some four inches taller, her hair a wild golden mane around her scowling face, was an intimidating sight.

However, the girl stood her ground and said meekly, 'I'm sorry, miss, I didn't mean to be rude.'

Betsy relaxed her grip, aware that perhaps she had over-reacted.

'The thing is,' the girl pressed on, 'I need some advice – how do I get to be a tart like you?'

Betsy couldn't understand why she had invited Amanda in, especially with Arnold asleep in the next room. Maybe it was guilt – she had nearly thrown the poor kid down the stairs – or maybe an instinctive recognition that here was a girl with possibilities. Those eyes, almost

272

black but flecked with hazel lights, were fabulous. Betsy had always been a good judge of the competition.

'Why,' she asked when she had sat the girl on her sofa and made her a mug of tea, 'should a nice kid like you want to be a prostitute?'

Amanda grinned, 'Cos I'm sick of handing it out for free – or near enough. I don't call a Four Seasons pizza and a tenner a proper return for letting a feller get his leg over.'

'Have you had lots of boyfriends?'

'Are you kidding? I'm very popular down our way, always was – even before I left school.'

Betsy nodded. She had been popular at school, too.

'But the men I know,' continued Amanda, 'only want one thing and they want it on the cheap. I was thinking of moving up west and putting it on a professional basis. Like you. Do you think I could?'

Betsy shrugged. 'Why not? The only thing that separates the amateurs from the professionals in this business is that we get the cash up front.'

'I mean, do you think I look good enough? You're so tall and blonde I can see why men would cough up to get at you. I'm worried I'm not special enough.'

Betsy laughed. 'Are you serious? You honestly don't know how gorgeous you are?'

'Well, my Uncle Danny says I'm the hottest little teenager he's ever had. But he fucks my mother too and she's gross, so I think he might not be the best judge.'

Betsy took a long look at the girl sitting next to her. She was bedraggled and nicotine-stained, her dress sense was abysmal and she continued to chew gum even as she slurped tea. She also mangled the English language in the funny London accent that Betsy still found difficult

273

to understand. Evidently this was not the most sophisticated lady in town. Nevertheless, there was something about her. The long dancer's legs, the big black eyes, the full red lips all screamed out that this girl was a guaranteed cock-stiffener at a hundred yards on a foggy night. A germ of an idea took root in Betsy's brain.

'Would you mind taking your clothes off?'

Amanda leapt to her feet and, without hesitation, began to strip. Betsy watched with half a smile on her face as clothes began to fly across the room – scruffy denim jacket, creased white blouse, garish red bra and pale green skirt – leaving her clad in just a pair of clumpy lace-up flat shoes and thick blue leggings that clung like a second skin to her hips. She wore nothing beneath them and a thick bush of flattened pubic hair bulged obviously at the junction of her thighs.

She kicked off her shoes and turned away from Betsy to bend over and slide the remaining garment down her legs. As she did so Betsy drew in her breath, 'Wow,' she said, 'that's a great ass!'

'Do you think so? I'm worried it's too big.' Amanda looked round at her rear end critically, grasping her left bum cheek so the creamy flesh spilled over her fingers.

'Honey, if you want to be a model or a dancer you're right – it's too big. But if you want to give a man something to hang onto in this crazy world then it's perfect. I bet none of your itchy-fingered "uncles" have ever complained.'

'I suppose not.' Amanda grinned sheepishly and ran her hands up to her breasts which were high and buoyant, each trembling orb topped by a cute red nipple standing out like a ripe raspberry. 'And what about my boobs?'

Betsy got to her feet. 'Child, you're a walking wet dream and you know it. And I can't hang around telling you you've got outstanding tits. How about going to work?'

'What? Right now?'

'Sure. I've got a guy next door and we'll soon find out whether you've got what it takes. You'll make money, too.'

'OK.'

'Good girl. I have a hunch you'll be fabulous. Now, you need some pretty things – let's see what might fit.'

Betsy turned to a large chest in the corner of the room and began to rummage through the drawers.

'Let's try these,' she said, and helped Amanda put on a white lacy suspender belt and matching stockings. The shoes she produced – elegant high heels in white leather – were too big but both agreed that that didn't matter much.

'That's great,' said Betsy, 'from the waist down anyway. The white garter belt sure sets off your little black muff. Let's see what else I can find. Unfortunately you'll never get those bazookas into any of my bras.'

She hunted some more and found a diaphanous pink top that fell in a tantalising gauzy screen over the girl's sumptuous tits.

'That'll do,' Betsy pronounced, having made Amanda parade up and down the room. She wobbled a bit in the unfamiliar shoes, setting her breasts quivering, but Betsy knew that was no disadvantage where men like Arnold were concerned.

'Two things more,' said Betsy.

'Yes.'

'Do you like big dicks?'

'You bet!' Amanda nodded her head enthusiastically. 'What else?'

'Lose that fucking gum. Forever.'

50

Tea at Brick Tempo's apartment was not an elaborate affair. He produced a large bottle of Thorny Cactus sour mash which he insisted that mother and daughter Knickerbocker drink neat. Of course, they'd have drunk neat bleach if he had asked them. In Billy's opinion the alcohol did not excuse what followed, the women were so fired up by events at Candy's that they were practically having orgasms just being in the same room as Brick Tempo. Nevertheless, Joanna attempted to observe the proprieties.

'It's so kind of you to invite us, Brick. Superstars like you must be constantly pestered by fans. It is a rare privilege for us to share a private moment or two with you, isn't it, Nicole?'

'Oh *yes!*' agreed the daughter.

'Believe me, ma'am, the pleasure is all mine. I just love to meet my admirers, that's how I learn about life. For instance, young lady, what exactly does that slogan on your shirt mean?'

Nicole pirouetted coyly, holding the T-shirt by its hem so all could see the words and the formidable swell of flesh beneath. She took a deep breath, 'Well – ' she began.

Her mother cut in quickly, 'Nicky, don't you *dare*!'

'But, Mummy . . .'

'I will not have you haranguing poor Brick with your infantile politics on such a nice afternoon.' Joanna turned to Brick, 'It's a badly made and horribly expensive piece of designer tat that has caused countless arguments in our house.'

Brick nodded sagely then smiled at Nicole who was on the point of tears.

'I see,' he said, 'but leaving politics aside it *is* rather unusual and I was wondering if I could buy it from Nicole.'

Mother and daughter regarded Brick curiously.

'I have a theory about clothes. I think fashion is a kind of material memory, if you know what I mean. Take that vest. It couldn't come from any other time or place in the history of this planet. Julius Caesar would never have worn it nor Napoleon nor even JFK, because it's a snapshot of *now*. Yes sir, I want it!'

Billy listened to this speech with admiration. There was no need for Brick to go through this elaborate charade to get Nicky's tits out into the open but he could see that the singer was enjoying himself.

'I tell you what,' continued Brick, bearing down on the open-mouthed girl, 'you can have my shirt in exchange. Or my jeans – or any of my clothes. Take your pick.' And he began to undress, unbuttoning his shirt and pulling it off his broad bronzed torso.

'C'mon, Nicky,' he roared, 'what are you waiting for?'

But the girl was frozen to the spot, mesmerised by the sight of her idol kicking off his cowboy boots and unzipping his jeans. He stopped when he was down to a pair of pale blue briefs that barely covered the straining bulge of his genitals. The bar of his big penis lay sideways across the flat of his stomach, almost poking through the material. He put his hands on his hips and gave a little pelvic bump in Nicky's direction, 'Don't be shy, honey, take what you want.'

Nicky swooned. She pitched straight forward into Brick's arms and he lost no time in peeling the T-shirt upwards and over her shoulders, at the same time appearing to administer to her the kiss of life.

The two of them stood there swaying in the middle of the room, joined at the mouth. Nicky's big breasts bulged out at the sides as she ground herself against Brick's chest, her arms wrapped around his neck.

The coveted T-shirt lay on the floor by Joanna's foot. Billy shot a glance in her direction to see how the respectable society mother was taking the sight of her half-naked daughter locked in the arms of one of the era's most celebrated degenerates.

Joanna smiled coolly back at Billy. 'She's not a bad girl really,' she said. 'I think a little rebellion is to be expected at her age, don't you?'

The teenage rebel now had one hand on the waistband of Brick's briefs, clumsily easing the elastic down over the stiff prong of Brick's cock. The unsheathed pink glans sprung into view and Billy could have sworn that Joanna's pupils grew twice as large at the sight. She gulped hungrily at her Thorny Cactus as the girl's eager fingers delved deeper to cup the singer's balls, revealing the thick stem of his prick as she did so.

Joanna laid a hand casually on Billy's knee. 'I'm so glad you could arrange this little tea party for us. It was really very kind of you, considering we had never met before.'

The hand slid upwards to Billy's thigh.

'Well . . .' he said, suddenly aware that Joanna's attentions were not, after all, entirely unwanted, 'I'm bound to help any friend of Candy's.'

In front of them Nicky's little shorts were being eased over her tight round bum as Brick's big hands swiftly undressed her. Obviously the old skills of girl-stripping had not deserted the rock star during his years of deprivation.

Joanna's hand had now unzipped Billy's trousers and his loins were alive with anticipation as her cool fingers slipped inside his fly.

'I adore Candy,' said Joanna, 'she does such good work, wouldn't you agree?'

Billy agreed – he'd have agreed to anything as Joanna's hand closed on him and began to work the slippery skin of his foreskin back and forth across the tingling head of his throbbing member.

In fact mother and daughter were manipulating cock almost in unison, as Nicky fingered Brick's big boner while Joanna wrapped her sweet fingers around Billy's agitated stem.

By now Nicky has been undressed down to her sheer black leggings which were stretched taut over the prominent ovals of her buttocks, revealing the pale gleam of white flesh beneath. The girl was on tiptoe, still hanging onto Brick's neck with one arm, her mouth pressed tight to his, wriggling her pelvis backwards and forwards. With a stab of excitement Billy noticed that there was a large hole in the crotch of her leggings through which, on the back thrust, he could glimpse short gingery pubic curls and the glistening pink lips of a well-lubricated vagina.

Brick's big hands were roaming over the girl's ripe arse, squeezing and kneading the pneumatic flesh, gripping the cheeks and pulling them apart, then probing lower between her legs. With a grunt of satisfaction he found the hole in the thin material and pushed a thick forefinger within, straight between the lips of Nicky's slippery pussy.

'Oh Mummy,' she howled, 'he's got his finger right up my twat!'

'Nicole,' replied her mother sternly, not breaking her rhythmic frigging of Billy's cock, 'you know I told you never to use that word!'

'Sorry, Mummy, but – ooh, he's found my clitty!'

'Nicky, please!'

'But he's rubbing my clitty – ooh, that's fantastic! Oh, Mummy I think I'm going to come!'

'Don't be disgusting!'

'But I can't help it! Brick Tempo's got his finger up my cunt! He's rubbing my clitty! Oh God, Brick Tempo's going to make me come. Oh, oh, OH!'

And the exquisite rounds of Nicky's bum, on a level with Billy's face as he sat beside her mother on the sofa, jerked backwards and forwards in a blur on the probing digits of Brick's big hand. Over her shoulder, hidden from the tight-lipped but dexterous Joanna, Brick grinned at Billy and winked.

Now Joanna was stripping Billy of his clothes, pulling at his shirt buttons and tugging at his belt, all the while maintaining her grasp on his erect cock. Nicole, too, was varying the action. Already recovered from her ecstasy and eager for more, she had wrestled Brick to the floor, swivelling her body so they lay head to toe, and slotted her pouting lips over the head of his cock.

It was obvious to Billy, as he too was laid on the floor and his penis engulfed in the hot mouth of Joanna Knickerbocker, that mother and daughter were in competition. For the moment, however, mother was allowing her offspring to make all the running.

But with the tight ring of Joanna's mouth squeezing the head of his tool Billy was happy not to dwell on female rivalries. It was time to take action himself, to explore beneath the thin shift that covered Joanna's trim thighs now arched invitingly over his head. He slid a hand up her flank, revelling in the feel of smooth, expensive flesh. To his surprise his fingers encountered soft pussy hairs and plump buttock flesh unencumbered by any sort of undergarment. There was nothing at all but bare skin beneath her dress – the randy mother must have removed her panties back at Candy's in anticipation of this moment.

Billy eagerly pushed Joanna's dress up to her waist to expose a lightly furred and thick-lipped pussy just begging to be tickled and licked and sucked. He applied his lips gently to her honeyed slot blowing warm breaths through her short pubic curls, making her jump and squirm in pleasure. Then he began to lick her slowly, lightly, from the base of her furrow up to the top of her crack, stopping just short of her clit to travel back down again.

Joanna went wild. She thrust her pelvis down onto Billy's face, capturing his head in the fork of her thighs, squealing with pleasure as he relented and took her prominent clit between his lips. There followed loud agitation and crisis. Billy could see nothing, imprisoned as he was in musky female flesh, but he could hear the keening of women's voices raised in orgasm. Mother and daughter, united in sex at any rate, were coming off together.

Brick and Billy, it seemed, were merely puppets, turned this way and that purely for the women's pleasure. Now they lay flat on the carpet, with Joanna and Nicky riding them side by side, each squatting on a penis, posting up and down, their faces rigid with concentration. It occurred to Billy that mother and daughter were a bit like a formation dance team, mirroring each other's movements with well-oiled precision. He wondered, in that case, how they practised their act . . .

But there was no time now for idle conjecture. The pressure in his well-exercised cock was mounting. It seemed unbelievable that he could come yet again after events at Candy's but there was no denying the rush of oncoming ecstasy building in his loins.

It was the sight of Nicky in orgasm that did it: her wild hair writhing, her ginger bush flowering from her black loins but above all the vision of her enormous breasts swinging and swaying in her excitement. They bounced up and down on her chest in such a riot of rolling nubile flesh that his spunk shot up his cock into Joanna like water out of a geyser.

But Joanna was not finished. She allowed Billy to fountain his pleasure into her and her daughter to flop forward onto Brick in post-orgasmic shock and then she went into action. In one movement she had pushed Nicky off Brick and was poised over him herself. Her well-juiced cunt was leaking sperm as she gripped the rock star's ever-rigid pole and thrust it deep within her, a smile of triumph on her face.

'Mummy,' wailed Nicole as she viewed events with dismay, 'I hadn't finished.'

'Hard luck, darling,' replied Joanna, settling into a steady rumba on Brick's stomach. 'I'm sure Billy will take care of you – won't you, Billy?'

Billy was too enfeebled to utter a protest as Nicole leaned over him and offered a swollen pink nipple to his lips. Then he heard the sound of Brick's voice.

'Hey, Billy, I think you need some of my nose drops.'

51

'Cor, he's got a big one!' shrieked Amanda in surprise. 'It's a fucking monster!'

'Ssh, he's asleep,' whispered Betsy.

Arnold was stretched out on his back on Betsy's bed, stark naked. His phenomenal penis, the object of Amanda's admiration, lay at rest along his thigh like a slumbering serpent.

'Blimey, Betsy,' hissed Amanda, 'you didn't tell me it was *this* big.'

'Chickening out?'

'No fear! I'd even pay to have a go at one like that.'

'Knock it off, Mandy. That's heresy, especially in a whore's bedroom. Besides, Arnold's going to pay you good money so you can stuff that sucker inside you. Think you can manage it?'

Amanda was standing by the side of the bed, gazing intently at the penis in question. 'I'll give it a good try,' she said. 'May I touch it?'

'Be my guest,' replied Betsy unnecessarily, for Amanda's hand was already gently stroking the length of Arnold's reclining tower, from base to tip and back again. Betsy watched intently as the girl grew bolder, fondling the great balls as they lolled between his thighs,

285

then curling round the stem and trying an experimental up-and-down jerk. The big cock soon began to respond to these ministrations of its own accord and she squealed out loud with pleasure as it lengthened in her hand.

Arnold's eyelids flicked open, then blinked rapidly at the sight of a half-naked stranger fingering his genitals.

'Hi, honey,' said Betsy, 'meet Amanda, she's on probation.'

'What?'

'I'm thinking of taking on an associate but first she's got to pass a test. You.'

Arnold sat bolt upright, a look of alarm on his face. 'You're not serious, Betsy?'

'Damn right I am. She wants to be a professional whore and I need someone to take over my regulars if I'm going off with you for the next few days. It makes sense, huh?'

Amanda looked backwards and forwards between the two of them during this interchange. Somehow her hand was still on Arnold's cock.

'But—'

'Come off it, Arnie,' continued Betsy. 'What are you complaining about? Isn't this girl adorable? Look at those great legs and her pretty pussy – I bet you can't wait to get in there. Anyway, you're stiff as a poker.'

It was true. Arnold's great member thrust up from his belly like a billy club, the whiteness of the shaft contrasting with the deep pink of the now-exposed helmet. Amanda was at work on it with both hands.

Arnold looked at her and she grinned back at him. She really was remarkably pretty and she did have a stunning body.

'Well . . .' he said, his resolve slackening as his cock

stiffened, 'provided Amanda doesn't mind.'

'Why should she? She's going to have the ride of a lifetime and you're paying. Where's your wallet?'

'Hey, Betsy—'

But Arnold had no choice in the matter or, rather, his willpower had evaporated as Amanda shrugged off her diaphanous slip and snuggled into his arms on the bed.

Meanwhile Betsy extricated a bundle of notes from the pocket of his trousers and placed them on the mantelpiece. 'Mandy, that's your fee. Now I want to see you earn it.'

'Betsy Toast, you're the bossiest cow I've ever met,' muttered Arnold.

'I bet you love it, though,' chipped in Amanda. 'I can tell. Here, how would you like to suck my nips?'

Arnold got his money's worth. Young Amanda was an enthusiastic fucker with elastic limbs and a dirty mind. Being on trial, she had not held anything back – she had sucked and tongued Arnold's dick, nipple-kissed his entire body by snaking her boobs lightly all over him, milked his penis with her breasts, ridden up and down on his huge cock with only minimal difficulty and had allowed him to plough her heartily in the good old missionary position. Given Arnold's physique this last activity could be construed as danger work but Amanda was well primed for action at that state and, to Betsy's surprise, had urged him on.

Though aware she wasn't supposed to come Amanda had done so three times and had had the nerve to claim that she was faking it. Betsy laughed and smacked her heartily on the rump which perked up Arnold's interest once more until he realised he couldn't afford any more of Mandy's favours.

'You can have me,' explained Betsy, 'provided I want you. But you can't have her unless you pay her.'

'So, are you going away?' asked Amanda. 'What do you want me to do?'

'Arnold's doing the catering for a charity concert in the country and I'm going for kicks. While I'm gone I'd like you to visit a couple of guys for me. They're dead easy, they probably won't even touch you. Wear your suspenders and buy some high heels and they'll let you walk all over them. They pay extra for that.'

'Great!'

'Half of what they give you is for me and I know just how much that is. OK? Will you do it?'

'Sure. This is terrific, I can hardly believe it. I get sent up here on some silly errand and I get a job! Just as well that Billy Dazzle wasn't there after all.'

Arnold, who had been listening sleepily, said, 'Are you looking for Billy? He's off with Brick Tempo at the moment. I saw them this morning.'

Mandy's jaw dropped. 'Cor, you saw Brick Tempo?'

'Yes. He's at this concert we're going to, Billy's taking him down there tomorrow.'

'Blimey!' Amanda was impressed. However, wheels were also turning in her brain. 'Where's this concert taking place?'

'At Bedside Manor. In East Sussex.'

Amanda grinned. Uncle Danny would be pleased.

52

'You know, Billy,' said Brick as they leaned side by side on the balcony watching the Knickerbockers climb into a black cab in the street below, 'I think I need more pussy.'

'How could you?' responded Billy. 'You've already fucked half of London society this afternoon.'

'You forget I've been released from the chains of enforced celibacy after five years. And it's all thanks to you.'

'Thanks to Arnold, you mean. I'd be cautious with his funny drops if I were you. Too many doses might finish your love life forever.'

'Who cares? I never thought this day would come along. That's why I want to make it last. And I want to show my appreciation to you, my boy. I've got a little hunch.'

Curious, Billy followed Brick inside and watched him pick up the phone.

'Hi, Imogen – how ya doing?'

Politenesses were exchanged. Brick waxed fulsome about everything, meeting Candy, the lunch party and, in particular, Billy's contribution to his contentment. 'There's one more thing I need, Imogen. It may sound strange but I wonder if you could spare the services of that fine young lady who does all your bossing around.'

Billy was taken aback. What was Brick up to?

'Yes, Katie Crisp, she's the girl. Would she mind stepping up here to keep us company for a spell? Tell her I'm writing a new tune called "Little Miss Fixit" and she's the gal who's gonna fire me up.'

Brick placed his hand over the mouthpiece and grinned at Billy. 'She's asking her now.'

'Brick, you're crazy. That bitch will never play ball.'

'Don't worry, I'll get her up here. She's my present to you. You've got the hots for her, right?'

That was true enough, if he cared to admit it, even if his interest was fuelled by the desire to even a few scores.

Brick was talking to Imogen again. 'She's not available? Now listen, Imogen, I suggest she makes herself available because if I don't get to finish my song I might not be able to perform tomorrow night. I'm like that. Once the goddess of creation lays her hand on my shoulder then she won't let me do a damn thing else.'

'You corny bastard,' muttered Billy.

Imogen was back on the line. Brick listened and smiled at Billy. 'She'll be up in ten minutes? That's terrific. I know her presence is really gonna inspire me . . .'

Ten minutes stretched into twenty before Katie appeared. Her face was dark with thunder and her mouth set in a mean slit as she marched in without a word and stood, bristling, in front of Brick.

'Why, Miss Chris,' exclaimed the singer, 'I'm delighted you could join us.'

'It's Ms Crisp, Mr Tempo, and I must make it plain
that I am here under sufferance.'

'Then we'll just have to try to ease your pain a little.
Allow me to pour you a drink. I can recommend the
Thorny Cactus whisky.'

'Anything, Mr Tempo, to make this ordeal less
tedious.'

'And, Billy, would you mind passing me my guitar?'

'Does that worm have to remain here?' said Katie,
regarding Billy poisonously.

'Now, Katie, Billy is crucial to my muse – just like
you. In fact I want you two to act out a little scenario
for me.'

'What!'

'Billy's going to be your boss and sit at that desk
there. And you, Katie—'

'I won't do it!'

Brick picked up the phone. 'What's Imogen's
number?' he asked Billy.

'OK, I'll do it. But I want you to know that I am a
highly qualified legal adviser and not somebody's secretary.'

'Katie, that's understood. Now would you mind sitting
on top of the desk just in front of Billy and sort of cross
and uncross those fine legs of yours. And would you
mind slipping your skirt off first? See, I'm getting
inspired already!'

To Billy's astonishment, Katie had gone along with it,
removing her clothing piece by piece till now she was
down to a half-slip, cream suspenders, stockings and
matching panties embroidered with pink roses. Her
bulging pubis clearly revealed the dark shadow of her

abundant pussy hair beneath the semi-transparent material.

She had posed in accordance with Brick's instructions, cursing and fuming as she did so, while he idly strummed his guitar, making up lyrics in her honour. All the same her hands had not been slow to unzip and unbutton and her sturdy but graceful limbs had been tantalisingly revealed to the obvious excitement of both men.

Katie now perched on top of the desk, her legs splayed apart and thrusting her pantied pudendum into prominence. Billy couldn't help observing that the material was damp with her juices.

'This really turns you on, doesn't it, Katie?' he said.

She didn't respond but turned her face disdainfully away from him. The skin of her shoulders and above the scalloped bosom of her slip was flushed and the distinctive perfume of her pussy – which Billy had cause to remember well – was thick in the air. Much as she may dislike the idea, the woman was on heat.

Brick had now put down his guitar and there was silence in the room.

'Well,' said Katie fiercely, 'can I go now?'

'Oh no, Ms Crisp,' said Brick, 'I've finished tinkering with the tune but now I'm looking for ideas for the video. Have you ever done any improvising? I'd like you to do whatever feels good, you know, just go with the flow.'

'I don't know what you're talking about,' she replied, however she was already tugging at the hem of her slip and lifting it over her head. She was now naked to the waist and her small but sweetly curving breasts shivered deliciously in their freedom.

'You're both disgusting! Foul!' But she was tweaking

her long pink nipples with one hand, going back and forward from left to right in an unconscious fever, pulling on them hard till they stretched into long stiff peaks quite out of proportion to her diminutive tits.

'Why don't you show us your pussy?' suggested Brick softly and no sooner had he said so than her other hand was between her spread thighs, pulling the panty material to one side to reveal the thick mop of black hair. Both hands were in her crotch now, delving for her slit and spreading her swollen labia to reveal her pink wet quim.

'I suppose you'd like me to kiss it,' said Billy, 'Like last time.'

'Yes!' she hissed, her fingers shamelessly at work in her crack. 'Yes, you revolting degenerate bastard, I want your mouth between my legs!'

'Well, hard luck, Katie. This time it's my turn and first you're going to have to suck my cock.'

Katie sucked more than Billy's cock, she devoured him with her mouth, kissing him all over, from his toes to his nipples, before thrusting his bursting tumescence between her lips. She clasped him to her fast, her hands beneath his buttocks, fingers dipping into his arse-crack to tickle his anus and finally push a finger deep inside him as he spurted his lust deep down her throat. The disapproving Ms Katie Crisp was a red-hot fellatrix at heart.

After that it was something of a free-for-all, with Katie on fire and eager for any games of lust though the only words she uttered were curses and insults. Stripped to just her suspenders and stockings she had turned into the antithesis of her severe everyday persona. But then

Billy had already been on the business end of those strong bulging thighs and the insatiable pussy mouth between. And, remembering the circumstances of his humiliation in the gym, he wanted even more from her. Though she was giving freely of her body, he desired the submission of her spirit.

He leaned back against the desk, his bum on the edge, his feet braced apart, his Arnold-inspired penis a raw and flaming sword curving up from his loins.

'Come here, Katie,' he commanded.

She came. 'What is it, you rat?'

He curled an arm round her waist and pulled her towards him so her belly rested against his, the barrel of his cock in the notch of her cunt.

'Put it in,' he said and she did so obediently, standing on tiptoe to slide the fat head of his member into her slot and screwing down onto it with a lascivious swivel of her pelvis.

Billy reached down to grasp her behind both knees and lifted her legs off the ground. She shrieked and flung her arms round his neck.

'You'll drop me!' she protested.

'I won't if you hook your legs round my waist. Besides, Brick is going to help.'

Brick approached wearing nothing but a smile, his big truncheon swinging before him. He wasn't sure exactly what Billy had in mind but the sight of Katie's large firm posterior thrust obscenely outwards in his direction was giving him a few clues.

'Have you ever had two men at once, Katie?' asked Billy.

'Put me down at once, you pervert!'

Billy's hands were on her broad creamy arse cheeks

and now he spread them wide, offering to Brick the dark hairy furrow between. The small brown pucker of her bumhole winked up at the singer invitingly and he stepped forward eagerly.

'No!' screamed Katie. 'Don't you dare! You'll never get it in – it's too big!'

Katie was wrong. Applying the buttery juices that flowed so copiously from her forward orifice, Brick lubricated her nether knothole and advanced the head of his prong.

'Oh my God!' cried Katie as she was breached.

Now the arms of both men were fast around her as she was sandwiched between their strong hard bodies. They proceeded slowly, Billy resting against the desk, taking the weight, allowing Brick to thrust his prick forward inch by inch, deep into the tight passage of Katie's luscious arse.

And Katie began slowly to respond, still cursing and complaining, but grinding her pubic delta down onto Billy's cock then arching back to take the increasingly urgent thrusts of Brick's shaft. She was completely smothered by male flesh, penetrated fore and aft, pinioned by two stalwart cocks who were able to give her everything her insatiable loins required.

'Oh God,' she wailed as their organs fenced within her and the momentum began to build, 'I hate you both! This is terrible! The most disgusting, ghastly, horrible – *wonderful* – thing I've ever done! OH!'

And her orgasm broke upon their ears like an explosion.

Imogen heard it in her office two floors below and stopped work for a moment to listen to the screams and bellows of ecstasy from above. She smiled contentedly to herself. She liked to know her people took pleasure in their work.

53

The day of the Gala broke upon a selection of interested parties with the brilliance of the best of English summer days.

In the Mayfair apartment, Katie Crisp rolled over in Billy's bed and thrust her broad bottom into his crotch. Still half asleep, he accepted this unspoken invitation to slide his morning stiffy home into the capacious and still-hungry mouth between her legs.

In St John's Wood, Candy Kensington inspected her new chauffeur as he paraded in his uniform. The peak of his cap shone brightly and his gold epaulettes did not look in the least ridiculous on such a broad and strong pair of shoulders. His trousers were in no need of Candy's attention for they hung neatly over a chair as she conducted an in-depth hand inspection of his throbbing cock.

In Hampstead, Patsy Fretwork gratefully sipped a mug of steaming coffee as Pandora Britches sat on the bed beside her and said, 'Poor darling, you shouldn't have drunk so much. I told you I'd be all right.' And Patsy made no objection as Pandora's long fingers began their familiar stroll across the soft and dimpled plain of her stomach towards her mound of pleasure.

* * *

In Soho, a further scene of sexual licence had just drawn to its conclusion when Sophie Stark knocked at Betsy Toast's door. It was eventually opened by a cadvaverous man of extraordinary height who had obviously just struggled into his jeans.

'I'm sorry to disturb you,' said Sophie, 'but I'm trying to contact Billy Dazzle and I wondered—'

The man held up his hand to halt her flow and yelled over his shoulder, 'Betsy, there's another recruit for your call-girl service. She looks even better than the last one,' he added under his breath.

'May I ask who you are, sir?'

'None of your business,' said the tall blonde who appeared at his side. 'And Billy's not here, so you can scram.'

The two of them towered over Sophie who nevertheless was not put out. She did what she should have done in the first place and produced her identity card. 'Do you mind if I come inside?'

The pair looked suitably chastened as Sophie took in the confusion in the tiny set of rooms. An empty suitcase lay on the unmade bed, other luggage stood in the hall.

'I didn't know Billy was such a popular guy,' said Betsy. 'You're about the fifth person who's come looking for him in the past twenty-four hours.'

'Did any of those people look like this?' And Sophie produced a photograph.

'You bet,' said Betsy at once. 'That big fellow came here twice. The second time he was wearing a false beard but he couldn't disguise his build. Who the hell is he, anyway?'

'You obviously don't watch the television or read the papers.'

'Sorry, I'm American. Your Brit papers are from Mars.'

'Well, this is a photograph of the country's most wanted man. We're looking for him in charges of racketeering, extortion, manslaughter and murder.'

'Christ!'

'If you've seen him, Miss Toast, I want to hear all about it.'

'Sure, sit down, Arnold will make us a drink. Why on earth is this guy looking for Billy?'

'I think he wants to kill him.'

'Oh my God!' cried Betsy, and ran into the toilet to be sick.

She was gone for quite a while during which interval Arnold handed Sophie a cup of instant coffee. As an afterthought, and because the policewoman had now discovered he was a celebrity chef, he also produced a homemade biscuit.

Betsy returned, her healthy tan dimmed for once, and sank into an armchair.

'I'm sorry, Sergeant—'

'Sophie.'

'OK. The thing is, Sophie, when he came back the second time I tried to get him to come inside to, well, you know. I vamped him up a little and pushed my bod into him because I saw something in his pants.'

'You thought he had an erection?'

'Right! In my line it's a handy indicator of business interest. He had a lump all right but it didn't feel like a dick to me. And I ought to know.'

'So what did it feel like?'

'A gun. Now that would make sense if he was going to kill Billy, wouldn't it?'

'Bloody hell!' said Arnold, who had been listening to this conversation with interest. 'What are we going to do about poor old Billy?'

'Do you know where he is?'

'Sure, he's going to the Gala at Bedside Manor with Brick Tempo. He's driving down this morning. And so are we.'

Sophie got Betsy to let her into Billy Dazzle's office with her spare key. She said she wanted to check it out but in reality she wanted to phone Ambrosia in private. The senior officer sounded pleased with her.

'Excellent, Sophie. So, our Danny is still in town, according to this witness. How reliable is she?'

'Very, I'd say. She identified him straight off from the photo.'

'And your theory is that Fretwork is after Dazzle because he bonked Patsy.'

'Yes. I think we've got to protect Billy Dazzle while using him as bait for Danny Fretwork.'

'Sounds familiar, Sophie. I remember your last scheme for luring Danny into our clutches. Danny doesn't know where Billy is, does he?'

'Not as far as I'm aware.'

'Good. I suggest in that case that you leave the rest of us to track him down. I'll put men inside Dazzle's office and step up the operation in Essex. He's putting himself about too much. He'll soon come unstuck.'

'But what about Billy? Danny will blow his brains out if he finds him.'

'He won't find him. Dazzle is much better off out of harm's way in the country. And don't worry, I will personally keep a discreet eye on things at Bedside.

It so happens that I have an invitation to the concert myself.'

'Ambrosia, Billy needs proper protection!'

'Forget it, Sergeant. You've done your stuff and just about saved your pretty neck. Don't spoil it, now. Take a few days off.'

'Ambrosia, please!'

'Don't be too disappointed, Sophie. You've done enough. Not even you can catch them all.'

Sophie sat morosely at Billy's desk. The thrill of latching onto Danny's trail had been swiftly cut off and she could hardly credit that Ambrosia had dumped her from the case. She must be feeling the heat herself.

As Sophie sat there she looked idly through the desk drawers. She had no doubt Fretwork would have gained entry and made a similar search. If there was evidence here that would have told Danny where Billy was then she'd get back to Ambrosia and insist she mount a big operation at Bedside.

She found nothing to link Billy to the Gala. But she did find something that brought her up short. An obscene photograph of a rounded female arse thrusting backwards to reveal a pouting pussy crack. It took her a moment to realise just whose arse and pussy this was. My God! The bastard kept a dirty photo of her in his desk drawer. It must have come from the poolside photos Sophie had told her about. Why had he kept this one? To jerk off over, she supposed.

The thought gave her a funny feeling. The notion of an unknown man regularly stroking his cock to solitary orgasm while fantasising over her disembodied bum was – well, she had to admit it – highly arousing. A bolt of desire shot through her like an electric current. God, she felt horny! Wildly, excruciatingly, heart-stoppingly horny!

Suddenly she knew what she would do. She would cadge a ride to Bedside Manor from Arnold and Betsy and she would keep an eye on Billy Dazzle herself. Patsy had spoken warmly of him. He sounded like a decent fellow even if a bit of a ducker and diver. And the notion of the boy wanking off to a picture of her thrusting arse – well, she had a duty to prevent him being blown away by a brute like Danny Fretwork!

She slipped the photo back into the drawer and got to her feet, trying to quell the lurid desires that stemmed from the crawling, itching feeling in the pit of her stomach. This was no time to think about sex – a man's life was in danger.

'Right, Sophie Stark,' she said to herself, 'on to Bedside Manor!'

Five

ORGY!

54

Bedside Manor, the former home of the Bedside family, enjoyed a naturally seductive location. Nestling at the foot of the Sussex Downs, it sat amidst fifty acres of neat green fields and rolling parkland. The Manor itself had been transformed by the stage-struck Belvedere Bedside in the years preceding the Great War. He had sunk the family fortune into a full-scale theatre which he had built a hundred yards from the house on the site of the old stables. His intention had been to run his own theatre company, attracting an audience from London and the nearby South Coast resorts. Unfortunately for him, war had intervened and he had thrown himself into a Greater Cause which had snuffed out his ambitions, along with millions of others, in a muddy bog somewhere in northern France.

But the legacy of Belvedere lived on in the exquisite little theatre he had built in the grounds of his family home on the banks of the whispering River Bed. This was now the home of the Bedside Opera Company, funded to a diminishing extent by the public purse and, increasingly, by a clutch of boring but profitable businesses who could afford to apply a little artistic gloss to their image. As a consequence of all this, throughout the summer months discerning patrons flocked in their thousands to picnic in the grounds and drink their fill of Culture.

On the night of the Poor Pussy Gala the regular company took a deserved mid-season break and yielded the stage to Imogen's carefully assembled roster of artistes. It was to be a glittering occasion, performed in front of an audience of the great and the good – including minor royalty. Dashing Prince Roger, twenty-somethingth in line to the throne, was squiring his latest exotic girl-friend, Inez de la Puta. The Spanish beauty was rumoured to have won his heart, or at least some other significant portion of his anatomy, by dancing the fla-menco in the nude at the Nuts Risborough Hunt Ball.

From across Europe the titled and the wealthy were making their way to Bedside. Candy Kensington's call had been loud and strident and many had answered. Some were driven by a genuine desire to support Poor Pussy, these were almost exclusively British patrons cap-tivated by Candy's image of a bandaged moggy adrift in a world without catflaps. The Continentals, who regarded most animals in simple culinary terms, were more interested in attending a social event. Some wished to visit Bedside without the tedium of actually sitting through an opera. Others were sufficiently attracted by the allure of Brick Tempo and Melissa Melone to aban-don their yachts and country retreats on an otherwise uneventful evening in the summer season.

Backstage there was panic. Voices were raised and shouts of anguish were commonplace as noisy people in designer clothes and silent ones in grimy sweatshirts mingled together. To Billy it had looked like chaos until

Brick explained that the smart ones were performers letting off steam and the scruffy ones were technicians who actually knew what they were doing. Having been chivvied out of several hidey-holes, Billy took refuge in a stairwell.

Katie Crisp joined him, dressed for once in jeans, and they sat companionably buttock to buttock on the steps. This was a changed Katie. It occurred to Billy that what she needed all along was an old-fashioned fucking. Nevertheless he was not so sure of his ground as to air this thought.

A particularly loud outburst broke out from the dressing rooms. Several voices were raised in outrage over a background of sobs and dark mutterings of a rebellious nature.

'What's that all about?' said Billy.

Katie grinned maliciously. 'That's the Marian Mucus *corps de ballet* discovering that their wardrobe is incomplete. The skip containing their costumes has got lost.'

'What will they do?'

'They've got to go on. Candy insists. They're going to dance in their body stockings.'

'Poor things.'

'Don't waste your sympathy. They're all so damned skinny they could dance naked and no one would notice. Unlike our friend Tracy. I'd steal her costume myself if I didn't think she'd just love to perform in the nude. What you men see in those wobbling jellies of hers I can't imagine.'

Billy hastened to change the subject. 'What happens now, Katie? I mean, this is complete pandemonium. I can't believe that a performance will possibly take place tonight.'

'Oh, it will. They may look like idiots but these people know what they're doing. So don't you worry your pretty little head. Your job is to keep an eye on Mr Tempo and make sure he keeps his pecker in his pants. And while you're at it' – she leaned across him and clapped a hand over his crotch – 'I suggest you keep yours buttoned up too.'

She kissed him with force, pushing her tongue deep into his mouth and massaging his loins meaningfully. Billy allowed his mouth to be raped and his cock leapt to attention as she slipped her hand into his trousers.

'Unfortunately,' she said, 'I've got to go. I must find out if Melissa Melone has arrived. Now you behave yourself.' And with a parting squeeze to his now rampant organ she exited up the stairs.

Leaving Billy with his fully erect penis thrusting up from his trousers in full view of two thin girls in leotards standing open-mouthed in the doorway straight ahead of him. He hastily stuffed his treacherous member back into his pants as he rushed past them. Maybe he had been better off when Katie was not being quite so friendly . . .

55

Sophie was in turmoil on the back seat of Arnold's car as the three of them drove through the ugly suburbs of south London. She couldn't understand the feelings of pent-up desire that were singing through her veins. She knew she was highly sexed, it had been an early item of self-knowledge and her adolescence had been one long battle with her sensual impulses. Since then, however, she had always managed to keep things in check. Correction – she had usually managed to keep things in check. The Crispin Kingsley incident had not been the only one to spoil her record. Nevertheless, she had always had some degree of choice when it came to sex. The fact that she said yes more often than no was irrelevant. But now, alone on the back seat of Arnold's much-prized secondhand Maserati, her heart was thumping and her pussy was drooling and she feared she'd be unable to say no to Hannibal Lecter.

Arnold was disturbed. The traffic was bloody and he really should have been at Bedside first thing that morning. He knew his team must have been at work since dawn preparing the evening buffet and he felt guilty.

Then there was the business about Billy. It was a bit hard to credit that some heavy was out for his blood but nevertheless it was not a pleasant prospect. What's more he had now been sworn to secrecy. Neither he nor Betsy was supposed to tell Billy his life was in danger. Sergeant Sophie had assured them both that since Danny Fretwork didn't know about the Gala then all would be well and Billy was better off in blissful ignorance. In which case why had she been so keen to drive to Bedside at once? It was all very complicated.

Arnold's most immediate concern, however, was the physical condition of the policewoman squirming on the back seat behind him. He observed her closely in the mirror, noting the flushed cheeks and heavy breathing and constant shifting of the hips. An awful thought was dawning. He hadn't, had he, given her the wrong biscuits? He kept some at Betsy's to inspire their midnight sex sessions. Had he then, in the confusion of learning about Billy, given this policewoman a Love Crunch Special? He must be going potty.

Which was exactly what Betsy was thinking. She too had noticed Sophie's condition, the way those lovely legs kept opening and closing and her hands fidgeted in her lap. At any moment the poor girl was going to start fingering herself. Betsy shot a venomous glance at her lover, she had no doubt who was responsible for this state of affairs.

'Are you all right back there, Sophie?' she asked. 'Want to change places with me?'

'Oh. I don't know. I mean, I am feeling a little odd . . .' Sophie floundered, unable to articulate, her eyes fixed on Arnold's long strong fingers wrapped around the gear stick, gripping it just below the bulbous end, so reminiscent of – 'Cock,' she blurted inadvertently. 'Oh, I'm sorry, I didn't mean. I—'

'Stop the car, Arnold,' ordered Betsy. 'Sophie and I are changing places so she'll be more comfortable.' Her tone was not friendly and Arnold did as he was told.

They resumed their journey with Sophie reclining on the front passenger seat which Betsy had lowered so that she lay virtually flat. Her skirt rose up over her trembling thighs and Arnold gazed with interest at the seductive expanse of flesh so close to his left hand. Betsy jabbed him in the back of the neck and hissed, 'Keep your eyes on the road.'

Sophie lay there, her senses on fire, her body thrilling to the smooth motion of the car and the throb of the engine. She looked up at Betsy, at the upside-down face now bent close to hers, at the full-lipped mouth which now whispered, 'I'm going to give you a massage, Sophie. You'll soon feel much better. I promise.'

Sophie might have protested but the touch of Betsy's fingers on her temples froze the words in her throat. They made circles on the skin on either side of her head, pressing gently and skilfully, banishing the tension in her forehead. Now, from her position seated behind her, Betsy moved her hands to Sophie's neck, relaxing her then titillating her nerve ends as she slid her fingers over her skin, pushing down to the base of her throat and sliding her hands beneath the thin cotton of her blouse onto the upper slopes of her breasts.

'Oh!' cried Sophie as Betsy's fingers reached her nipples. 'Oh yes!'

'Relax, Sophie,' said Betsy, leaning forward so her hair hung in a yellow sheaf over Sophie's face while her hands grasped the fullness of Sophie's big tits.

'Oh!' screamed Sophie again as the magic of Betsy's touch washed over her. 'Ohh!'

Betsy lowered her head and fastened her lips over the open mouth beneath. Sophie reached up through the golden curtain and gripped Betsy around the neck, locking them into a long and passionate upside-down kiss.

By now the car was off the main road, Arnold considering it prudent to take to the lonely lanes. He looked down with longing at the heaving loins of his passenger, the skirt riding high on widespread thighs to reveal a thin strip of white panty at her crotch.

He slowed the car so he could give more attention to the action beside him. The kiss still endured and Betsy had stripped open Sophie's blouse to reveal a sumptuous pair of creamy titties lolling half out of a lacy white brassiere. As Arnold sneaked glances to the side he saw Betsy's hand reach further, over the bunched skirt and under the band of Sophie's tiny panties. The long thighs snapped shut on the questing fingers and then sprang open again as Sophie thrust her pelvis up off the seat to try and capture as much flesh as she could in her hungry snatch.

Arnold pulled the car off the road into a wooded layby.

Betsy pushed the flimsy panties to one side revealing two fingers already sunk to the knuckle inside Sophie's long-lipped quim. Arnold shifted uneasily in his seat and unfastened his seat belt.

'What are you doing, Arnold?' said Betsy.

'I thought I might be able to help.'

'I bet you did. Well, you're not needed.' Betsy's fingers were still working in Sophie's spread pussy, jabbing into her in a steady rhythm that was being answered by Sophie's upward thrusts.

'I think she wants a man, Betsy.'

'Don't be stupid. Stick that big thing of yours in her and you'll be up on a charge of assault with a deadly weapon. Now drive on.'

A bemused Sophie, her senses tingling as she teetered on the edge of orgasm, half-heard this exchange. Only one thing was clear to her, a cock was on offer and, if that was so, then she wanted it.

'Yes,' she said feebly, 'give me that big thing. Stick it up me, please!'

But Arnold didn't hear as he gunned the motor and Betsy had other ideas. With her free hand she had managed to rearrange her own clothing and now, as the car resumed its journey, she insinuated her long body along Sophie's to bring her mouth to the spot where her hand was working so energetically.

For Sophie the yellow screen of hair over her face had vanished to be replaced by slim thighs and a pink-lipped pussy mouth ripe for kissing. And as the first ripples of orgasm broke over her aching body she began to kiss Betsy as fiercely as she had ever kissed anyone in her life.

56

Coincidentally, on a separate stretch of road bound for Bedside Manor, another act of sexual licence was taking place.

Sebastian Silk, king of the musical theatre, had been as nervous as a kitten throughout the press conference at Heathrow. It wasn't the massed ranks of the fourth estate that unnerved him – he was used to them – it was the woman at the centre of it who was to accompany him in his chauffeured limousine to the Gala. To Sebastian, Melissa Melone was more than simply the world's greatest soprano, she was a goddess. Her agreement to sing his new song cycle at the Gala eclipsed all his previous successes. The West End smashes, the Broadway hits, the clutch of chart-topping albums – all faded in comparison with Melissa Melone's approval. For Seb Silk, formerly Cedric Damp of Ball's Pond Road, Melissa Melone represented an entree into the world of proper Art.

Melissa had stepped off the plane from Rome in the midday heat of August dressed in an ankle-length sable coat. The journalists flung themselves at the bait; in the no-news silly season Melissa was guaranteed good copy.

'How come, Miss Melone,' asked the *Blizzard*, 'you

are here to support the cause of feline welfare and you are wearing a fur?'

'Because my coat is not real, it is for fun – a fantasy. I think the real pussy should keep its coat but we women must be allowed our fantasies too.'

'But it's nearly eighty degrees, aren't you hot?' From the *Rabbit*.

'You don't know what I am wearing beneath this. Maybe it is nothing.'

'Go on, Melissa, let's have a look. Strip off!' This from the *Dog*, which didn't merit a reply, just a finger-wag of disapproval and a saucy smile.

Melissa Melone was a creature of legend. Her origins were obscure – the dozen biographies disagreed on fundamental points – but from her first performance in the great opera houses there was no disagreement. Here was a Voice that could act and seduce the hardest of critics. Her looks helped, of course. She was big and blonde, a Valkyrie in scale, yet thoroughly Italian in her warmth and passion. She was a fixture in the artistic firmament and had been for more than twenty years. Only her five ex-husbands, their dependants and lawyers, a few hundred jealous women and the majority of her fellow performers had any cause to hate her.

And now she sat beside Sebastian in the back seat of the limo.

'At last,' she said expansively, 'we are alone.' Which was true if you discounted the chauffeur. Her secretary and hairdresser were making their way separately.

Sebastian was overwhelmed. He had the impulse to fall on his knees before her.

'This is a great honour,' he began.

'Bull,' she said quickly. 'We are artistes, we don't

have to talk bullshit to each other.'

Sebastian's heart sang – if only his critics could hear that Melissa Melone regarded him as an equal. He'd make some of those snobs eat their reviews . . .

Melissa fixed him with her mysterious sea-green eyes. 'You are a very naughty boy, Sebastian.'

'Melissa?'

'Don't you act innocent with me. Though this is the first time we meet I know lots about you. Not just the rubbish in the newspapers. I have been singing this new music of yours for two weeks now and I know you are a naughty boy.' She chuckled, a low throaty gurgle that turned Seb's stomach upside down. 'Do you want to find out what is beneath my coat, like those lecherous reporters?'

Sebastian was confused. He had spoken to her on the phone frequently during the past few weeks, being unable to get away to Rome and assist in the rehearsals. She had been charming and businesslike, now she was implying an intimacy that surely wasn't possible and yet . . . His eyes were transfixed as she began to unbutton her coat, still holding it closed over the mountains of her chest.

The car was moving fast in the outside lane of the motorway, the world flashing by in a blur through the tinted windows. Cocooned in the air-conditioned interior, drinking in the musk of Melissa's perfume, Sebastian felt suddenly liberated. The daily politics of his four current productions, the sniping of his ex-wife and the nagging of his present one, all vanished from his mind. In this brief time-capsule with the exotic goddess of his dreams at his side he felt blissfully free.

The coat was now gaping, offering tantalising glimpses

of creamy flesh. A firm thigh in a sheer stocking breached the fur on her lap. Seb was tumultuously erect.

'That doesn't look like a fake fur,' he said.

'Of course it's not. I have a wardrobe full of furs. Real ones. I love the touch of fur on my body. I have a real tiger-skin rug, too. I keep it to make love on.'

'You'd better not tell Candy Kensington.'

'Don't try to change the subject, Sebastian. I want to talk about you.'

The coat was now unbuttoned, it fell open sufficiently to set Seb's imagination running riot. The most famous bosom in opera, celebrated throughout the world on album covers and posters, spilled out of a peach satin half-cup bra. The shadow between these magical globes promised a ravine of cleavage into which Sebastian longed to plunge. He stared agog at the great right breast, so close to him, which threatened to burst free from its support, its milky upper reaches billowing over the edge of the undergarment.

'You see,' she said, 'you are staring at my teats like you have never seen a woman before in your life. I know you are a wicked man in your mind.'

'Melissa,' panted Seb, 'any man would feel wicked looking at you right now.'

'OK, but let's talk about this music you have written for me. I know what it means. It is saying come and make fuck with me, yes?'

Seb gulped. 'Actually, it's a tonal poem.'

'Maybe, but the poetry says come fuck with me. Like a lady cat in her season calling the male cats. Tonal poem – pah! That's what the music professors say. You are not that, you are from the guts – yes? That's why you are such a big success.'

Sebastian flushed with pleasure. Though he was used to compliments, to receive them from this quarter was thrilling.

Melissa began to sing a phrase from his composition in a hypnotic purring tone that filled the small space and sent a message of pure joy down his spine.

'I am right, yes? This is a song of a cat on heat.'

It was true, it had seemed appropriate given the Poor Pussy cause but it was inspired by the overwhelming feeling of lust she stirred in him and – he'd bet on it – every red-blooded male who had ever heard her sing.

'That is why there are no words, yes? Just sounds.'

'Do you like it?' he asked nervously.

She threw back her head and laughed. Seb's thirsty gaze drank its fill of her shaking bosom. 'It's not a matter of like,' she said. 'It is perfect for me. Shall I show you?'

Seb nodded.

She began to sing very softly. The notes rose and fell, controlled and soft then suddenly harsh and loud. There were indeed no words, just sounds, pure and liquid, wailing and guttural. Her eyes were closed, her feet were planted firmly on the floor and the sound flowed up from her belly, twisting and spiralling around Sebastian as he sat, enthralled.

As she sang her bosom seemed to flex in her bra as if it were seeking to burst out and her hands rose to her breasts and began to make little circles round the satin cups.

Then the music swelled and she poured out a torrent of naked emotion, as if she were stripping herself bare. *She's right*, he thought, *it's just an outright plea to be fucked!* And he was aware his cock was pulsing in his pants, threatening to poke a hole clean through the material.

Now it was as if she were in pain, some terrible bowel-wrenching pain that she could not contain and the sound she made drowned out the throb of the engine, the rush of the wind and the sound of the wheels on the road. He watched completely mesmerised as, almost of their own accord though her fingers must have released them, her fabulous breasts burst from their prison. Breathtaking hills of flesh, still stupendous in her middle years, they shifted outwards and downwards, their turgid chocolate-brown nipples erect and inviting.

And as Seb stared at these bounteous glories unveiled for him alone and her voice hit the long concluding top note that only the truly blessed could ever hope to reach, he had the most blissful orgasm of his life.

'Sebastian, are you all right?' asked Melissa long moments later.

He stirred slowly from his prone position on the seat and opened his eyes to see that she was holding her arms out to him. He allowed himself to be pulled into the exotic warmth of her embrace and pillowed his cheek on the magical flesh of her bosom.

'You see?' she said triumphantly. 'I shall have a great triumph. I shall make them all come in their pants!' And she stroked the composer's curly hair and delicately fed a big brown nipple into his mouth.

In the front seat the bewildered chauffeur drove on, plucking at the material in his crotch as it lay in a sticky mess over his slowly deflating penis.

57

'I don't care what you say, Billy, I don't want anything to do with him.' Tracy Pert looked thoroughly indignant. As indignant as anybody could look wearing tight leather shorts and a long furry snake between her legs.

'I understand how you feel, Tracy. By any normal standards the guy behaved like a pig. But he's not normal, he's a superstar.' Billy edged to the side of her in the cramped confines of the tiny dressing room and peered at her rear. 'What is that thing sticking out of your bum?'

'It's my tail.' Tracy presented her derrière to him and shook it saucily. The woolly growth projecting from between her buttocks flipped from side to side. 'It's part of my costume – do you like it?'

'To be honest, Tracy, I don't see why you want to dress up as a monkey.'

'I'm not a monkey, you berk, I'm a cat. Poor Pussy Rescue – get it?'

'And what goes with it – whiskers and a flea collar?'

'Oh, fuck off, Billy Dazzle. And tell Brick Tempo to fuck off, too.'

'Calm down, Tracy, it was only a joke. You look fantastic in those sexy shorts. You'll knock 'em dead.'

Tracy's murderous expression turned instantly to one of anguish. 'Billy, I'm so nervous. I'm going to muck it up, I know it. My song's going to seem so silly amongst all this ballet and stuff. They're making fun of me already.'

Her ravishing blue eyes suddenly swum with tears and she fell into Billy's outstretched arms.

'Who's making fun?' he asked, not slow to cup her perky bum cheeks in the palms of his hands.

'Those little bitches next door. Marion Mucus and her dancing snotbags. They were giggling about my boobs. One of them asked me if they were real.'

'Envy,' said Billy, 'there's not a tit worth touching up amongst the lot of them. And they'll take you seriously when you sing with Brick Tempo.'

'What?'

'It's difficult to explain, Tracy. Believe me, he wants to sing with you. He's changed since you first met him.'

'But that was only yesterday morning!'

'Nevertheless. Anyway, he asked me how he could make it up to you and we hit on the idea of a duet. He's writing it now.'

'Are you having me on?'

'Come and talk to him. He's down by the river. He says it inspires him.'

'Billy Dazzle, if you're joking I'll rearrange your private parts.'

'When you're around, Tracy, they do that of their own accord.'

'There's Billy Dazzle,' said Betsy, 'the guy with the blonde heading across the field.'

'That figures,' said Sophie, 'from what I've heard about him.'

They were looking out from a room on the second floor of the Manor itself. Arnold and Betsy were to use it as a bedroom.

'Do you want to meet him? Shall I call him over?'

'No. I just need to be able to identify him. Besides, it looks like he's busy.'

Sebastian Silk was an averagely endowed fellow. Better than average, according to his wives and girlfriends, if they were of a mind to be honest. However, as his limo approached Bedside Manor, Sebastian was kneeling on the floor between Melissa Melone's vast white columnar thighs feeling utterly inadequate.

'You see, *cara*? I warned you,' said the diva. 'It is not possible for you to satisfy me with a staff such as you possess. I am built on a grand scale, only a truly outsize penis can fill me as I need to be filled.'

It was true. Between her long strong legs was a cavern in which Seb rooted ineffectually. He felt as if he were stoking a fire with a toothpick.

'Don't worry, my darling, it is not your fault. I arouse lust in others but cannot satisfy it in myself – that is my curse and my gift. It is the reason I am such a big success.'

'No, Melissa, you sing like an angel—'

'Ssh, Sebastian, we are nearly there. You must come to your climax at once.' And she closed her mouth over his, her big mysterious eyes staring deep into his as her hands clasped his buttocks and pulled him into her. Sebastian was lost. He felt as if some great sea current had swept him away and he was powerless. A finger suddenly penetrated his anus, pushing deep inside him in a hideously skilful caress that had him bucking and moaning and shooting his spunk into the depths of her as the car purred slowly up the drive of Bedside Manor.

Tracy was enjoying herself, for once someone was taking her seriously as a performer. Brick was fingering his guitar, explaining his new song and demonstrating where she should join in. He was a clever player, the melody flowed effortlessly and he soon coaxed Tracy into passable harmony. It was a seductive tune, Tracy threw herself into it and he smiled encouragement, his craggy face crinkling with warmth. Billy was right, he was a changed man from the day before.

Only one thing puzzled her – the words to this new song. 'How I long to roam your valleys/And paddle in your creeks/To dabble in your bushes/And lay my head between your peaks.' But why should she worry?

'You're not such a bloody awful bastard after all, Brick,' she said cheerfully.

'Why, thanks, ma'am,' he replied, 'does that mean you'll come up and sing with me tonight?'

'OK, why not? What should I wear?'

'Anything that shows off that gorgeous body of yours.'

'Don't worry, I know what my main selling points are.'

Sophie was feeling quite pleased with herself. Arnold had fixed her up with a ticket for the performance and Betsy had supplied an evening gown. To be more accurate Betsy had bullied, cajoled and flirted her way into the Opera Company wardrobe. There they had selected a low-cut cocktail dress in jade green which clung to Sophie like a second skin and was set off by a necklace of artificial pearls.

'Wow! You look fabulous,' said Betsy enthusiastically.

'Isn't it a bit tight? I feel like I'm going to burst out of it.'

'Women have always had to suffer in the cause of glamour. You know that, Sophie.'

'Well, I don't see how anyone could sing in this.'

'Just thank your stars you're not Melissa thing. She'd never stuff her Melones into a smart little number like that.'

Then, having arranged to change in Betsy's room before the performance, Sophie inspected the premises. No one bothered to ask her what she was doing, they were all too busy. She ambled the grounds and spotted Billy, Brick and Tracy sitting on the river bank. She poked her head into the marquee on the lawn where Arnold's army of caterers were setting up the buffet tables. She even ventured into the auditorium but retreated swiftly, not wishing to be involved in a screaming match between a statuesque Italian woman and a harassed electrician.

The sun shone, the setting was idyllic and the excitement of the evening's performance was infectious. Sophie was rapidly coming to the conclusion that Ambrosia was right. Danny Fretwork would not show. This was a world far removed from villains of his ilk. Even if he had discovered Billy's whereabouts he'd never follow him here. Not even Danny Fretwork was crazy enough for that.

At that moment, on a train leaving Victoria Station, a burly man took his seat amongst an elite throng. Like many of his fellow travellers he wore a dinner jacket and black bow-tie – though from the way he tugged at his collar this was obviously not his accustomed garb. He was on his own but it soon transpired he was a sociable fellow, something of an expert on Spanish property values and Scuba diving if a little shaky on the staging of *Aida* at Verona. Contrary to Sophie's expectations, Danny Fretwork fitted in rather well.

58

The evening's entertainment began slowly. Murdo Cameron, the Scots baritone, was not known as the most exciting of performers. Candy and Imogen had been at a loss where to hide him on the bill but had concluded he would do least damage if he came on first before anyone had had time to get bored. Fortunately, his Wagner solo and arrangements of Celtic folk songs were over while the audience were still eyeballing each other.

Next up was the Drax Trio – three sisters who played avant-garde violin music in sequinned halters and black mini-skirts. They had a strong appeal to the young, the trendy and the simply lecherous. The arts critic of *The Rag*, Pandora Britches, was seen to applaud enthusiastically.

There followed another longueur in the programme – Cecily and Archibald Cherry, the husband-and-wife team who specialised in duets from operettas. With many an arch twinkle and coy glance, the leathery pair hammed their way through the greatest hits of Lehar and Offenbach. In her seat at the back of the circle Sophie stifled a yawn.

The Cherrys finally relented and gave way to the first of the evening's widely touted events – The Marian

Mucus Ballet. They were dancing a new piece specially devised for the occasion. It told the symbolic story of a lost cat: a pampered fireside moggy who had strayed from home to be confronted by the horrors of the Real World such as Cars, Pollution and Big Business. Finally the abused hero met up with a band of gypsy cats who rescued him from capture by a man with a bowler hat and they all frolicked happily together in the finale.

That was how the programme explained matters but, to Sophie's eyes, the stage was simply filled with leaping and prancing females who were almost entirely nude. After the first shock she realised that they were just wearing flesh-toned body stockings. Sylph-like creatures that they were, they nevertheless displayed sturdy thighs and temptingly rounded buttocks to full advantage. At their appearance the hitherto comatose gentleman on Sophie's left jerked into life. 'Amazing what you can get away with in the name of art,' he muttered loudly to his wife. All the same he applauded loudly as, after an energetic ten minutes, the panting dancers flitted from the scene.

By now many of the audience were thinking ahead to the sumptuous buffet which awaited them in the brilliance of the summer evening. However, there remained one more act to endure before the first half drew to a close. Rebellious patrons shuffled in their seats. How much was one expected to suffer in aid of a good cause?

Halfway back in the stalls Pandora Britches tightened her grip on Patsy's hand. In her function as critic she would be entirely objective, within feminist parameters of course, as to the merits of the performance that was about to take place. Personally, however, she hoped that her former lover, Tracy Pert, would play her allotted role in life and make a right tit of herself.

Loud rock suddenly blasted through the air, cruelly jerking some from their slumbers as the curtain rose to reveal a gyrating Tracy, microphone in hand, swivelling her notorious curves on top of a hastily erected dais. She wore tiny tight black leather shorts and thigh-high leather boots that glistened in the spotlights. Her amazing bosom was cupped in shiny black latex with crossover straps which moulded the twin globes upwards into two firm bowls of flesh.

Tracy wailed unintelligibly against a down-and-dirty barrage of electronic noise, giving it her all. She dipped and swooped, posed and preened, brazenly displaying every pouting inch of her spectacular form. She turned upstage and presented her pumping buttocks to the audience of the great and good who sat frozen in their evening finery, mesmerised by her lewd display.

The bum cheeks wiggled and wobbled, the pussycat tail flicked saucily from side to side. Then she swung back to the front, bending low so that her big breasts threatened to topple free from their constraints. Then she straightened up, rocking back on her heels and bumping her pubis forward in unmistakable copulatory invitation. Grabbing her tail with her free hand she pulled it upwards between her legs, closing her eyes and moaning in fake ecstasy as she sawed it suggestively across her pubic delta. With a final squeal, her hand yanking on the woolly limb springing from her bulging crotch, the lights went out and the curtain descended in deafening silence.

'Fantastic!' cried Billy, waiting in the wings to throw his arms round Tracy in a hug of congratulation. 'That woke the stuffy bastards up!'

'Good God, that was obscene,' said the woman on the right of Sophie. The man on the left was pounding his palms together, adding to the growing tumult of applause in defiance of the icy glare of his wife.

Patsy pulled a stunned Pandora to her feet, 'Let's get a drink quick. You look like a woman in need.'

59

Amidst the bustle of the long supper interval Arnold Brie was in his element. He was the master chef, the wizard of the kitchen who could wave a magic wand and make people happy. People adored his food and they were wild about his Bedside Summer Punch, specially concocted for the occasion. Candy had requested a cocktail to make the evening go with a swing and Arnold had complied. He knew what was required. What's more, the fizzing, ice-cold creation tasted damned good. He allowed himself another glass.

The first person to feel the full effect of Arnold's punch was Lavender Roe. Overtaken with a coughing fit during the ballet, she had made an early exit. Consequently she was two glasses up on her mother by the time they were reunited in the interval crush on the lawn outside the marquee.

'Lavender,' barked Lady Roe, 'what have you done with your wrap, you look positively indecent.'

There was some truth in this, the cerise swatch of silk was intended to be worn over a flimsy top suspended by two thin straps and cut low beneath the arms to allow for maximum air circulation on a hot night. The garment could hardly be worn with a brassiere and was only suitable for women who had no breasts or those with a firm and youthful pair that could stand up for themselves. The fair Lavender fell into the latter category.

'Don't fuss, mother, it's far too hot to wear anything unnecessary. *You* don't think I look too naughty, do you?' She addressed this to the tall waiter who was busily recharging her glass.

'I think you look gorgeous,' said he, openly ogling her half-exposed bosom.

'Well, I think you look gorgeous too. Will you come and help me look for my wrap? I think I dropped it over there in the bushes.' And she sailed off with the waiter in tow, leaving her mother, for once, completely speechless.

The new Minister for the Arts was another who felt the early benefit of the Bedside Punch. It was well-known that Godolphin Sumner hated anything of a cultural nature and he particularly resented boring evenings at the theatre and the opera. It was all right for Henrietta, she could sink three gins in the interval and go straight to bed. He, on the other hand, still had to face those bloody ministerial boxes no matter what time the fat lady put a sock in it.

Tonight, however, he felt different. Perhaps it was the effect of the beautiful evening amid perfect surroundings though, to be fair, he wasn't usually affected by mawkish considerations of this sort. If he were honest he'd put it all down to all those little ballet girls prancing around almost in the buff. They were artistes, of course, and he knew he wasn't supposed to think naughties about them. But that Tracy female, all leather and rubber and bulging boobs – there was no doubt what a chap might think about her and, by George, he was thinking it! It was a pity her contribution hadn't lasted longer.

'Minister – I'm delighted to see you here!'

Sumner grinned and extended his hand to the stunning woman who had appeared in front of him. She wore a black-and-white striped stretch cotton dress with an embroidered bodice that thrust out an inviting expanse of golden breast-flesh. The Minister had a feeling he ought to remember this filly – she was a hell of a looker.

'You remember Candy Kensington, don't you, God?' said Henrietta Sumner on cue as usual. 'She's the clever lady who has made this wonderful evening possible.'

'Marvellous!' he boomed. 'Let me bestow a kiss upon you, Candy, courtesy of HMG.' And he did so, making a big fuss of placing the ministerial lips on both of Candy's cheeks, sneaking a long look down her cleavage as he did so.

'I say, God, steady on,' said Henriette, adding to Candy, 'I haven't seen him so enthusiastic for years.'

Candy turned her smile on Sumner at full beam and placed a slender hand on his arm. 'Who have you enjoyed most so far?'

'Why, Tracy, of course,' shouted Sumner and gulped a glass of punch in one go. 'That girl's got talent! She's a great ambassador for British culture.'

Curious glances were cast amongst the knot of people which had formed around the Minister. Usually voluble critics were struck dumb. Then came a cry of 'Hear! Hear!' from the fringe of the group and Prince Roger pushed himself forward.

'Couldn't agree more, God. A most stimulating performance.'

Thus Tracy Pert from Stratford East received the seal of approval from God and the Crown – a unique accolade that spread amongst the assembly like bush fire.

Danny Fretwork looked through the throng with a keen eye, his glance passing swiftly over the elegantly attired women. For once, an abundance of alluring feminine curves did not hold his interest. His mind was focused on a man – Billy Dazzle. Though he had never wittingly clapped eyes on the detective he had studied photographs. So far his quarry had eluded him.

Danny grabbed two glasses from a passing waiter. He didn't intend to drink them – he needed to keep a clear head – but it gave him a pretext to roam the lawn peering at the crowds as if in search of a missing companion. In fact, he rather wished he had brought one – young Amanda, say, she would have been good cover. Not that he wouldn't have felt bad about involving Amanda in a hit. However, he had only been able to turn up one ticket. He grinned to himself. Amanda was a stunner, he'd have enjoyed rigging her out in posh togs and setting her loose at this fancy do. She'd have turned a few heads.

'Basil, hello!' cried a voice by his side and a small brown-haired woman in a cream suit stood on tiptoe and kissed him on the cheek. As she did so she whispered in his ear, 'For God's sake, pretend that you know me!'

Danny's first impulse was to tell her to piss off but he was suddenly riveted by two bird-bright eyes, a full kissable mouth and, looking down from his height into the shadows of her jacket, a fully exposed and perfectly formed left breast.

'Hello yourself,' he replied and relinquished a glass

to her. She drank deeply. Danny took in the petite curves and slim brown legs set off enticingly by the lightweight summer suit. The breast was now no longer in view but the notion of its availability sent a surprising shiver down his spine.

'I'm sorry to thrust myself upon you,' she explained, 'but I can't stand the old goat who brought me here. He's been fingering my arse ever since the lights went up. I told him I'd spotted an old flame and fled.'

'Do you want me to sort him out for you?'

'Don't be silly, he's a superintendent in the Metropolitan Police. He's my boss.'

Danny's shock was evident. The woman placed a slender hand upon his arm and squeezed, 'Don't worry, tonight's my night off. My name's Ambrosia – what's yours?'

Backstage in her cramped dressing-room Tracy carefully tucked the tails of her white silk shirt into the waistband of her short black skirt. She had decided that classic simplicity would be suitable for her appearance with Brick. The thought of it made her head spin.

There was a knock at the door. She swore under her breath. It was probably Billy but, much as she liked him, she couldn't afford to be distracted by him now. She knew just what he'd be after but he'd have to wait. Tonight Brick came first.

It wasn't Billy, it was one of the ballet girls from next door. 'Won't you pop in and have a drink with us?' she said. 'They've sent some goodies round from the buffet in front.'

'Oh,' said Tracy, caught completely off-guard, 'I don't think so, I've got to get ready.'

'Rubbish, darling,' cried the dancer, grabbing Tracy by the hand and tugging her out of the door, 'we insist.'

'But I thought you didn't like me,' spluttered Tracy, unable to resist the other's surprisingly strong grip.

'Don't be daft. We think you're fantastic. And we just love your fabulous figure. Don't we, girls?'

'Yes!' they cried, surrounding Tracy as she allowed herself to be pulled inside their dresing-room.

'Don't you realise,' said a thin elf as she pushed a glass of fizzing punch into Tracy's hand, 'we'd all die for tits like yours.'

'But you do fancy me, don't you?' said Ambrosia, edging Danny up the staircase that lead to the darkness of the balcony overlooking the gardens of Bedside. 'If you don't, why do you keep looking down my front?'

'Look, Ambrosia, of course I fancy you but it's just not on! We'll be seen.'

'No, we won't. Besides, so what? I'm a senior police-woman. You're safe with me. Live dangerously for once, Basil. Forget your boring office job, seize this romantic moment.'

She flung her arms around his neck and kissed him passionately. They were at the top of the stairs now and he couldn't help kissing her back just as ardently.

'This was meant to be,' said Ambrosia, 'I know it. When you told me your name really was Basil I knew something special was about to happen to us.'

She turned her back to him and bent forward over the stone balustrade of the balcony. 'Put your arms around me,' she instructed, 'cuddle up close from behind.'

Danny did so, dazed by the sequence of events. He

couldn't believe he was about to be seduced by a police inspector on her night off. But what could he do about it now? Her hands had reached behind her and she was already fumbling in his fly for his prick.

Danny was not a man to look a gift-horse in the mouth where crumpet was concerned. Besides he was feeling incredibly randy. So what if the woman currently tugging his cock from his trousers was a policewoman? There was no denying she had a tidy little arse and he was going to enjoy unveiling it.

His big hands were now under the hem of her skirt, bunching it up over her hips to reveal smooth firm thighs and a tight bottom encased in silk french knickers. He savoured the sight of the twin cheeks stretching the material taut over her outthrust seat.

'Come on!' hissed Ambrosia, pulling aside the flimsy fabric of the gusset to reveal a pink and hairless pussy slit. 'We've not got much time. Stick it up me quick!'

Danny did not fail her. His iron-hard shaft slid up her channel in one delicious thrust. She was warm, wet and very willing.

'Ooh,' she moaned, answering his pelvic jabs by wiggling her arse back into his crotch. 'Ooh, yes, you don't know how badly I need this!'

Her need, in fact, was a complete puzzle to Ambrosia. Twenty minutes ago, with the ghastly Armstrong leering at her, she could have sworn that the entire process of sexual connection was repellent. And now here she was, with a complete stranger rodding her from the rear and she was revelling in it!

As the orgasm hit her, the whole scene – the jostling crowds on the lawn, the lush green valley, the fading pink of the evening sky – seemed to go fuzzy at the edges. It may have been the booze or the fact that vanity dictated she keep her spectacles in her pocket but it added to the unreal magic of the moment. It was a joy to be relieved, if only for one evening, from the pressure of tracking down Danny Fretwork.

She remembered her conversation that day with Sophie and she laughed out loud. Danny took this as his cue to slide a hand round her hip and down into her split from the front.

'Silly Starkers,' muttered Ambrosia to herself as a coarse finger strummed across her clit, making her shiver, 'as if that ape Fretwork would ever show his face at a classy event like this.'

'What's that?' whispered Danny into her ear, his fingers teasing the neat crop of fur at the head of her crack, his belly thumping into the soft cushion of her arse-cheeks in a steady rhythm.

'Forget it, Basil, just bring me off again with your beautiful prick!'

And he did.

Further along the same balcony a pair of women stood dumbfounded, their intimate tête-à-tête irrevocably disrupted by the arrival of Danny and Ambrosia.

'My God,' said the small blonde one, 'that's my two-timing bastard of a husband!'

'I know,' said her tall dark companion, 'and he's bonking Detective Chief Inspector Spicer.'

And for once Patsy and Pandora were incapable of doing anything but spectate.

60

Brick's performance was simple and effective. He sang his songs at the front of the stage, a lone figure picked out in the crossbeams of two spotlights. In the dimness upstage could be seen the shadows of a handful of musicians – though for the most part Brick accompanied himself on his guitar.

He talked a lot too, some twenty-five years in the business of making popular music had given him plenty to talk about. It soon transpired that he was in a mellow mood – and so was his audience. Wealthy industrialists and their wives, trendy culture-vultures and chattering taste-makers, high-brow critics and snobbish patrons of the arts – all had at some time thrilled to a Brick Tempo hit.

So when he began a long monologue about his first girlfriend and her spectacular legs and how she put her foot through the window of his daddy's Cadillac and *then* played the opening bars of 'Making Out on the Back Seat', a collective shiver of delight ran through the audience. Sophie was amazed to see the stuffy couple on her left – Mr and Mrs Merchant Banker as she now knew – fall into a clinch and begin energetic French-kissing as if they were teenagers.

They were not alone. All around her Sophie was conscious that hands were being held, thighs being stroked and breasts being surreptitiously fondled. The worst of it was that she too was feeling incredibly horny. She wouldn't mind spending an hour or so on a back seat with hunky Brick. It seemed she was permanently on heat these days. She squirmed uncomfortably in the too-tight dress.

Brick was continuing to delve candidly into his love life and had shifted to the late seventies and his notorious union with anorexic punk-rocker Mandi Nickers.

'I never did go for skinny women,' he drawled, 'and when Mandi took her clothes off for me the first time I nearly ran out of the room. But she had one thing that stopped me and I'd like to sing you a song I wrote about it.' He paused in mid-strum and added, 'Given the nature of the occasion I'd like to dedicate it to Candy Kensington.'

Then he began a song familiar to almost everyone in the hall. At the time of its release the childish words and simple tune had made it seem a most unlikely Brick Tempo record – factors which had doubtless contributed to its enormous success. Billy had always been puzzled by 'The Cutest Little Dimples in the World' but now, as Brick substituted 'pussy' for 'dimples' all became much clearer.

The audience loved it, clapping in time and singing the new words with gusto. In the royal box Prince Roger led the audience participation while, out of sight of the throng, his hand roamed boldly across the silky delta between his Spanish companion's long legs.

By the time Tracy hit the stage to sing her duet with Brick, the house was bubbling. So, too, was Tracy. The ballet troupe's hospitality had been exhaustive and punch had been downed in quantity. So thrilled had Tracy been to be feted by the dancers that she had thought it only fair to satisfy their curiosity about her incredible body. Thus she had allowed herself to be undressed and paraded around the dressing-room and finally reassembled in a way they deemed satisfactory.

Now she stood in the spotlight by Brick's side wearing her shirt knotted tightly beneath her swollen bust, a black mini-skirt, suspenders and stockings. This was not a costume designed to conceal her abundant charms, especially when perched on top of a tall stool in front of three hundred people all of whom appeared to be looking up her legs. Tracy didn't care. Tracy had drunk a lot of punch.

Brick had announced her to a great whoop of applause – predominantly from the males in the audience, though by now almost everyone was caught up in the fever of the occasion.

To the surprise of many, Tracy could hold a tune and though she faltered at the beginning of 'True Love', Brick's hit with Tania Tingle, by the end her voice was ringing out clearly and sweetly. The audience roared their approval, the men and the women this time. Brick threw his arms round her and gave her an enthusiastic hug which somehow stretched into a frankly open-mouthed kiss. Whistles blended with the applause.

Then they launched into Brick's new song, Tracy sitting perkily on her stool facing straight ahead while Brick stood behind her, an arm loosely draped across her shoulders.

Billy watched from the wings, feeling proud and proprietorial. Tracy was doing really well.

'I didn't know she had it in her,' he muttered.

'I did,' whispered a voice in his ear.

Billy turned to study the woman by his side. The neck was long, the hair elaborately coiffured, pearls glinted in the lobes of her ears and the eyes looking into his in the half-light were, as he well knew, a cool stony grey.

'So you should,' he replied, 'you're her agent.'

Imogen chuckled softly, the sound audible only to Billy as the musicians swung into the number. On stage Brick was nuzzling Tracy's neck and both hands had found their way around her waist onto her bare midriff. Tracy, singing out to the manner born, did not appear to notice.

'I suppose you are about to remind me that it is thanks to you that Tracy is still my client. Don't worry, I haven't forgotten.'

Tracy and Brick were warbling on about roaming in each other's valleys and his hands were now toying with the knot in her shirt.

'Now you come to mention it, Imogen, I was thinking of asking for a bonus. After tonight Tracy is going to be hotter than ever. Especially if what I think is going to happen, happens.'

'And what's that?'

There was really no need to ask, for at that moment Brick and Tracy hit the climax of the number. As they both belted out the final refrain about love among the peaks and Tracy flung her arms wide, the tails of her shirt parted to display her fabulous hills in all their pink and heaving glory. To the readers of the *Daily Dog* this was a familiar sight but the assembled company were thunderstruck.

'What bonus did you have in mind?' asked Imogen

coolly as the applause hit them like a wave.

Billy placed a hand on her hip and slid it very deliberately over the firm spheres of her buttocks, savouring the smooth swell of flesh beneath her satin sheath.

On stage Tracy had only just realised that she was displaying her magnificent mammaries to the world. Covered in confusion she turned to Brick and threw herself into the sanctuary of his arms.

'How about it, Imogen? I reckon you owe me a favour.'

She took no steps to remove his exploring hand from her buttocks, indeed she seemed to rub her arse against him, but she said, 'Isn't Tracy enough for you? Or Katie? Or Candy?' Then her fingers were in his groin tracing the outline of his erection through his trousers. But when the curtain fell and a giggling Brick and Tracy stumbled from the stage wrapped in each other's arms, she was gone.

61

The buzz of conversation was loud in the short intermission following Brick's performance. There was much shifting of bums and crossing of legs and craning of necks to ogle fellow spectators. The effect of Arnold's punch was evident in sudden bellows of rude laughter and spontaneous displays of affection nor normally witnessed in public. Nevertheless, for the moment, the lid was still on the powder keg . . .

In a small side box lady Carmella Mills found herself happily participating in an unlikely conversation. She was flanked by her young nephews, Giles and Thomas, nineteen and seventeen respectively. She had known them all their lives – she had changed their nappies, for God's sake! – and yet here she was earnestly discussing with them the varied shapes of women's breasts. Their faces were flushed, as was her own, and their beady curious eyes kept straying to her bust. She should never have worn this dress, it was much too décolleté. And yet it *was* pretty and her bust, as many could attest, was her very finest feminine attribute.

'I bet yours are just as big as hers,' said Thomas.

'And just as firm, Aunt Melly,' said Giles, already an

adroit flatterer. 'You must have broken lots of hearts.'

'Stop buttering me up, boys,' she said, wondering why her heart was racing quite so fast, 'or I'll tell your mother.'

'You'll tell Mother we said you had the best tits in the house?'

'Thomas! How dare you?'

'Don't be angry, Aunt. After all, it's perfectly true.'

In the aisle seats of the front stalls Araminta Hush tut-tutted her disapproval to her escort and live-in lover, Lionel Broth.

'It's not the sight of mounds of puppy-fat that puts me off, it's the coarseness of it all I find offensive,' she said.

'The crudity not the nudity, you mean,' responded the Irish novelist, who was something of a media face in his own right. 'Personally, I thought it was rather touching. He handed to her the mantle of his amour with Tania Tingle and she accepted it. He gives her a lifeboat to a musical career, she gives him her bountiful breasts. It seems a perfectly fair bargain to me.'

'Well, it would appeal to you, wouldn't it? It's just the kind of thing you go in for yourself. Don't think I haven't noticed your new researcher has udders that wouldn't disgrace a Guernsey cow.'

'A cruel shaft, my uptight beauty. I don't think you of all people should be making comparisons with cows.'

'Fuck you.'

'—especially when you are looking such a picture. You are easily the most desirable woman in the room and beside you neither Tracy Pert nor my poor slandered researcher are worth a second glance.'

'You slimy bum-sucking Irish bastard.'

'That's better. Now, why don't I slip off during this lull in the entertainment and see if I can find us a drink. You should have had one in the interval, you've got to learn to relax.'

'OK, Lionel, but you'd better hurry, you won't want to miss Melissa Melone. I hear she makes Guernseys looks under-developed.'

'Pandy, what the hell is he doing here?' Patsy was agitated and upset. It was not the first time she had posed this question since they had witnessed Danny's tryst with Ambrosia Spicer. Pandora was getting fed up.

'For God's sake, Patsy, how should I know? He's a cheeky bugger, that's all I can say. Perhaps he's just cocking a snook at authority – or snooking a cock, in his case.'

'*Pandy*! This is serious. My husband's on the run. The place is crawling with police. Sophie Stark is snooping around. Danny's just betrayed me with that horrible Ambrosia Spicer. And those people in front of us are virtually doing it in public! Everything's going crazy!'

'That's true but there's nothing we can do about it. Just think what a great book we'll get out of all this at the end of the day.'

'What a great book you'll get, you mean. I'll be stuck visiting Danny in Parkhurst for the rest of my life, I can see it. That's if I can bear to face that bastard ever again.'

'Rubbish, Patsy, don't be such a wimp. You're with me now. And you've got to admit that your Danny is good for something.'

'What's that?'

'Shafting the police. I took great pleasure in seeing DCI Spicer get her comeuppance.'

Danny was astonished at what was going on. All around him people were kissing and cuddling and flirting out-rageously. The most staid middle-aged worthies seemed to have their arms draped around one another and everywhere he looked hands were dipping into bodices and sneaking beneath hems. Surely it wasn't normally like this at these fancy occasions?

Danny couldn't help but stare as he systematically combed the seated throng in search of his quarry. Unfor-tunately, from his position halfway back and to the side of the dress circle, there was a large proportion of the audience who were not in his line of sight. Billy Dazzle must be amongst them, he decided, and that horny police-woman too. For this he was most grateful. Exciting though the encounter with Ambrosia had been he had had no wish to prolong it. Especially since her physical approach would doubtless have soon lead to the dis-covery of the pistol strapped to the small of his back.

Beside him, a well-built young woman with bare shoulders and flawless creamy skin began to laugh hys-terically. As she did so she dropped a hand onto the thigh of the man on her other side. Danny watched closely – he couldn't help himself – as she slid her fingers into her companion's groin and shamelessly began to massage an obviously appreciative erection. The girl laughed on, her dimpled shoulders rippling enticingly. And as the lights began to dim, without once glancing in Danny's direction, she dropped her other hand into his lap. Danny gently removed it, he'd had enough of unsolicited approaches from strange women. But later, when Melissa began to sing and the hand reopened negotiations with his loins, he didn't have the strength to resist.

62

Melissa's first notes, loud and pure and unaccompanied, rang through the darkness and instantly stilled the shuffling buzz of conversation. It was as if a great hand had reached down from on high to touch each and every member of the audience on the forehead, bringing instant peace. There was a collective sigh of contentment and then a gasp of delight as the stage was suddenly illuminated.

Melissa Melone was an acknowledged expert at manipulating stage lighting – the best since Dietrich, it was said. However primitive the conditions, however mulish the local technicians, Melissa always appeared a divinity under lights.

Tonight she radiated sex. Dressed in a flesh-pink sheath that clung to her like a coat of paint, she seemed almost naked. Her statuesque form – the tall columns of her legs, the swollen sweep of her hips, the twin cupolas of her breasts – dominated the stage. Even the memory of nubile Tracy faded from the mind when confronted with these lush curves. Melissa was a combination of exaggerated feminine characteristics that set every man in the audience on fire and filled every woman with pride in her sex. That was the magic she exerted –

everybody in the audience loved her.

Her voice had many colours and she used it to unveil a variety of songs from the most simple to the most dramatic, from peasant serenades to arias from Verdi and Puccini. Behind her the Bedside Orchestra responded to every twitch and swoop of the baton wielded by Sebastian Silk. And then she embarked on the new song cycle, the Poor Pussy Suite.

The audience was bewitched. Even the Philistines were transported.

God Sumner stared bug-eyed like a beached cod, glorious visions of the Pert mammaries already fading. In the cultural stakes, he concluded, this Melone woman was a world-beater. Pity she wasn't British. An unfamiliar condition afflicted his nether regions, tenting his trousers – to the excitement and perplexity of Mrs God, his beloved Henrietta.

In the royal box, Prince Roger for once sat completely still, oblivious of all but the intoxicating vision on stage. Her wonderful voice thrilled even his impoverished musical soul. By his side Inez fingered the royal erection which, while never exactly princely in size, was at the moment bigger and harder than it had ever been before. She promised herself she would have it up her bum later, she was sure she could take it comfortably. She'd bet he'd never done that before. It ought to be worth a diamond bracelet at least . . .

In the dress circle Danny Fretwork was being torn in two. He was here to find Billy Dazzle and blow his brains out, yet he was paralysed! His eyes were glued to the erotic vision on the stage and his penis was poking out of his pants, throbbing to the ministrations of the young woman in the next seat. Danny shot a swift glance to his right. Her pretty pouting face was a picture of concentration as she stared straight ahead, chewing her lower lip. Her left hand was busy with Danny and her right was performing the same service for the man on her other side who, in turn, had his hand up her skirt. It dawned on Danny that throughout the theatre men and women were masturbating each other to the golden voice of the woman on stage.

Melissa was now approaching the climax of the piece. Just as she had promised Sebastian, it was to be a literal climax for many present. As she hit the final sequence, holding on to the incredible top note at a volume that swelled and obliterated the orchestra, all over the theatre men ejaculated.

Henriette Sumner was astonished to feel the growing pool of wetness beneath the hand she had affectionately placed over God's tented dress trousers. In the royal box Inez de la Puta hastily reached for the mirror in her handbag to wipe the royal spunk from her eye. In the circle the pouting girl next to Danny swore to herself she would never, ever forget the night two men came simultaneously all over her hands.

And next to Lady Carmella Miles a subdued voice whispered, 'I'm sorry, Aunty, I've wet my trousers.'

'Well, you'd better take them off then, Thomas,' she replied. 'And you, too, Giles. At once!'

There was tumult in the auditorium. Men were recovering from the spasms in their loins only to leap to their feet and applaud. Women clambered on seats to see above the throng. The noise of whistles and shouts and clapping was deafening. On stage Melissa was surrounded by well-wishers. Seb leaped to kiss her on both cheeks. Candy and Imogen were there, pushing back the over-eager and trying to organise an orderly curtain call for the great diva who blew kisses and smiled and basked unashamedly in the approbation.

Then came the bouquets, for Sebastian, for Candy, for Brick and Tracy who had emerged hand in hand and finally for Melissa herself. This last was a gargantuan bouquet of red and white roses proudly carried by Arnold. He presented them with a flourish and bent to kiss her on both cheeks – the only man on stage who was taller than she was.

It seemed to Billy, watching from the wings, that they were engaging in quite a conversation. As Arnold whispered in her ear the singer's eyes opened wide with surprise and she clapped a hand to her mouth to stifle a giggle. The chef spoke again, he was smiling but Billy could see that, for him, this was no light-hearted matter.

The applause had now turned to a rhythmic handclap, accompanied by foot-stamping. An encore was required. Melissa gracefully allowed herself to be persuaded and the stage cleared. The musicians regained their places, Sebastian picked up his baton and the opening bars of the Poor Pussy Suite once more floated through the theatre.

Melissa began to sing but she was not alone on stage, she had Arnold by the hand and addressed the song to him. She sang it differently too, at a faster tempo and Seb could be seen casting anxious looks in her direction as he urged the orchestra to keep up.

The audience were with her. They had not regained their seats, indeed they had pushed towards the front and were clapping in time. Some of the women at the back had climbed on men's shoulders, many stood on seats and waved their arms in the air. Wraps were cast aside, jackets shrugged off and ties unfastened. This was party time . . .

On stage Melissa began to strip Arnold. First his bow-tie, then his cuff-links, then off with the jacket. Her singing got raunchier, she began to bump and grind, Arnold shimmied back, the temperature rose.

Billy had a strange premonition about what was going to take place. But then he knew what kind of weaponry Arnold carried in his pants.

In the crowd many breasts were bare, strapless gowns had slipped unheeded and blouses had been magically removed by eager hands. Few erections had subsided, the Bedside Punch had seen to that, and those that had were revived by the display of flesh – both on-stage and off.

Melissa was an innate show-woman and she turned Arnold's back to the audience as she eased his thin briefs over his firm buns, keeping the discovery of his penis to herself. For a moment her voice faltered and then swelled in triumph as she took in the unique proportions of what she had uncovered.

There were shrieks and yells from the women in the crowd. They were impatient to see it, too, and so she teased them, prolonging the moment before she slowly, tantalisingly, turned him round.

Billy thought he saw two women in the crowd faint but he ccouldn't be sure. The collective gasp at the sight of Arnold's gargantuan dick drowned out the orchestra and then things got a little out of hand.

Melissa pushed Arnold onto his back, hoisted her dress and impaled herself on his rearing cock. She sank down on it in one movement like a disgraced Roman on his sword. But the smile that split her face as she did so was that of a woman who had found the answer to her prayers.

And then the mass fucking began.

63

Arnold's punch was not intrinsically strong – at least according to his calculations. His aim was to loosen a few inhibitions, to provide a way of slipping free from the straitjacket of polite society. He wanted an evening of midsummer madness. It could be said that he got it.

In the event, Arnold's punch was more powerful than planned, the night was hotter than he had foreseen and the audience drank like fishes. Even the teetotallers. 'Have you tasted it, darling? It can't be that strong. Lovely evening. Think I'll have another.'

The consequence was that by the time Melissa Melone had pulled her dress up her statuesque thighs and fed all of Arnold's tremendous pole into her gaping pink split, the audience were in a frenzy of excitement.

In the aisle by Henrietta Sumner a tall thin blonde crouched on all fours, her black sequined skirt pulled up over her bare and quivering buttocks.

'Stick it in, Hugo,' she commanded her boyfriend who knelt behind her, fumbling, 'and hurry up, for Christ's sake!'

Henrietta coolly bent over, took hold of his big penis and helped him to ease its length into the girl's impatient hole. Then she slipped her arms from her crepe bias-cut gown and pulled the boy's head into her still-girlish and trembling bosom. 'Oh yes,' she cried. 'that feels wonderful. Suck my tits, you naughty boy, and promise you'll fuck me next!'

The orchestra played on as the stage filled with bodies, many naked, many still clinging to incongruous bits of finery. Seb Silk was wearing just his socks as two of the mini-skirted Drax sisters, now minus their halters, took it in turns to mouth his cock. While they did so he moved his left hand backwards and forwards across their dangling titties and conducted the orchestra with his right.

Candy Kensington, down to just her suspenders and stockings, took on all-comers on top of a dais at the back of the stage. It cannot be said, however, that she had lost all sense of the occasion. Assisted by a naked Katie Crisp she demanded money in aid of her cause before allowing admirers to place a finger on her seductive form. A naked suitor protested that he had no means of payment to hand. Katie produced a camera and took a full-frontal shot. 'A cheque in the post tomorrow, or else,' she said as Candy twined slim fingers round his bobbing member, 'made out to Poor Pussy.'

'It'll be Filthy Rich Pussy by the time the night's out,' he muttered as he allowed Candy to guide his aching hard-on between her legs.

In the small box above the stage young Thomas and Giles would have had a terrific vantage point from which to add to their store of sexual knowledge. However, they only had eyes for their shapely aunt who had now stripped to the waist to allow each of her young admirers to suckle on a swollen tit. The boys were trouserless, as she had decreed, and so her hands were able to roam at will over two firm and springy erections thrusting up from their youthful loins. Such bliss!

'Bite harder on my nipple, Giles, don't be afraid. Oh, that's so nice!'

Which one, she pondered, would she have first? Thomas, the younger, was bigger and she longed for the full-up feeling she knew he would give her as he stretched wide her long-neglected cunt. It might be best, however, to let Giles fuck her first and then big Thomas, coming second, would open her further. What a problem for a maiden aunt! Perhaps she'd let them choose, she didn't want to show favouritism.

Minty Hush had her eye on the royal box. The drink Lionel had brought her had not had an effect for a while. And when things began to hot up, clothes began to fly and a flushed Lionel had turned to her expectantly, she had pushed him away.

'Ask her,' she had said, angrily pointing to a buxom nymphet congoing raunchily in the aisle amidst a crunch of groping bodies, 'she's just your type.' To her chagrin Lionel took the rebuff in his stride and now, as Minty was only too aware, he was fucking the nymphet doggie-fashion over a row of seats, his hands juggling the generous pears of her dangling breasts.

It was while watching this display that the urge had hit Minty, like a match flaring in her loins and lighting a fire that now raged unchecked throughout her body. God, she needed a fuck!

But Minty was not someone to throw herself to the mercy of chance, even in the throes of lust she calculated. She had not been to bed with anyone who wasn't worthy of a colour-supplement profile for years and she wasn't about to start now. Which was why she slipped out of the auditorium and crept up the stairs to the royal box.

Her luck was in. The detective assigned to Prince Roger now lay on the lawn outside on top of Lavender Roe, his trousers round his size-fourteen feet.

Minty boldly entered the box and found herself witness to an act of royal buggery. Inez lay across two chairs, her rosy rump thrust upwards to receive Prince Roger's diminutive but willing member in the tight little hole of her anus.

'Good gracious,' he said, 'it's Minty Hush. Where did you spring from?'

'I wondered,' said Minty, seizing her opportunity, 'if I might have a private word with you, sir.'

'You can have anything you like. I'm a great fan of yours, you know. But just at the moment I'm a bit tied up.'

Minty bent her mouth to his ear and whispered, 'I'm surprised you want to put your cock in that particular orifice, sir, you don't know who's been there before you.'

'Eh?'

The Prince stopped pumping.

'We ran an investigation on Inez for the programme, sir, but we didn't dare show it. There's been an army of Spanish playboys up her bum before you.'

'Good Lord.' The royal dick jerked rudely backwards, vacating its cosy home in some haste. Inez cast a bemused look behind her and was obviously surprised to see they were not alone.

'Get lost for a bit, will you, Inez? I've got some things to discuss with Miss Hush.'

Inez opened her mouth to protest but the royal hand fell with a smart slap on her exposed buttocks. It rose again but Inez had got the message and she scampered out of the door clad in nothing but her blouse and suspenders, shooting Minty a venomous glance as she did so.

Minty was unfazed. She presented her back to the Prince, her curves tightly delineated in form-hugging satin of canary yellow.

'Perhaps, sir, I can provide a substitute for your attentions.' And she began to pull the material of her dress upwards over the backs of her thighs to her hips, revealing a deliciously curved derriere, whose twin cheeks were flimsily veiled by matching yellow knickers. She bent over to present her bottom to its best advantage, the sheer material stretching taut over the full moons of her buttocks. And as she felt rough fingers tugging the underwear impatiently down her thighs, then delving feverishly between the tender rounds of her cheeks, she thought to herself, 'Scoop!'

64

Billy Dazzle watched in amazement as members of the Marian Mucus troupe, this time authentically naked, twirled and pirouetted in the centre of the stage. He compared legs and breasts and pubic muffs – or the absence thereof – while at the same time marvelling at their grace. They flew through the air as light as thistledown, their long legs scissoring open, their little buttocks twinkling, their high small breasts scarcely wobbling on their chests. Two of the girls had shaved their pussies and, though he was a good twenty feet away, he imagined the neat pink valves between their legs opening and shutting with each bound of their buoyant limbs.

A knot of admirers avidly watched the show. Every so often one of the dancers would twirl away from the group and pick herself a man from the crowd to exercise her lithe skills upon. Then she would return to the dance, her thighs glistening with a film of spunk, a satisfied grin upon her face.

'What a remarkable scene, dear boy,' murmured a gravelly voice in Billy's ear. 'It's positively Dionysian, isn't it? We are privileged to be present at one of the great orgies of our age.'

Billy immediately recognised the fruity tones of Peregrine Carstairs, the television arts presenter. His was a name to conjure with, a profile on one of his programmes was a passport to celebrity on the Hampstead dinner-party circuit. Billy, fortunately, had no such ambitions.

'You ought to make a programme about it,' he replied.

'Alas, the forces of repression would rise against us. We'd probably lose the franchise. I am, however, thinking of featuring the Mucus nymphs. They are remarkably talented.'

At precisely that moment, as if to demonstrate his point, the tallest of the dancers beckoned to a trouserless man in the crowd. Ushering her chosen partner to the centre of the stage, she instructed him to lie flat on his back and hold his penis perpendicular to his body. Then, with a skip, a run and a flying leap she did the splits upon the lucky fellow, skewering the head of his impressive member in the moist little notch of her hairless cunt. She sank upon it with the grace of a future prima balerina, her arms describing a classic arabesque, her large pointed nipples dark smudges in the half-light.

'I see what you mean,' said Billy.

'You are a discerning young man. I've been watching you. You stand aloof from the crowd and observe. However, I wonder if I could persuade you to participate on this memorable occasion? How would you like to suck my *thing*.'

Billy was suddenly jolted from his envious contemplation of the dancer's undulating buttocks.

'I'm sorry, Perry,' he said. 'Though naturally I'm flattered, your kind of thing is not mine.' And he fled, fast.

* * *

Billy was not remaining aloof for any particular reason. He had not abstained from Arnold's punch – far from it – and desire burned in his loins just as furiously as it did in others. However, this was indeed a unique occasion. All around him were luscious women – beautiful, expensive, pampered, exotic women – and, for once, they were stripped of their inhibitions. He could have almost any of them for the asking. So he looked around for one he really wanted.

He found her in a box at stage level which was partly filled with lighting equipment. Imogen sat in the near darkness coolly smoking a cigarette. There was an empty chair beside her and Billy subsided into it.

'I've just been propositioned by Peregrine Carstairs.'

'Poor Perry,' said Imogen, 'he's having a tough time finding a partner tonight. I had half a mind to tell him to try Prince Roger but Minty Hush has jumped the queue.'

'My God, I didn't know the Prince was gay.'

'According to Inez, he's a latent bumboy. Apparently he tried to bugger her so she ran off and left him to Minty.'

'She'll soon straighten him out.' Billy had no doubts on that score. He knew for a fact that Minty Hush was a persuasive performer once she had warmed up.

'I suppose you've come to claim your bonus,' said Imogen, blowing a cloud of smoke in his direction.

'Well . . .' Faced with her imperturbable stare, Billy was struck by a sudden failure of confidence.

'Get on with it, then,' said Imogen. 'Fuck me if you want to, I won't stop you.'

She took hold of the bodice of her white satin dress and jerked it down to her waist. Her soft ripe breasts spilled out, the long pink tips firm and pointed. She continued to smoke. With her free hand she cupped her left breast and squeezed, pushing the nipple into greater prominence. Billy remembered how she had displayed her breasts for him before.

She smiled. 'You like them, don't you?'

'Yes.'

'I suppose you want to see the rest.' She didn't wait for a reply but reached down and pulled the hem of her dress up to her waist so that the expensive gown lay bunched in a band around her waist. She braced her feet apart on the floor and thrust her pelvis forward. Her legs were long, her nylons were sheer, her thighs were firm. She wore no panties and her cunt was framed by the thin white straps of her suspenders. She ran a hand through her bush, fluffing the hair up and out, teasing it away from the long crack that ran from north to south between her legs.

Billy sat motionless, his eyes focused on those teasing fingers, his heart pounding in his chest.

The half-slumped figure of Imogen slowly finished her cigarette while she played with her pussy for Billy's pleasure. She was excited now, he could see that. Her vaginal juices glistened on her probing fingers. She dropped her cigarette butt and ground it out with her heel.

Both hands were now in her wide-open crotch, one at the top of her split, two fingers splayed downwards in a vee, opening her treasure to his gaze. She plunged the fingers of her other hand into the pretty mouth of her cunt, in and out in an obvious rhythm, her top hand rubbing over the hood of her engorged clitoris.

Billy watched her inviting bosom rise and fall as her breath came harder and faster. He resisted the temptation to reach out and grasp those tempting, trembling mounds of flesh. He was determined to wait until he had seen iceberg Imogen melt completely.

She came in a frenzy, her hand buried almost to the wrist within her, her left forefinger flicking over her clit. Her head tossed from side to side, disturbing her elaborately styled hair which now tumbled down her swan-like neck. Her eyes were closed and her mouth hung open and she made no sound apart from a succession of breathy grunts which were swallowed up in the tumult around them.

Billy waited until she had completely finished and she lay slack and dull-eyed in front of him. Her thighs lolled apart, revealing her wet and puffy pussy lips.

He got to his feet and began to undress.

'Don't take your clothes off,' she said, 'take your cock out.'

'You do it,' he said, stepping close to her, his bulging crotch on a level with her head.

She did as she was told, unzipping him in a trice and prying his whole tackle into the open. One hand was around his shaft, the other cupped his balls. Her eyes sparkled.

'My secret weapon,' she said. 'I'd better show my gratitude.'

She lowered her head and sucked his aching knob into her mouth, running her tongue around the cap. She let it slide from her mouth and licked the length of his shaft to take first one ball, then the other into her mouth.

'Mmm,' she said. 'I think you do deserve your bonus after all.'

Billy fell to his knees between her thighs and held the head of his penis against her enlarged clit, thrilling her sweetest spot.

'For God's sake, put it in!' she hissed.

'You really want me to, Imogen?'

'Yes, I do. I want that big thing in me to the root.'

Billy could not hold back any longer, sliding his swollen member down the length of her split and thrusting it between the lips of her gaping pussy. She twined her legs behind his back, locking her ankles together, whimpering with pleasure as she did so. Her arse was now completely off the seat, giving him free access to fondle and squeeze her firm bum cheeks as he swung his big tool deep into the delicious channel between her legs. Their mouths locked and they kissed hungrily.

It did not last long. The pent-up passion could not be restrained for more than a minute or so. She began to come first, this time in a long sustained moan that rang out through the auditorium, and his groans mingled with hers as the two of them shivered the course of a cataclysmic orgasm.

When it was over she pushed a lock of hair from out of his eye and kissed him tenderly.

'I'm sorry to tell you this, Billy, but you're fired.'

'What do you mean?'

'What I say, that's why I was reluctant to grant you your bonus. You see, I never fuck the help.'

She jostled her loins companionably against him. His cock was still hard within her.

'However, now you're off the payroll, I don't see why we can't socialise.'

'Is that what you call it?' said Billy, grinning now, after all he had only lost a client, not a career.

Her hand was now between their bodies, ringing his cock at the base where it thrust between her pussy lips. 'Come on, private dick, socialise me again . . .'

65

Danny was flagging. In order to keep a clear head he had laid off the booze and so had failed to benefit from Arnold's inspirational punch. And the more he flagged the more in demand he appeared to be.

First had been Ambrosia, of course. Leaving aside the dubious nature of her profession, he had been delighted to explore her sumptuous rump and service the shaven-lipped split between her legs. Then the girl in the next seat had brought him off by hand while simultaneously wanking the man next to her to orgasm. He couldn't deny that that had been exciting.

He had also risen to the challenge when, during Melissa's thrilling encore, the girl had taken him in her mouth. Once the orgy proper began, she had pulled the dress off her back, stuffed her panties in her bag and climbed purposefully onto his lap. It would have been churlish to have refused her the use of his big penis, not when she was so evidently in need. Besides, fucking was obviously expected of him and he didn't want to draw attention to himself.

So fuck he did, holding her flaring hips as she bounced up and down in his lap, riding his rod as if she were on a steeple-chaser. Next to them her girlfriend performed in a similar fashion on top of the other fellow. All three knew each other and they brayed loudly in upper-class tones as they fornicated.

'I say, Monica,' cried the second girl, 'what's yours like?'

'Super!' shouted Danny's girl. 'He's got a bloody sight bigger willy than Nigel. You've got to try him next!'

Danny would have protested but Monica pulled his face onto her dancing white bosom, pushing a ripe red nipple into his mouth as she bucked into her first orgasm.

By the time Monica let him go, Danny was as wrung out as a dish cloth. He lurched away into the dark, tucking his limp cock into his trousers as he went. As he made for the exit he heard cut-glass tones raised in complaint.

'Where did he go, Monica? I want that big cock you promised me!'

Danny hurried along, aware that he was losing his grip. So far he had failed to catch even a glimpse of his intended target, Billy Dazzle, and he had had an encounter with the law that could only be termed 'close'. However, there was still time to put matters right. Now, surely, was the moment a randy rat like Dazzle would emerge from his bolt-hole. In the prevailing chaos it should be easy to deal with him and make a quick escape.

But even getting down to the stalls proved difficult. On the stairs Danny was waylaid by two groups of women. The first comprised society matrons wearing little and caring less. They pinned him to the steps and pulled his trousers to his ankles, big titties billowing and swinging as they set about him. He was kissed fervently while insistent hands rummaged in his trousers.

There was some disappointment amongst the ladies that his joystick was not instantly rampant but they worked on him for a while and their fearsome enthusiasm was such that he found himself responding. He allowed himself to be ravished, with one woman's meaty thighs on either side of his hips, her big slack breasts shaking like jellies in his face. Then they took turns, the last one coaxing from him a shot of sperm that he felt had come from the very bottom of his locker.

It soon transpired that it hadn't. Soon after his release, two nude ballet dancers wrestled him to the ground and practised their pirouettes in unison on his body, one sitting on his face, the other reviving his exhausted member with her mouth. Such were their skills that Danny once more responded.

He entered the rear of the auditorium naked from the waist down, an ache in his bones and a limp in his step. Soft hands helped him to a seat and a gravelly voice said, 'Feeling a bit pooped, are we? You look like you could do with a rest.' With relief Danny noticed that his benefactor was a man. Only for relief to turn to outrage as those same soft fingers crept onto his thigh.

'Get your fucking hands off me, you pervert,' he growled, thrusting the fellow away and lumbering off into the dark.

Danny stumbled between the seats, avoiding sprawling bodies, trying vainly to detect the hated figure of Dazzle. Then he saw him, a broad-shouldered young man with a shock of black hair, his face caught for a moment in a spotlight that some joker was playing across the bodies on the stage. The boy's head fell back, out of sight.

Danny picked his way forward with a purpose. The

gun, which he had so far managed to conceal from his admirers, now burned a hole in the small of his back.

Another teetotaller at the feast, and one who had so far managed to avoid unwanted attentions, was Sophie Stark. For two pins she would have launched herself into the fray in search of a lusty fellow. Tonight, however, she had a mission.

She had seen no sight of Danny Fretwork at any point during the evening. But once the free-for-all had started she had spotted Billy Dazzle at the side of the stage ogling the dancers. She had kept an eye on him as he clambered into the box with Imogen, then found a vantage point, in a box above and to the side, from which she could monitor his activities. They were not designed to ease her frustrations. It took all her self-control not to go down there and join in.

However, that would not have been smart. If Danny was here he would surely see Billy and make his move. Then Sophie had to be ready. Billy's life – and her career – depended on it.

Nevertheless when she saw the large barrel-shaped figure moving carefully but purposefully between the bodies in the centre aisle of the theatre it was a shock. The kind of surprise a fisherman feels on getting a bite after an eternity of staring at the empty water. She could not believe it.

Danny was halfway down the stalls now and Sophie watched, frozen to the spot, as he reached behind him and took a small object from beneath his jacket. For a moment it winked in the light but she already knew it was a gun.

Sophie unzipped her dress and her flesh sang as the

restricting garment fluttered to the floor. She had no choice, she could not go after Danny in clothes that inhibited her every movement. So Sophie went after her man in her favourite battledress. Stark naked.

66

Danny screwed the silencer onto the gun barrel as he made his progress towards Billy. The boy was no longer visible but Danny's plan of action was clear: get as close as possible, just to be sure it was him, and then plug the little shit in the head. He could be off before anyone realised what was up. The car park was stuffed full of fast motors. Within ten minutes he'd be long gone.

He made his way along a row of seats to the side aisle. From there he could look straight into Billy's box. He boosted himself up on the seat at the end of the row and looked down into the small space.

It was Dazzle all right. He was sitting by himself, naked but for an open shirt, calmly watching the progress of the orgy on stage. On the chair by his side lay the crumpled remains of some female's evening finery.

A sudden feeling of revulsion swept over Danny. The dinner jackets and the yah-yah accents, the snobbish entertainment that was really just a leg show, all these stuffed shirts dipping their aristocratic wicks – it pissed him off. He was an outsider, condemned to jail or exile, while dear old Blighty went to the dogs in the hands of these decadent piss-artists. This Dazzle was a fast-buck yuppified con-merchant who seduced other men's wives and frolicked with the upper classes.

Danny took aim. From this angle he could blow the bugger's head off and it would be morning before anyone noticed.

Billy was taking a breather. The long-awaited encounter with Imogen had left him replete – for the moment. And so he surveyed the crazy scene around him: the flailing, dancing bodies on stage, the knots of revellers in the aisles and the orchestra who played on, many of them in an admirably inventive fashion, under the erratic baton of a naked Seb Silk.

The whole scene was like a wild fantasy from the depths of his subconscious. So it should not have been a surprise for him to recognise a face from his dreams: a big face set on a huge bulky body last seen awesomely naked by an outdoor pool in Kent. Danny Fretwork. The evil bastard was standing on a seat in the stalls looking straight at him, with murder his his eyes. And, just as in Billy's nightmares, with a gun in his hand.

Oof!

An excruciating pain erupted in Danny's loins and a hand grasped his wrist, forcing the gun up into the air. Then he was flat on his back wrestling with a soft and perfumed bundle of nude female flesh.

But the bundle was strong and sinewy and Danny was in agony having been clouted between the legs with what felt like a sandbag. It was, in fact, a small but heavy ladies' purse.

They wrestled on the floor, a trouserless man and a naked woman – a common sight by this stage of the evening. Sophie felt herself succumbing to Danny's vastly superior strength. She yelled out to Billy.

For a moment Billy was paralysed. The awful vision of Fretwork standing not ten feet away aiming a pistol at his head had vanished. It took him a moment to realise what was going on. That Danny really had aimed a gun at him and that he had been saved by a naked woman who was now wrestling with the gangster on the floor and calling out to him for help.

Billy scrambled over the front of the box and jumped down into the aisle. He was not a fighter. He was not trained in boxing or hand-to-hand combat or karate. However, he had played a bit of football at school. So he kicked Danny in the head.

Billy's foot landed fair and square and smacked Danny's skull solidly against the metal base of the seat next to the aisle. The gangster collapsed like a felled ox.

Together they hauled the big man out of the emergency exit at the front of the stalls and found themselves in the gardens at the side of the theatre.

'Over there,' ordered Sophie, pointing across the moonlit lawn, 'we'll tie him to the fence.'

'What with?' asked Billy as they reached the iron railings that marked the boundary with the adjacent Bedside Park.

Sophie opened her purse and produced a pair of handcuffs. She snapped one jaw round one of Danny's wrists and threaded the other through the bars before attaching it to Danny's other hand.

As she worked, kneeling over the supine figure with her back to Billy, he couldn't help admire her curves, so thrillingly illuminated in the moonlit. In particular, the full swoop of her luscious bum cheeks stirred a chord within him.

'Do you always carry a set of handcuffs?' he asked as she sat back on her haunches and surveyed a surprisingly peaceful-looking Danny Fretwork.

'Always – you never know when they'll come in handy.' She was now taking Danny's pulse to assure herself all was well. 'He's asleep. I don't think there's any damage done.'

'That's a pity – the sod was going to kill me. Don't you think we should call the police?'

'There's no need,' said Sophie, turning to look at Billy. 'I'm Detective Sergeant Sophie Stark of the Met.'

'Good God!' Billy was contemplating her rear as it thrust back at him, the cheeks rounded and voluptuous and suddenly familiar. 'I think I recognise you.'

'You bloody well should do. You've got a photo of my arse in the desk in your office.'

'You were at the swimming pool!'

'When you fell out of a tree and ruined my last attempt to arrest Danny Fretwork. You've caused me a deal of trouble, Billy Dazzle.'

'How do you know my name? And what were you doing in my office?'

Sophie was now standing by his side, the pale moonlight shimmering on her mane of hair. The globes of her big tip-tilted breasts were so close they almost grazed his bare chest.

'Don't be boring,' she said, looking down at the slumbering form of Danny, his tree-trunk thighs spread wide to reveal a shrivelled and slack sex organ. It nestled limply amongst the coarse hair of the gangster's groin, as useless as he was. On the other hand the staff of her new acquaintance rose stiff and strong just inches from her itching pussy. She curled her fingers round its swollen tip.

It was good to have a man's penis in her hand again and she ran her fingers urgently up and down the thick shaft.

'Come on, Billy,' she said, pushing him down onto the grass and spreading her long legs wide, 'I've had enough of being the only wallflower at the biggest orgy since the fall of the Roman Empire!'

Billy needed no persuading. He eagerly fed his tool into her hungry pussy and as he filled the void within her Sophie cried out in triumph and celebration.

'That's it, Billy, fuck me! Fuck me all night long!'

By her side an exhausted Danny Fretwork slept the sleep of the vanquished.

Once more Sergeant Sophie Stark had got her man.

More Erotic Fiction from Headline:

FAYE ROSSIGNOL
PEARL OF THE HAREEM

The sensational story of life
in a high-class house of pleasure

**'Here I am – the girl who hit
Constantinople like a sexual
earthquake!'**

Kidnapped in Vienna in 1904, shipped to the
Orient and sold into slavery by the most ruthless
rogue in the land, though she does not yet know
it, the beautiful young American Pearl Keefer is
on her way to becoming the most famous
courtesan of her day. Her new home is the French
Hareem, the most fabulous brothel in Turkey, and
it is there that her magical talent for the
pleasuring of men is honed to the heights of
artistry. Here is her story and these are the erotic
secrets of a lifetime of love!

Also available from Headline by Faye Rossignol:
SWEET FANNY
SWEET FANNY'S DIARY
LORD HORNINGTON'S ACADEMY OF LOVE
A VICTORIAN LOVER OF WOMEN
FFRENCH PLEASURES
THE FFRENCH HOUSE

FICTION/EROTICA   0 7472 3779 4

A selection of Erotica from Headline

FONDLE IN FLAGRANTE	Nadia Adamant	£4.99 □
EROTICON DESIRES	Anonymous	£4.99 □
LUSTFUL LIAISONS	Anonymous	£4.50 □
THE ROYAL SCANDAL	Anonymous	£4.99 □
FRENCH FROLICS	Anonymous	£4.50 □
EROS OFF THE RAILS	Anonymous	£4.99 □
CREMORNE GARDENS	Anonymous	£4.99 □
ECSTASY ITALIAN STYLE	Anonymous	£3.99 □
MY DUTY, MY DESIRE	Anomymous	£3.99 □
IN THE MOOD	Lesley Asquith	£4.50 □
KISS OF DEATH	Valentina Cilescu	£4.99 □
THE LUSTS OF THE BORGIAS	Marcus Van Heller	£4.99 □

All Headline books are available at your local bookshop or newsagent, or can be ordered direct from the publisher. Just tick the titles you want and fill in the form below. Prices and availability subject to change without notice.

Headline Book Publishing PLC, Cash Sales Department, Bookpoint, 39 Milton Park, Abingdon, OXON, OX14 4TD, UK. If you have a credit card you may order by telephone — 0235 831700.

Please enclose a cheque or postal order made payable to Bookpoint Ltd to the value of the cover price and allow the following for postage and packing:
UK & BFPO: £1.00 for the first book, 50p for the second book and 30p for each additional book ordered up to a maximum charge of £3.00.
OVERSEAS & EIRE: £2.00 for the first book, £1.00 for the second book and 50p for each additional book.

Name ....

Address ....

....

....

If you would prefer to pay by credit card, please complete:
Please debit my Visa/Access/Diner's Card/American Express (delete as applicable) card no:

Signature ....Expiry Date ....